Combine one adventurous young lady, three homeless kids from the New York slums, and send them out West on an Orphan Train in 1873. Throw one totally unsuspecting rancher into the mix, season with plenty of mischief, a few growing pains, a dash of pepper, allspice, salty tears, and loads of laughter. Stir together well, and voila! you have a...

'Sure-Fire' Recipe for Happiness!

Home is where the Heart is
Copyright © 2015 by Barbara Dan
All rights reserved
ISBN 13: 978-1514730904
ISBN 10: 1514730901

Presented by *Spring Mountain Publications*
268 NW Hayden Court, Hillsboro, Oregon 97124

Cover Design and Interior Layout: Laura Shinn Designs
http://laurashinn.yolasite.com

The jean quilt on the cover of this book was made by Carolyn Turner of Salem, Oregon.

Registered with the Library of Congress Control Number 2015913081

> 1. Wyoming Territory, 1873-74
> 2. Homesteading by women
> 3. Roles of women in settling the West
> 4. Wyoming Cattle Ranches

Trade Paperback, $14.95

Home is where the Heart is

Historical Western Romance

BARBARA DAN

DEDICATION

This book is dedicated to a very special friend of mine: Carolyn Turner, of Salem, Oregon. No stranger to personal tragedy, Carolyn lost her truck-driver husband, Byron, in a head-on collision with another big rig many years ago, and later nearly lost her own life in a similar accident, while driving a smaller truck. A true survivor, she beat incredible odds and has devoted herself to serving others in her community ever since.

Over the past forty years—when she wasn't busy raising her five children and, later, enjoying all her grandchildren, great-grands, and great-*great*-grands—Carolyn has made literally *thousands* of wonderful quilts, including her totally unique jean quilts, for family, friends, wounded veterans, and homeless individuals.

Over the past twenty years she has also organized weekly blood drives for the American Red Cross. Like the Good Samaritan, Carolyn has a real knack for showing up wherever a need presents itself. Thanks, Carolyn, for being such a wonderful inspiration to us all. We love you!

And now, dear Reader, with Carolyn's kind permission, I have interjected a bit of fun by using her name and her late husband's as secondary characters in **Home is where the Heart is**. Enjoy!

—*Barbara Dan*

RECENT REVIEWS OF
BARBARA DAN'S NOVELS:

REVIEWS of *PETTICOAT WARRIOR*:

"**Barbara Dan's** Civil War historical romance is a fast paced, adventurous novel which will appeal to readers of all genres. Gabe and Sarah are a terrific pair who love to disagree almost as much as they adore being in love. The author's references to the late 1800s are on-point, factual and quite interesting. This story is engaging from start to finish and contains a perfect blend of history and intrigue, which will warm the cockles of your heart and excite you all at once."
— *Romantic Times*, **4-1/2 Star Top RT Rating**

"Fast-paced romance with lot of fireworks and humor. Sarah and Gabe are a fascinating mix of hot-headedness and attraction. I laughed a lot as Sarah fought to maintain her independence as a feminist during the Civil War era."
— **S. Habegger, Amazon.com 5 Star Customer Review**

"**Barbara Dan** does her homework! The historical detail is impressive ad vividly colors the romantic story, which is full of surprising twists of fate. I felt the urgency of being so close to a Civil War battlefield. Sarah is there disguised as a male doctor desperately hoping to find her father, who's been imprisoned by the Confederates while serving as a Union Army medic. Drs. Gabe and Sarah are complex characters, her women's lib ideals in sharp contrast to his views of male superiority. From the southern woods, to a visit with Susan B. Anthony, to an elegant New York City mansion, Sarah is swept along on a journey she never expected to take."
— *Laureltree Books*, **Amazon.com 5 Star Customer Review**

REVIEWS of *MacGREGOR'S BRIDE*:

"**A high spirited romance** about a strapping sea captain and his love-starved war bride during the War of 1812."
— *Las Vegas Review Journal*

Amazon.com 5-Star Reviews for *MACGREGOR'S BRIDE*:
"I absolutely *adored* MacGregor! He is not the typical "dark, foreboding, mysterious" type that many novelists choose to portray [as] their male love interests. He is gorgeous, yes, but he is also happy, upbeat and absolutely lovable!!!! This story is very satisfying

from beginning to end. If you like a story with a great ending, you will really like this one!!!!"
— *"Romance Lass," Jennifer*

Wonderful writing . . . full of detail and research. The hero is a happy-go-lucky all-American hero. Usually I go for the dark tormented hero, but Bruce is so handsome and lovable that I fell in love with him instantly. The heroine, Lydia, is also great . . . I really can't rave enough about Barbara Dan's superb prose.
— *P. G. D.*

"**One of my all-time favorite romances**. LOVE IT, LOVE IT, LOVE IT! This is one great book. I've read it twice, and I never do that. I couldn't put it down. It's a must-have for all romance story lovers."
— *David B. Yerkie, Spring Lake, MI*

"An old-fashioned roller-coaster ride with a strong hero and heroine who come alive on the page. If you enjoy an adventure-filled story, this is for you."
— *Romantic Times 4-Star Review*

REVIEWS of *SILENT ANGEL*:

"*Silent Angel* is a touching, compelling love story. A wonderful romance! Barbara Dan is a terrific storyteller."
— *Bobbie Smith, NY Times / USA Today Best-Selling Author*

"*Silent Angel* is a delightful novel. [The way] Barbara Dan describes the lives of pioneers [is] the next best thing to being there. I love the way she develops her characters and storyline — it will make you laugh and cry. She keeps you on the edge of your seat until the very end. Once I started reading this, I couldn't put it down. She is truly an artist who paints with words."
— *5-Star Customer Review (arlomore) at CreateSpace.com*

"What a pleasant surprise! When I started reading, I couldn't stop. My husband would say, 'Are you coming to bed?' I'd say, 'In a minute.' Even 2 or 3 hours after I finished reading *Silent Angel*, it was so real that I kept wondering about the twins growing up and weather in Montana. A most enjoyable read!"
— *Customer Review (jchapman)*

REVIEWS of *O'ROURKE'S BRIDE* (1864 Historical Romance):

"A fun, fast-moving read. Barbara Dan is a talent to watch!"
— *Bobbi Smith, NY Times bestselling author*

"An enjoyable marriage of (in)convenience set amid a majestic mountain range . . . funny and entertaining, as the battle of the sexes heats up in more ways than one. Hot!"
— *Romantic Times*

Amazon.com Customer Reviews: 5-Star Reviews:

"**Witty, Sexy, Irish West Romance!** Barbara Dan treats romance fans with a brand new rip-roaring western romance with sexy passionate Irish characters that are very much like a mixture of two all-time favorite John Wayne movies, *The Quiet Man* and *McClintock*."
— **Beverly Romance Books, St. Petersburg, FL**

"**Great Characterization**. I haven't enjoyed a book so much in a long time. It is set in a part of the country I know, so that was fun, but there is nothing trite or contrived about how this book unfolds. I especially enjoyed O'Rourke."
— **Jane Jordan, Boise, Idaho**

"**A Delightful Romp!** You will not be bored with this book! [It's] romantic, humorous, and hard to put down. You wonder what the beautiful, hot-tempered, impetuous Kate is going to do next? From start to finish, the book entertains, while giving you your money's worth (and then some!) in the romance department. On a scale of milk toast to hot chili peppers, this book's romantic heat leans more toward the peppers. A spicy romance with wit aplenty!"
— **"Tigger," Wood Village, OR**

"**Barbara Dan** has written about cultures clashing: western vs. eastern vs. British cultures, all set in the bawdy, boisterous and booming times of Virginia City (NV), 1864. There is a good deal of passion and wit in this fun book."
— *Love Western Romances Book Review Online*

"**Barbara Dan's** Western romance, *O'Rourke's Bride,* is set in Virginia City during the mining boom of the 1860s, [and] involves a sham marriage, lumbermen, miners and the theatre."
— *ROUNDUP Magazine, Feb. 2007*

Home is where the Heart is

*"The most precious jewels you'll ever hang around
your neck are the arms of your children."*

Prologue

Dear Aunt Gladys,

Surprise! I am only minutes away from Cheyenne and the new life that awaits me there.

By the time this relentlessly long train ride crossed into Wyoming Territory on the fifth of June, 1873, I confess I was pretty much "tapped out," to borrow an expression from the crusty old bugler who heralded our arrival at every whistle stop—until he abandoned our great cause and left the train at Omaha.

I never imagined how much work it would be to supervise thirty orphans en route to prospective parents scattered all across this great land. Besides feeding and comforting these poor lost lambs, wiping running noses, and keeping the peace whenever squabbles break out, I must also make certain the children look presentable, so that good-hearted folk along our route will find it in their hearts to provide homes for these unfortunate orphans.

Many of these poor, homeless children lost their parents during the War between the States. With families broken up and the nation's economy in ruins, they had fallen on hard times. Abandoned to a life of poverty and starvation on the streets of New York and Philadelphia, they faced a bleak future, indeed, before being rescued by the Children's Aid Society.

Of course, not everyone who adopts children off the Orphan Train has the best motives for giving these previous waifs a home, but it is my earnest hope and prayer that most, if not all, of the children who came West with me will fare better in their new homes than they did back East.

As I write this, my journey is nearly over. But alas! Even though nearly thirty orphans have been placed with farmers and town folk over the past few weeks, I have little hope of finding a loving home *for the sweet little girl who is still in my charge as we approach our final stop, Cheyenne.*

In addition, I am soon to meet my prospective employer, a rancher with whom I have tentatively accepted the position of housekeeper. Yes, I must apologize, Aunt Delia, for keeping you in the dark about this latest revelation. At least you will be relieved to know that I am not a mail order bride!

However, being a war orphan (like my charges) and having been reduced to dire financial straits since Mama passed on, I not only agreed to escort these unruly, insecure children on this perilous journey, in exchange for my train fare and food, but I made so bold as to answer an advert. in the *Times* from a Mr. Samuel Gallagher, who was seeking a housekeeper.

Now, Auntie, I hope you won't be too shocked upon learning this. You and Uncle Henry have enough troubles without worrying about me. However, a person must eat, and since I have good health and all my faculties, I might as well take my chances out here in the "Wild West."

Oh— Did I mention how impressed I was by this gentleman's kind response to my letter? (His reply caught up with me in St. Louis during my two-day layover with Cousin Albert.) Anyway, I was pleased to see that Mr. Gallagher writes with a bold hand—quite literate really, and businesslike—indicating that the job was mine, if I still wanted it. Since he has business in Cheyenne anyway, he plans to meet me at the depot. He assured me that living on a cattle ranch with a bunch of hungry "cowpokes" should suit me perfectly. (I blush to admit that I described myself as an "adventurous young woman in my twenties." Oh, I do hope he doesn't take me in dislike or misinterpret what I meant by "adventurous"!)

Anyway, I am about to embark on my grandest adventure yet. So why, I keep asking myself, am I quaking in my shoes, as the train chugs relentlessly down the track toward the station? Hopefully my fears are all for naught. Until I write again, I remain

Your affectionate niece,
Margaret

P.S. I should add that Mr. Gallagher sent me travel money. However, not wishing to place myself under obligation until I have actually set eyes on the man, his money is safely hidden away amongst my unmentionables. If we do not suit, I am fully prepared to refund his money and to seek gainful employment elsewhere.

Chapter One

"Now dry your eyes, Susie." Margaret Wolverton—known as 'Meg' to family and friends back East—bent down and with her handkerchief gently dried the grubby, tear-streaked face of the youngest orphan in her charge. "Everything will turn out all right, you'll see."

"B-but nobody w-wants me." The little girl poured out her grief, her chest heaving with distress. "Th-they took my b-brother Chester, 'cuz he's big and strong, but wh-what can *I* do? I am only little."

"You are just the right size for *you*," Meg said, giving her a reassuring hug. The distraught three-year-old in her lap had just awakened in a near panic, because all the other children on the Orphan Train were gone, and she and Meg were the only two passengers left from their group in the railway car.

"B-but what w-will happen to me?" Susie's big brown eyes looked up at her so trustingly that Meg's heart fairly turned over.

"Isn't it obvious? *You*, my precious, will grow up to be a beautiful young woman and—"

"No! I mean right now!" Susie kicked her feet, connecting with Meg's shin. "I need a Mommy! And a Papa, too. Why can't I be like other children?"

Ouch. Meg winced, then got a firm grip on her growing frustration. "Why don't we wait till we get off the train in Cheyenne and see? Perhaps someone will—"

"I know!" A dancing light of inspiration flashed in the tiny child's eyes. "I will adopt *you* as my new mother."

"Well, if nobody else comes along, that sounds like an excellent idea," Meg replied, tidying the child's pigtails and retying her shoelaces.

"Yes, you can be my new Mama," Susie declared triumphantly. She folded her arms across her chest, just as if the matter had been settled to her full satisfaction.

Meg sighed and looked out the soot-streaked window to watch their approach.

Suddenly the locomotive surged forward, overshot the depot, then came to a screeching, grinding halt a hundred yards past the baggage handlers' cart. A shudder went through the entire train in a series of jerks that nearly flung Meg and her one remaining charge from their seats. Righting herself, she straightened her hat, got a firm grip on Susie's tiny hand, and picking up their meager belongings, walked to the end of their coach.

No sooner had she reached the exit door to debark when two ragged boys—both orphans placed with a South Dakota farmer by Reverend Lowell—came scrambling out of the forward railway car. "Miss Wolfie! Miss Wolfie!" they yelled, beaming. Sure enough, they were headed straight for her.

Her heart sank. David Hale and Jimmy Baxter were two of the most incorrigible children she had *ever* met—constantly fighting, shirttails flying, blackened eyes, bloodied noses. It was beyond imagination how these two hooligans could find trouble at the blink of an eye. Indeed, Jimmy was sporting a black eye right now!

"Hello again," Meg said, opening her arms to the two boys. Some might describe them as damaged goods, the result of a lifetime of neglect, but she only saw them as being more needy than most. The right family would surely overlook the mischief this noisy pair constantly stirred up. Unfortunately Reverend and Mrs. Lowell had left the Orphan Train in North Platt, so that left her responsible for finding suitable homes for these two ragamuffins, as well as for Susie.

"Miss Wolfie! Miss Wolfie!" Jimmy shouted, again taking liberties with her last name.

"Saints preserve us," Meg said under her breath. *Does trouble always come in threes?* she asked herself. "Where did you two come from?"

"We ducked out on that mean ole farmer and hid in the baggage car," Jimmy explained with a crooked, but endearing grin.

Davey, his expression blank as a stone wall, rocked back and forth agitatedly, bumping against Meg and whimpering, almost like an injured animal.

Jimmy, a product of New York City's worst slum, Hell's Kitchen, clapped a filthy hand over Davey's mouth so *he* could talk. "Quiet!" He gave the younger boy a shake. "Miss Wolfie, you gotta help us. That ole man was gonna beat us for sure!"

"We ain't slave labor," Davey mumbled.

"Of course, you're not," Meg sympathized.

"Comin' through!" growled a scraggly looking cowboy, pushing them aside, using the bedroll and saddle on his shoulder as a battering ram.

With an indignant huff, Meg gathered all three children in close, while several cowboys, reeking of whisky, staggered down the steps on unsteady legs. As the exit began to clear, she picked up her straw valise and satchel, in which she kept travel necessities, a few toys for her orphans, and emergency food for the trip. Owing to a problem on the tracks along a deserted stretch of the Nebraska prairie, they were fully seven hours late arriving in Cheyenne. She only hoped the delay wouldn't leave them stranded in this rough looking town. When she had agreed to meet Mr. Gallagher at the station, she naturally assumed the train would arrive on time. But lately nothing seemed to be turning out quite the way she'd planned.

"Come along, children." Ready to debark, she inched forward, the children clinging tenaciously to her skirts, ostensibly fearful of being abandoned. Murmuring words of encouragement, Meg glanced around, hoping to catch a glimpse of her new employer—a daunting task since she had not the slightest idea what he looked like. All she knew was that he was delivering a herd of cattle to Cheyenne and planned to meet the train on Tuesday, the fifth of June.

Well, it was still the fifth, though just barely. So where was he?

Meg narrowed her eyes, impatient to catch sight of anyone remotely matching the self-described "middle-aged rancher" who'd outlined her wages and duties as housekeeper and cook. From his letter she gathered that Mr. Gallagher was absent from home a good deal of the time, riding the range and tending to business. That suited Meg just fine. She was looking forward to the peace and quiet of country living. It would certainly be a welcome change after her long train ride and dealing with so many noisy children for weeks.

As she handed her belongings down to the conductor, nine-year-old Davey clutched her skirts fearfully and balked about getting off the train, no doubt dreading his new surroundings. He was a strange, rather unsocial child, often living in a world apart.

Making soothing sounds, Meg shooed him along in front of her. "Come along, Davey. Time to get off the train."

Resisting, he whimpered and clung even more tightly to her. Clearly he wasn't about to walk down the steep metal steps on his own, she realized with a sigh. She already knew he reacted badly to loud noises. The train ride hadn't have been at all easy on him—just one clattering noise after another. As she gathered him close, hoping to reassure him, he slumped like a stolid, unresponsive weight, making her progress down the steps precarious, though she made it with a little assist from the conductor.

"Thank you, sir," she told the conductor, still a little breathless from wrestling Davey, who weighed close to sixty pounds, more than half her weight. Not making life any easier, Susie still hung around her neck. Sensing that Davey was nearly frozen with fear, Meg gave him a series of gentle nudges with her knee through the heavy serge of her traveling skirt to get him moving.

Her heart full of misgivings, Meg paused to get her bearings. A huge cloud of choking coal soot poured from the train's smokestack, drifting with the wind and raining down on passengers as they made their way toward the depot, juggling suitcases, satchels and herding small, sticky-fingered children. Suddenly the train whistle let out a shrill blast. Startled, Davey clapped his hands over his ears and took off running like a scared jackrabbit. Jimmy lit out right behind him. Leading Susie, fiercely sucking her thumb, Meg limped after the two boys, her tight shoes pinching.

"Davey, Jimmy, wait!" Meg called, to no avail.

Both boys were already inside the waiting room when she finally caught up with them. She spotted Davey perched on the high back of a wooden bench, playing peek-a-boo with his own reflection in the dirty window. Completely oblivious to the fright he'd given her.

As for Jimmy, he had abandoned her suitcase and was hustling other passengers for money, offering to carry their bags, and in general putting to use the aggressive survival skills that had kept him alive on the streets of New York.

In other words, he was a quart-and-a-half sized hustler.

With no idea how to deal with three such needy and apparently unadoptable children, Meg carried Susie over to a hard wooden bench and sat down. Things weren't exactly looking up at the moment. What she needed was a miracle. *Even a small one will do, Lord,* she silently prayed. Though a great big one would be even more welcome, she had to admit.

~ * ~ * ~ * ~

Some distance away on a side rail, a handful of trail-weary cowmen, twirling ropes over their horses' heads and whistling shrilly, herded cattle from a holding pen toward the last in a long line of open-slatted cattle cars. During the grueling process, the men had been eating dust for several hours. Their mouths were dry as sand, their bodies covered with a thick layer of alkaline silt.

As always, a few stubborn strays balked, as if sensing that they were headed for the stockyards in Omaha. But for the most part, the men's work was about finished for the day. And high time, too. Their muscles were aching, their bellies empty, and tempers just a touch edgy. After a trip to the nearest saloon to wash the dust out of their throats, they planned to head back to the hotel for a well deserved rest.

Only one man out there, riding herd on a mean steer, had other plans. That was Sam Gallagher, a man who wasn't usually averse to a few drinks and a hand or two of poker when he rode into town. But not tonight. He had other plans, and they didn't include whiskey, saloon girls, or cards.

Hunching his shoulders, he clenched his teeth around the loop in his lasso and steered his horse through the swirling dust toward the long horned steer that was holding them up from calling it a day.

"Hi-yah!" he bellowed and gave his raw-boned neighbor, Len Peterson, the signal to come up on the steer's blind side. Once they dropped a couple of ropes on this stubborn maverick and got him into the chute, he'd be docile as a kitten.

Well, maybe as tame as a cougar, he allowed.

Cattle bawling so loud they could barely hear each other, he and Len sent their ropes singing through the air. Len's rope fell over one horn. The steer tossed his head and slipped free.

Whomp! Sam's rope caught the steer around the neck, and his horse dug in its heels, adding sufficient traction to stop the cussed animal in his tracks. Len, standing high in the stirrups, threw again, this time successful. A cheer went up from the men milling around, but the struggle wasn't over—not yet. Exploding with energy, the steer lunged first one way, then the other. Cowboys scrambled to save their mounts and themselves from its tossing horns. Sam and Len stubbornly hung on, men and horses pitted against two thousand pounds of ferocious animal prowess. The blur of mahogany hide bucked and thundered, tearing up the ground, and filling their nostrils with the smells of sweat and earth and sheer animal fury.

It seemed like an eternity, but in actual fact, the whole process took less than four minutes. Finally, with an added assist from the wrangler, the steer lunged forward through the gate. Moving quickly, Sam and Len made sure the animal was headed inescapably up the chute before freeing their ropes.

Another two dozen cows followed without a hitch. The boxcar door slid shut, and they were able to call it a day. Trading lighthearted banter, they beat the worst of the dirt from their chaps, then the cowmen broke up into twos and threes and started down the street.

"See you in the morning, Sam," Len called, walking backwards across the tracks, leading his horse toward the livery stable.

"Thanks, neighbor! Couldn't have wrestled that ornery son of a tornado into the chute without you."

"Sure thing." Len gave a nonchalant wave, turned at the corner and disappeared.

Barbara Dan

Finally alone, Sam slowly rewound his lariat and slung it over his pommel. Pondering his next move, he jammed his hands in his pockets and scuffed his way tiredly through the tumbleweed and dandelions poking up here and there beside the tracks. His horse ambled along behind him, untethered.

Even though the sun set late in these parts in the summer, the sky already glowed softly, a painted canvas of pinks and purples and a touch of orange. He thumbed back his wide-brimmed hat from his forehead and, rocking back on his boot heels, watched the train from back East pull out of the station. Heading west to California.

That could only mean one thing: He was already in the dog house with Miss Wolverton. Right now, she was probably cooling her heels inside the train depot, and none too happy that he hadn't shown up yet. *I am sure in for it now!* he grinned.

Aware of his disreputable appearance, he plunged his calloused hands into the horse trough next to the train station hitching post, then ran blunt fingers through his hair. Not much he could do to improve his looks, short of a full body bath, he reckoned. But he supposed any woman willing to take him up on his job offer, sight unseen, and traipse halfway across the continent, wasn't likely to kick up a fuss over a little dirt. Well! He'd soon find out, wouldn't he?

Patting his horse's neck, Sam raised his head, inviting the breeze flowing down off the mountains to cool his sun-burned face. Then, with a resolute stride, he set out to meet Miss Margaret Wolverton. He sure hoped things worked out between the two of them.

Chapter Two

Not wishing to be conspicuous, Meg turned aside and opened her purse, giving her sparse collection of coins a nervous jingle. Barely enough for a single night's lodging for the four of them. A quick glance at the railroad clock over the ticket master's window caused her heart to plummet. The advanced hour only confirmed her worst fears. The train being so late, Mr. Gallagher must have decided she wasn't coming. Otherwise he would surely be here by now.

Handing Davey and Susie her last two apples to stave off their hunger, she began to pace. *What to do, what to do?* Since the train had pulled out, headed for the West Coast, the station had pretty much emptied out. Soon it would be time to close—not a welcome prospect for a lone woman with three children.

She took a turn around the waiting room, pausing now and then to glance hopefully out the window. Still no sign of Mr. Gallagher. More and more he was starting to feel like a promise in the wind; a phantom. Yes, he'd sent money for her trip, most of which she'd used to buy food for her orphans at various whistle stops along the way, but except for his bold, scrawling signature on the letter in her purse, the man's existence seemed as hard to confirm as that clump of tumbleweed rolling helter-skelter across the open track.

Where, oh, where can he be? she fretted, biting her lip.

Another half-hour passed. Pacing, Meg tried not to panic. *Mustn't worry!* Yet she couldn't stay here all night. Nearly frantic, she planted her bustle on the bench between Davey and Susie, and began to run through her options again. Jimmy had made two bits helping two female passengers with their bags, but when he mentioned that he was available for adoption, they had pulled their shawls around their bony shoulders like ruffled hens and suggested he apply for a job at one of the saloons down the street. Meg shuddered at the thought. What these children needed was the steady guidance of a loving mother and a kind, but firm father.

Barbara Dan

I need to focus on what to do right now, she reminded herself. Perhaps if she sought lodging before it grew any later—yes, perhaps that would be best. Having the boys bed down in the same room with Susie and her might prove a bit awkward, but in a pinch, how else could she keep an eye on all three?

What she and the children needed was a hot meal, a good wash, and a place to bed down. In that order. After being tossed about like for peppercorns in a shaker for the past few weeks, a real mattress would be simply heavenly.

Yes, Meg decided, she must take charge of the situation at once. Mr. Gallagher was undoubtedly an unreliable sort, or he would have been here to greet her by now. She would leave word with the station master, in case their arrangement finally dawned on Mr. Gallagher. In the meantime, she must seek out an inexpensive, but respectable boarding house.

Her mind made up, she tucked a rebellious strand of her dark auburn hair into her tidy bun and bent down to wake Susie, who was nodding over her snack. As she straightened, adjusting the child's weight on her shoulder, she caught a glimpse of the strangest grizzled visage—a ghostly apparition, actually—peering in the station window through cupped hands.

Backlit by a yellow lantern, the man loomed large against the gathering twilight. He was so large, in fact, that she shrank back, instinctively protective of the child in her arms, and pressed her gloved fist against her trembling lips.

This only seemed to amuse the great hulking creature, for he grinned—a most hideous sight, for his smile made every line in his face crack, leaving reddish fissures in his grey death's mask. He grabbed his battered hat and raised it in greeting, while his eyebrows—nearly indistinguishable against his grey pallor—lifted inquiringly.

With a small squeak of dismay, Meg shot to her feet, her heart banging wildly against her ribs. Was *this* her future employer? Or was it some lunatic figment of her imagination?

Holding her breath, she clutched Davey and Susie to her tightly. Hopefully Jimmy was big enough to fend for himself! She had expected "middle-aged," but nothing so antiquated! She gave a tiny shake of her head in denial. What had she gotten herself into? Or maybe she should be asking, *"Lord, what have You gotten me into?"*

The man looked old enough to be Methuselah's grandfather!

He knocked on the windowpane and cocked his head, mouthing the words, *"Are you the one?"*

Winging a quick prayer, Meg gave a brisk nod. He responded with a rascally wink, then disappeared from view, a fact that only heightened her level of anxiety. Had she been hired to care for an invalid? True, he *appeared* large and well muscled, but having nursed her father through his final illness, Meg knew that looks could be deceiving. With a ghostly complexion like Mr. Gallagher's, he probably had one foot in the grave already! And if that were the case, there was no point in accompanying him to his ranch, because she simply could not take care of an ailing widower and properly attend to the needs of three precious children, too!

~ * ~ * ~ * ~

Pursing her lips, Meg was all set to beg off when the railway station door opened, and in walked this same tall gentleman, hat in hand. The lighting being somewhat better inside, she knew at once that she *may* have misjudged the situation. His eyes appeared dark; though she couldn't discern the color, his eyelids were rimmed with pink. A thick layer of gray dust coated his eyebrows, his eyelashes—in fact, everything from the thick mane of hair on his head to the crusty leather boots on his feet.

Startled, she took in his odd appearance, totally unaware that her own mouth was hanging open in astonishment. Mr. Gallagher, however, had the presence of mind to reach out a large dusty knuckle and close her mouth for her.

"M-Mr. Gallagher?" she stammered.

"In the flesh, dear lady," he replied, with a merry twinkle in his eyes, which she now saw were a warm chocolate brown. "Miss Wolverton, please forgive me for not getting here sooner. I got tied up loading cattle—completely lost track of the time. I trust you haven't been waiting very long?"

"Uh, no." For some reason she was tongue-tied. She shook her head, trying to clear her mind. What had she expected? Besides being frightened out of her wits by the sudden ghostly apparition at the window, that is. Underneath all the layers of dust was a man with a sense of humor. And he spoke English like an Easterner! Now why should that come as such a surprise? Everybody came to the Territory from somewhere else; she knew that.

She cleared her throat, trying to figure out what he looked like beneath all that dirt. Clearly her job as housekeeper would include many hours bent over a washboard! "You startled me," she said softly. "I don't know what I expected, but—" She lifted her hands in a helpless shrug.

Sam Gallagher had been studying her, too. "I don't know why, but from your letters I thought you'd be a bigger woman. Are you sure

Barbara Dan

you're up to working on a ranch?" He frowned, and a crater of new lines formed in the dust covering his face.

"I'm fit," Meg replied in emphatic tones. Now that he was here, she didn't want to give him an excuse to send her packing. "I-I've worked hard all my life, sir. I know how to keep house and preserve food, and I bake the best apple pie you've ever—"

"Whoa!" He raised a large hand, effectively putting a period to her list of qualifications. "I believe you! I got your two letters, remember?"

"Well, then, I'm surprised you would even comment on my size!" Meg said with a show of spunk. Besides being fatigued, she was more than a little annoyed by his being late.

"How old *are* you?" He peered at her, the same way a horse trader might examine livestock.

"Not that it's any of your business, sir, but I'm...twenty-two," she snapped back, adding two years just in case he thought twenty was too young and sent her packing. To put him on the defensive, she threw the question right back at him: "How old are *you*, Mr. Gallagher? It's a little hard to tell under all that sand."

Sam let out a guffaw. "I'd say *you're* the one who's got sand, little lady," he retaliated in a dry, raspy voice. Chuckling, he whacked his hat on his chaps, raising another cloud of dust. He clapped it back on his head and looked her over with a touch of admiration in his eyes. "As for your question, I'm old enough to know better, Miss Wolverton. But come along. I reckon you'll do." He bent to pick up her suitcase.

"W-wait!" Meg said. "What about the children?"

He looked around, puzzled. "What about them? Where are their parents?"

"That's just the point," she said. "They have none! I've been taking care of them all across country for the Children's Aid Society. I started out with thirty orphans, and these three are still homeless. I-I confess I find myself in a bit of a quandary, Mr. Gallagher. You wouldn't happen to know a loving family who'd be willing to adopt three children, would you?"

Sam scratched his head, a little thrown by this slight change of plans. He studied the bedraggled assortment standing before him.

"First things first, Mr. Gallagher," Meg planted her hands on her hips to show she meant business. "I can't just abandon them," she said.

"No, of course not," he agreed.

- 12 -

Susie pulled her thumb out of her mouth with a pop and stared up at him with serious brown eyes. "Miss Wolfie is *my* Mama," she said, clinging to Meg's skirt.

Sam looked startled. "Your letters said nothing about—" He cleared his throat. "Miss Wolverton, did you not tell me you were a single lady?"

Blushing, Meg didn't want to wound Susie's feelings, but she had to set the record straight—right now! She pried her skirt loose from Susie's grubby little fingers and drew her employer aside. "I am nobody's Mama, Mr. Gallagher, and I'm unmarried. However, I *do* feel an obligation to these children, After all, they *were* placed in my care," she whispered.

The look of utter consternation on his crusty face made her realize that she had no choice but to confront the situation head-on. Also, discussing this might delay her being able to tend to the children's needs for quite some time.

"Mr. Gallagher, I'm truly sorry that circumstances force me to be blunt, but the hour is late, and the children and I are hungry and exhausted from our trip. They need a home, so unless you are willing to help me find suitable parents to raise them, I cannot possibly accept your kind offer of employment." She folded her arms and patted her foot, awaiting his decision. "The children's needs *must* come first," she told him in a no-nonsense manner. "It is of no great consequence to me whether you decide to discharge me, or not."

"Really?" he said, and frowned.

"I am a woman of my word," she added, raising her chin. "Will you help me?"

His mouth twitched in a cocky grin. "Are you sure you're not an orphan yourself?"

"As a matter of fact, I *am*," Meg admitted, suddenly hot under the collar. "I was only ten when my Daddy died of his wounds during the war. That's why I care so deeply about what happens to these children!"

"Let me see if I've got this straight." He hooked his thumbs in his chaps belt, cocked one knee, and looked her over, his dark eyes glinting with amusement. "You're threatening to back out of our agreement, if I don't find a home for these kids?"

She stuck out her pointy little chin. "I am fully prepared to refund the money you wired me." She held her breath, awaiting his response.

"Don't that beat all." Shaking his head in dismay, he picked up her suitcase and tucked her satchel under his arm. "Come along." Taking her elbow, he escorted her out the door.

Suddenly wary of going *any*where with a stranger, especially after dark, Meg signaled the boys to stay close. Scooping up Susie, she gazed up at this shambling giant of a man, as he silently marched them down the railroad tracks and into town.

Sensing danger, the boys tried to tackle Mr. Gallagher, hoping to impede his progress. Susie, hanging on Meg's neck, started to bawl.

"Hey, pipe down," Sam told the little girl, which only made her howl louder.

"What did you expect?" Jimmy said. "She's scared, bein' a girl."

"Where are you taking us? And don't think you can have me arrested for breach of contract," Meg warned, a little scared herself.

"Yeah," said Jimmy. "If Miss Wolfie goes to jail, we're going, too."

"That right?" Sam grinned like a friendly ghost.

"She's *my* Mother, too!" Davey asserted.

"Will you relax?" Gallagher said, clearly the only one who seemed to find their situation the least bit amusing. "I'm sure we can work something out." He began to herd all four of them toward his horse.

"Where are you taking us?" Meg tried to break free, but he was bigger than her and his fingers were like a steel trap on her upper arm. The tight strings on Meg's corset made her quite breathless. Indeed, it was hard for her to keep up with his long stride.

"I booked us rooms at the Pioneer Hotel nearby. If you have any more baggage to claim, we'll pick it up in the morning," he informed her.

"Oh. That was thoughtful of you." She still didn't trust him, but at least she and the children would have a place to lay their heads tonight.

Sam didn't say a word, just handed Jimmy the reins to his horse. Then he secured Meg's suitcase and satchel to the pommel with a rope and slung a sleepy-eyed Davey up in the saddle.

Ignoring the rowdy cowboys lounging outside a nearby dance hall, he dropped off his horse at the livery stable two blocks down. Lifting his saddle to one shoulder, he handed Meg's suitcase and satchel to Jimmy to carry, half-drag. Sam picked up his Henry rifle and saddle and proceeded to shepherd Meg and her drooping, stumble-footed brood up the street.

Out of the corner of her eye, she noticed he was studying her. "You're certainly a man of few words," she observed.

"No, just hungry. It's been a long day, Miss Wolverton," he said gruffly. "For all of us, I expect."

After a long silence, punctuated by the clack of cowboy boots and the boys' scuffing shoes on the boardwalk, Meg couldn't resist asking, "Does this mean you'll help me find parents for my orphan kids?"

"Let's discuss it over dinner, shall we?"

"As you wish." She gulped, totally thrown off balance by his terse manner. *He must be seething inside at getting saddled with three unexpected children*, she thought, trudging along at his side.

"I-I hope you're not too disappointed, Mr. Gallagher," she said, "I mean, I can't help my age. But I'm a real hard worker. And the children won't be a bit of trouble. They're very well behaved, and they can help with chores," she said, talking fast to cover her nervousness. "I promise you, sir, you won't be sorry. I won't let you down."

When he still said nothing, she rushed on. "I suppose a lot of women responded to your advertisement for a housekeeper."

"A few." He frowned at her. "I liked your letter the best."

"I'm so glad." Meg paused to retie the trailing sash on Susie's rumpled dress. "I'd hate to think I came all this distance, only to find out you've hired somebody else."

He heaved a great sigh. "Relax. You're hired. Haven't I said so? I just didn't expect you to be so young."

"I suppose your other applicants were older ladies?" She hated being such a chatterbox, but she just couldn't seem to stop talking. Taking their clue from her, Jimmy and Davey sat down on the boardwalk and solemnly examined the holes in their shoes. "Now, boys," she cautioned.

"Is there some reason you can't keep walking while we talk?" her employer asked, his voice like rusty iron. "If we don't make tracks, the restaurant will be closed before we get there."

"Oh, I'm sorry!" She picked up Susie again and, picking up the pace, continued to interrogate her employer. "You *did* say you preferred a single lady, didn't you?"

"Yes. An *unmarried* woman."

"And why is that, if I may be so bold as to ask?"

His lips tightened with impatience. "It's quite simple actually. I'm a widower with no children, Miss Wolverton. In the event we hit it off—I mean, you being a single lady, and all—I thought in time we might marry and raise a family."

"But you never said a word about marriage in your letter!" Her eyebrows knit together furiously, while she pondered this unexpected revelation. He hadn't advertised for a mail order bride, but clearly that must have been in his mind all along. *This will never do!* she decided. He was not at all suitable. She was aware that men far outnumbered women in the West, but this was *beyond* devious and underhanded of him! It almost made her want to resign on the spot! And she might have done so, were it not for the children being homeless.

Gazing down at the boardwalk, she realized there were other questions she needed to ask, such as whether a widower might consider adopting the three orphans in her charge without making a wife part of the deal. Since he'd probably had marriage in mind from the get-go, she decided to approach the subject in a roundabout way.

In a way, it would be a test of his character. Hers, too, for that matter.

"So you *do* want children?" she asked.

He stopped in his tracks and stared down at her. "Eventually."

"Well, then," she said pertly, "perhaps you'd like to adopt these three and get a head start on having a family."

Sam Gallagher looked her over thoughtfully, drawing his own conclusions. "When I advertised for a housekeeper, I had no idea things would get so complicated."

Meg choked on a nervous laugh. "Neither did I!"

Usually when she asked a question, she got a direct answer. It appeared the man was something of an artful dodger. She also realized that she lacked sufficient experience to play his game.

Sam passed a hand over his grizzled jaw. Life up to now had been riddled with sorrow and hardship, but he'd never expected such a winsome young woman, or the offer of instant parenthood. "I grant you, a ready-made family would be a radical change from the quiet life I've led up to now."

Struck by the enormity of what she'd just said, Meg blushed. "Would you at least consider the idea? Jimmy and Davey have had such a hard life. We must consider what's best for them," she said earnestly. "They need a loving father to guide them—"

Sam smiled, admiring Miss Wolfie's brass, not to mention her practical common sense. "*And* a loving mother," he reminded her, as they resumed their short walk to the dimly lit café. "Don't forget that."

Meg's cheeks grew warm with gratitude. At least he hadn't turned her down—yet! "As I said, Mr. Gallagher, we have much to discuss."

Sam glanced down at the little tyke nodding sleepily on her shoulder. "I believe this one has already adopted *you*, Miss Wolverton," he said, his manner deceptively calm. "I reckon it all depends on how the boys feel about things."

Davey, rocking and bumping between the two adults, gave Sam a silent, questioning stare. He was a handsome youngster, though all the horrors of living on the streets showed in his hollow blue eyes and solemn features beneath the shock of brown hair drooping over his forehead. He and Jimmy seemed like the type of sons a man would be proud to call his own. All they needed was a little settling down, he suspected. A month of hot meals, plenty of room to run and let off steam in the great outdoors, and the knowledge that they were safe should do the trick.

Noticing the direction of his gaze, Meg smiled and ruffled Davey's hair. "Davey is the best little boy, just bursting with energy! I promise he won't be a bit of trouble, Mr. Gallagher."

"And what about this young fellow?" Sam nodded toward the towhead who was industriously lugging her suitcases and absorbing every word that passed between them.

"Jimmy is a hard worker, Mr. Gallagher. There's not a mean bone in his body."

"Ah." Again he nodded, wise to her attempt to wrap him around her finger. "Don't soft-soap me, Miss Wolverton, or I'll start thinking you were a snake oil saleswoman before you hired on as my housekeeper."

"No such thing, I assure you!" Meg blushed at such an idea, then sobered, gesturing to the children. "There, but for the grace of God, go you and I, Mr. Gallagher!"

"Amen, sister," he said softly and, pushing open the café door, ushered everyone inside.

When Sam unburdened himself of his saddle, dropping it on the floor with a loud thud, Jimmy dropped the straw suitcase and satchel. Sticking his thumbs in his patched back pockets, he struck a similar pose. Meg was still mulling over how quickly the boys aped her employer's mannerisms, when the owner of the café stepped out of her kitchen.

"She cooks the best Southern fried chicken," Sam informed the boys with a wink, and stepped forward to shake the cook's hand. "Hello, Miss Betty. I brought you some hungry customers!"

"Why, Mist' Sam! You look a mite peaked yourself!" Betty said, beaming.

"Starved," he admitted, patting his stomach.

"Well, grab yourselves a seat, and I'll be right back to take your orders." Betty disappeared into the back, shouting to her helper, "We need three tall glasses of milk, you lazy no-account, and some of them hot rolls. Hurry up now! Mist' Sam's done found hisself a pretty li'l gal and three of the hungriest lookin' chil'ren you done ever seen!"

Sam grinned at Meg apologetically. "The food here is out of this world, at least judging by Cheyenne's standards." He pulled out a chair, but before he could seat her, Davey threw himself against the backs of her knees, causing her to totter unsteadily.

Expecting to see her fall over in a dead faint, Sam hooked an arm around Meg's slender waist. "Hold on, Miss Wolverton. Boys, sit yourselves down." Frowning, he pointed to two chairs across the table.

Quickly regaining her balance, Meg began to push against his chest to avoid inhaling all his dust. "Mr. Gallagher, cease and desist! I am perfectly able to take care of myself." She twitched her skirts aside and seated herself.

Sam raised his hands defensively. "Whoa. What was that all about?" he asked, surprised by her show of temper.

"Davey was only attempting to seat me like a gentleman," she explained, smoothing an untidy wisp of hair back from her face. "Children learn by example." Smiling at them, she spread her napkin across her lap. "Isn't that right, children?"

"Well, he sure could use a few lessons on how to seat a lady!" Sam eased her chair into place. "As for the children's needs and requirements, we can discuss those later. In private," he added in a low, gravelly voice that reverberated up and down her spine, and left her feeling more than a little nervous.

Chapter Three

Fortunately the children were too hungry to misbehave. The boys packed in the food as if they didn't know where their next meal was coming from. And Miss Betty, who had a heart of solid gold, kept them so entertained that the time passed quickly. As a result, Meg and Mr. Gallagher never did find a spare moment to discuss the children's future or the specific requirements of her employment.

Throughout most of the meal, when he wasn't masticating what appeared to be a thick steak, her employer was close-mouthed—until finally Meg began to think he was having second thoughts about hiring her. Well, at least she could thank her lucky stars that she and the children would be sleeping in real beds tonight. Perhaps she was letting her fears run away with her?

Didn't the Good Book say, *"Sufficient unto the day are the troubles thereof"*? If only she wasn't such a worry-wart! She really must cultivate the habit of being more thankful for each day's blessings, and not worry so much about tomorrow.

After dinner, she stood waiting with Susie in her arms, while Sam Gallagher paid for their meals. The boys were watching his every move intently. No doubt measuring whether they could trust this taciturn stranger. And hoping they wouldn't be let down again, the way so many adults had done in the past.

"All right, everybody. Let's mosey." Stuffing his wallet in his back pocket, Sam picked up his rifle and his saddle and gear.

Galvanized into action, the two boys nearly bowled Meg over in their hurry to follow him out the door. "I got Miss Wolfie's suitcase," Jimmy said, grabbing it.

"Me, too!" Davey excitedly commandeered Meg's satchel.

"Whoa. Easy, men. Slow down," Sam laughed. "Ladies first." He bowed politely to Meg, indicating the door. "After you, ma'am."

Shaking her head over the boys' eagerness, Meg smiled. "Since you know where we're going, Mr. Gallagher, and I don't, perhaps you should lead the way?"

Barbara Dan

A wide grin spread across his face. "Yes, ma'am. Reckon I'm stuck with being the point man," he drawled. "We'll be heading due north to the Pioneer Hotel, ladies and gentlemen. Follow me."

~ * ~ * ~ * ~

Like most of the hotels located near the train station, the Pioneer Hotel had definitely seen better days. *And hopefully a more reputable clientele,* Meg thought, glancing around the lobby. Her employer shouldered his way past the garishly dressed nightingales loitering on the steps outside. Cigar smoke and loud talk enveloped them, as he escorted his new housekeeper and her brood of orphans over to the registration desk. He dinged the bell with his fist, interrupting the clerk, who was engaged in a dispute of some kind with a rummy-eyed character in coveralls.

"Remember me? Sam Gallagher," he growled. "I came in earlier today and reserved two rooms for tonight. Upstairs in the back, where it's quieter."

Eyes popping with curiosity, the clerk stared at the cattleman covered with dust, then at the prim and proper young lady in travel clothes standing next to him—and three children, each with a smear of cherry pie on their lips.

Catching Sam's warning glower, he squinted at the register, then scrambled for keys. "Here yah go, Mr. Gallagher. That'll be two dollars a room. Fifty cents more if you want water brought up."

Sam paid up and, being weighed down with gear, signaled Meg with a jerk of his head to take possession of the keys. "Send up plenty of water, and make it hot," he barked at the clerk, his voice raspy with trail dust.

"Sure thing, Mr. Gallagher."

They hiked up three flights of stairs to their rooms, which overlooked the back alley. He dropped his saddle in front of his door and followed Meg and Susie over to render any needed assistance. Jimmy and Davey trailed behind him like shadows, carrying her luggage.

Tongue between her teeth, Meg worked the key feverishly in the door lock. She wanted nothing so much as to escape the looming Mr. Gallagher and his brooding silence. He'd said very little during dinner, and considering the disreputable people loitering in the hotel lobby, she hesitated to mention the need for a trundle bed. Davey and Jimmy would just have to bed down on the floor in her room.

"Here, Miss Wolverton, allow me," Sam offered, taking the key from her.

In need of a good oiling, the lock finally clicked, and she stepped past him into a dark cubbyhole of a room. While she set Susie on the bed, the boys trooped in with her suitcase and satchel and dropped them like a bomb. Taking charge, Mr. Gallagher lit the lantern and raised the window to air out the pungent, musky odors that lingered, left behind by the room's previous occupants.

Having led a fairly sheltered life, Meg blinked in disbelief at the gaudy red drapes and purple flocked wallpaper. She could only imagine the types of debauchery that regularly took place in this hotel. Frankly shocked, and hoping this was all a terrible nightmare, she glanced at her employer, who stood rubbing the back of his neck, a sheepish expression on his face.

"I apologize. All the rooms in this district are decorated pretty much the same," he said.

"District? Are you saying this is a . . . Red Light District?" she whispered, holding her hands over Susie's ears.

"Most all the hotels near the railroad and livestock pens are pretty raunchy," he admitted. "With the round-up in full swing, there wasn't anything else available."

"Oh, dear God!" As the truth began to dawn, she felt her head start to spin and her knees turn wobbly with fright. "Surely there's a decent boarding house nearby?" She gazed up at him imploringly.

"No, ma'am. I checked those first— *Whoops!* Hold on." Catching sight of Jimmy hanging over the window sill, trading insults with a drunk in the alley, Sam nabbed him quick and hauled him back inside. He slammed the window shut and gave the squirmy kid a stern look that took the fight right out of him. "Kid, I am speaking with Miss Wolverton. Now *sit!*"

In two quick strides he had young Jimmy sitting cross legged on the floor and came back to Meg, who sat on the edge of the bed, biting her lip and close to pitching a full blown conniption fit. No stranger to dealing with female troubles, Sam went down on one knee in front of her. "Now, Miss Wolfie," he said in a soothing voice, taking her hands in his. "Let's not start getting cold feet! Especially since you've made it all the way across country with a passel of lively young mischief makers."

She nodded. "Thirty in all."

"You helped twenty-seven orphans find homes?" he said admiringly.

"Yes." She straightened her shoulders. "Of course, I did have help. Reverend and Mrs. Lowell dealt with town officials along the way. My job was mostly seeing that the children were on their best behavior and got enough to eat."

"There you go." A big smile spread over his face. "And down to only three now."

"I know, but this place gives me a really bad feeling." She gave an involuntary shiver and looked at him, seeking reassurance.

"There's a good strong lock on the door," he said. "And I'll be right next door with my trusty Henry rifle."

Gazing into his smiling eyes, Meg began to regain a smidgeon of courage. *Everyone feels afraid from time to time,* she told herself. It didn't mean she was a coward.

"It's only for tonight," Mr. Gallagher reminded her.

Rising, she moved to the window, swept aside the tacky red drapes, and peered into the darkness. At least the only balcony was on the front of the building, and she needn't concern herself with peeping Toms and other undesirables. Her gaze dropped directly down to the alley below. A couple of wagons and a half-dozen horses were tied to drain spouts and anything else a cowboy could wrap a pair of reins around. The upshot of this was that the alley was pretty effectively blocked off, except for foot traffic.

"The outhouse is out back in the alley," Sam said, appearing at her elbow. "Considering the distance at night, it's probably best if you and the children make use of the chamber pots."

Blushing at such frank talk, Meg nodded. "I'm sure we'll manage somehow, Mr. Gallagher," she said with as much dignity as she could muster.

She hated to think how noisy the rooms facing the street must be, if the hotel clerk considered the alley quiet! Sounds of a rinky-tink piano pounding out a discordant rendition of "Old Brown's Daughter" floated up from below, along with the odors of refuse and untended horses. Cheyenne's saloons were certainly going full throttle, accompanied by raucous laughter, the clink of empty bottles, and the out-of-tune shrill of a chanteuse. The scrape of stomping boots against wooden floors confirmed the dance going full swing in the saloon across the alley.

Forcing a smile, she met her employer's gaze. He lingered in the open doorway. "I'll take the boys off your hands so you can get a good night's sleep." He grinned wryly, stepping into the hallway. "Again I apologize for not having time to get cleaned up before— well, Jimmy and Davey and I are definitely due for a good scrubbing. See you in the morning."

"Good night, Miss Wolfie." Jimmy darted forward and threw his arms around her in an impulsive hug.

"Good night. Sleep well, boys." She waved to them; then remembered: "I have an extra bar of soap in my satchel, Mr. Gallagher, if you need it."

"Thanks. I'll let you know." Sam chuckled, recalling the children's nickname for her. "Good night, Miss Wolfie. See you in the morning." He bowed slightly, and keeping a firm hand on each boy's shoulder, herded them into the room next door.

Shaking her head over the day's unsettling turn of events, Meg closed and bolted the door, then went to help Susie out of her travel-stained clothing. "Let's get cleaned up, shall we?"

Susie sniffled. "I gots no nightie, Miss Wolfie."

"Well, perhaps something in my suitcase will fit." Meg tapped one finger against her lips, then smiled. "I know just the thing." Rummaging around, she produced a delicate chemise trimmed in pretty lace.

Susie's eyes grew wide; then she shook her head. "Too fancy for me."

"First we'll have a thorough wash," said Meg, ignoring the child's woebegone look.

A knock on the door announced the arrival of hot water, and she quickly unlocked the door. Sam handed over two pails of water. "The desk clerk brought these up to my room. Careful, this one is really hot."

"Thank you." She carefully set both pails on the dresser, next to the pitcher and basin. "I can't begin to tell you how much I appreciate this! Goodnight, sir."

Closing the door, Meg smiled at Susie, who looked intimidated by so much water. "Off with those clothes, young lady. Time for your bath."

"Oh, no," Susie whispered, drooping pathetically.

Placing the wash basin on the floor, Meg poured water and tested the temperature with her elbow, then beckoned. "You're small. You should fit with no trouble," she urged the child.

"Won't I get drownded?" Susie asked wistfully.

"Nonsense. I'm an expert swimmer." Meg laughed. "I promise to save you, if you get soap in your eyes, or—"

"You are so funny." The little girl shyly buried her face against Meg's skirt. "I love you, Miss Wolfie. I want you to be my Mama forever!"

"Yes, well, right now we need to scrub you clean, so your pores can breathe." Meg gave Susie's armpit a little tickle. "And then you can wear this lovely chemise of mine, and sleep like a real princess in this bed."

"Like a princess?" Susie's eyes goggled with happiness. "Oh, Miss Wolfie, that would be swell!"

Laughing, Meg made Susie sit down, inwardly cringing at how thin the child was. "Yes, but remember, you must never say 'swell,' if you want people to think you're a *real* princess. It's simply not done in the best circles," she joked in a hoity-toity voice. She handed over the soap and a washcloth. "Do a good job now. Don't forget to wash behind your ears."

Susie heaved a dramatic sigh. "Yes, Miss Wolfie."

While Meg searched through her suitcase for suitable attire for the trip to Mr. Gallagher's ranch in the morning, a large puddle of water formed on the floor around the basin. Finally calling a halt to the splashing, she toweled the little girl dry and dressed her for bed. She was about to draw up the covers to Susie's chin, when the child tugged on her sleeve.

"What is it, darling?" she asked.

"I gots to say my prayers," Susie said. "Reverend and Mrs. Lowell said as soon as I got me a new family, I should thank Jesus." She knelt down beside the bed and began to pour out her heart in earnest to God.

Listening, Meg knew it was premature to assume that Mr. Gallagher would adopt all three children. But he might take the boys. When they grew up, they could be a real asset on his ranch. As for this little sprite? She seriously doubted his generosity would extend that far.

Even so, she hated to say anything that might squelch Susie's optimism. These orphans had suffered enough already, and it hardly seemed right to dash their hopes. Deeply conflicted in her heart, Meg dropped to her knees beside the little girl.

"...and bless my new Mama. Amen!" Bright-eyed, Susie threw her arms around Meg.

"Oh, darling. You are the sweetest little girl!" Her voice broke, as she returned the little girl's fierce hug. "Whoever adopts you will be the luckiest person in the world."

"Yes," Susie agreed smugly. "You *are* lucky to have me, aren't you?"

Choking back a tearful laugh, Meg suddenly caught sight of a nasty critter crawling along a strand of Susie's hair. Alarmed, she jumped back. "Oh, dear! We need help, Susie, because you have—" she gulped— "How can I put this delicately? You have—head lice!"

"Uh-huh," Susie nodded. "We *all* do, Miss Wolfie."

Meg regarded her with horror. "Who's 'we,' darling? You mean, the other orphans—?"

"Well, Jimmy and Davey have cooties—"

Meg jumped up. "Don't move," she ordered, pointing a finger at Susie, who stood by the bed with dripping wet, scraggly hair. "I'll be right back, I promise!" And she fled out the door.

Susie let out a howl. "Did I do something wrong, Miss Wolfie?"

"No, darling. Stay right where you are!"

Banging on Mr. Gallagher's door, Meg needed to find out if he'd made a similar discovery about the boys.

Standing shirtless in the doorway with a towel slung around his neck, Sam raised his eyebrows inquiringly. "Miss Wolverton?"

"Susie has lice!" she blurted out.

"So do these two." He jerked his thumb at the two emaciated boys, standing in the altogether, clutching towels around their privates.

"What are we going to do?" she whispered furtively.

"Kill the lice." He shrugged. "I'd invite you in to inspect their heads, but none of us is properly attired to entertain a lady."

Meg blew her cork. "This is no time for foolish talk, Mr. Gallagher! Just tell me where to find the nearest pharmacist."

"Miss Wolverton, *I* am not going out at this hour to beat down doors looking for a patented cure, and neither are you. Tomorrow morning the boys and I plan to visit the bath house. We'll take care of the problem then."

"What about Susie?" She planted her fists on her hips and tilted her chin at him. "I-I assume this— er, bath house you speak of caters strictly to men?"

"Women, too. You'll have to take her, because that's where I draw the line. I'll delouse the boys, but I think it best if we divide up the sexes."

"Yes, of course." Her face reddened with embarrassment. "I never meant to imply—"

His laugh lines emerged, as he regarded her persnickety stance. "I know you didn't, Miss Wolverton." His voice was kind, and for the first time Meg realized what a difference soap and water had made in his appearance.

She squinted, not trusting her vision in the dimly lit hall. "Mr. Gallagher?" She gawked, wanting to make absolutely certain she had the correct room. The transformation was that profound. He was not an old man, not at all. He was deeply sunburned, with sandy blond hair and lively brown eyes, just brimming with intelligence and fringed by thick dark russet eyelashes and eyebrows. With the dirt gone, he was—she swallowed hard—why, he was downright handsome!

Flustered, she retreated into the hall. "Very well, then," she said primly. "Please knock on my door tomorrow morning, when you're ready to set out for the—uh, bath house." She jerked a quick nod and fled.

Safe once more behind her locked door, Meg carefully wrapped Susie's damp head in a dry towel. Hopefully it would keep the critters from traveling! Besides, keeping busy seemed the best way to distract herself from harboring improper thoughts about the man in the next room. *Old man—hah!* She shook her head in amazement. He was nothing like she'd imagined!

And he was patient with the children. In fact, the boys seemed amazingly meek and well behaved under his supervision, and yet— Meg swallowed down a lump of fear. Considering the quizzical look in his eyes, which she now knew were a deep velvety brown, she almost wished *he* would vanish into the night, leaving her stranded, for never in her life had she felt such a strong tug at her heartstrings!

Certainly she had never reacted to a member of the male species like this before. A stranger, too! Could his being partially undressed account for her irrepressible urge to giggle? And all that hair on his chest! Did men have hair all over their bodies? And what amazing muscles! Why, even his nipples had muscles. His arms, too. No wonder he could carry a saddle one-handed with such ease!

Oh, what is the matter with me? she chided herself. It was best not to examine some things too closely. Otherwise, she'd never have the courage to look Mr. Gallagher in the eye again!

Nevertheless she vowed to maintain constant vigilance and watch every move she made around her new employer. Otherwise she had a pretty good idea where this all might lead. *Dear God in heaven!* From the moment she agreed to come West, a whole series of events had been set in motion, until now she was assailed by a strong conviction that this little 'adventure' of hers was likely to develop into something far more challenging than she'd ever dreamed!

Wringing her hands, she paced the room, wondering how a worldly man like Mr. Gallagher felt about having three children and an inexperienced housekeeper dumped on him all at the same time. Preferring not to ponder what tomorrow might bring, she tucked the covers around Susie, who blinked sleepily up at her. Braving a kiss, Meg bade her goodnight.

Nearly slipping on the puddle of water, she wiped up the floor with a towel. Intent upon disposing of the bath water, she flung open the window. Seeing only darkness below, she snatched up the basin Susie had used, with all those disgusting, dead critters floating in a scum of dirty water—*ugh!* Hardening her heart against any drunks loitering in the alley, she threw the contents out the window. Sure enough, an angry curse promptly floated upward.

Intent upon stifling the profanity, Meg closed the window and closed the curtains. Dreading the prospect of a long wakeful night, she tiptoed around to the other side of the bed and stretched out, fully clothed, on top of the quilt. She snuffed the lamp and stared into the dark.

In case a dire emergency should arise during the night, she thought it best not to disrobe. In a wild town like Cheyenne, one never knew what to expect. Full of speculation about the children's future and living on a ranch, she closed her eyes. Almost immediately she fell into a deep sleep.

Chapter Four

Daybreak came too quickly. As Meg lifted the window, the cool air in her face filled her with renewed energy and excitement. This was the first day of the rest of her life, she realized. No matter what came her way, from this day forward, she vowed, taking another deep breath, life was going to be...well, different.

The past year had been lived mostly hand to mouth, at times not knowing where the next meal would come from. Often stretched to the breaking point, she had taken one low-paying job after another to help make ends meet. Sewing, cleaning other women's houses, running errands, baking pies—whatever it took to pay the rent on her tiny basement apartment.

Now, suddenly, she found herself responsible for the care of three orphans as well. But at least she had a paying job. Steep responsibilities for a lone woman, true, but she was well able to meet the challenge, she told herself. Perhaps her optimism stemmed from the spirit of the West, where the "rules" governing the role of a woman appeared...well, more respectful. She had seen it already in the deferential behavior of men toward women. Of course, that might be partly due to the scarcity of women, but here, at least, a woman had a chance to prove herself.

Pondering that thought put Meg in an extra cheerful mood, as she prepared for the day. She no sooner finished brushing her hair when a knock on her door interrupted her tendency to daydream. Smiling, she opened the door and encountered Mr. Gallagher and the boys, each with a sheepish grin on his face. "Good morning, gentlemen!" she said with a bright smile.

"Good morning, Miss Wolfie! You look mighty sharp this morning," her employer responded with a bow. "I was going to say, 'Don't bother to get dressed,' but I see you already have."

"And why would I *not* be properly attired, Mr. Gallagher?" she answered pertly. "It's morning! And I am eager to seek out the bath house and take care of a certain unpleasant task before breakfast."

He held up a large olive green tin and pointed to several ominous bugs on the label. "I have the magic elixir right here."

"Ah!" She smiled approvingly. "I see you found an apothecary."

"We'll take the children down the back stairs and through the alley. Shortcut," he added, by way of clarification.

"Yes. An excellent idea," Meg agreed. "I'll wake Susie. We'll only be a minute."

"Don't worry about bringing towels," he told the already closing door. "The bath house provides clean ones."

"Thanks." She poked her head out the door and nodded. "What a lovely morning it is, Mr. Gallagher," she said, surprising him by her cheerful mood, and closed the door. Quickly buttoning Susie into her dress, she quickly rejoined her employer, and together they took a brisk walk down the alley with the boys racing on ahead.

One block up, they entered the bath house and were met by a sleepy-eyed attendant. With no other customers at such an early hour, they had the place to themselves. Meg and Susie disappeared through the partition to the women's tubs, while Sam, Jimmy and David entered the men's area.

The furnishings were crude, but after a month long train ride, Meg didn't hesitate to avail herself of a full body soak. Susie, on the other hand, balked. "I took a baff last night," she protested, squirming. The woman in charge soon put the little girl at her ease, and before long she and Meg were both submerged in tubs of lovely hot bubbly water, scented with spices and oils.

"Just for the ladies," the woman attendant confided. Whatever the establishment used to scent the water on the men's side, Meg was grateful for the special pampering and the privacy she and Susie enjoyed. It had been ages since she'd felt so pampered!

Through the thin walls, she could hear her employer and the boys having a raucous good time. Judging by the caterwauling, Sam Gallagher was actively involved in the scrub-down of two very grimy young fellows. Jimmy was twice as vocal as Davey, but they both took ear-cleaning and smelly shampoos with less hollering than she expected.

Eventually it was Susie's turn to undergo delousing, a task Meg had been dreading. When the attendant brought in the tin of fumigating powder, Meg hastily stepped out of the tub, wrapping a towel around herself, and prepared herself mentally to do battle.

"Time to be brave, Susie darling," she said.

"I will stink. I just know I will!" Susie wailed, shivering despite the tub's hot steam.

"Yes, but only for a few minutes," Meg promised. "After we're finished, this nice lady will pour rose water on you, and you will *love* how wonderful you smell."

"If I don't die first." Susie held her nose and closed her eyes. "Ugh!"

"Such a prima donna," Meg laughed.

After reading the instructions on the can, she handed Susie a wet washcloth to cover her face. Standing as far back as she could and still administer the powder, she slowly began to work the powder into Susie's hair. "Hold very, very still," she cautioned. "It says to keep it on for five minutes. I know it smells terrible, but try to be brave, sweetheart!"

Sam knocked on the wooden partition separating the men from the women folk. "How's it going?" he chuckled.

By now Meg was gagging with the smell. "Are you sure there isn't a less noxious cure?" She coughed, furious with him for laughing.

"We *could* try kerosene," he yelled back, "but that nearly always damages the lungs. Plus it's highly flammable."

"Fancy that," she quipped. "By the way, does anyone have a clock around here?"

"I do," said the female attendant, coming back. "Time's up. Time to rinse off that poor child."

"Thank you, God!" Grabbing a clean bucket of warm, not scalding, water, Meg sloshed it over the drooping figure standing before her. She combed through Susie's hair to make sure the lice were dead and gone. To make absolutely certain, she gave her a second rinse.

Finally Susie revived enough to demand, 'Where's my roses? I can't smell the roses."

Meg gave her a quick hug, and with a conspiratorial wink, the attendant added some attar of roses to the next bucket. "Coming right up, missy!" the woman sang out cheerfully and gave the little girl a thorough dousing.

~ * ~ * ~ * ~

Celebrating clean, healthy scalps, Sam marched everyone over to Betty's Café for a big breakfast of pancakes, sausages and juice. The children's voices grew boisterous, as they joked about their harrowing experience with the "bug powder."

Smiling at her charges, Meg realized that truly this *was* the first day of the beginning of *all* their lives. Not just hers, but all five of them. The emotions that filled her felt...glorious! Wyoming Territory—what a perfect place to test her mettle as an independent woman. Just thinking about it felt liberating!

She was still smiling at everyone gathered around the table and pondering her exciting life, when her confidence received an unexpected shock that sent her spirits plummeting.

Suddenly, without warning, Davey went into a full blown seizure.

Overwhelmed by all the laughter and confusion, the unfamiliar sights and smells, the loud *clink* of silverware, and foot traffic passing back and forth from the kitchen, Davey began to thrash around uncontrollably and utter incoherent cries of distress. Sliding beneath the table, he got tangled up in the calico tablecloth, upset the coffee pot and knocked over several water glasses.

Sam's plate of fried eggs and grits landed in his lap. This inspired a startled expletive from the only ally she and the orphans had.

First things first, however. Her employer was big enough to fend for himself.

Going to the rescue, Meg grabbed Davey's flailing legs and hauled him out from under the table—hopefully before Davey could do any serious damage to himself or anyone else. Alas, her efforts only made matters worse. In the struggle the table got turned upside down!

Davey lay convulsing in a full-blown *grand mal* seizure. Crawling to him on hands and knees, Meg envisioned all her bright hopes for the future disappearing down a black hole of despair and humiliation. Her employer's knees were at eye level, and for a fleeting second she couldn't help but wonder what he must be thinking, and how much he must regret hiring her.

Frantic to help the nine-year-old, she groped about on the floor for an implement to keep Davey from swallowing his tongue. Abruptly the wrecked table was swept aside, and Sam dropped to one knee beside her. "I'll take it from here," he said quietly.

His face was surprisingly calm, as he rammed a large spoon between the boy's clenched teeth, forcing it over the tongue, and held it in place. "Hang on, Davey. You're going to be all right, son. It'll be over in just a minute."

Davey's rigid body arched and jerked spasmodically, while Meg focused on not letting go of him. He was, after all, *her* responsibility. In her head she felt like yelling at the rancher, *"Go away! Leave us alone! Can't you see this is an emergency?"* If Mr. Gallagher couldn't stomach one of Davey's little episodes, perhaps they should part company right now. Yes, she needed a job, but she could handle this without outside interference.

She felt so helpless, waiting for the seizure to pass. Finally the tremors stopped and Davey went limp. She'd only seen him in seizure twice before, but after each of his fits, he had fallen asleep, worn out by the violent force that held him in its grip. As his eyes began to flutter and close, Meg heaved a sigh of relief. Each time he suffered a seizure, she felt a tiny piece of her heart break. Not that she understood the cause of his illness. All she knew was that she must help him get through it without hurting himself.

As the crisis passed, Gallagher's strong hand clasped her elbow and lifted her to her feet. Seating her in a nearby chair, he returned to the child lying on the floor. Stooping, he gathered Davey up in his arms and, fishing in his back pocket, brought out some bills and pressed them into the café owner's hand. "To cover the cost of the meal and the damage," he said apologetically.

With a quick nod, he indicated that Meg, Susie and Jimmy should follow him outside as he headed toward a nearby chuck wagon. "Archie," he called to the driver. "Keep a close eye on the boy while I take care of business." Effortlessly and without consulting Meg, he passed Davey's limp body up to the grizzled old driver. Stepping over the front seat, the man named Archie laid the boy on a stack of flour sacks in the back of the wagon.

"Mr. Gallagher—" After all the embarrassment he'd been subjected to, Meg felt the least she could do was give him a chance to back out of their agreement. "I am *so* sorry about your breakfast," she apologized.

With surprising good humor, he patted his trim belly and rocked back on his boot heels. "I can afford to drop a few pounds," he said lightly. "Besides, Betty's eggs were runnier than I like 'em. I distinctly remember ordering 'sunny-side up.' And those grits—why, they had more lumps than the tick-infested hide of a buffalo!" Ignoring her startled look at his picturesque speech, he leaned his face down close to her ear. "I'm counting on you, Miss Wolverton. I like my grits *smooth.*"

Meg tilted her head to one side. *Goodness gracious!* If she didn't know better, she might think he was trying to sweet-talk her. "Are you quite sure you even want to risk a sample of my cooking?" she asked. Hadn't he seen enough trouble for one day? Any sane man would have the good sense to 'git' while he still could. "I completely understand if you find Davey's problem—"

He hooked his right thumb in his gun belt, calling her attention to his revolvers for the first time, and making her wonder if she might not be getting the worst of the deal, if life on his ranch required him to wear such an arsenal.

"Lady, I already told you. I like your sand. And I want you working for *me.*" He pointed his other thumb at his heart.

Meg gulped. "But what about Davey?"

"I plan to address that problem in a minute."

"Well, I certainly hope so!" she snapped, confused by his cavalier attitude.

"We'll stop at the druggist and pick up some belladonna, plus some tonic for Jimmy's rickets." Sensing that she was less than thrilled by his plan, he added, "Relax. I used to be an army doctor, Miss Wolverton—before I turned rancher."

"Oh." Shocked by this latest revelation, and wondering why he gave up doctoring in favor of raising cattle, Meg wasn't sure how to respond. His assessment of her housekeeping skills, while flattering, in no way matched her own opinion. Right now she was quaking in her shoes following Davey's seizure. She was mighty glad Mr.—or should she call him Doctor? Anyway, she hoped he hadn't noticed how uneasy she felt around him, not to mention the rough band of slightly hung-over cowboys riding up the street toward them. It suddenly dawned on her that she might wind up being the only woman for miles around! How did he intend to guarantee her safety?

Hopefully not by using violence. "Mr.—uh, Dr. Gallagher?" she stumbled over his name.

"Call me Sam," he said.

She cleared her throat. "Might we speak privately for a moment?"

"Certainly." He gestured toward the boardwalk, and she followed reluctantly, careful to keep an eye on Jimmy and Davey. Susie clung to her skirts like a large, sticky-fingered beetle.

"What's on your mind?" He seemed surprisingly open and cheerful, considering the ruckus that had just taken place in the café.

Since last night Sam Gallagher had undergone an amazing transformation, including a change of clothes. Suddenly it occurred to her, rather forcefully, that for a man in his thirties, he was actually quite— Well, he was nothing like the ancient embodiment of Doomsday that had confronted her at the train depot the night before! All the more reason to think twice before traveling into the untamed wilderness with him and his men, she now realized. Especially in light of the strong mutual attraction that seemed to be developing between them.

She clasped her hands primly and gave him her sternest look. "Mr. Gallagher, I cannot go with you, unless you stick to our original bargain."

He shooed away an annoying horsefly, only half-listening. "Sure. I'm a man of my word."

"I'm delighted to hear it, sir. Now about my living accommodations—"

"I'll take care of it," he interrupted. "I've got it all figured out."

Glaring up at him, she decided that his reassurances left much to be desired. "And what, pray tell, have you got 'all figured out'?"

"The boys and I will sleep in the bunkhouse, and you and Susie can live in my line shack until I rebuild the ranch house." He pulled on his left ear and gave her a sheepish look. "It kind of burned down a couple of weeks ago."

"Your house burned down?" She narrowed her eyes at him. "That sounds like a tall tale to me."

"Well, it's not," he said, looking her straight in the eye. "We had a violent lightning storm, and my house burned to the ground."

"I see. And how long will it take to rebuild?" she pursued.

"Not long." The glance he slanted her way revealed his impatient nature. "Anything else you want to ask, Miss Wolverton?"

Pursing her lips, she folded her arms over her chest. "Precisely *how* long, Mr. Gallagher?"

"The name's Sam," he reminded her.

"Whatever." She couldn't call him Doctor, because evidently he was no longer a practicing physician. And she absolutely refused to call him Sam, because that would encourage unwelcome familiarity between them.

They stood toe to toe, nose to nose, in a clear standoff.

To her surprise, his gaze shifted first.

She certainly hadn't expected him to back off. After all, he held the purse strings, which gave him a superior bargaining position. He swept off his hat, wiped his perspiring forehead on his shirt sleeve, then plunked it back on his sandy blond hair. He stared at the horizon, frowning. "Ma'am, it's getting late. Are you coming with me, or not?"

"It's barely eight in the morning!" Meg planted one foot on the boardwalk. She wasn't about to budge unless there was a meeting of the minds. "I want your solemn word that the children and I will have our own quarters, separate from yours."

"There's not a whole lot of lumber available in these parts," he stalled. "But I'll see what I can do."

"That's not good enough." She tapped her foot. If he wanted a housekeeper and cook, he must humor her on this point. *Oh, Satan, get behind me,* she thought, for when this man got stirred up, his eyes took on a liveliness that was downright provoking!

"I'll have you all fixed up in a day or two," he assured her. "Unless you prefer to stand here butting heads all day? But I'm warning you," he wagged his finger under her nose, "we need to get moving before that sun starts burning a hole in the sky."

"You're quite certain you won't find the children too much of a nuisance?" she asked.

"What do you want, Miss Wolverton? Do you want me to adopt them? Or are you getting cold feet?" he asked, confronting her fears head on.

"Why— I guess, if you're willing to— Oh, Mr. Gallagher, thank you!" She grabbed his hand in both of hers and gave it a vigorous shake. "I shall be pleased to keep house for you and the children! I promise, you won't be sorry."

He thoughtfully examined her hand, as if testing it for strength and flexibility. His own hand felt warm and calloused in hers. "What about this business of building a second cabin?" he asked, making her wonder if he meant to go back on his word. "How the devil do you expect to take care of me and these hooligans, if you're running your legs off, keeping house for yourself besides?"

The directness in his tawny gaze made her blush. "Mr. Gallagher, I'll do whatever it takes to give those children a good home," she said, fighting the emotional lump in her throat.

"Good! We'll stop by the justice of the peace on our way out of town."

"What?" she squawked.

He moved in close, murmuring in her ear. "Let's be practical, Miss Wolfie. It's going to take a father *and* a mother to raise these kids properly."

"That is not what I meant, and you know it!" she choked, suddenly blazing mad. "Now I will be happy to—"

"Fine." He turned abruptly and began issuing orders to his men. "You better ride on ahead. Miss Wolverton and I have a few errands to take care of before we hit the trail."

Aghast, Meg stood with her mouth hanging open. *Again!* The big lout actually thought she had agreed to marry him! *"Not a chance!"* she wanted to yell and shake her fist at him, but of course he was too busy *jawing* with his driver Archie and his men to pay attention to a mere *woman*!

Great balls of fire! He probably thought he'd get out of paying her for services rendered, if he sweet-talked her into marrying him! Oh, he was one sly dog, that man! She wondered if she could trust anything he said, including about his house burning down. *Hah! One thing I am* not *going to do is lie down with the devil,* she thought, and went to check on the boys.

Fortunately Davey was awake now and jumping up and down, testing out the chuck wagon's springs. Jimmy had climbed in back with him and was egging him on. Still her shadow, Susie was scuffing her feet in the dirt and talking to herself.

Meg tapped her employer on the shoulder to remind him to get Davey's medicine. "Excuse me, shouldn't we buy Davey some—what did you call it?—*bella* something?"

"One thing at a time," he told her. "We need to stop by the dry goods store and pick out suitable clothes for the children." *Finally* he spared her a sweeping glance. "I assume you already have a full wardrobe?"

Grinding her teeth with exasperation, Meg gave him a curt nod. "I won't be walking around naked, if that's what you're thinking." Shocked by her own boldness, she clapped her hand over her mouth. *Did I really say such a thing?* she thought, mortified.

~ * ~ * ~ * ~

Getting a head start, the men of the S-G-S Ranch departed on horseback, following a buckboard driven by his foreman and loaded with roof trusses.

Ready for the next item of business, Sam held up a large hand. "Instead of jawing ourselves to death, let's divide up," he said. "Young Jim, you go with Archie and pick up Miss Wolfie's trunk at the train depot. Davey and I will visit the local pill pusher. And *you*, Miss Wolfie, can take Susie and get a head start buying the children new clothes at the Emporium. We'll reconnoiter back at the store in half an hour." He gestured toward the mercantile down the street. "Can we agree on that much?"

Meg opened her mouth to object to being called "Miss Wolfie." The children used it as a term of endearment, but she hadn't given him permission to address her with such familiarity!

Without waiting for her response, Sam untied his horse from the hitching post and led it over to the chuck wagon. "Gimme the kid, Archie." He reached out and snagged Davey, who let out a squeal of surprise. Sam tossed the boy in the air, seated him in the saddle, and strode away, leaving Meg staring after him.

Who does he think he is, ordering everyone about that way? she fumed. *"Come back here with my child,"* she wanted to shout, but Sam Gallagher was already halfway down the block, each long stride taking him and Davey, bobbing along on his horse, farther away from the reach of her voice.

Furious at such high-handed tactics, she hiked up her cumbersome skirts and petticoats and took off running after him, her shoes clacking against the wooden boardwalk.

Susie let out a terrified squawk and came charging after her. "Wait for me, Miss Wolfie!"

Hearing Meg sputtering like a mad hen behind him, Sam spun around, walking backwards with a grin. "Hey, Archie!" he yelled to the man driving off in the chuck wagon. "After you collect Miss Wolverton's trunk, round up the kids at the Emporium and start on home. Just be sure you leave an extra horse for Miss Wolverton. We should catch up with you on the trail around noon."

Chapter Five

Meg stomped after him, anger radiating off her like hot sun bouncing off a corrugated tin roof. Even without looking, Sam could hear every peevish breath she took, as she pursued him down the rutted road with those ladylike fists of hers pumping.

Her protectiveness of the children didn't surprise him. He'd had a hunch about her just from reading her letters. And the minute he laid eyes on her interacting with the orphans, he knew she'd make an outstanding mother. Less than a day after meeting her, he was sold on "Miss Wolfie"—the kids' nickname for her sure tickled his funny bone! He kept walking, not because he wanted to test the strength of a mother's love, but because he flat out didn't have time to convince her how wrong-headed she was about his intentions.

Miss Wolfie needed to take a man at his word and cooperate without constantly falling into disputes about, well, darn near everything! Being committed to the children's welfare was admirable and praiseworthy. Being unwilling to accept help from others was just plain pig-headed. Grinning, Sam shook his head. He'd been on enough college debating teams to know it made more sense to *do* than to *say*. Especially when dealing with a woman. Once he got her and her brood settled in, he predicted she'd become as conformable to his wishes as soft riverbed clay in a potter's hands.

But enough about his growing obsession with Miss Wolfie. He had no intention of riding out to the remote valley he called home without first making sure Davey had proper medication. A shiver ran down Sam's spine. Suppose he had a fit and choked to death before he or Meg could get to him? No, whether she liked it or not, he was taking the boy to the local sawbones. Maybe some better cure had been discovered since he left the doctoring business. The boy needed the latest scientific help available, and by all that was holy, he was going to get it. Sam knew he was better qualified than most, in terms of training and experience, to care for this ragtag bunch. But it just made good sense never to assume. Besides, having them around was guaranteed to lift his lagging spirits.

"Where are you taking him?" Meg demanded, getting closer. She snatched up Susie and dodged around a lumbering wagon carrying a load of roof trusses.

As usual, Miss Wolfie kept talking a blue streak! As soon as all three waifs were properly outfitted, he was sending them home with Archie in the chuck wagon. Then he was tying the knot with his housekeeper. He wasn't born yesterday. No woman was going to stick him with three young pups and then leave him high and dry when the notion struck her fancy.

Two blocks up the street, Dr. Thaddeus J. Meade's sign swung gently in the breeze. Behind Sam and Davey came those same two rambunctious females, hot on his trail. Thankfully, his petite, auburn-haired housekeeper was slowed down some by the freckle-faced three-year-old in her arms, or he'd sure be catching hell about now!

Out of the corner of his eye, he noticed what a high old time Davey was having, bouncing and rocking in the saddle, yanking on the horse's black mane and laughing up a storm. No, he didn't anticipate any serious problems with Davey over the long haul. He was just a regular kid who happened to be wired a little different. No problem, he told himself.

Miss Wolfie, on the other hand, was a genuine spitfire. Her color was high in her cheeks as she advanced, no doubt aiming to get her hands on him and throttle him. If she did, Sam chuckled, he'd be a goner, right then and there. She had all the makings of a scrapper, that one! Her fierce tenacity radiated off her like a Roman rocket going off on the Fourth of July. He'd never seen a woman so passionately committed to her brood. It was a quality he greatly admired in any woman, but especially in this one.

Whatever else he was yet to discover about Miss Wolverton, she was a stayer and a goer; not a quitter. As protective as a mama mountain lion—no, there wasn't anything lukewarm about her! Those flashing blue eyes really raised his temperature. She had a fine pair of ankles, too.

As if she could read his thoughts, Meg stumbled, catching her toe in the hem of her skirt, and hopping like a one-legged bunny rabbit. *Still* she refused to slow down. Just kept dogging his tracks. *Whoo-o-ee!* He had found himself a warm one, for sure.

A quick, determined burst of speed took her and little Susie into the path of a horse-drawn wagon on a collision course with a mule skinner driving a pair of mouse-grey pack animals. Alarmed, Sam held his breath, as his tiny but athletic housekeeper leapt nimbly out of the way, narrowly escaping the horses' hooves and, still carrying Susie under one arm, made her way to safety. To his amazement, she took up the chase again, without even blinking an eye.

Shaking his head, Sam marveled at her tenacity. He had greatly underestimated the lady. Of course, he wasn't really trying to *lose* her, although she seemed to think he was. He was just doing what came naturally to him: *See a problem; fix it.* Hopefully Dr. Meade was up on the latest patented medicine to prevent seizures.

For his own peace of mind he needed to make sure Davey would be safe on the ranch. Suppose the boy had a spell while he was riding horseback? Or the horse spooked and he fell off and broke his neck? Now *that* was a scenario Sam hoped he never had to deal with. Life was tough enough without a child having epilepsy. Even if he had to hog-tie and gag that fiery housekeeper of his—*oh, dear Lord! She was gaining on him*—he planned to rifle through Dr. Meade's latest medical journals and get his friend's opinion on the best treatment for Davey.

Pausing beneath the physician's shingle, Sam tied his horse's reins around the hitching post and hauled Davey out of the saddle. The boy held himself stiffly, hanging over Sam's arm like a sack of potatoes. As he worked to free the boy's tight grip on the horse's mane, Meg finally caught up with him. She darted around the physician's shabby black buggy, parked at an angle against the boardwalk, and grabbed Sam's arm.

Panting and disheveled, she glowered at him, her auburn hair tumbling around her shoulders. "Mr. Gallagher, I will *not* have you ignore me!"

"Didn't think I was." Ignoring her pugilistic stance, he nodded toward the flight of stairs leading to the second floor. "I want Doctor Meade to check Davey over. His office is upstairs."

"Well, why didn't you say so?" She clutched the stitch in her side caused by running so hard. 'Davey is—" She gasped, trying to catch her breath. "He is *my* responsibility!"

"No, he's *our* responsibility." He tossed Davey in the air and with the boy hanging over his shoulder, headed for the stairs. He only took two steps before she pounced again.

"That remains to be seen!"

Sam swiveled, nearly colliding with her. He took a purposeful, almost menacing step toward her, just to test the fire in her belly. Waiting for her to give way to the better man. Instead she straightened her upper torso haughtily, refusing to back down.

"You might at least include me in whatever decisions you make for the children." Lifting her chin defiantly, she glared at him.

"Great balls of fire! Use a little common sense, woman! We can't put this kid's life in jeopardy. There are wild animals on my ranch: snakes, coyotes, wolves, all sorts of danger," he said. "Only think what might happen if he had a seizure in the corral and got stomped. Or suppose he was drawing up a pail of water and fell down the well? Or tumbled out of the hayloft?" He fell silent, letting her picture in her mind's eye the hazards. "Living on a ranch is the complete antithesis of living in New York City," he added, trying to get a grip on his temper. Before he did something radical, like pull down her drawers and blister her bottom.

As the truth began to sink in, Meg nodded with dawning respect. "I appreciate your concern, Mr. Gallagher. I just don't want you treating my kids like they're your hired hands. Davey's only eight years old, and Tom is barely twelve."

Sam Gallagher threw back his head and laughed. He wondered if she knew how aroused he got when she was spitting mad. For an Eastern born and bred female, she sure had spirit. "Just trying to help," he said in a lighter tone. "I want to get Davey the latest medicine available before we set out for the ranch."

"I'm going with you," she informed him, climbing the stairs, holding Susie by the hand. Reaching the landing, she reached out for Davey. "I'll take him now, Mr. Gallagher."

Without protest, Sam surrendered the boy. He knew better than to separate a mother in the wild too long from her cubs. Miss Wolfie definitely had strong mothering instincts, and he wasn't about to cross her. Besides, watching what she did next was more entertaining than anything he'd done in a good long while.

Holding the door wide, he ushered her into the doctor's crowded waiting room. They took a number and found their seats. He sure hoped Doc had updated information on epilepsy and its treatment. He wanted to believe Davey's problems were mostly due to insecurity and being shuffled about from place to place, but it paid to err on the cautious side. He wondered about Davey's blank stare and whether he'd suffered some trauma early on in life. Hopefully, once he settled down, the fresh mountain air would do wonders for him.

~ * ~ * ~ * ~

Coming out of the doctor's office an hour later, Meg felt it was time for a frank discussion with her employer. "I realize you weren't expecting me to show up with three homeless children. And certainly I have no desire to take advantage of your good nature. I think it's only fair, under the circumstances, if you want to deduct the doctor's fee from my first paycheck."

Having said her piece, she marched down the steps, her back rigid with disappointment. Dr. Meade had taken a kindly interest in Davey. He'd even admitted to having seen another similar case in his long medical career. But aside from medication to control the seizures, he had nothing new to suggest.

"Davey is different. You mustn't expect too much," Dr. Meade had advised.

Too much! All she wanted was to be able to hold a coherent conversation with Davey, maybe share a hug now and then. Was that too much to ask? Fighting back her tears, Meg trudged down the street toward the Emporium. All she wanted was some assurance that Davey would be able, in his own unique way, to experience joy and love, like other children.

Touching her elbow, Sam removed the prescription fluttering from her nerveless fingers. "Nobody said he's mentally retarded, Meg. He's—just 'different.' Try to remember that."

"What does 'different' mean?" she asked forlornly.

He scratched his ear. "How the heck do I know?"

"You have medical training. Shouldn't you know?"

"All I know is that we all have problems or shortcomings we struggle to overcome." He sighed. "Davey seems to be going through a rough patch right now. Like Doc said, 'It's going to take a heap of patience.'"

"Well, I refuse to give up," she said, dashing a tear from her cheek. "He's only a child! And he deserves a loving home, just as much as Susie and Jimmy do."

"You head over to the Emporium with the kids, while I fill the prescription," Sam interrupted—his way of cutting off the pity party before it became a flash flood. "And don't give me any malarkey about paying for these kids' upkeep out of your salary." He gave Davey a light tap on the backside to get him moving in Meg's direction, and disappeared into a nearby druggist's shop.

Spotting a land assayer's office two doors past the Emporium, Meg wandered across the street, her curiosity piqued. She had no idea how the idea of filing a homestead claim got stuck in her head, but she decided to investigate. She and Mr. Gallagher seemed destined to clash—no doubt set in his ways, being a widower. Being a boss in charge of a bunch of rough cowboys was enough to make a man difficult to deal with, she supposed.

Or maybe he'd locked horns with so many steers that he only saw things one way. *His* way. Living in the wilderness, a man was bound to focus on survival and hard work and totally overlook a woman's tender feelings. Yes, that probably explained what kept her stirred up and agitated around him. Right now he was trying his best to be accommodating and make a good first impression, but just how long *that* would last was anybody's guess.

He surely must be desperate to promise me a cabin of my own, she mused. In fact, the more she thought about homesteading, the more the idea appealed to her. Maybe she didn't have enough money to file just yet, but it gave her a dream for the future. Actually, it was the first attainable goal she'd been able to grab hold of in a good long time.

Taking Davey and Susie by the hand, she strolled along the wooden boardwalk, assuming an air of nonchalance she didn't really feel. The closer she got to the land office, the faster her heart raced. Brimming with curiosity, she cupped her hands and peered through the dusty windowpane. Everywhere she looked, there were rolled up maps stuck in cubbyholes or scattered over the top of a beat-up old desk.

After a few minutes, two men came out, heads together, talking excitedly.

Furtively Meg glanced across the street toward the druggist's shop. This might be her one and only chance! All she wanted was information. At least she could ask for a pamphlet telling her more about homesteading. No sin in asking. Squaring her shoulders, she herded the children ahead of her through the open door and startled the clerk behind the desk.

"Is this where I see about filing a claim?" she blurted out before she lost her nerve.

The clerk's mouth fell slack. 'Why, right here, ma'am." He looked at the children and then behind her, before stating the obvious: "But you need to bring in your husband."

"I don't have one," Meg said, her voice tight with annoyance. She lifted her chin proudly. "Don't have one, don't want one, and I most certainly don't need to be told that I do!"

Her forthright response set the clerk back even farther on the rungs of his rickety chair. He blinked, clearly bowled over by her vehemence. "No offense, ma'am, but homesteadin' is back-breaking work. I ain't never had no lone woman come in here before, expectin' to make a success out of—"

Suddenly, out of the corner of her eye, Meg saw a large male shadow stride past the window, then backtrack. Clearly she didn't have a lot of time to get the information she sought. Not about to miss her chance, she set her jaw and stared the clerk down. "I want to file a homestead. There's just me and these—uh, my three children. Now I would like one of your government pamphlets and a list of available properties in the territory. And don't bother showing me anything stuck in some god-forsaken drought area. I want something with water flowing through year-round!"

"Show the lady the parcel next to mine, Harold," an all too familiar deep voice said behind her. Her employer came alongside, set his elbows on the counter, and gave her a magnanimous smile. "There's no sweeter piece of land in the territory," he told her, "with the exception of my own spread, of course."

Caught red-handed, Meg fought to quell the heat wave sweeping over her. "I-I'm only looking for information, Mr. Gallagher. In case things don't pan out between us," she added through clenched teeth.

Handing her Davey's sack of medicine, he assisted the clerk by lifting a large book of plat maps onto the counter. With surprising dexterity, he thumbed through until he came to the map of his own ranch and the land adjoining it. "Now *this* is the property you should file a homestead on, Miss Wolverton. My late wife was all set to file, but she died before—" Gallagher cleared his throat. "You won't find better grazing land in the territory. A creek runs right alongside my property line, see?" He tapped his finger on the much abused vellum map. "You could plant yourself a nice orchard right here and enjoy fresh fruits and vegetables all summer long. I'll even lend you my mule and help you cultivate the ground." His warm brown eyes gazed into hers, keen with speculation. "What do you say, Miss Wolverton?"

His description of the land and his enthusiasm proved too contagious to resist. Her eyes met his, and her spirits lifted like a wellspring of water flowing clean through her. "Why, yes—" She gazed eagerly at the map, suddenly unwilling to let such a promising opportunity pass her by. She gave a quick nod, her mind made up. "What have I got to lose?" With a soft laugh, she gave Susie and Davey each a little hug in celebration.

"All you need is the filing fee," Sam Gallagher said, his eyes crinkling with shared enthusiasm.

The mention of money made her smile fade. 'How much will it cost me?" she asked, already knowing it would cost more than she carried in her purse.

"Twenty bucks, and a whole lot of hard work," the clerk answered.

Meg did some fast calculating. Even though her employer said he didn't expect her to pay the doctor's bill and the medicine, it was a debt she felt honor-bound to pay. That must surely come out of her pay first. So if she filed her homestead papers today, and instead of him building her a cabin on *his* land— *Goodness gracious*, she thought. *At this rate, I'll be up to my ears in debt to him for a good long time.*

"Don't worry about a thing," Sam said. Providing an instant cure before she got cold feet, he slapped down a twenty dollar gold piece. "That should cover it."

"I-I'll pay you back," she promised. "I'll put it in writing, if you want."

"Shouldn't be necessary," he said, calmly scrutinizing her from beneath the wide brim of his hat. "Not having to eat my own cooking makes you one of the best investments I've made in a *long* time."

Flustered, but eager to take advantage of his generosity, Meg held out her hand and shook on the deal. "I am not a commodity, Mr. Gallagher, or an 'investment.' And don't you forget it!"

Ducking her head to avoid his rascally smile, she leaned over the counter and directed the clerk to begin filling out the homestead papers to her land.

~ * ~ * ~ * ~

As soon as they finished shopping for new clothes for the children and bought additional food staples to see them through the summer months, Meg and Sam waved goodbye to all three children, as they rumbled down the street, hanging on for dear life in the back of the chuck wagon. Whipping up his mules, Archie could still be heard singing "Camptown Races" for the children's benefit, long after he turned the corner and disappeared out of town.

Watching them depart, Meg fought a stomach full of nervous butterflies. Careful not to look Sam Gallagher in the eye, for fear he was thinking the exact same thing she was, she slipped her hand inside her reticule to make sure her homestead papers were still there. It was hard to believe her incredible luck. She was now a land owner!

And already in debt. She turned with a friendly smile, expecting him to be standing beside her. After all, that's where he was a second ago, when she last looked. Only he was on the move again. Clearly this was not a man who let a lot of grass grow under his feet.

Retrieving their horses from the hitching post in front of the Emporium, Sam noticed her sudden skittishness. "Relax, your papers are perfectly safe," he grinned. "Now, can you think of anything else we need to take care of, while we're still in town?"

A tiny frown puckered her brow. 'Nothing comes to mind."

He tucked her slender hand around his muscular bicep and, leading the horses behind them, strolled around the corner and down a side street, so that while she was straining to catch one last glimpse of the children, he was taking her in the opposite direction.

"I find a leisurely walk helps me think more clearly," he began calmly, noticing that the farther Meg got separated from the children, the more anxious she became.

Steering her past a few shops and a few modest homes, he paused in front of a small white church surrounded by a picket fence. "Now this place looks promising. What do you say we step inside and meet the pastor?"

Sorely tried by his lack of transparency, Meg tugged her hand free. She'd had a sinking feeling all along that he had more in mind than a simple employer-employee relationship. While not wishing to offend him—he *was* her benefactor, after all!—she felt the need to be on firm footing with him from the start, or he just might wind up walking all over her. "Now, Mr. Gallagher, I have a pretty good idea what's going on in that devious mind of yours," she began.

"Aw, shucks!" he exclaimed, with a teasing glint in his dark brown eyes. "Here I was hoping to surprise you, and all along we were of like minds!"

"No, sir, I-I am shocked and dismayed by the assumptions you make...on such short acquaintance, too!" She planted her fists on her tiny waist and glared up at him. "What unmitigated gall, sir!"

"Who, me? *I* have *gall?* Listen, Miss Wolfie," he waggled his finger under her nose, "just once I'd like to get married without the bride being in a family way—"

"What *are* you talking about? How many wives have you had, anyway?"

"Only one. Not counting you, I mean." Seeing her look of mounting dismay, he grinned boyishly and ducked, raising his arms to shield his head—in case she planned to strike him—an act of desperation she felt closer to committing than he could imagine! "I never got to court you properly." He sighed apologetically, but she wasn't buying his foolishness for a minute.

"I don't *wish* to be courted, you—you great *buffoon!* Moreover, sir, I refuse to be intimidated, or—" She spluttered, rendered speechless with indignation at his outrageous ideas of how to treat a lady.

"Good! Now shut up and kiss me!" Taking matters into his own hands, he swept her into an amorous embrace that set her heart to pounding. Her legs felt wobbly clear down to her toes.

The instant she stopped offering resistance, Sam released her and assisted her up the church steps. "I've met the pastor here. A very agreeable fellow," he informed Meg, as if she had actually agreed to his insane plan to get married.

Goodness gracious! Was this how men behaved in Wyoming Territory? Why, they were total strangers! Still in a daze, Meg stepped past him inside the church and grabbed hold of the back pew to steady herself. This could not be happening!

Hearing them come in, the plump woman playing "Bringing in the Sheaves" on the organ halted on a sour note. "Oh, my! Looks like I'd best fetch the minister," she said breathlessly and scurried away.

Meg glared at him. "You cannot be serious."

"I am not raising those kids alone," he warned.

Minutes later, Pastor Schroeder, a well rounded cleric wearing a black suit and string tie, walked in and greeted them as if he and Sam had been best friends all their lives.

Doing all the talking for them both, Sam introduced Meg and explained that he had hired her as his housekeeper, but when she got off the train yesterday with three orphans in tow— "From that moment, I saw no alternative but to make an honest woman of her," he explained, gazing down at her with a rascally smile.

"This is totally unnecessary!" Meg's temper exploded. "It's not as if they're *my* children, Pastor," she explained, seeking to salvage her reputation. "I offered Mr. Gallagher a chance to adopt the children, as any decent humanitarian would, but now, it seems, he wants to make it impossible for me to quit my job, ever." She glared at her prospective bridegroom, with an unmistakable promise in her blue eyes: *Oh, he will rue the day he ever placed her in such an untenable position!*

Convinced that his leg was being pulled, Pastor Schroeder chuckled. "What an charming tale," he said with a twinkle in his grey eyes. "Simply delightful! I wonder how I might work it into my sermon next Sunday—"

Sam cleared his throat. "I'd rather you *didn't* share it with your congregation just yet, Pastor. The lady is a little hyper-sensitive. Not much sense of humor," he added.

Meg stomped her foot. "*Ooh!* This is intolerable!" she raged.

"Young lady," the pastor said, his demeanor unruffled. "Are you willing, or not?"

"I *do* want the children to have a good home," she allowed, with a righteous nod.

Pastor Schroeder rubbed his hands together. "In that case, what are we waiting for?"

Taking her trembling little hands in his, Sam raised them to his lips, and asked rather compellingly, "Miss Wolverton, will you do me the great honor of becoming my wife?"

"Oh, all right. I suppose I must," she snipped. "As long as you promise to observe the proprieties and honor the conditions of my employment."

Sam winked at the pastor. "She seems willing enough. Let's tie the knot."

If only I could fall through a trap door in the floor, she thought, feeling faint.

The pastor opened his Bible. "Dearly beloved, mindful that the state of holy matrimony was instituted by our Lord, and blessed by His presence and by His first miracle at the wedding in Cana of Galilee, we rejoice in this most honorable pact between a man and a woman. It is not to be entered into lightly or inadvisedly, but reverently, discreetly, and soberly." He cleared his throat. "Samuel Gallagher and Margaret Wolverton, I charge you both, as you will answer on that dreadful Day of Judgment, when the secrets of all hearts shall be revealed..."

At this point Meg's mind began to wander. Everything was happening much too fast. She lost track of the pastor's exhortation as she stared at the strong hand clasping her own. *Who is this man in whose hands I am about to place my entire future?* she asked herself. *Have I completely lost my mind?*

When she'd written Aunt Gladys about seeking adventure in the West, she never dreamed how quickly her life was going to change. From whence had this reckless spirit arisen? She wasn't behaving at all like herself! For here she stood alongside this complete stranger, and by her very passivity seemed to be agreeing to marry a man who punched cows for a living! Certainly no rational person would describe their relationship as love at first sight. It was mind-boggling how this had come to pass.

Yet here stood Sam Gallagher, handsome, healthy and—yes, she conceded, he had a strong, heroic looking chin—and for reasons yet unknown to her, seemed perfectly willing to take on three orphans and a wife. And what about her? Did she have sufficient courage to be a wife and mother in this untamed wilderness?

Unable to answer any of these outrageous questions to her full satisfaction, Meg stared at the pastor while even more butterflies darted around in her stomach. The Reverend Schroeder looked expectantly at Sam, waiting for his response to the question he had just posed.

"I do." Sam turned and grinned at her. "I take you, Margaret Wolverton, to be my wedded wife, to live together in the holy estate of matrimony. I will love and protect you, comfort you, honor and keep

Home is where the Heart is

you in sickness and in health, and forsaking all others, keep myself only unto you, for as long as we both shall live."

Deeply moved by the sincerity in his voice, Meg was *almost* tempted to fall into his arms on the spot. Almost! But then it occurred to her that any man who could rattle off his vows so glibly had to be slightly suspect. After all, they barely knew each other! And she really ought to question her own motives, too. What on earth was she doing, standing up in church with a 'perfect' stranger? Since neither of them was even close to perfect, that left a whole lot of room for error.

Truthfully she might be better served if she turned tail and ran back to the train station. And she might have done just that, if it weren't for the children, already on their way to his ranch.

How *could* she have allowed this to happen? But she was clearly "in for a penny, in for a pound," as the old saying goes. She stood frozen to the spot, trying to weigh all her options, and the consequences if she did *this*, or did *that*.

Damned if I do. Damned if I don't! Light-headed, she sank her teeth into her lower lip and let out a soft moan.

Pastor Schroeder leaned forward expectantly. "And do you, Margaret Wolverton, take this man to be your wedded husband, to live together after God's ordinance, in the holy estate of matrimony? Will you love and comfort him, honor and keep him in sickness and in health, and forsaking all others, keep yourself only unto him, so long as you both shall live?"

Oh, help. The preacher wants an answer, she thought. "As God is my witness, Mr. Gallagher, I will... l-l...r- uhm, r-respect you, in sickness and in health—" Stumbling over her words, she blurted out, "I w-will do everything in my power, uh, not to b-burn your supper, and—and to be a good and faithful wife!"

"What? No 'obey'?" Sam lifted his eyebrows at the pastor, who began leafing through his Bible frantically to see if he'd left anything crucial out.

"That, too," Meg snapped, impatient to end this farce. When Sam rolled his eyes, she hastily added, "to the best of my ability, for as long as we both shall live."

By now she was so confused that she almost wished she would drop dead on the spot. Only she was boiling mad, too, for getting railroaded into marriage, even if it was for a good cause. But then, if she dropped dead, she'd never be able to get even with the grinning ape—!

"Good enough!" Smiling, the pastor closed with a prayer and pronounced them man and wife.

The organist rushed over, mopping her eyes with her lace hanky. "Such a lovely wedding! Didn't you think so, Pastor?" she gushed.

"Indubitably." Pastor Schroeder closed his Bible. "Let's walk over to the parsonage next door, shall we?" He gestured to a door near the altar, and they filed out silently. "We'll have a cup of coffee, while we fill in the details on your marriage certificate..."

Later, after they'd signed the official papers and toasted each other with a cup of lukewarm coffee in the Schroeders' cluttered parlor, it suddenly dawned on Meg what *else* had been missing from the ceremony:

Samuel Gallagher had neglected to kiss his bride. She wasn't sure why such an omission should bother her, considering the circumstances, but it did. It most certainly did!

Chapter Six

Just coming over the hill, the dirt road dipped down sharply, and a thicket of spirea and stunted birch trees boxed them in on either side. Recognizing their surroundings, the horses eagerly shifted to a swinging gait, and Meg, completely out of her element on a horse, clung to the saddle horn and followed Sam's lead through the narrow pass. When finally they emerged into the open, they found themselves on the edge of a high bluff.

Below a broad valley stretched almost as far as the eye could see, covered with tall prairie grass and, here and there, cattle grazing. Bathed in brilliant sunlight, patches of purple lupines and stunning red and blue wildflowers dazzled her senses. Meg breathed deeply, trying to absorb the beauty of it all—from the hypnotic drone of bees and locusts to the lazily soaring eagles in the hot cloudless sky overhead.

The chuck wagon driven by Archie and conveying Susie, Jimmy and Davey to their new home was a mere speck in the distance. She barely made out the winding ribbon of creek water as Sam Gallagher pointed out the dividing line between his ranch and the homestead she had filed claim on. Squinting into the sun, she wouldn't help but wonder how such a narrow creek could provide sufficient water for livestock and wild life. Not to mention enough to sustain settlers—if there were any.

Suddenly struck by the rugged, semi-arid climate and the isolation of her surroundings, she searched the horizon in vain for a glimpse of chimney smoke rising out of the raw landscape to signify the existence of neighbors. Meg dragged in another deep gulp of pure mountain air, filing her lungs and nostrils with the pungent smells of sagebrush, prairie flowers and pine. What a grand country! Never had she seen such a vast, untamed wilderness. In the far distance majestic mountain peaks surrounded the open range and, above it all, brilliant blue skies stretched from here to eternity.

Against this vast panorama, she found little to calm her womanly fears. So far as she could tell, Sam Gallagher—her new husband, she kept reminding herself—owned the only ranch for miles around. She was beginning to wonder if he and his men might not be the only neighbors she and the children would have!

Studying her nemesis out of the corner of her eye, her suspicions mounted.

"How far to the nearest church?" she asked with a lump in her throat.

Sam shrugged. "Fifteen...twenty miles, maybe."

"Oh, but I am accustomed to Sunday worship!" she exclaimed. "What remedy would you suggest, Mr. Gallagher?"

He adjusted his Stetson over his eyes. "Why, read your Bible, do a little psalm singing and pray, would be my guess."

"But what about fellowship and...and sharing? There *are* other women in these parts, are there not? You know—friends?" The thought of being deprived of meaningful human contact caused her to grow even more alarmed. She'd had no idea how cut off and isolated his ranch was until that very moment!

He gave her an indulgent smile. "If you like, I'll sit on the front porch after Sunday dinner and let you preach at me."

Meg's lips tightened at such levity. Though charming when he had a mind to be on best behavior, Mr. G. was clearly baiting her. Oh, he could be a tricky devil, no doubt about it, and probably as dangerous as a two-headed rattlesnake. *Probably thinks he has me over a barrel*, she thought. Well, maybe he did; maybe he didn't. But even though she'd grabbed at the chance to homestead and was now in his debt, that didn't give him the right to make light of her feelings.

She wouldn't soon forget his remark about "psalm singing" either. It would be folly to encourage his irreligious attitude. "Sorry to disappoint you, Mr. Gallagher, but I am no preacher!"

He raised his hands toward the sky. "Glory to God! And here I was hoping I might worship at your feet."

"Do be serious!" Blushing, Meg flapped her hand, eager to discourage such foolish talk.

Still chuckling, Sam urged his horse through a hillside of wildflowers and down the trail toward the valley below. "We'd better get a move on," he called back to her. "Watch those boulders on the left, now."

Meg knew they had plenty of things to iron out before they proceeded any further with this so-called marriage. But how could she argue effectively with the man, when his horse was quickly leaving her behind? Considering how fast he was going, he might lose her altogether!

Clenching her teeth, and giving her horse its head, she carefully picked her way through the rocks and sagebrush. She had no intention of letting this stranger run roughshod over her feelings, her wishes, or her wants. On one thing she must stand firm: Were it not for the children, she would *never* have exchanged vows with the man. *Never!* This marriage was purely a matter of expediency, and nothing more.

Inside she felt confused and unsettled—more than a little scared, too, though wild animals would never drag such an admission from her lips! She had no real reason to fault the man, yet. But out here in the middle of nowhere, it wouldn't take much for a lonely man to misread a friendly gesture and try to cross the line. Determined not to borrow any more trouble than she already foresaw, Meg dug in her heels and goaded her horse to a brisk trot.

~ * ~ * ~ * ~

Though outwardly he passed for a man who enjoyed nothing better than the steady gait of a strong horse beneath him, Sam's thoughts were racing. As his horse's nostrils picked up the familiar scents of home ground, it began to pick up the pace. And the closer to home they got, the more Sam questioned his actions. It wasn't like him to make spur of the moment decisions. Had he made a serious miscalculation by bringing Miss Wolverton and her orphans out here to live in near isolation? Why, hell. The nearest neighbors lived five miles away, and already she was acting like she had a burr under her saddle.

Five years had passed, and he still hadn't forgotten what store a woman set in being able to visit back and forth with other womenfolk. *Thunderation!* He should have thought about *her* needs more, instead of focusing on what *he* wanted when he wrote those *dang-fool* letters. He felt lower than sand beneath a toad's belly for not asking Meg what was important to her. He should have romanced her a bit in town; told her how pretty she was. Maybe if he had, they wouldn't find themselves at a near standoff right now.

Right now, she was probably wishing she'd never answered his advertisement. But he wasn't sorry, the way things had evolved. He wasn't disappointed with his choice either. In fact, he considered himself damn lucky. Especially considering the harpy his neighbor Len Peterson had married, sight unseen. He should feel downright elated. He couldn't ask for a finer woman than Meg Wolverton. She was caring, intelligent, strong. She had backbone, and she was a damn fine looking woman, too.

Whatever fate had brought them together, he knew she was the one for him. Thank God, he was done writing strange women. Cute little "Miss Wolfie" suited him just fine. Needed a little breaking in, he had to admit, but he was in no hurry.

Now all he had to do was convince her to stay. Getting her to marry him hadn't been all that difficult. Her concern for the children overrode personal choice. Encouraging her to sign that homestead agreement was another step in the right direction. Oh, sure, she got prickly as a cactus pear when it came to maintaining separate quarters—couldn't blame her for that. He still hoped she might see her way clear to move in with him, but even if she didn't, having her and the children closeby would make life a whole lot more interesting.

After all the struggles he and his late wife Amie had shared, a bachelor's life just didn't sit well with him. And though the pain of losing Amie and little Beth had eased somewhat over the past five years, he lacked the stomach to live out the rest of his days eating biscuits burnt black as charcoal, and a stewpot of vittles so full of soot and smoke as to defy description. *No, sir.* If the Almighty had intended him to cook and darn his own socks, He would've made him with female parts. But since He hadn't, Sam had finally figured out it was up to him to change his own dad-blamed luck. Hadn't done half bad for himself, either. Oh, yeah, Miss Wolfie was quite the find, and when a man stumbled onto a gold mine, he wasted no time staking a claim!

He shuddered to think of the mail order brides some of his neighbors had got stuck with. Len Peterson's wall-eyed wife Leona had a temper worse than a crazed cow on locoweed. And Mike Gehrhart, who lived six miles down river, wound up married to a temperance worker twelve years older than himself. Sure put a quick end to Mike's carousing. The woman saddled him with four little cowpokes in record time, though, which came as an even bigger surprise.

Sam uttered a sigh, thinking about his new family, especially the children. What a hardscrabble life they must have experienced in the New York slums. He could only imagine the emotional scars they carried. Hopefully he and his new bride could establish a home full of love and laughter, and maybe, over time, erase some of the insecurities and nightmarish memories from their past. He was relying on Miss Wolfie to help him create such a home, a place that was safe and full of comfort and tender understanding. In his gut he sensed that she'd be on the same page with him about that. Just the way she acted sometimes told him that she, too, knew how it felt, to be alone and poor and slightly desperate.

Being alone was something Sam could relate to right well. It lived inside him like a hollow place that needed filling. Like a hunger that gnawed inside him nearly every waking hour. No matter how hard he worked, there were things he could never atone for. There was always that yearning to fill the void, find someone to love, and share his life with. That's what finally drove him to take the desperate measures he had.

WANTED: Housekeeper, strong, healthy, honest.
Prefer single woman, 25-30 years old.

Looking back, taking out that advertisement had probably not been the act of a completely sane man. Maybe it might work for a high risk-taker like his neighbor Mike Gehrhart, but not for a chap like himself. Sam never could get up the nerve to come right out and advertise for a *wife*, even though he needed one badly.

Later he figured the loneliness had finally warped his reason. Well, maybe so. But once he met Meg and her three orphans, Sam figured maybe he hadn't done so badly for himself. Having four people to take care of already made him feel happier, more hopeful about the future.

He gave a grim chuckle, remembering Meg's rebuff, that he shouldn't try to turn Jimmy and Davey into ranch hands. She had no idea what it took to commit one's energies fully to the task of carving a life out of unbroken wilderness. It meant constantly pitting one's strength and know-how against the unpredictable elements of nature, wild animals, rustlers, and the occasional flare up among restless hostiles. Oh, sure, recent treaties had eased tensions somewhat between the Indians and white settlers on the high plains, but he'd had his share of trouble in that department, too.

If only he'd seen it coming years ago, and knowing what he knew now, he might have moved on, rather than risk harm coming to Amie and little Beth. As it was, he'd paid dearly for his complacency. While he was rounding up strays one hot summer afternoon, the two people he'd loved most in all the world had died. Their life's blood had been spilled on this land, making his attachment to the land irretrievably precious.

Sun-up to sundown, running a ranch put tremendous physical and mental demands on a man. That's why he welcomed the chance to start over again. Now, thanks to Miss Wolfie, he was getting a new family and a fresh start.

A strange ache settled in Sam's chest, as memories of the past came streaming back to haunt him. He'd never fully appreciated how important a role Amie and little Beth played in his life until it was too late. If only they hadn't quarreled that fateful morning. But they'd had words, over something so petty he no longer remembered what it was all about. Then he'd ridden out. Those words, spoken in anger so long ago, could never be taken back. He had lived every day since, convicted by the knowledge that he'd placed a higher value on his pride than on his marriage. Sam could only speculate on what the outcome might have been, if he had stayed home that day.

Suddenly the sound of gurgling water tumbling over rocks broke in upon his thoughts. The horses, smelling water, broke into a full gallop toward a cluster of tall cottonwoods, and thundered across the wooden bridge that spanned the creek bordering his property.

"Welcome to the S-G-S Ranch!" Jubilant with anticipation, Sam reined in his horse, waiting for his Eastern tenderfoot of a wife to catch up. Convinced that his vast holdings would minimalize any qualms she might have about living this far from civilization, he greeted her with an eager smile.

While they paused to let the horses drink, he began to describe the type of cattle he raised, and how many. Fully focused on her lively expression, as her eyes darted from one landmark to another, he deliberately delayed mention of the ranch house itself...until at last they rode past a clump of trees and the burned-out front verandah came in view.

Meg's smile faltered. She blinked, clearly in disbelief. "Oh, Mr. Gallagher." Her voice grew quietly strained, as if she was fighting off a siege of panic. "Please tell me this isn't where you live," she said.

Sam guiltily wrenched his gaze from the look of horror on her face. Trying to see the burned-out shell of a house through his young wife's eyes made him downright queasy. After railroading her into exchanging marriage vows, would this be the straw that broke the camel's back? Would she wash her hands of him altogether?

"What did you say the name of your ranch was?" she asked, pointing to the dilapidated sign hanging lopsided from the gate.

"The S-G-S Ranch." He scratched his head. What a question, when the ranch house had been completely gutted by fire only two weeks ago! He'd tried to warn her when they were back in Cheyenne, but perhaps she thought it was just a small, one-room cabin?

"I suppose 'S-G' stands for your initials." Meg said, shaking her head sadly. "What does the other 'S' stand for?"

Though tempted to say a cuss word, he refrained. "Oh, I suppose you could say 'S-G-S' stands for "Still Going Strong." He chuckled self-consciously. "Barely hanging on by a thread at times, but never completely broke."

He squinted from beneath his broad hat, willing to concede that even before the fire, the house had looked a little rough after five years of benign neglect. One good thing: That inferno of heat and smoke had destroyed all the spiders and wasps' nests that used to make sitting on the porch in the evenings such a dad-blame nuisance. *Yes, what the place needs is the diligent care of a woman, to give it that homey look,* he thought. Of course, he and his men needed to level the place to the ground first and then rebuild. But that would take a lot more work than he had time for right now.

"Seems like you've been having a streak of bad luck," she said, glancing around.

Sure, rub it in, lady. Did she think he was blind? Yes, the house had been gutted by fire. The windows were smashed in, the calico curtains consumed by flames. Even though the fire had burned itself out, even before he and his men finished rounding up the cattle, the acrid stench of burned horsehair-stuffed upholstery and charred timbers still hung in the air.

Viewing the devastation through her eyes for the first time, he understood why seeing it for the first time would come as such a shock. Justifiably upset with himself for not being more mindful of her feelings, he dismounted and tossed the reins to Meg, who sat motionless on her horse.

"Wait here," he ordered curtly and strode toward the blackened shell—all that was left of the house he'd built five years ago with the help of neighbors and friends. The front door stood ajar, creaking ominously back and forth on a broken hinge in the faint breeze. Ducking his head, he cautiously looked inside. What he encountered was a gaping black cavity formed by the scarred skeleton of charred and broken timbers. The roof and most of the interior walls had been consumed by fire. Only a few large support beams on the front verandah appeared to be salvageable. Thank God he had the foresight to buy more lumber while he was in Cheyenne.

Fighting nausea, Sam unsheathed his rifle from his scabbard and walked around back. Spotting a coyote scavenging through the wreckage, he pumped off a round to send the animal loping through the brush. He was grateful the fire hadn't spread to the barn and other outbuildings, because he had enough fodder stored in the barn to burn down every building on the place and start a forest fire raging out of control across the open range. Just one more lightning strike could have put him out of business.

To his relief, the barn and corral were intact. His primary concern was the breeding stock he'd left grazing in the south pasture.

The whole damn lot must have broken through the fence and disappeared. Probably headed downstream for water.

Shaking his head in dismay, Sam spun around and nearly ran over his diminutive wife.

"Mr. Gallagher, I am *so* sorry for your loss." Meg laid a small, consoling hand on the muscles bunched with tension in his arm. "It seems we have our work cut out for us," she said softly. By including herself in the equation, she hoped to show him that she regarded the problem as mutual and not a tragedy to be borne alone.

"We?" His look of incredulity made her take a step back, though she continued to regard him steadily from beneath the brim of her sun bonnet. "Miss Wolfie, unless you're handy with an axe and a hammer and a saw, I think *we* had better get you and the children back to Cheyenne in a hurry."

"Why? Are you expecting an Indian attack?" She squinted up at him with a worried frown.

"No, no. You're perfectly safe on that score, believe me," he said, mentally chastising his lack of foresight. Where was he going to house one lone female and three children?

"How can you be so certain?" She was a persistent little creature, if nothing else.

"Because if Indians had anything to do with this, believe me, their bellies would be too full of my beef to be able to walk, much less ride back here for many moons to come." He shook his head, not in the mood for chatter and too ashamed to burden her with the truth, that he would never fully understand why his first wife had decided to kill herself and their only child five years ago. And he for damn sure didn't have any control over random Acts of God either!

"Well, it looks highly suspicious to me! It would take something much bigger than a spark flying up the chimney to catch an entire house on fire," she said, gesturing toward the burned-out shell of a house.

"I totally agree, Miss Wolfie. As I tried to explain to you in Cheyenne, the house was struck by lightning. We sometimes get violent thunderstorms in the summer. Unfortunately this one occurred just as we were about to drive cattle to market, so it was too late to warn you not to come."

"Yes, but you also mentioned a line shack in your letter. Where is it?" She gazed up at him trustingly, like he could just snap his fingers, and the line shack would instantly appear.

"Up in the hills. A few miles away." Sam realized what a fool he was not to have thought things out before dragging her out here. "I apologize, Meg. I don't know what I was thinking when I wrote you about the line shack, but I see now it would be totally unsuitable for a new bride to live in, even short term."

But she seemed not to be listening to a word he was saying. She walked around for a few minutes, lightly tapping her pursed lips, almost as if she was a detective investigating a highly fascinating crime scene. Meanwhile Sam was starting to get edgy. He needed to come up with a way to put a roof over her head, while she— "You actually *saw* the lightning strike?" she asked.

Under any other circumstance, the fetching scatter of freckles on his bride's nose would have been prompted him to pull her into his arms and kiss her into submission, but not now. During his absence, all the livestock he'd left grazing near the creek that separated their two properties had vanished. At least the fire hadn't spread to the barn and outbuildings, but the damage was serious enough.

But his wife had asked him a question. Not a very helpful question, but the least he could do was try to answer it. "Why, yes, Miss Wolfie, I did see it. From a distance, of course. Lightning strikes can burn down an entire forest. Or in this case, a house."

Meg straightened her shoulders and faced him squarely. Oh, she had a glow about her, like a benevolent aura shining in her eyes. For a second, it quite took his breath away.

"Well, then," she smiled with determined good cheer, "that leaves us with the task of repairing your house and also building a cabin for the children and me. I realize it may take some time—"

"Ma'am," he sighed, "The house is beyond salvaging. I appreciate your willingness to help, but with all the work that regularly needs to be done around here, rebuilding my house is going to be a major undertaking. I'll be lucky to build you a small cabin before the early snows come."

"Oh." Completely missing the point that he could never meet all the conditions of employment that she'd set before him, Meg went on. "I just want you to know I don't hold you responsible for—well, *any* of this." She gestured toward his ruined domicile.

"I'm quite willing to have one of my men escort you and the children back to Cheyenne tomorrow morning, if that's what you decide," he said, reluctant to subject her to such Spartan living conditions. "I'll pay for food and lodging, of course."

"Mr. Gallagher," she was starting to sound perturbed, "must I remind you that we are now married with three children? And that I plan to homestead the property just beyond that creek?" She pointed toward a thick stand of birch trees. "I am not leaving, sir. Though I *do* require a few trees to be cut down on my side of the creek. Otherwise building my cabin will be well nigh impossible."

"Come back next spring," he said, wondering if all his dreams were about to go up in a puff of smoke. "I'll keep a close eye on things for you."

"Oh, so now you intend to jump my claim," she said, tilting her chin defiantly.

Overcome by the unsettling shock to his system of taking on a young wife and having three orphans foisted upon him, all in a single chaotic day, Sam began to laugh uncontrollably, almost to the point of tears. "I can't jump your claim, Miss Wolfie, because it isn't mine!"

Meg planted her hands on her hips, fingers drumming furiously. "Read my lips, Mr. Gallagher. I'm not leaving!"

"Oh, yes, you are." Sam glared at his stubborn tenderfoot wife. "It's only a piece of raw land, woman. It will still be here next May. Now you do just as I say—"

But if he hoped to win her cooperation, he was doomed to disappointment. Meg wasn't listening. In fact, her full attention was suddenly riveted on Archie, as he whipped up the horses and drove the chuck wagon up to the bunkhouse.

Hanging on for dear life, Davey and Susie and Jimmy let out great whoops of laughter every time the rear wheels on the wagon hit a rut in the road. Seconds later they all piled out, breathless and chattering at the same time.

Susie made a beeline for Meg. "Miss Wolfie! Miss Wolfie! Look what I found," she said, holding up a giant pine cone. Also overjoyed to see her, Jimmy and Davey tackled Meg around the waist, greeting her with crushing hugs.

"I like this place," Jimmy declared, planting his hands on his skinny hips and looking about.

Off in his own little world, Davey studied the sun's rays through his laced fingers.

Abandoning the housing question as a lost cause, Sam came forward to greet his driver. "I see you survived, Archie," he said out of the corner of his mouth.

"Just barely." His driver spat a chaw of tobacco at a nearby locust nest. "I could sure use some help unloading supplies," he hinted.

"I'll help!" Jimmy yelped.

"Thanks, son," said Sam, ruffling the towhead's hair. "But as you can see, the main house burned down in a recent thunder storm. I need you to help me convince Miss Wolfie that this is no place for a bunch of tenderfoots—"

Meg stepped between Sam and her brood. "We're here now, children, and *all* of us, Mr. G, are going to stay and make the best of things!"

Sam's jaw dropped in surprise. "Oh, so now I'm 'Mr. G,' am I?"

"Since the children call me 'Miss Wolfie,' and even *you* have taken to abusing my name, it only seems fair that you should have a nickname, too." She folded her arms and gave a pert nod. "Fair is fair, Mr. G."

"Well, damn, woman. I like my new name." Sam grinned approvingly, causing her to blush. "I like it just fine. But that still doesn't mean you can stay."

Jimmy looked crestfallen at the idea of leaving the minute they arrived. "Even if you send Susie and Davey back to town, I can stay, *can't* I?" He dragged a thirty pound sack out of the chuck wagon and staggered toward the bunkhouse with it clasped in his scrawny arms. "I can do a man's work."

Sam decided that a boy with such a willing spirit deserved a grown-up name. "Well, I like your attitude!" he said heartily. "In fact, I think it's time we started calling you 'Big Jim.'"

"Cuz I'm all growed up?" said Jimmy, puffing out his scrawny chest.

"Yup."

Jimmy looked up at Sam with worshipful brown eyes. "Gee, thanks, Mr. G."

Alarmed, Meg came close to losing her composure. No way was she going to let her boys be exploited. "Mr. Gallagher!"

"Call me 'Mr. G.'" Sam grinned, admiring the way her blue eyes flashed, and raised his hands in a gesture of peace. "Just saying."

"Mr. G." She cleared her throat, determined to stay on task. "You made a lot of promises when you hired me as your housekeeper. You made even more promises when you and I exchanged marriage vows this morning."

Susie popped her thumb in her mouth and studied these two adults, who weren't exactly seeing eye-to-eye. Davey bumped his head against Sam's chaps belt, moaning, "No, no, no."

"Exactly! *You're* supposed to obey." Sam shook his finger under her nose.

Meg didn't even bother to answer such an absurd remark. "I expect things may be a little inconvenient for a while, but we will all manage somehow!" she told him.

"Yeah," Jimmy shouted and grabbed another sack of flour from the chuck wagon. "If we're gonna be your kids, you gotta give us a chance!"

Sam shook his head, admiring the boy's pluck. "It would only be temporary, I assure you. Just until I rebuild my house."

"We'll help you do that, too," Meg said. Standing her ground, she slowed Jimmy down by placing her hands on his shoulders. "You have several men working for you, and the children and I are more than willing to do our fair share."

Sam smacked his dusty hat against his chaps. "Guess I'm outnumbered. Can't fight all four of you."

"No, sir!" Jimmy grinned. "Four to one is hard to beat."

Sam decided he had better things to do than argue with three scrawny children and a woman who looked as contrary as a wet hen. Picking up three sacks of flour, he shouldered past his new family and headed over to the bunkhouse to recruit help from his ranch hands.

When he paused to adjust his next load, his new bride came over and wiped the sweat from his face with her linen handkerchief. While she fussed over him, he felt himself start to weaken, but caught himself in time. *I had better keep a tight rein on yon vixen,* he decided, *or watch my brains turn to jelly.*

"I wear the pants, Miss Wolfie," he growled softly, just to show who was in charge, "and what *I* decide goes."

Meg smiled sweetly. "I see no point in disagreeing over which of us wears the pants in this family, Mr. G. As for everything else you have to say, I wait with baited breath to discover what you have in mind."

"Don't tempt me, woman," he warned. And then, to keep the peace with this opinionated young lady, he began barking orders to his men, and everyone got busy unloading food supplies.

Chapter Seven

Clearly, until Sam Gallagher got around to building her a cabin, she and the children would be totally reliant upon his resourcefulness. *Foxes have holes, but the son of man has nowhere to lay his head.* Considering their current circumstances, Meg had a whole new appreciation for that Scripture. But experience had also taught her not to sit back and hope against hope that life would be kind to her. For now, she must put on a cheerful face and make herself useful. For *all* their sakes.

Cautiously she shifted her attention to the ranch hands and noticed the look of frozen disbelief on many of their faces. Most of the men had ridden in ahead of Sam and her, and the damage caused by the fire seemed to have dealt them all a demoralizing blow, just as it had to her and her employer. Sobered by the destruction, the ranch hands silently put their backs into the task of unloading the chuck wagon. It was almost as if they understood that the boss needed time to assess the situation and absorb the full impact of what had occurred just prior to the cattle drive.

Meg glanced over her shoulder, curious to see how Mr. G would handle things. At first he seemed like a man not easily discouraged by misfortune. In fact, if she were to describe his demeanor in a word, as he hauled up buckets of water, hand over hand, from the well to refresh the horses and livestock, that word would be *nonchalant. Too* nonchalant, as far as she was concerned. Here he was engaged in the most menial of tasks, as if the terrible fire that had destroyed his home had never happened. On top of that, he had her comfort and the children's to see to. Instead of assigning such menial responsibilities to his men, *he* chose to tend the horses! Yes, she decided, Mr. G acted as if he hadn't a care in the world. Most men would be tearing their hair and cursing their misfortune. Mr. G, on the other hand, acted as if he didn't have a care in the world.

Meanwhile Jimmy was busy trying to strike up a rapport with the men and imitating their mannerisms, as they carried sacks of beans, flour, and other basic supplies into the lean-to behind the bunkhouse. Clearly he was hungry for male approval and acceptance. So maybe it was a good thing they *were* staying. He and Davey would have given her a merry old chase if they'd gone back to Cheyenne.

Holding Susie by the hand, Meg wondered what she could do to make a difference. The animals were being well cared for by her taciturn husband, and the food supplies were being quickly stashed for future use. For a moment she felt like a fish out of water. But then she recalled that she had hired on with this outfit as the cook and housekeeper. So be it. Even if the house was gone, she could still feed people, couldn't she? Hoping to restore a degree of normalcy, Meg walked briskly over to bunkhouse, her city-bought shoes raising tiny puffs of dust in the dry sage.

"Which of you gentlemen is the foreman?" she asked the ranch hands quietly, so as not to disturb Mr. G, who was now busy unsaddling the horses they'd ridden in on earlier.

A razor-thin, lanky cowhand paused in the rolling of his smoke. His faded blue eyes met hers below the floppy brim of his hat. "That'd be me." He held out a leather-tough, scarred hand. "Slim Rowlands, at your service, ma'am."

Meg gave his hand a business-like shake. "Pleased to meet you, Mr. Rowlands. I'm Mrs. Gallagher, and these are my children." She nodded toward Jimmy, who was trying so hard to fit in as one of the ranch hands. "Jimmy is twelve. And this little one is Susie; she's three. She's going to be a big help to me, aren't you, darling?"

"I'm sleepy, Mama," the little girl said, stroking her cheek with a bedraggled scrap of blanket.

"Of course, you are, darling." Meg turned to Slim with a friendly smile. "Is there somewhere I might put her down for a nap?" she asked.

Daniel, a fledgling cowboy of perhaps fifteen, volunteered his cot in the bunkhouse.

Thanking him, Meg stepped inside, only to find the bunkhouse in complete disarray, clothing and personal belongings tossed helter-skelter on the bunks and floor.

Immediately several of the men, eager to make a good impression, came in and started tidying up their own bunks. One cowpoke introduced himself as Jelly Belly. "Thet poor kid's plumb wore out!" He shook his head sympathetically, chewing on a plug of tobacco.

Slim the foreman had a better idea. Looking up at the sky, he suggested they hurry up and empty the chuck wagon. "Hey, Big Jim," he beckoned to Meg's oldest orphan, "Fetch us a clean mattress from the shed. We'll let the little Miss bed down in the buckboard, while the boss gets things figured out."

"Oh, thank you, Mr. Rowlands," Meg beamed.

Looking around for Davey, she spotted him clinging rather comically to one of Mr. G's muscular legs, as he carried his saddle into the barn. "That's our Davey," she said, amazed how quickly Davey had become attached to Mr. G. To his leg, at any rate.

One of the ranch hands nodded. "Makin' hisself right at home. Smart little fella, latching onto the boss thet way."

Oh, dear, Meg thought. And here she'd hoped to keep Davey from pestering the man, especially when he had so much on his mind.

Archie gave her and Susie a wink. "We'll get the chuck wagon unloaded in jig-time, ma'am. You just tell us what you want to cook tonight, and I'll fetch the fixin's for supper to you right quick."

She looked at him, astonished. "Why, I hardly know— Doesn't that depend on what supplies you have on hand?"

A couple of cowboys exchanged a glance. "Makes a powerful lot of sense, don't she?"

Not wishing to appear ignorant, Meg planted her fists on her hips. "What do you usually eat for supper?"

Young Daniel rolled his pale blue eyes. "Oh, mostly we eat squirrel or possum meat, beans, and biscuits with bacon gravy. And for dessert we generally have Johnny cake an' hot apple pie or corn fritters—"

"Every night?" She tucked in her chin, instantly suspicious.

"Well, maybe not *every* night." Caught in a harmless lie, Daniel stared at the ground and scratched his ear apologetically.

"Not in a month of Sundays," Rowlands broke in. "These fellows are just dreamin,' ma'am. Biscuits and beans'll do just fine."

Meg smiled at the lanky cowhands surrounding her. "I'll see what I can come up with," she promised with a friendly nod.

"We ain't hard to please," another man added. Doffing his hat, he introduced himself as Walker.

Instantly the other men doffed their hats, and in record time, Meg found herself shaking hands and trying to keep all the names and faces straight. Bill, self-conscious about his missing two front teeth, wore red suspenders over a plaid shirt on which no two buttons matched. Mort was the bald, potbellied one. Jelly Belly had a bull neck and obvious upper body strength, despite his short stature.

Zeke, sporting waxed mustachios and long flowing hair to his shoulders, clearly saw himself as a lady killer. Cory was a loose-jointed black man with a ready smile. Pete walked bowlegged with a limp, like he was recovering from an injury, and Tobias dressed all in black, right down to his silver-tipped boots. Manuel displayed his proper Spanish upbringing by saluting her with a gallant bow and a compliment: "*Bella señora.*"

Meanwhile Archie continued to supervise unloading the wagon. As soon as the introductions were over, Meg was headed for the outhouse with Susie, when a change in the men's rhythm, as they passed food sacks from man to man, caused her to turn around.

Shading her eyes, she spotted Davey's hind end scooting under a wire fence into an area so odorous it could only be...the pigpen! "Oh, no!"

Leaving Susie to fend for herself, Meg hiked up her skirts unceremoniously and raced after Davey. A blur of slender ankles in black stockings caused almost every male on the place to stop, frozen in admiration.

Bill whistled through the gap between his teeth. "Look at the missus go!"

"Davey, no!" she hollered. "Come back here, sweetheart!" Swallowing back her gorge, she climbed the rickety fence, freed her skirts from the barbed wire, and made her way gingerly past a trough of pig swill.

Bending down, she peered under the shed, where a huge freckled sow lay flopped on her side, suckling a litter of piglets. "Davey," she crooned. "Yuck! Leave that horrid animal alone, do you hear me? Come out of there, this instant!"

"Better let me handle this, Miss Wolfie." Abruptly Sam picked her up and moved her aside—careful not to knock her into the pig trough, she noticed gratefully. He dropped down on all fours, wincing slightly as the soft ground seeped through his tough denim trousers. Stretching out on his belly, he reached a long arm into the dark recesses beneath the shed's raised floor.

Choking on the stench and reaching blindly, he cursed softly under his breath. Then his hand closed around Davey's flailing foot, and he hauled him out. Davey slid backwards through the mud, his small body wriggling. He had both arms tenaciously wrapped around one of Lulu's squealing piglets.

Sam dragged the pair into the daylight and held Davey up for inspection. "I do believe he's found a new friend," he announced.

Meg clapped her hands and beamed. Judging by the huge grin on Davey's face, this was a banner moment. He looked happier than she'd ever seen him.

"Oh, Mr. G!" she exclaimed through tears produced by a mixture of joy and overwhelming stench. "You cannot imagine how happy this makes me!"

Standing there with pig slime dripping down his front, Sam wasn't sure who was crazier: him or Meg. Under one arm, he held a piglet with a corkscrew tail, and under the other a squirming mud-ball of a boy. "Huh?" was his brilliant response.

"Just look at him," she grinned excitedly. "He is *so happy!* I cannot thank you enough, Mr. G, for inviting us to live here on your ranch!"

Somehow Sam maintained enough presence of mind to escort everybody, including the squealing piglet, over to the well. As he lowered the bucket down the well and raised it full of water, his heart began to warm even more toward this vivacious young woman and three abandoned orphans. *Who'd have thought it possible?* he marveled, half in love already.

As each new bucketful of water came up, he upended it over Davey's head, washing away more and more slime with each dousing. Enjoying all the splashing, the little fellow clung to Sam's thoroughly wet trouser leg, rocking and bumping and jabbering excitedly in that strange little sing-song voice of his.

Finally Meg retrieved a towel from her suitcase and wiped Davey down. She wished she had a clothespin to pinch her nostrils and block out the smell. Gulping and holding her breath, she worked as fast as she could. The minute he was passably dry, Davey and the pig took off, running toward the barn, and she was able to draw a breath of fresh air again.

Seeing the funny side of things, she wiped her hands, then handed Sam the towel for his own use. "Sorry that impromptu bath got you so wet," she gasped, sounding more amused than apologetic.

Soaked to the skin, Sam slung the limp, wet towel around his neck. He frowned at her, as if trying to solve a puzzle. "I still think I should send you and the children back to Cheyenne."

"Yes, but you won't," Meg told him and sashayed away with her nose in the air.

Oddly enough, the idea of staying filled her with a great sense of relief. If chasing through the pigpen had accomplished nothing else, it had at least settled one dispute between herself and Mr. G. She and the children would be staying. Cheyenne might be a wild and woolly town, but it was nowhere ready to take on three such lively orphans! Especially not Davey. She could put up with a bit of inconvenience, as long as living here was good for her orphans.

Smiling, Meg realized how much Davey and Jimmy needed a strong man in their lives. A man who wasn't averse to laughter and didn't flinch at the usual scrapes young boys often get into. Misadventures were a normal part of growing up. She couldn't describe the thrill of seeing Davey smile—his first real smile. Oh, how it made her heart rejoice!

One of her deepest concerns on the trip had been never seeing a glimmer of happiness in his angelic face—until that tussle in the mud. Hopefully that impish little grin was a positive sign of better things to come. She wouldn't trade that smile for a dozen well behaved children in spit-and-polish Sunday School outfits, ears reamed out, hair slicked and every freckle gleaming, as they marched piously off to church.

Yes, she decided, she was in Mr. G's debt more than he knew. She must begin at once to include him in her nightly prayers.

~ * ~ * ~ * ~

Not wanting to make too obvious a display of her elation, for fear of being thought odd, especially in light of the destruction of the ranch house, Meg shifted her gaze to the horse fly buzzing over Sam's bare head in the sun.

Doing his best to ignore her and still keep his feelings private, Sam kept bringing up water, bucket after bucket, his powerful arms flexing in the hot sun, until he had filled the corral trough. Except for the scrape of ropes against the well's wooden casing, and the quiet splash each time the bucket went down the well, everything around the place was conspicuously tranquil, as his men went about their usual business.

As soon as the chuck wagon was empty, Archie drove it under the shade of a large cottonwood and secured the brake. He hopped down, unhitched the mules, and set them loose to graze. Meanwhile Zeke and Cory led four horses over to a buckboard parked next to the barn and hitched them up to the whiffletree.

Meg, who hoped to put Susie down for a nap in the buckboard, soon realized that Sam had other plans for it.

"Archie, you stay and help Mrs. Gallagher," he said. "Bill, you, Zeke, Manuel, Pete, and the rest of you men, I need you to give me and Slim a hand. I promised this lady a proper roof over her head tonight, and I never go back on my word. So that means we've got a bit more work ahead of us that needs to get done before dark."

Meg swallowed a protest. With the ranch house burned to the ground, placing her comfort ahead of others' more urgent concerns took her completely by surprise. "Why, thank you, Mr. G. That is most kind of you!"

"Don't mention it." Picking up Susie, he handed her over. "I don't envy you one bit," he said softly. "You'll be feeding a pack of ravenous wolves tonight."

"That's why you hired me, isn't it?" she said pertly.

Sam swept his gaze in a challenging fashion around the circle of admiring cowboys. "Yeah, I reckon," he said laconically, and Meg, her eyes growing wide, realized that he was daring any of his men to challenge the boss's plans.

"Fine. I'll have supper ready when you return from...wherever you're going."

"Thanks. See that you do. My men and I work best on a full stomach."

Meg's cheeks grew warm under his piercing gaze. Perhaps, considering the fact that she was one lone woman among all these roughnecks, she should feel grateful for his proprietary manner, but it still made her uneasy. While she expected to be shown respect, she also meant to *earn it*, not be made to feel like she wore his brand, like some cow. She lifted her chin, hoping to convey both an independent spirit and her desire to be treated with dignity.

"I think I might even find time to bake a few pies," she said, baiting him.

Gallagher tipped his hat, then settled it low over his eyes. "Keep the coffee hot, an' plenty of it." Having made it clear who ran the outfit, he pivoted on his boot heel and strode away, taking with him the entire population of the bunkhouse, except Archie.

"Do you like your coffee black, or with cream?" she called after him.

He turned his head, moving so fast that his men were hard pressed to keep up with his swift stride. "Black, unless we come across a fresh cow and her calf."

Well. The man seems to have an answer for everything, Meg thought, watching the boss man and his ranch hands enter the corral and catch fresh mounts. Next the men rummaged through the barn, coming back with an assortment of saws, hammers, tools, pulleys and ropes, which they tossed in the buckboard.

All afternoon Meg peeled, chopped, cooked, stirred, and baked. Davey soon succumbed to exhaustion and slept next to Susie on an old Army cot in the bunkhouse, so she could keep an eye on them. 'Big Jim,' anxious to prove himself indispensable, had ridden out with the men, his bony hind end bouncing on the backside of a fat black pony.

Watching her and fetching whatever she required, Archie straddled a chair backwards, playing mumble-de-peg with his bowie knife. He volunteered a time or two to help, but she declined as politely as she could. After all, this was her job, not his. Once she made that clear, he resigned himself with a grunt to keeping a sharp eye on the boss's new wife. Even so, every twang, as his blade hit its target, made Meg nearly jump out of her skin.

The old vulture's disapproving silence filled her with uneasiness. Clearly he'd been left behind to stand guard over her and the children. That in itself made her spirit chafe. She hated having every move she made watched. And that knife! Although acknowledging the usefulness of weapons in the wild, she cringed inwardly. Every twang of metal reverberating against wood made it harder to relax and act natural.

Amazed that Davey and Susie could sleep so soundly, Meg tried not to overreact. Archie's one eye glittered, giving him a dangerous aspect. Even so, she didn't find him nearly as terrifying as the prospect of an outlaw band riding into camp. Despite Sam's reassurances, she was *not* comfortable in her new surroundings, not one bit.

Seeing her flinch again, the old frontiersman let out an amused grunt. His fingers deftly lofting the knife, he flicked his wrist, this time hitting a knothole on the table where she was working. "Bulls-eye!" he softly breathed.

With a shiver, Meg plunged her hands into flour dough up to her elbows and began to roll out another pie crust. Even though she sensed old Archie was only testing her mettle, this little war he was waging was starting to get on her nerves. Truly, living in the West promised to be a challenge in more ways than one. She hoped Mr. Gallagher and his men were in a good mood when they returned, because she was making no guarantees about the state of her nerves. Especially if supper didn't turn out just right.

Chapter Eight

Suppertime came and went, while the pies cooled on the shelf. Her beans, seasoned with wild onions and bits of rehydrated beef jerky, had thickened and turned slightly mushy. Her biscuits had trebled in volume under a towel and stood ready to stick in the oven the instant the men returned.

Meanwhile Archie had disappeared on another of his long stalks around the perimeter. Worn out, both children lay curled in a ball like two kittens, fast asleep. Yawning, Meg stoked the fire to keep the coffee hot for a bunch of ranch hands who, despite the late hour, seemed impervious to hunger pangs.

The sun set. The moon rose. Finally the clock on the wall inside the bunkhouse chimed ten o'clock, and Meg, her eyelids heavy with fatigue, stumbled to her feet and peered through the dust-streaked window. It was still unclear where she and the children would be sleeping that night. She stretched, easing her tension with a long shudder from head to toe.

What could be keeping them? she asked herself for the umpteenth time.

She glanced at the table, set with plates and unmatched flatware of a strictly utilitarian variety. During the late afternoon, Davey had wandered in with clumps of black-eyed Susans and wildflowers, pulled up by the roots. Touched by the gesture, she'd arranged them in a jar, and placed it on the table, which was made of rough-sawn boards and set up on saw horses. The flowers did little to beautify their primitive surroundings, but perhaps they might brighten the men's spirits a little at the close of a long, long day.

Wishing she had proper napkins for the table, Meg turned back to the window. The bunkhouse was strewn with dirty laundry, ample proof of the men's careless habits. She vowed she would always set a proper table. Even the simplest fare tasted better when served in an eye-appealing way.

But such a resolution was for the future, she conceded. Tonight her legs ached, and she would be content with almost any place to lay her head. In a haze of fatigue, she leaned over Susie and Davey, watching them sleep. *Such sweet innocents,* she smiled, wishing that she, too, could curl up and sleep. But one lone woman must never relax her guard around strange men. And even though Archie, the strangest of the strange, with all his menacing knife work, might turn out to be perfectly harmless, she preferred to err on the side of caution.

Yawning, Meg sat down on the cot next to the children's, and resting her elbows on her knees, buried her head in her arms. *I'll just rest for a moment,* she told herself. Gradually the tension in her neck relaxed, and her eyes closed...

Her next awareness of her surroundings came with the loud rumble of what sounded like an avalanche of boulders rolling down the hill behind the bunkhouse. This was followed by a sudden frightening crash.

Terrified, Meg leapt to her feet. Her head jerked around, eyes straining to discover whatever fate awaited her. Instantly her ears picked up the stealthy noise of bodies moving around in the darkness. Every nerve in her taut body quivered with fright. Her sleep-clouded brain fought to make sense of things and prepare for whatever danger lay ahead. Amazingly, Susie slept through all the noise, but Davey sat up, rubbing his eyes and looking all around. Crooning soft reassurances to both children, Meg picked up her rolling pin and tiptoed to the door.

The kerosene lantern flickered, a dull yellow light, as the door slowly creaked open, letting in a cool blast of mountain air. She raised her rolling pin, ready to jump into action. Fortunately she was deterred from violence by the look of fright in Cory's rolling white eyes and Zeke's bold smirk, as they and a dozen other men came crowding through the door.

"Hold on, missus!" Cory raised his hands over his head to ward off a blow.

Meg dropped her arm. Her face grew pale, then flushed with surprise and acute embarrassment. She barely had time to get out of the way, as the entire crew trouped past her into the bunkhouse, drawn by the aroma of coffee and flavorful, if slightly overcooked hot stew. Sam Gallagher came in last, looking pleased with whatever he and his men had been up to. She could have throttled them all for giving her such a fright.

Someone turned up the lantern. Young Daniel began throwing sticks of kindling into the potbelly stove, creating quite a clatter. Amidst laughter and trading jokes, they made a beeline for the coffee, which she was sure must have boiled down to the consistency of mud after simmering for hours on the back burner. But before she could open her mouth and offer a word of caution, Toby was gulping down his second cup and exclaiming her virtues as the outfit's new cook. "This lady can cook!"

Convinced that they were hopelessly uncivilized, but grateful nonetheless that they were willing to eat whatever she dished out at such a late hour, Meg stuck the biscuits in the Dutch oven. Then she began to ladle out beans with a giant ladle. She only got the first bowl filled when someone grabbed the entire pot and plunked it smack-dab in the middle of the makeshift table. Someone else grabbed her pot holders and carried the succotash to the table.

Taking that as the signal to eat, every male present, including Jimmy, who was quick to ape his elders, stepped over the benches and sat down. An instant free-for-all ensued, with long hairy arms grabbing left and right for food. All her careful preparations went unappreciated, even Davey's wildflowers. Everyone was talking a mile a minute, with mouths full. Taken aback by their lack of manners, Meg stared aghast at the free-for-all of cowboys devouring her food like hungry wolves! Sam Gallagher had not been exaggerating about their manners. It was a feeding frenzy like nothing she had ever witnessed before.

Not one person even thought to offer a word of thanks to the cook—or, more importantly, the Almighty! If Meg was upset earlier by their showing up late for supper, their coarse manners were more than she could bear. Grabbing hold of the potato masher, she clanged it against an empty pot.

At first her furious clanging went unnoticed amidst all the guffaws and wild talk and slurping. So she picked up *another* empty pot and clanged the two pots together. By now she knew her own behavior was anything but dignified, but she simply couldn't help it. Observing the proprieties was never a mistake, nor was such uncivilized behavior to be tolerated! Somehow she had to make these men realize that they weren't pigs lined up at a slop trough.

Finally her loud banging and clanging got through to these sleep-deprived, food-crazed cowboys. Finally she got their attention...*finally!* They stared at her, many with bits of food hanging from their lips.

Meg folded her arms across her chest and pursed her lips. "Gentlemen," she announced, with only a trace of nervousness in her voice, for she noticed her employer was among the worst trespassers, "I think you have overlooked something important."

"Yeah? What might that be?" Mort raised his bowl, slurped down the last of its contents and let out a belch.

"We neglected to ask the Lord's blessing on the food," Meg said.

If she had dropped an elephant through the roof, they could not have looked more dumbfounded—or more sheepish.

Sam Gallagher's face turned an apoplectic red beneath his sunburn, though he held back from voicing his own personal opposition to prayer. After all, it was important that his men show his new wife proper respect. Resolved to take up the issue of prayer with her later in private, he set his hat on his knee and studied the slightly rumpled young woman standing at the foot of the table. Since she wasn't aware of his feelings on the subject, this might prove a testing ground for future discussions. However, considering the men's extreme fatigue and need for food, he decided to go along with her, in this instance.

"Mr. Gallagher, would you care to ask the blessing, or shall I?" she asked, only confirming his suspicions that she had a mulish streak and wasn't likely to give up easily.

He acceded to her wishes with a polite gesture. "Since you were so kind as to remind us, Mrs. G., perhaps you will oblige us?"

"Certainly, sir." Meg clasped her hands together and waited while, one by one, the men doffed their hats and bowed their heads. "Heavenly Father, Bless each of us under this roof. We thank Thee for Thy bounty and watchcare. In Jesus' name. Amen."

A few mumbled "amens" followed before the men resumed the serious business of filling their bellies. Though the mood was slightly more subdued, appetites remained hearty. Refilling coffee cups, Meg spotted out of the corner of her eye a whiskey flask being passed from Jelly Belly to Pete with a wink. Setting down the coffee pot, she rescued the pan of biscuits from the oven with a wadded up dishtowel. "I'll trade that bottle of hootch for these nice hot fluffy biscuits," she sang out, holding the pan of aromatic biscuits where all could smell and salivate, but not close enough to encourage thievery.

"No use arguing with the lady," Zeke said, smoothing the corners of his mustache with his index finger.

"Smart thinking," Sam Gallagher seconded the motion. "No hootch tonight, boys." His tawny gaze met Meg's with a decided lack of humor.

"But my rheumatism," Bill muttered.

"Maybe a nip at bedtime. After we get Mrs. G and the children settled in," Sam said with a firmness that put an end to the complaints.

Feeling as if she'd won a major victory, Meg relaxed her grip on the tray of biscuits. She set them down gently at her husband's elbow. "Eat hearty, gentlemen," she said with a smile. "There's apple pie for dessert, and all the coffee you can drink."

"Thank you, ma'am," her husband said meekly, and immediately a chorus of male voices chimed in, expressing their appreciation as well.

A little surprised at herself for resorting to bullying, yet proud of her success, Meg poured herself a cup of coffee and sat down at the far end of the table facing Mr. G and his cowpunchers. The men devoured everything in sight like a horde of locusts, and were cutting wedges of apple pie when the biscuit pan finally reached her end of the table.

She stared at one lone biscuit. In a way, it seemed to represent her own isolation among a baker's dozen of disorderly, yet hard working men. Not wishing to push her luck too far, she gingerly rescued the leftover biscuit, broke it in two, and slowly buttered a portion with her knife. She was just raising a morsel to her lips when her husband dropped his fork with a clatter onto his metal plate and stood to his feet.

Meg looked up expectantly.

Sam puffed out his chest and gave his foreman a slow wink. "What d'you say, men? Shall we escort my bride to her cabin? Or does anyone wish to volunteer as dishwasher?"

Being manly men, they all declined the dubious honor of washing dishes. That left only one option: Archie would do the honors that night.

Leaving Davey and Susie blissfully sawing logs in the bunkhouse, Meg allowed herself to be escorted out the door. Gallagher, coming up behind her, held the lantern high to light her path. Three hundred yards away, the silhouette of a small cabin loomed against the sky, and behind it, the dark, burned-out shell that had once been the main ranch house.

At last she understood the strange rumbling of rocks earlier, and the sudden violent crash.

The men had been rolling the cabin downhill on logs, until the steep incline proved too difficult to control speed, and the forces of gravity won out. Picking up speed as it thundered down the hillside, the cabin had finally met resistance and come to rest against the stout trunk of a large cottonwood tree. And there it sat, a pattern of silver-leafed moonbeams dancing over the moss-covered roof through the fluttering leaves.

Meg's jaw dropped. "Oh, my stars!" she exclaimed, amazed by their resourcefulness. "How far did you have to move it?"

Slim chuckled. "No more'n maybe two or three miles."

"Shook up the spiders a bit," Pete contributed.

Cory rolled his eyes until only the whites were visible in his dark face. "Ain't fit fer a lady in its current condition, that's fo' sure."

"I am truly beholden to you gentlemen," Meg assured them. "Mr. Gallagher, thank you, sir. I can't tell you how grateful—" Deeply moved, she shook his hand, then looked around the circle of men with tears in her eyes. "Thank you all, so very much!"

Before her tongue got any more tangled up, Sam handed her the lantern. "Wait here." He retraced his steps to the bunkhouse. "I'll get the children," he called over his shoulder. "Bill, you and Jimmy grab a few blankets. We'll move the cabin the rest of the way after breakfast tomorrow."

Surveying the eager faces clustered around her, Meg had no idea their industry could accomplish so much in so short a time. "I'm sure there's no need to move it right away. At least not until— well, it should do just fine, right where it sits, at least for the time being," she tried to assure them, but Walt spoke right up.

"When the boss says 'move something,' it gets moved."

A quick glance around the circle confirmed the men's "can-do" spirit. "Yes, I suppose you're right," she said with a nervous little laugh. "The children and I will be ready to move—again— right after breakfast."

Sensing the approach of her employer's large shadow, followed by two shorter ones, she turned to discover Sam carrying a sleeping child on each shoulder. Bill, his arms piled high with blankets, stepped past her and kicked open the shack's door. 'Big Jim,' as her twelve-year-old now preferred being called, stalked past, toting a bucket of water. "For washing up," he told her and set it down beside the bed.

"Thanks, Jimmy," she said, as he stepped outside again. When she and Jimmy were finished sharing a quick good-night hug, Sam handed Susie over to Meg and, supporting Davey in his arms with surprising gentleness, ducked beneath the low doorway, entering the ramshackle cabin.

Unsure of his intentions, Meg followed him just to the doorway. "Mr. G?" she asked, a little breathless.

He stuck his head out the door and fixed her with a tawny, cat-like stare. "Yes, Mrs. G?"

Her face felt like it was on fire, and she bit her lip. "I just wanted to say that it took a great deal of hard work to move this cabin, and I want you and your men to know how grateful I am." Her feet, indeed her entire body, seemed stalled on the threshold. "I-I know we exchanged vows for the children's sakes," she whispered.

He smiled, catching her meaning. "Just trying to live up to our bargain, Mrs. G," he said with a reassuring nod. Taking Susie from her, he carried the three-year-old inside, and settled her on the far side of the bed, next to Davey. "Rest easy, Mrs. G." He gently tapped her chin with his knuckle, closing her open mouth. "Jim and I will bed down for the night in the bunkhouse. We'll be within shouting distance, should you need anything."

As he brushed past her in the dark, Meg let out a slow sigh of relief. *Thank you, Lord!* Her instincts about this man had been correct. Sam Gallagher would look out for her and the children—nothing to fear where he was concerned. And being under his protection, she needn't worry about his men stepping out of line either.

Chapter Nine

As soon as the door was barred, Meg carefully shook out the blankets, as a precaution against any hidden spiders or tarantulas. Then she spread the covers over the cornhusk mattress, where Susie and Davey lay sprawled in open-mouthed oblivion. In the eerie yellow lantern light, she studied her rustic abode. The walls were seriously out of plumb, no doubt knocked cattywompus when the cabin came to rest against the large cottonwood tree.

A misshapen branch stuck through a shattered window, barring anyone from making it inside past the twisted wreckage. Silky grey cobwebs swung from the rafters, drifting back and forth like moss dangling from a spooky tree in the bayous. It kind of gave Meg the willies. Of course, having read tales as a young girl about the foggy Louisiana swamps during the battle of New Orleans in 1815, her imagination began working overtime. Even so, looking back over the past couple of days, Meg was quite certain this was as bad as things could possibly get.

Snuffing out the light, she cautiously climbed in bed between Susie and Davey and lay down, fully dressed. Crickets chirped in concert and sang from log chinks around the room. She crossed her ankles, tucking her skirts snuggly around her legs against any possible invasion of spiders. Closing her eyes tightly, she put her fingers in her ears to block out vague, persistent scurrying sounds in the dark. Presently what she imagined to be the faint scrabble of small rodents began to grate on her nerves. Wilderness living certainly left a lot to be desired. Even so, she was determined not to give way to unfounded fears.

While she sought to talk herself out of such irrational fears, the strangest dry rustling noises began to come closer and closer across the floor boards. The rustling noise grew louder—*could it be mouse claws?*—until finally her blood ran cold in her veins. She lay rigid beneath the scratchy wool blanket, praying for dawn and, hopefully, the departure of all her restless nocturnal visitors.

Suddenly, in addition to the cabin's other rather disturbing creaks and groans, a strange flapping noise roused her to full alert. Her heart nearly leapt out of her chest. Cautiously Meg opened one eye. Perched directly overhead, a pair of large, unblinking yellow eyes stared down at her from the rafters. Hot gorge rose in her throat. Jerking bolt upright, she clapped both hands over her mouth, stifling her scream and turning it into a gurgle. The air over her head stirred, as a large barn owl swooped down, its talons narrowly missing the hair standing straight up on her head. She closed her eyes, as it pounced on some unseen creature of the night.

Nearly swooning with fright, Meg fell back against her pillow. Vowing she'd never sleep a wink, she curled her body protectively around Susie. Somehow she must survive this terrible night, but at dawn she would insist that Mr. G return her and all three children to Cheyenne. Though a rough frontier town, it was a palace, compared with this horrible place!

She was still rehearsing how to justify her decision to Sam Gallagher when sheer exhaustion and fright overtook her, and she fell asleep.

~ * ~ * ~ * ~

The sun beat through her eyelids, forcing her to emerge from a semi-conscious state. With a dry mouth and a throat burning for lack of water, Meg sat up slowly. Still not certain if she had fainted or fallen into a stupor the night before, she gingerly moved away from Davey. To the touch, his body radiated heat. Checking him for fever, and having reassured herself that he was merely warm from sleep, Meg proceeded to smooth the wrinkles from her travel clothes.

As she bent to tighten the laces on her ankle-high shoes, a disturbing pattern of spiraling arcs on the dusty floor caught her eye. Her curiosity heightened, she hesitated, as her gaze followed the slithering trail. Holding her breath, she lifted the edge of the blanket from the floor beside the bed where she and the children had slept.

She gasped, scarcely believing—yet realizing once again the miracle of God's love and great protection. A large diamondback rattlesnake lay headless beside the bed. Instantly she realized the role the owl had played during the night, quite possibly saving their lies. If she *had* given into her fears and gone screaming out into the night, chances are she, or Susie, or Davey might have suffered a fatal strike from the rattlesnake's deadly fangs.

As she stooped to examine the rattlesnake's lifeless but still twitching carcass, she realized her panic the night before was well justified. Amazed and grateful that she and the children had escaped harm, she rushed to the bed with praise in her heart and began to tickle the children in the ribs to waken them.

~ * ~ * ~ * ~

Sending Davey and Susie ahead of her out the cabin door, Meg carefully scooped up the snake's carcass with a shovel and carried the eight-foot rattlesnake across the clearing to the bunkhouse. Even though it *seemed* to be dead, she didn't feel brave enough to carry it dangling like a bullwhip from her fingers. Still, she was looking forward to flaunting it under Mr. Gallagher's nose.

As she marched up behind him, parading the snake in plain sight, she wondered if seeing her trophy might give him an attack of apoplexy. "Good morning, Mr. Gallagher," she called out.

"Ah, 'tis Miss Wolfie herself." Focused on shaving, he raised an eyebrow at the provocative tone of her greeting, but went on shaving.

Meg walked up behind him, swinging her shovel gently back and forth. She was determined to get a rise out of him.

A couple of cowboys coming back from the outhouse spotted the snake and nearly jumped a mile trying to get away from it, but Sam kept right on shaving.

Exasperated, Meg raised up on tiptoe and stared at him in the small cracked mirror nailed to the bunkhouse wall. Momentarily distracted, he paused, his lathered left cheek only half done.

"Turn around and stop ignoring me," she said, peeved.

He spun around, and grabbed her by the shoulders to avoid colliding. While he had no particular objection to having such an attractive pair of bosoms pressed up against his chest, she didn't appear in the mood for early morning sweet-talking. In fact, she seemed downright irate.

When she let out a startled huff and took a step back, teetering on the edge of the step, he politely stepped aside, hoping to ease the sexual tension.

"Yes, Miss Wolfie?" he grinned. "What can I do for you?"

"I-I thought you should know that this snake was in my cabin last night," she said, waving the evidence around.

He examined it calmly and gave an approving nod. "I'd say you took care of the situation quite handily."

She let out an exasperated squeal. "What do you want me to do with it?"

"Should cook up mighty tasty," he said, deadpan.

"Perhaps you'd like me to serve it to you in an omelette?" she countered, with a flash of sarcasm.

"With plenty of hot sauce." Grinning, he playfully flicked a speck of lather on her nose, then picked up his razor and resumed shaving.

Wiping her face, Meg stood behind him, tapping her foot. Rattled by her heavy breathing, he nicked his chin.

Muttering under his breath, Sam hollered for a clean towel.

Knowing there wasn't a single clean article of clothing in the bunkhouse, Meg dropped her shovel in the dirt and made a beeline for the line shack. When she got back, several of his men were standing around, admiring the dead rattlesnake. Half of them giving Mr. G credit for killing it!

"Here, Mr. G." She handed him a clean towel and a jar of salve from her suitcase. "Wouldn't want you to get lockjaw."

Still miffed, she stooped to grab the writhing rattlesnake by its tail, but Archie quickly stepped between her and the snake, moving her gently to one side. "Let me deal with this here snake for you, missus," he said in his gravelly voice. "Let me show you how to strip the guts and debone it. Otherwise, you're like to get poisoned."

"But it's already dead," she protested. Already she had visions of cracking it like a bull whip over Mr. G's head.

"The head on this here snake has already been lopped off, but unless it's handled jus' right, you can still get mighty sick. C'mon, I'll show you. Beckoning for Meg to follow him, Archie picked up the twitching snake by the rattles in its tail with the other hand.

Glancing around at Mr. G. and his men, Meg turned up her nose. She would show Mr. G! No matter how nonchalant the boss man tried to act, he'd better think twice before he *ever* put a woman and two innocent children in a rattlesnake-infested line shack again!

Meanwhile she was having a few second thoughts of her own about the correct way to prepare wild game. Maybe, just maybe—being a tenderfoot and all—she'd be wise to take advantage of Archie's long years of surviving in the wilderness.

"Archie, what do you think about cooking it up in a batch of chili?" she asked, following him down to the creek to wash and prepare it for dinner.

~ * ~ * ~ * ~

After a hearty breakfast of grits, bacon, pancakes and hot coffee, served up through the combined efforts of Meg and Archie, the really hard work of clearing the way for a new house began. Using mules and a team of oxen, several men set to work salvaging whatever timbers they could from the ranch house.

While they were busy doing that, Meg and Jimmy searched through the ashes and wood scraps for bits of hardware and any personal effects that might have survived the fire. Gradually, as the morning wore on, the charred remains were hauled off, until all that remained was a large black patch of level ground.

When Meg questioned why they didn't just set fire to the pile of rubble and save themselves a lot of unnecessary work, Archie's reply quickly sobered her about the dangers of living in this lone region: "Smoke from a fire that size would surely bring even more trouble down on our heads."

When she frowned quizzically, he spelled it for her: "I can see how a city woman might think such a thing, but landsakes, woman! You don't never burn nothin' out here, just to get rid of it. Come winter, every scrap of wood's gonna be needed to keep us from freezin' to death. Why, I thought even a greenhorn could figure that out!"

Her cheeks flaming, Meg hastily apologized for her ignorance. "I guess I have a lot to learn about living out West," she admitted. "I appreciate your candor, Archie."

"Yes, ma'am," he said gruffly, and then, to make up for venting such harsh criticism, he gently relieved her of the bucket full of salvaged hardware. "I'll take care of this. Besides, I expect the men would appreciate a pot of your hot coffee about now."

Recognizing his good intentions, and glad to be let off the hook, Meg hurried back to the bunkhouse to get lunch on the table.

~ * ~ * ~ * ~

An hour later, after dragging the line shack, bumping and careening across the yard on ropes, the men pulled the supporting logs out from under it. The structure stood cattywompus and wobbly, badly needing to be shored up at one end of the newly graded patch of charred earth formerly occupied by Mr. Gallagher's ranch house. Moving it that last twenty or thirty feet had proven almost as difficult as rolling it that last mile and a half downhill. By the time the men got it positioned, they were covered with dirt and grime and eager to get back to tending cattle.

While Meg passed among the men, serving coffee, beans—no rattlesnake meat, not yet anyway—and biscuits to tie them over until supper, she figured it was as good a time as any to remind Mr. G that her homestead lay across the creek. Since he seemed to have commandeered the line shack for his own use, she needed clarification on this vital issue.

Not wishing to have her housing situation become a sore spot in their relationship, she asked as politely as she could when he intended to get around to building her a cabin on her homesteaded land.

When she persisted, her employer only shook his head and winked at his foreman, as if to say that only a "dang woman" would have difficulty comprehending an undertaking of this magnitude. "For the time being, you'll stay here," was his only comment.

Meg was still contemplating the mixed blessings of her situation, when her employer jerked his chin toward the saddle bags hanging over the corral fence. "I'll take care of Jimmy and Davey, Mrs. G, providing you rustle up a few clean towels and a bar of soap from those bags," he informed her.

She stared at him. "I beg your pardon?"

"The boys and I could do with a quick dip in the creek," Sam grinned. "If we stand around yammering much longer, I doubt *any* of us, once the mud dries on our clothes, will be able to move a muscle."

The underlying sarcasm in his picturesque speech brought Meg down to earth with a jolt. "I'll be glad to bathe the boys," she offered, thinking he wanted her to take the boys off his hands.

Gallagher stepped aside, easily eluding her. "No sense ruining your dress. I'm already a mess, so I might as well take a good dunking. It'll save you getting wet."

He spun on his boot heel and strode toward the creek, catching Davey up in the air and dangling him over one shoulder. "Come on, Big Jim," he called to the older boy. Davey threw his arms around Sam's neck and twisted around, looking scared. Up, up he went again, as Sam Gallagher flipped the boy in an overhanded somersault.

Suddenly Davey shrieked.

Alarmed, Meg hiked up her skirts and ran after them, her knees pumping up and down like pistons. "Mr. Gallagher! Not so rough!" she gasped, hoping to rescue her boys.

"Relax." He shot her a sidelong glance. "Jimmy and Davey can survive a bit of rough and tumble."

"Oh, but you mustn't!" Had he no idea what these orphans had already been subjected to? Nearly breathless with fright, she latched onto his forearm in mute appeal.

"Look," he said, "it won't do him any harm. Besides, Davey seems to like getting tossed around a bit. Boys need to kick loose now and then. It frees 'em up after all the fussing lavished on them by women folk."

"Is *that* what you call it?" Meg drew herself up to her full height of five feet one and balled her fists. To her mind, Sam Gallagher had the sensitivity of a goat. If she weren't so needy financially, she would just love to tell him off. But being responsible for three orphans, including one who had problems enough without her sticking her foot in a quagmire, she decided to reason with him. "Davey is not like other boys, Mr. G. And while I appreciate that you're a man of good intentions, I must ask you not to interfere."

"Interfere!" He looked up at the only cloud in the blue sky and addressed it. "Women!" With an exasperated snort, he sat down on a large rock and started pulling off his boots. Then he stripped the boys down to their smalls and resumed walking along the creek, looking for a good place to have a water fight with two frisky young boys.

"Mr. G," she warned, racing to keep up with the trio. "You don't know your own strength. I must ask you to cease and desist. Davey and Jimmy aren't used to such rough play! You cannot—"

"Hold your nose, Davey," was his response. "On the count of three. One, two, three!" He flexed his muscular knees and jumped in the water, still holding Davey, and dunking Jimmy with his other hand.

Davey let out a squeal of surprise. Then the waters closed over their heads. Not to be outdone, Jim entered the water with a splash and began instinctively to dog paddle.

Pacing the bank, Meg wrung her hands, as she waited for Sam and the boys to surface. They shot up, spouting water, like three bull frogs in a jumping contest.

"Whaauugh!" Sam roared, shaking water off his head and shoulders like a wet bird dog.

"Waaa—" echoed Davey, flapping his hands wildly and trying to capture water droplets on his tongue. "Waa—"

Still secure in her employer's arms, Davey spotted Meg crouched a few feet away on the sloping bank and laughed out loud. Grinning, he leaned over and splashed water at her.

"Oh, very well," she conceded. "I'll go fetch you some towels."

"Might check on little Miss Susie-Q while you're at it." Sam gave Jimmy a good-natured knuckle sandwich and promptly got rushed by both boys.

"I'll be right back," Meg warned, so he wouldn't think she was turning a blind eye on all the hijinks going on in the creek. Well, maybe she *was* a little jealous. Males seemed to have all the fun, whereas she still had a ton of laundry and supper still to be done.

As she hurried over to the corral, she saw Susie, seated on a slow moving, pregnant mare, getting put through their paces by Daniel. She waved to the teenager, who was helping the three-year-old get used to riding. "Thanks, Dan," she said, admiring his gentleness with Susie.

"Happy to oblige," he grinned, tipping his Stetson. "It's a nice change of pace, helping with the kids."

Being an orphan himself, and only three years older than Jimmy, Daniel seemed an ideal choice, chores permitting, to help with the children. Meg knew from personal experience how hard it was to get through her teen years without parents. At least she had her aunt and uncle.

Having found what she needed, she closed the saddle bags. "I'll be back soon," she promised and headed back to the creek, her arms piled high with towels. Still preoccupied with thoughts of Daniel, she thought perhaps he might find a quick dip in the creek refreshing, too, but decided to consult "the boss man" before saying anything.

She found Jimmy and Mr. G busily scraping caked mud off themselves and their clothes, and Davey joining in with shrieks of laughter. Amazed by Davey's vocalizations, Meg ducked the avalanche of water headed her way—they were amazingly accurate for three such unrepentant males! Cupping her hands in the fast flowing creek, she threw water at all three. though her attempts were pretty lame, she had to admit. All she did was get herself soaked. Still, it was worth it, just to see Davey's unexpected attempts to engage in play. His face was wreathed with smiles, and his continual cries of "Wa— Waaaugh!" filled her heart with happiness.

Oh, Davey, Davey! You sweet, precious boy, she rejoiced. Daring to hope it wasn't an isolated attempt at speech, she splashed vigorously, encouraging Davey to express himself. Never had she seen him so expressive and involved with other people.

Suddenly a barrage of cold water hit her in the face. As she wiped her dripping face, Sam Gallagher laughed and ducked below the surface. Then he grabbed Davey's hands, and conspiring with Jimmy, all three began splashing water for all they were worth, drenching her in a wild deluge of spray.

"Cover your eyes, Miss Wolfie," Sam advised. "These boys play for keeps."

Entering into their play wholeheartedly, Meg gave equal treatment. Standing on her dignity presently gave way to helpless laughter, as she leaned over, scooping water with her hands. Davey howled and slapped the water. Watching his face light up, and seeing Jimmy's delighted grin made her forget to uphold her dignity. It was the most fun she'd had in ages.

Looking up at the sky through the sparkling shimmer of aspen trees and sunlight, she felt as if the whole world was suddenly filled with light. It was as if a tremendous weight had been lifted from her young shoulders. For years she had been weighed down by adult responsibilities, long before she came of age.

Now, suddenly, in this uncivilized wilderness, while she clutched at tree roots and tufts of grass to keep from tumbling into the swiftly moving stream, she felt the most indescribable joy overtake her.

The feeling came so unexpectedly, filling her with unspeakable happiness. Quite in contrast to the agitated stirring of water drenching her. The rain of warm tears and splashing prisms of light danced over her skin, accomplishing infinitely more than the mere washing away of her cares. The ice cold run-off from the mountains left her breathless and refreshed. It was as if something deep inside her spirit had been liberated.

And in that breathless moment, she forgot to worry about having the proper decorum, or worrying about the future, or even the children. She let go of her bitterness because her parents had died and left her destitute so many years ago. Even Mr. G's obstinacy no longer intimidated her. None of it mattered, she realized, as she stumbled backward on the grassy bank and lay there, gazing up at the sky, and laughed out loud.

Never had she felt so free! Slowly sitting up in a daze of wonderment, she was still dimly aware that the water fight between Jimmy and Davey and Sam Gallagher continued. The boys' high spirited young shouts intermingled with Sam's playful, stentorian roars, followed by even more vigorous splashing. *When had she forgotten what it felt like to play?*

Knowing the boys were safe, Meg finally picked herself up and walked back to the cabin, her wet skirts dragging through the tangled rustle of parched summer grasses. She wondered what, exactly, had taken place back there at the creek. Minutes before, she'd had her hackles up, like a fiercely protective mama lion, ready to do battle with Mr. G. for the souls of her orphans.

Now, the strangest feeling came over her: That innate compulsion always to be the one in charge—knowing—or perhaps more accurately, *assuming*—that nobody else understood how it felt to be the underdog, carrying all the cares of the world—suddenly all that was gone. Vanished! Like a schoolmarm's slate—wiped clean. And in its place she recognized a new and abiding conviction, that *this* was her destiny, and she must embrace her life here, and never be afraid of it again.

Chapter Ten

Meg's spirits continued to climb to new heights, as she recalled Davey's startling vocalizations and Jimmy's wide, happy grin, as they tried to dunk Sam during the water fight. How this rambunctious man could so effortlessly win a very special place in the boys' affections seemed truly amazing to her.

And so in the days that followed, Meg found herself warming toward Sam more and more for taking the boys and Susie under his wing.

Soon Davey and Jim could be seen tagging along with the ranch hands, carrying tools, or leading a tame horse, or toting a milk pail back from the barn. The bond between the two boys and Sam made her heart swell with hope, as she came to realize how much Davey and Jimmy must have missed, growing up without a father's love during those formative, early years. Yes, she conceded, as important as a mother's role was, her orphans also needed a father to look up to.

But she couldn't afford to dwell long upon the past. For one thing, she didn't have *time* for idle speculation. She had more than enough work to do, what with cooking, baking, washing, keeping the cabin swept and tidy, and seeing to the needs of three lively children. Fortunately Archie handled a fair amount of the cooking for the cowhands, or she'd have been buried under an avalanche of housework.

With agonizing slowness, the site where the ranch house had once stood got cleared and leveled. Trees were felled. Logs were split and fresh lumber was hauled in and stacked, whenever the demands of running a ranch permitted a few spare hours to work on the house.

For now Meg was pretty much resigned to living in the line shack, which seemed destined to become a spare bedroom on the end of Sam's house. If it ever got rebuilt. Meanwhile she and the boys, when they could be lured away from shadowing Mr. G, spent a little time every day, daubing mud into cracks in the drafty cabin walls to keep out insects and vermin.

Gradually Davey began to take a greater interest in his new surroundings. He often wandered off on little adventures and returned slung over the saddle of one of Sam's ranch hands. Occasionally he brought home rocks or arrowheads he'd found. In no time, his collection of 'treasures' had grown to the extent that she sometimes stumbled over a rack of antlers, a chunk of obsidian, or a tortoise shell in the grass.

Finally she dragged a couple of empty boxes out of a shed and set them on end under the porch eaves to display his treasures. Almost immediately the pile grew, as one by one, the cowboys discovered a "perty rock" to add to the items Davey proudly had on display.

Then came the day Davey dragged home a cougar's newborn kit.

Seeing the boy all scratched up, yet stubbornly hanging onto his latest trophy, Sam laid down the law. Not only did he confiscate Davey's latest acquisition, he delivered a blistering lecture.

"No more wild critters," he said flatly. "They spook the horses, raid the chicken coop, and eat my livestock." He strode outside, the snarling cat swinging in a burlap sack at the end of his fist. Mounting his horse, he rode off.

Meg stood on the porch step watching him go. She hadn't the courage to ask what Sam planned to do with the animal, but she wasn't the least bit sorry to see it go. Even so, she still had to contend with Davey, who was registering his displeasure with a full blown temper tantrum. Used to getting his way, he threw himself face down in the dirt, and began kicking and bawling at the top of his lungs.

For once, Meg chose to ignore him. She worried about the scratches, but pitching a fit that way was clearly an attempt at emotional blackmail. Having better things to do, she calmly stepped over his prone body, went back inside the line shack, and quietly closed the door.

Without an audience, Davey soon gave up his incoherent crying. An abrupt silence fell, and Meg smiled, watching from the window. There he sat, brushing himself off. His cheeks were streaked with tears, but he was making a valiant effort to reason things out.

Oh, how her spirits rose, as it dawned on her: Having a tantrum was normal behavior for a child his age. *Normal!* It was the first time she'd seen Davey throw a tantrum and then make a conscious effort to control his emotions. *Oh, Davey, Davey.* How she longed to kiss away all the tears and grime from his face. Though still protective, some deeply engrained instinct restrained her from trying to console him.

He took a few hesitant steps, as if he meant to follow Sam, but then he dropped his head and turned back. Smiling, Meg bit her lip, watching him struggle for self-mastery. As much as she wanted to show sympathy, she was careful not to say anything.

Finally he mounted the porch steps. She saw that tiny scowl—so deep in thought. Shoulders slumped, he trudged past the window where Meg stood, half-concealed, watching and praying for wisdom and forbearance.

Solemn as a pallbearer, eight-year-old Davey walked over to his rock collection. After some pondering, he picked up a chunk of grey rhyolite. He turned it in his hands, staring intently at it. Suddenly he opened his pudgy fingers and dropped it with an explosive crash.

Startled, Meg stuck her head out the window.

Dave's shock of brown hair concealed his face from her, as he stooped to pick up the broken pieces. *What could he have been thinking, to drop that heavy thing?* she thought. It was a wonder he hadn't smashed his toe.

Oblivious to her concerns, Davey picked up one of the larger broken pieces of rhyolite. He jiggled it up and down, watching the amethyst crystals catch the sun's rays and sparkle. Slowly he turned his new discovery over in his hands, touching the brilliant points of light.

Meg's breath caught. Hidden inside the rough, grey exterior of lava rock was great beauty. Quartz crystals. Only when it was broken could the rock properly display its wonders.

How like our lives, Meg marveled, sharing Davey's wondrous discovery. *Until we let go of pride and come broken and willing to receive spiritual sight, our lives are as lackluster as volcanic ash. Oh, dear Lord, help me to shine for you in this place,* she fervently prayed.

How much she had to learn! About each of her orphans, and about herself. About life in general. Leaving Dave to explore his latest discovery, Meg began to prepare supper with a lighter heart. She had plenty of time to ponder her great good fortune.

~ * ~ * ~ * ~

As grateful as she was that Sam had disposed of the cougar, she dismissed all thought of it as soon as it was out of sight. She might never have learned what he did with it, had not one of the men mentioned it in passing at the dinner table later that night, while passing the potatoes: Sam had reunited the wild kit with its mother in the wilds.

Meanwhile every time Davey saw Sam, he remembered that he'd been deprived of his pet cougar. Clearly holding a grudge, he steadfastly ignored all Sam's overtures of peace. Everyone wisely ignored his pouts, and eventually Davey resumed his daily routine, just as if he'd never had a falling out with Sam.

Sam Gallagher's patience with the boys continued to amaze— and often put her to shame. No matter how tired or busy, he invariably found time to set aside his work, hunker down beside the boys, and show them how a job should be done. He always impressed upon them that every task, no matter how small, was important and deserved their best effort.

Watching from the sidelines, Meg watched the boys' confidence grow. She prayed that the bond between man and boys might stimulate further speech and social skills in Davey, and help fill the emotional void in Jimmy's upbringing.

Though extremely busy herself, she kept a close eye on the bond forming between the children and her employer. Unlike her attempts to nurture the children, Sam made no effort to shield the boys from the consequences of being clumsy, or of not being alert to their surroundings.

"Haven't time to coddle the boys," he told her late one afternoon. He leaned down from the saddle and dropped a squalling Davey into her outstretched arms. At first she focused on his curtness, but as she reflected on the incident—Davey was howling about a barely skinned knee—she soon began to question whether some of the children's insecurities might not stem from her being overly protective. Knowing how vulnerable these orphans were, she realized she was often guilty of trying to shield them from the challenges of everyday life and its harsher realities.

Now, sensing positive changes in the boys, Meg consciously relinquished her fears to the Lord. When Sam joined her and the children for breakfast the following day, Jimmy and Davey eagerly demanded to be included in the outfit's plans for the day. Giving Davey a pat on the backside, she was able to send him racing out the door with a lighter heart.

And so the days passed. While she washed and baked, cooked and swept, fed the chickens and slopped the hogs, Davey and Jim tagged along with the ranch hands, proud to be doing "men's work." She just hoped they didn't pick up the men's rough manners. But then she asked the Lord's forgiveness, because their kindness far outshone their lack of social polish.

Occasionally she picked up a hammer herself, or a paint brush, and made a minor repair to the cabin, but mostly she relied on Sam and his men to set the place to rights. Of course, the men had given the ramshackle cabin a thorough shaking up right after they got it repositioned. Emptying it out to the bare walls, they had swept out the spiders and cobwebs. They'd shot two rats that attempted a stand-off, rather than give up their turf. A scaly lizard, seeing the rats' fates, scurried off into the sagebrush.

Then cowboy Bill climbed up in the rafters to remove the owl's nest. Minutes later, he marched outside, the owl secured in a burlap sack, its nest and three eggs in the bottom of his hat.

"This here Mama owl will keep a close eye on things at night." Giving Meg a wink, he removed the owl's nest to the barn loft. When he released the owl, she rewarded him by trying to bite him.

"Sentry duty," Moses said with an approving nod.

Sam said very little—until he added his own surprise touch to making the cabin more homey. Reaching into his loosely buttoned jacket, he pulled out a small tawny pup dog.

"Every family needs a good watch dog," he told Meg.

"Are you sure that thing is housebroken?" Full of doubts, she folded her arms over her chest and eyed his gift with distaste. It was kind of cute, but the size of those paws made her less than enthusiastic.

Sam shrugged. "Give her time."

Typical man, Meg thought. How she wished she had a choice, just once, instead of being presented with something else to keep track of.

Sam reached and rubbed the puppy's soft floppy ears. "My first wife used to put an old rag rug on the porch, just till a new pup got the lay of the land. Prevents accidents indoors," he added.

"Really!" Meg was tempted to remind Sam that it didn't necessarily follow that what his late wife did to break a dog of bad habits was how *she* would handle the situation. Why, if it were up to her, she'd just send that pup and all its fleas down to the bunkhouse!

But before she could open her mouth and flat-out refuse to add one more nuisance to the long list of chores she already had, Jimmy came barreling around the corner. The minute he saw that puppy, he dove headlong into the dirt, tangling with the yelping pup and rolling over and over in the grass. Drawn by the puppy's excited barking, Susie and Davey let out wild whoops and began running in circles around the dog, and there ensued a noisy free-for-all.

Sam's eyes—a close match for the puppy's tawny coat—gleamed with amusement. Meg was sure he knew how much she dreaded taking over the training of that mongrel pup.

"Guess that settles it," he chuckled. "The kids are plumb crazy about Dusty."

"Dusty!"

"Yup. It's a female." He leaned one shoulder against the outer wall of the cabin and crossed one boot over the other, while he watched the children hug and laugh ecstatically over the puppy. "I've found that females stick around home better," he added.

Since the children had fallen in love with Dusty at first sight, Meg threw up her hands in defeat. What choice did she have? Their radiant smiles overruled common sense. She could not spoil all their fun, even though Dusty with her oversized paws, long floppy ears, and pumpkin head was clearly destined to grow into a very large, slobbery dog. The instant her orphans spotted Dusty, her wishes had no more substance than the smoke drifting up the chimney stack.

With as much good grace as she could muster, Meg said, "All right, thank you—I think. Just tell me one thing: How *does* one raise a half-breed pup?"

Seeing how reluctant she was to take on the raising of a hyperactive young pup, Sam casually reached out and ruffled her soft hair, gathered loosely at the nape of her neck.

"Let Dusty inside for only a few minutes at a time," he suggested. "At night, make her sleep outside. Before winter, she should be pretty much finished chewing and digging and making a general nuisance of herself."

"Sounds like I just traded one bunch of wild critters for another pest," she said.

"She'll make a fine watchdog," he assured her, then switched subjects. "Ready to inspect your new home?" He leaned close, his eyes gleaming with fresh mischief.

Not trusting him a bit, Meg drew in a deep breath and braced herself. Sam and his men had barred her from the cabin all day, while they made essential repairs. Clearly he'd forgotten his promise to build separate quarters for her and the children across the creek.

Not having got her way regarding the dog, she figured it made no sense to beat a dead horse. "I'm as ready as I'll ever be," she said.

Chapter Eleven

After being made to wait outside with the children until the men were satisfied that the cabin was safe, finally it was time to inspect her temporary new home. Shielding her eyes, Meg stepped across the threshold and instantly felt an unmistakable peace settle over her spirit. The children clustered around her, anxious to hear her reaction.

Standing just outside, Sam and his men appeared to be holding their breath—they were that quiet, while she pivoted, admiring the men's handiwork. She could not get over the improvements in their living quarters! Instinctively her nose crinkled up at the damp coat of whitewash that now brightened the log and mud-chinked walls. Yes, dust motes still drifted in the air from the rigorous cleaning the men had given the place, but the windows were sparkling clean and the floor spotless. The furniture, such as it was, had been repaired, and a small cot had been carried in from the bunkhouse for Suzie.

Among the hearth stones, somehow having escaped the men's housecleaning, a cricket chirped its merry tune.

"Oh, my stars!" Meg breathed, close to tears. "I can't believe you did all this for the children and me!"

Self-consciously Sam doffed his hat and poked his head through the door. "I know it's still a little rough—" But then he fell silent, watching Meg tiptoe around the room, touching various objects and setting them down almost reverently.

"Dear Lord," she whispered, "bless these men for seeing to our needs so beautifully, and especially bless Mr. G for inviting us here and making us feel so welcome—"

An unintended eavesdropper, Sam felt his insides begin to squirm like a passel of raccoons fighting in a burlap sack. Though he knew she meant no harm, any mention of the Almighty made him uncomfortable. Reminders of the hereafter still didn't sit well with him. Fact was, he and the Man Upstairs hadn't been on speaking terms in quite some time.

Still carrying a grudge since the loss of his wife and child, Sam decided to stop Meg before her prayers got the Almighty all stirred up, and he found himself roasting in the hot seat of God's wrath.

"Excuse me, Mrs. G," he broke in, "you're not exactly my invited guest. I hired you as my housekeeper, remember? And when you kind of sprang three extra mouths on me to feed, I just naturally did the decent thing and married you."

Startled, Meg turned to face his thunderous scowl. Suddenly aware that he'd overheard her praying, she blushed. "Oh! I'm sorry. I had no idea I wasn't alone," she stammered.

"Maybe we should make one thing clear, right from the get-go," he said, his ruddy cheek bones burning. "I'd prefer not to be the subject of a lot of holier-than-thou prayers!"

Taken by surprise, Meg felt her dander rise in defense of her faith. "Are you saying that I am not allowed to pray?" she challenged him in a dangerously quiet voice.

"Pray to the wind for all I care." He shook a slightly shaky finger under her nose. "Just leave my name out of it!"

The oddest sensation, like a deep shock, settled in her bones. Too stunned to speak, she sat down on a straight-backed chair, her knees suddenly weak as dishwater. His reaction to prayer seemed so sharply at odds with his many kindnesses to her and the children. Almost she wanted to weep, for despite his rejection of God, she felt the strangest urge to comfort him.

How lost he must feel, she thought. A great wave of pity swept over her, for it occurred to her that any man who feared the mention of his name in prayer must be in dire need of God's intervention.

"Would you mind telling me why you feel that way?" she gently probed.

"Don't care to discuss it," he said gruffly. "Just don't pray for me." He jammed his Stetson on his head, and ducking his head to avoid the low doorpost, glared at her. "That is not a request. It's an order!"

Her curiosity piqued, Meg touched her forehead in a mock salute. *Aye, aye, sir,* she thought. Clearly Sam Gallagher was embroiled in a very private controversy with God. She shivered involuntarily, and in her heart she vowed to *double* her prayers for him.

In fact, it might be interesting to see how God intervenes. After all, she didn't need to let Sam know she was praying for him. She would just keep it between her and the Lord. Because regardless of how Mr. Gallagher and God were getting along, Meg knew she'd be hard pressed to survive this untamed wilderness without being able to pour out her heart to the Lord—often.

She clapped her hand over her mouth to stifle a guilty laugh. Her employer should be praising God, instead of going off like that about prayer. Why, if he only knew how often she was *this close* to giving him a good swat with her frying pan! *Oh, my, yes.* No telling how many lumps he'd have now, if it weren't for the grace of God restraining her hand.

Clearly God had a purpose in leading her here. Whether to homestead and raise three orphans, or to help a hard-headed rancher come to know God was his friend, she knew she must rely on *His* strength and wisdom to "live at peace with all men."

~ * ~ * ~ * ~

From that day on, Meg ceased to harangue or even drop hints to her employer about the need to build her a separate cabin on the land she planned to homestead across the creek. Sam never brought up the subject either. Indeed, he seemed well pleased with their arrangement. He respected her need for privacy and made no further attempts to set foot inside "her" line shack. While much remained unspoken between them, he seemed content to let matters drift along as they were, and Meg, for her part, decided to let God work in His own mysterious ways.

Of course, there were times when she missed the beauty of fine furniture and the easy access to friends, neighbors, churches and stores she had enjoyed back East. Here she had no women folk to keep her company, and few of the luxuries she had taken for granted prior to moving here.

By far her worst challenge as a housekeeper centered around the problem of cleanliness. Dust created a never ending problem here on the Wyoming plains. When she wasn't planting and weeding the garden, she was busy keeping up with an endless round of cooking and washing dishes. She was constantly drawing water at the well to scrub floors, do laundry on a scrub board, and hang another batch of clothes out to dry. What the men didn't bring back to the bunkhouse after a day of rounding up cattle and riding horses, the winds did. No other chore taxed her energies like the daily round of waging war with all the dirt that got tracked in.

In the evenings she sewed and mended by firelight, often patching her employer's torn clothing, or the children's. Now that she was eating regularly, she ripped out the seams on a gingham dress that fit too snugly, and made curtains with the material. When she finished hanging them, Meg tucked her work-roughened hands under her chin and turned slowly in a circle, admiring the changes she'd made to the cabin with satisfaction. It wasn't fancy, but it felt like a place where she could put down roots, for now anyway.

Flaunting her private disagreement with Sam, she placed her Bible on a side table made from an empty nail keg and covered with an embroidered cloth she'd brought from back East. The small child's rocker she'd rescued from the barn became Susie's very own chair.

All her kettles and pots hung in neat rows from nails she'd pounded into the wall, all by herself. Her dishpan, doubling in duty on days when she baked bread, sat on a shelf near the potbelly stove, which had survived the ranch house fire and a vigorous scrubbing with steel wool. Sam had installed the stove, repaired with odds and ends of wire and a vent pipe that exited out the line shack's roof.

The cabin seemed fairly solid now. Hopefully it would withstand the deep snows when winter finally arrived. The cabin was crudely built by modern standards, but for the first time in many years, Meg felt a deep abiding happiness that exceeded all her original expectations. It seemed inconceivable that she could feel so blessed, especially amongst the harsh surroundings of pioneer living, but it was true. She was happy.

Nearby Susie jabbered to herself, playing a game with marbles. The warble of a harmonica drifted on the evening breeze from the bunkhouse, surrounding Meg with dreamy musings, as she worked her needle in and out, darning the heel on one of Mr. Gallagher's socks. He brought his torn shirts to her with such regularity that she almost felt married! Well, they *were* married, at least legally. But nothing in their dealings with each other hinted at the slightest impropriety. Even so, now and again she did sometimes wonder...

Suddenly the new pup Dusty began barking, off in the distance.

After a moment the pup quieted.

Meg lifted her head, listening intently.

Barking at the wind, she thought absently, and resumed her sewing. The lantern shone through the lace cap she wore to keep dust off her hair and cast distorted patterns on her handiwork. Her eyes tired from so much close work, she rubbed them and yawned.

Presently a disquieting prickle of apprehension stole over her. , Unable to ignore the feeling that she were being watched, Meg set aside her handiwork and rose to her feet, stretching to get the kinks out. As she passed the window, she glimpsed Sam's tall silhouette etched against the night sky, as he climbed the hill behind the cabin. Against better judgment, Meg lifted the bar from the door and stepped noiselessly onto the porch.

Wagging her tail, Dusty ambled across the yard to nudge Meg's hand with her cold wet nose. Together they stood scanning the stars. When the winds picked up, Meg retrieved her woolen shawl and wrapped it tightly around her against the cool mountain air. An icy chill ran through her, touching the very marrow of her soul. Knowing what it was to grieve the loss of a loved one, Meg respected Sam's privacy during his lonely night vigils at his wife Amie's grave.

She never spoke of it to him, but watching him ascend the hill, she wished she had a magic elixir to mend his broken heart. Too well she knew the ghosts that kept vigil with him up there. Their names were legion: Regret. Guilt. Pride. Failure. Loss. Emptiness. Unforgiveness—most often directed inward.

Meg privately acknowledged that she would never have survived the loss of her parents without a personal faith in God. Sam, for reasons known only to him, preferred to wrestle with his grief alone, rather than look to the only One capable of carrying the crushing weight of his burdens.

Oh, how she yearned to share God's promises with him! If only he was willing to open his heart to the Lord. But he wasn't ready. The timing was not right.

Slowly Meg walked back inside. Closing the cabin door behind her, she stood with head bowed, her thoughts in a muddle. Even with the door safely shut, her heart was pounding. More than sympathy was behind her sudden desire to seek Sam out. *Be still, my wayward heart*, she thought, shocked by the direction her wayward thoughts were taking her. No longer could she deny her growing attraction to Sam. But neither was it an impulse she should encourage, at least not yet. Knowing that God was her true refuge, Meg sank to her knees in a rustle of crinoline and woolen skirts.

"Please, Lord," she whispered, "I need your help! I feel so desperately alone and vulnerable. Grant me a pure heart and the strength to walk in righteousness. I am thankful for all that Mr. G has done to provide the children and me with a home, but I am also a woman, Lord, with a woman's heart. Please strengthen me to discern your will...

"Help Sam to experience your peace and forgiveness. Without your intervention he never will. And he certainly won't, if I give in to the foolish inclinations of my heart," she confessed. "Don't let me stray from following you, Lord! I dare not look to anyone but You for help. Sometimes I feel so abandoned. Yet even if Sam should—" She broke off, unable to express the deepest yearnings of her heart. "Forgive me, Lord, I know I mustn't assume that he and I— that we are intended for each other. Please, Lord, whatever you ask of me, whatever the cost, guide me in Your ways." Meg dashed a tear from her damp cheek. "And please bless Sam. Not because I ask it of You, but because he seems so lost and lonely."

Already stronger for having admitted her own shortcomings, Meg got to her feet and snuffed out the lantern light on the table. "Guess that's about it for tonight, Lord," she said softly. "Thanks for listening, and amen!"

Chapter Twelve

Awakened by the rooster crowing outside her window, Meg dragged herself out of bed at the crack of dawn. Yawning, she let Susie sleep a little longer while she dressed and got mentally organized to face a busy day.

Bending over the wash basin, she splashed cold water on her face, then patted her skin dry. Peering at her image in the small cracked mirror, she was shocked by her puffy eyes, caused by secret bouts of weeping. *Where has my bright and shiny outlook on life gone?* she wondered. *Where's my sense of humor?* Two weeks of frontier living was starting to take its toll on her. What she wouldn't give for a heart-to-heart talk with another woman! Always before she'd had cousins, aunts, and women friends to share common interests with.

Vigorously brushing out the tangles in her long auburn hair, she hurriedly pinned it up and donned a serviceable dress and clean apron. After tickling Susie awake, she gave her a big hug and helped the little girl don a clean pinafore apron. Then, working as a team, they clanged the bell on the front porch, informing the rest of the world that it was time to rise and greet the day.

This day began like so many others before it. After stoking the stove with wood, Meg fetched water from the well to make coffee and oatmeal. While Susie ground the coffee beans, Meg sliced bacon strips and measured out the dry ingredients for biscuits. Soon she had two skillets sizzling with bacon and pancakes, a bubbling pot of oatmeal, and the kettle of hot water on a simmering boil. All she was waiting for now was a slight assist from her two helpers, who, for lack of room in the cabin, regularly slept in the bunkhouse with Mr. G and his men.

Sure enough, Jimmy and Davey, hair and faces still dripping, came racing out of the barn, each unsteadily sloshing a pail of milk. Right behind them trotted the mama goat, bleating unhappily over their inexperienced handling of her tits. Jimmy carried his pail to the bunkhouse, where Archie kept a pot of coffee going from dawn to sundown. Meanwhile Davey, beaming with pride, brought his milk pail up to the cabin. Then off he went, hand in hand with Susie, to gather eggs in the hen house.

While Meg mentally organized her tasks to feed a crowd, she stoked the fire, turned bacon strips and flipped a second batch of pancakes. She stirred a large wooden spoon through the oatmeal, added cinnamon, sniffing the rising vapor with an approving nod, and set it aside. When the Dutch oven was just the right temperature, she slid two trays of biscuits inside, closed the door, and set the timer.

Seeing Susie and Davey through the window, she hurried outside. As they carefully set down their basket of eggs beside the porch rocking chair, she opened her arms and gathered them close. "Good job!" she exclaimed, needing hugs as much as they to start the day.

Before Meg cracked the first egg into the frying pan, she was surrounded by a dozen hungry males, all talking a mile a minute about cattle and horses and chores. With so many mouths to feed, it only made sense to let the men help themselves. She was glad she already had everything laid out on the table: bacon, pancakes, oatmeal. As soon as the timer went off, she rescued the biscuits from the oven, set out the blackberry jam, molasses and butter, and started taking orders for eggs, sunny-side up or scrambled. She was getting to be a real expert, using two skillets to keep up with this hungry crowd! All they had to do was grab their plates, bowls, and silverware and get in line.

Lately she felt as if she was in danger of withering on the vine. Not that Sam and his men would understand a woman's needs for sociability and conversation with other women. They just saw her as "one damn fine cook." As far as she could tell, even her so-called "husband" fell in that category.

Most of the time the ranch hands watched their language and deferred to her with respect, treating her the way they would treat their own sisters or mother. But none of them seemed comfortable carrying on a real conversation with a woman. That's why the prospect of passing the time in the company of other women seemed like such a precious commodity. A real necessity, if the truth be known. Because, yes, one friendly smile from another woman would do sp much to lift her sagging spirits. Yet here she was, one lone woman among many men.

It was an awkward and unenviable position in which to find oneself. Of course, she had no complaints where Sam Gallagher was concerned. It wasn't as if she expected him to carry on a courtship, or treat her like a real bride, or pick wild flowers, or whisper romantic words in her ear. She was not so foolish as to expect such nonsense as that! No, no. Mr. G was too practical-minded for such foolishness.

Helping her file the homestead next to his land was simply good business. Besides, he had taken in her three orphans without raising any fuss at all. That was worth a good deal more than if he started making eyes at her, or took her for walks in the moonlight.

The ranch hands seemed a decent sort, but she held herself a little aloof around them, lest they mistake friendliness for something else. It was unnerving enough when she caught Mr. G's eyes roaming over her, when he thought she wasn't looking. A tiny shiver ran through Meg. Sometimes she felt as if she might jump right out of her shimmy. Well, she refused even to think about *that*, she told herself sternly. She should just count her blessings, which were many.

Making another pot of coffee, she set it on the back of the stove and walked outside to cool her warm cheeks in the breeze, while the men finished devouring their breakfast. Rescuing her comb from her pocket, and palming the hairpins that held her long auburn hair in place, she began to braid it into a long coronet.

Through the open door came a burst of masculine laughter, as the men laughed about some sheepherder's wife who'd lost her mind after months of isolation. "Plumb loco she was," Slim said, relating how some woman had shot her three sons and new baby girl. "Sat there a-rockin' and a-starin' into space. Eventually her husband came home, seen what she done, and kilt her dead."

Meg shuddered. *God forbid she should ever share that poor woman's desperation*, she thought, walking back inside to refill the men's coffee cups. *Listen to them!* she fumed. She couldn't begin to imagine what would drive a woman over the edge to commit murder, but it made her blood boil to listen to them to sit around joking over the misfortune of some poor daft woman!

Closing her ears, she retreated outside again. *Men—bah!* She'd better not even think about making this a permanent arrangement. Sam Gallagher knew how to get under her skin without half trying, that one! True, he showed great kindness to the children, but he was not for her. The only thing she should concern herself with was getting the children raised. They were the light of her life, God's perplexing, yet wondrous gift to her. In time, perhaps she would understand His wisdom in sending her to this desolate place.

Right now she had too much work to trouble herself with the whys and what-fors that so frequently robbed her of sleep. Besides feeding the men, whose appetites rivaled a pack of starving wolves, she planned to set snares for the pesky rabbits that persisted in nibbling tender green shoots and spoiling her vegetable garden.

With the men talking about the long dark winter ahead, it seemed only practical to make provision early. She had found candle molds and a sizable drum of lard in the storage shed next to the barn—probably belonged to the late Mrs. G—a woman of industry, judging by the men's constant praise for "Amie's" cooking.

Could she help it, if they preferred Amie's Southern fried chicken to her Yankee pot roast? Meg never seemed to use enough peppers in her bean casserole to suit them either! Always needling her about this and that; 'twas beginning to get on her nerves.

One of these days she would climb straight to the top of that hill, where she so often saw Sam pacing in the moonlight. And she was going to have a long talk with the Lord. She was getting sick and tired of everything she cooked being compared to a dead woman's!

Pursing her lips, Meg wound her braids around her head, secured the coil with a bone hairpin, and jabbed a dozen more pins in place for good measure. *There!* she thought, examining her unsmiling face in the mirror over the wash basin on the porch. She patted the coronet of braids and tilted her chin for a critical look. *Not exactly a raving beauty, but respectable, at least.*

She smoothed the prim white collar around her throat, then waited on the porch till the last cowboy trooped outside to pick his teeth. Praying that she could maintain her composure, she walked back inside. She rolled up her sleeves, no longer taken aback by the wild array of dirty dishes. *Men!* With a sigh she began to clear the table.

~ * ~ * ~ * ~

Stuffed with flapjacks, bacon and eggs, fresh blackberry preserves and biscuits, Sam and his men mounted up and rode away. Most times they took Jimmy and Davey with them, but not today, for some reason. Archie drove the wagon out of the yard and slowly turned down a rutted road that was barely distinguishable in the tall overgrown grass. Five men headed out to check on a salt lick for the cattle. Meanwhile Sam and four hand-picked men headed through the woods, taking a more direct route than Archie, but aiming to meet up on the other side of the hill around noon.

Even with leftover biscuits and beef jerky in their saddle bags, Meg knew they would return for supper in their usual ravenous, slightly edgy mood. Quickly she cut up several wild onions, put the leftover pot roast from last night through her meat grinder, added sage, rosemary and wild parsley, and sautéed everything before adding it to the large kettle of pinto beans she'd left simmering since early morning.

Still smarting over Juan's critique of her cooking—"ah, so very bland, senõra"— she chopped up a handful of small peppers. Normally she avoided over-seasoning food, but somehow she needed to show that she was willing to accommodate the men's taste buds. Having done all she could in good conscience, she stirred everything together and clapped on the lid.

"Come on, Susie, let's play outside, while I set a few snares." Meg held out her hand to the child who was her constant shadow. "We'll make a little game of it."

Sue went willing enough, still clutching the cornhusk doll that Moses, one of the black cowboys, had made for her. Jim and Davey were already down at the corral, working on their riding skills that morning with Zeke. Before she set out, Meg waved to the two boys and told them where she and Susie would be.

"Watch me, Miss Wolfie!" Jimmy yelled, drawing back on the reins and making his horse rear up on its hind legs.

"Very good. Have fun, boys," she called. "I'll see you soon."

She noticed that Davey didn't look up or acknowledge her at all. It was almost as if he suffered periodically from mind blindness. Sometimes Davey's mind seemed so narrowly focused on a single tiny object, that he never seemed to grasp the vastness of the universe around him, or its wonders. Still, he *was* making progress, slow but sure. He also seemed to revel in the sheer physicality of learning to ride.

In her canvas shoulder bag, Meg carried the snares she had prepared late last night. Hiking up her skirts to avoid cockleburs and thistles, she set off with Susie for a nearby meadow. She hoped the rabbits would be drawn by the abundance of leafy green clover and grasses fed by the creek. When she reached the water's edge, however, she discovered that Sam Gallagher's testy old bull had been moved to this field.

Being nimble, she might have attempted a snare or two, but with Susie along, invading the bull's territory was out of the question. The animal was known for sudden bursts of speed and for tossing its horns at the slightest provocation. More than one cowboy on the place had had his backside sown up by Sam, or so she'd been told. Since Meg had no desire to test the bull's unreliable disposition, she quietly drew back from the wire fence.

Searching for a safer alternative, she spotted a large jackrabbit raised up on its haunches, nose twitching. It was staring right at her through a clump of tall buffalo grass.

"This way, Susie," she whispered, ducking low.

Assuming it was all a game, Susie shook her cornhusk doll like a rattle and let out a piercing scream. Then she ran straight at the rabbit, which took off over the hill. It was the same hill on which Amie Gallagher and her little daughter Beth were buried.

Heart pounding, Meg grabbed her bag of snares and took off running after Susie. Her ears rang with the buzzing of katydids and the drone of bees in the tall grasses all about. Being small, Susie soon disappeared from sight.

Shading her eyes from the sun, Meg turned in a circle, searching for the little girl in a thicket of scrub oak. Where had she gone? she wondered. The fields and gullies were a haven for rattlesnakes and all manner of small creatures, including opossum and skunk. Larger wild life, as well. Only five days ago a weasel had broken into the chicken coup!

Ahead of her, the child's gleeful shrieks flushed out all manner of small birds and game on the parched, grassy slope. The sun's rays beat down relentlessly. Her face flushed from her exertions, Meg climbed, bareheaded, to the top of the hill, hoping to catch a glimpse of the child.

From the crest of hill, she looked out over a vast panorama of grasslands intersected by shallow rivulets of water that coiled like the backbone of a snake, feeding this fertile area. She gasped, in awe of the sheer magnificence that stretched for miles in every direction. For the first time she understood why her employer so frequently visited this spot at sunset. No cathedral fashioned by human hands could approach the glory of this place!

The purest blue sky formed an enormous canopy that arched gracefully down to touch piney green forests at the higher levels, while fleece-white clouds, faintly tinted with pink, chased across the valley floor and cast elongated shadows up the canyon walls. Whatever she had expected to find fell far short of the beauty that met her wondering eye.

Ahead of her, perched on a rock, Susie was intently gathering a pile of red and blue wild flowers in her lap. As Meg's breathing slowed, her gaze fixed on the child, and all the splendid energy of childhood just crying out to be shared.

Not wishing to startle Susie, Meg made her way carefully along the rocky slope. She pushed aside the low branch of a quivering birch and there, just beyond a clump of stunted scrub oak, she spied two mounds, side by side and covered with rocks on a grassy knoll. Drawing closer, she knew at once that these must be the graves of Amie Gallagher and her daughter Beth.

Had she not first spotted the graves from above, she might have overlooked them entirely. She couldn't imagine leaving the graves so untended. So many years! Such neglect. Before long, all traces of their existence would vanish. Standing in that desolate spot, she decided the dead deserved more respect than that.

Sorrow flooded her heart, as she walked slowly toward the two unadorned, unmarked graves. As she stood there, absorbing the peaceful beauty of the place, her thoughts strayed to Sam, and for the first time she thought she understood what drew him here so often at day's end. Such a place surely afforded a splendid view for a man who owned such vast holdings, yet intuitively she sensed that the time he spent up here alone had little to do with the land.

Oh, he might fool his men with his usual pleasant banter, but a woman had a second sense about such things. A woman usually knew when things weren't quite right.

Meg suspected he carried within him a private sorrow that he found difficult to express, even after all this time. His long silences spoke volumes to her heart. Inevitably a bleakness would come over him at nightfall. Long after his men retreated to the bunkhouse, she often spotted the yellow glow of a kerosene lamp bobbing, as he trudged up the hill on his lonely pilgrimage. So often his loneliness called out to her, and yet she hesitated to intrude.

Whatever preyed on Sam's mind, it seemed best to lay his cause before her heavenly Father. Let Him deal with it. Besides, she was hardly in a position to offer advice or judge. She had enough problems of her own without taking on his burdens as well.

Sensing that Susie had followed her to the gravesite, Meg reached down and smoothed a soft lock of blond hair back from the child's forehead. "How peaceful it is." She breathed deeply, taking in the clean mountain air. "How beautiful everything is!"

Squinting up at her, Susie tugged on her skirt. "Here, Mama." She solemnly thrust a clump of uprooted yarrow, daisies and columbine at the slender woman standing beside her.

"Why, thank you, precious!" Giving her a hug, Meg dropped to her knees beside the graves. "I have an idea: Why don't we plant these flowers for Mr. G's wife and baby girl? As a token of our love. To show that they're not forgotten."

Susie nodded solemnly. "I used to have a Mama." Her pudgy little fingers tugged on a tall, unwieldy thistle. "Only she died, and I can't remember what she looked like any more." She yanked impatiently at the prickly weed, again without success. "Ouch!" She fell on her rump and held up her finger for Meg to see.

Setting aside the wild flowers, Meg pulled the squirming little girl onto her lap. "Let me see. Oh, my! What an impressive *ou-wie*." Pouring water from her canteen on the tiny cut, she began digging around in the bag she'd brought with all its snares and what-nots.

Waving her finger, Susie tearfully burrowed her face against Meg's neck. "Kiss it, Miss Wolfie."

"Oh, very well." Smiling over such a fuss about nothing, she pressed a kiss in the child's palm. "For good luck."

"Again!" the child demanded. "You kissed the wrong place."

"We need to keep your wound clean, sweetheart." Finding a jar of salve, Meg applied the green salve her boss swore by, then wrapped it up with a clean strip of cloth and tied it. "There, that should make it all better, until we get home and show it to Mr. G."

Rummaging in her bag again, Meg gave the three-year-old a drink of water from her canteen and a cookie. "Consolation prize," she said. "Now, why don't *I* clear off the weeds, while you take a little nap?" She folded her shawl into a pillow to make Susie comfortable and hopefully take a nap.

With time on her hands, she picked up her all-purpose bag and began to search out suitable places to set her snares. Certainly there was plenty of small game in the area. She had sighted four rabbits during the brief time she and Susie had sat together, enjoying the view.

Burrs, briars and coarse weeds from the field clung tenaciously to her practical brown skirt, ignoring the tug of bramble bushes and tangled wildflowers, as she waded through weeds that grew knee-high. Reaching the rocky mounds, she began pulling up fistfuls of weeds, straining to uproot them from the drought-hardened ground.

The sun beat down upon her head and shoulders, yet she persisted. She pulled out the small claw hammer she carried in her bag and began to hack at the weeds that choked the larger grave. When she had finally cleared a small border, she straightened, wiping perspiration from her forehead with her sleeve. Her progress, though tedious and slow, seemed a battle worth waging. Already she had begun to regard this young woman and her daughter as part of a growing sisterhood of lonely pioneer women, many unappreciated by their menfolk, and an alarming number of them consigned to an early grave.

No woman should lie forgotten beneath a weed patch. Meg decided to return the next day with better tools and a pail to water to soften the hard ground. It seemed only right that the passing of these two precious souls should be marked by a proper show of respect.

Chapter Thirteen

All her plans to tidy up the tiny graveyard went out the window before Meg even got the children out of bed and dressed the next morning. Sam, eager to make an earlier than usual start, came banging on her cabin door before dawn. "Coffee ready yet?" he queried, sticking his head around the door when she didn't respond quickly enough.

Hampered by a mouthful of safety pins, Meg paused in the midst of pressing Davey's shirt. Where the buttons had disappeared still remained a mystery, though she'd spent a half hour last night down on hands and knees searching every dark corner.

"Mmfph!" she said, gesturing toward the cold stove.

"Sorry to barge in so early," he said with an unrepentant grin. "We've got one more load of timbers to bring down the mountain before everybody gets here."

Meg spat out the pins before she choked on them. "What do you mean, 'everybody'? What's going on that I don't know about?"

She tucked Davey's shirt into his trousers and sitting on the cot, began putting on his socks and shoes. Davey stared stolidly at the wall, offering no resistance. Neither did he seem inclined to help.

Sam was already busy poking around in her cupboards. "I hope you have a few cakes and pies stashed around here," he said, too preoccupied with his search for food to notice that she had no clue what he was talking about, or his plans for the day.

Uninvited, Archie trooped in and lit the stove with a stick of flaming kindling, while Slim and Juan got out her mixing bowls and a large skillet.

Perturbed by this high-handed invasion of her work space, Meg elbowed her way past the ranch hands taking over her kitchen, gathering flour, lard, and a slab of bacon as she went.

"How 'bout one of you fetches water, while the rest of you men wait outside?" she huffed. "It won't take but a few minutes to prepare breakfast. Daniel, here—you grind the coffee beans." She handed the sack of coffee beans to the outfit's youngest cowboy—another orphan Sam seemed to have added to his collection of strays years ago.

"Sure thing, Mrs. G," he grinned.

As soon as she got the cabin sufficiently cleared out, Meg tied on her apron. While Daniel vigorously turned the crank on the coffee grinder, Davey, fascinated by the grinding noise, climbed up on a stool to observe.

Sam sat down at the table, stretched out his legs, and crossed his boots at the ankle, like a true man of leisure.

Meg cocked her head and looked pointedly at his spurs digging into the floor. "Since you're in such a hurry this morning, maybe you'd like to set the table," she suggested.

One corner of his mouth kicked up a notch. "That's what I have you for."

"Is that so?" Cracking an egg, she dropped it in the pancake batter she was mixing. Her face grew warm, more because of his teasing smile than the fire now crackling inside her stove.

"Len Peterson and his crew should be riding in any minute," he mentioned casually. "Everyone else promised to get here by nine."

"That's nice," Meg said, stirring like mad. 'Mind telling me what's going on?"

"You mean you haven't noticed all the cut timber we've been hauling in here over the past few days?" He fell silent, as if no further explanation was necessary.

"You'll have to be more specific, Mr. G." She accepted the water bucket from the cowboy standing in the doorway. "Thanks, Bill. I'll let you know if I need anything else."

Daniel finished grinding the coffee beans. Sensing an unusual amount of emotional static in the room, he scooped up Davey. "Why don't I just take this li'l cowpoke outside with me?" he said and headed out the door.

"Thanks, Daniel." Meg gave the pancake batter a final stir and picked up a knife to slice the bacon. She glanced at her employer. Something was definitely going on behind that rascally grin. Though tempted to demand what he was up to, she held her tongue. No use getting all stirred up because company was coming.

Instead she hacked off a dozen or so strips of bacon and threw them in the frying pan. She banged lids and stirred, all the while seething inside. The bacon hissed and sizzled, sending up a mouth-watering aroma toward the ceiling, while she braced herself to play hostess to his friends this morning. How many were coming was still anybody's guess.

After watching her a few minutes, Sam chuckled. "Looks to me like you got up on the wrong side of the bed this morning."

"If you mean, did I start off the day in prayer, the answer is no. I definitely did not get off to the good start I intended, Mr. G." Nose in the air, Meg poured off the fat into a jar and drained the bacon.

"I thought a visit from the neighbors might perk up your spirits, not get you all riled up," he said with an amused shrug.

Meg's ladle paused over the skillet, interrupting the pouring of pancake batter. "Mr. Gallagher, I am not 'riled up.'" Hand on hip, she took a deep breath. She was perfectly willing to take him on, if the stakes were high enough. "I'm amazed that you neglected to mention last night that we have company coming this morning. Now, I am no mind reader, sir! And while I welcome the prospect of entertaining guests—"

Before she could mention her concerns about preparing a suitable amount of food and refreshments to serve, his chair tilted back and he nearly fell over laughing.

"Entertain!" he hooted.

Alarmed, Meg ran around the table and began pounding him between the shoulder blades. In seconds he recovered enough to catch his breath. "Nobody expects you to *entertain* them, Meg!" His shoulders heaved with silent laughter.

Badly shaken by the unexpected strength she felt radiating off Sam Gallagher's body, Meg stepped back quickly, her face flaming with embarrassment. Shocked that she'd laid hands on him in such a familiar manner, she stared at him, unable to define her true feelings.

"Oh, sir, I do apologize!" *What is wrong with me?* she asked herself, blushing. Indeed, they'd had absolutely no close physical contact up to now, except to shake hands when they entered into this awkward matrimonial arrangement. Her hands still smarting from the pounding she'd given him, she hid them in the folds of her apron. Somehow she needed to make amends for her behavior.

Fortunately the acrid smoke of burning pancakes jarred Sam into awareness first. He grabbed a spatula and began flipping flapjacks. Recovering what good sense she still possessed, Meg reached around him with a wadded-up dish towel and grabbed the skillet by the handle. "Here. This is what you pay me for."

Walking briskly around the long table, she pitched the charred pancakes out the door. Whistling for Dusty and leaving the pup to dispose of the mess, she marched over to the stove and began preparing a proper breakfast for her employer and his men.

Surprised to see her all fired up, Sam stepped aside and watched her work her magic, moving like a whirling dervish. He shook his head, not quite sure what to make of his new housekeeper, aka wife.

As a precaution, least the dog get too fat on her cooking, he waited until she finished making breakfast; *then* he told her the rest of his good news: "I don't mean to set you off, but we may have as many as forty people dropping by this morning."

"Forty!" Meg nearly lost her grip on the platters stacked high with flapjacks and bacon. She blew a rebellious curl off her forehead. "Am I to understand this is not entirely a social call, Mr. Gallagher?"

He grinned like a kid. "Nope. We're building us a brand new house today!"

"I see." She nodded, finally getting the message. "A house-raising."

"I knew you'd catch on eventually."

On that happy note, Sam called his men in to breakfast.

Amidst all the noise of scuffing feet as they came inside, he poured himself a cup of coffee and sat down with an air of satisfaction. "The women folk will be happy to lend a hand with the extra cooking," he added, just to gladden her heart.

Seeing that he was serious, Meg rolled her eyes toward the ceiling and winged a quick prayer. *Oh, dear Lord! I don't know what this day will bring, but I'm willing to do my best. But just in case, how about multiplying a few loaves and fishes?*

Sam and his men had no sooner finished breakfast when the first buckboard, driven by a slender, watery-eyed young woman wearing a yellow poke bonnet, rumbled in the front yard. In the back of the wagon, two squirmy toddlers thrashed their chubby legs and hollered, straining to escape from three adolescent girls in calico, whose unenviable job was to keep the younger children from falling and just possibly getting run over by a wheel.

The woman hauled back on the reins, bringing the team to a halt beside the cabin steps, where Meg stood ready to greet her first visitors. Noticing that the woman's skirts rode high, indicating another baby was on the way, Meg hurried forward and grabbed the horse's lead rein to hold him steady, so the woman could safely get down from the high seat.

"Howdy! Be right with you." The woman set the brake and then, one hand pressed against her swollen belly, gingerly leaned over the front seat and picked up yet *another* infant, under one year in age. Meg marveled that the baby had slept through the ruckus the other children were making.

"Now hush up, you two, or I'll box your ears," the woman warned her two sons, and ran her fingers affectionately through the chief noisemaker's unruly yellow locks. Despite her stern warning, her voice betrayed no harshness, only slightly frayed nerves.

Meg stepped to the side of the buckboard and reached out her arms. "Here, let me help," she offered.

Leaving the teenage girls to fend for themselves, the two women unloaded the two little boys, followed by the baby, whom Meg handed off to one of the girls. Next the mother handed down a baby's sleeping basket, followed by a cloth bag full of diapers and replacement clothes—"for when the boys need sprucing up," she explained. These provisions were followed by four large picnic baskets full of preserves, baked pies, two quarts of buttermilk, and other treasures from her kitchen.

"I'm Leona, Len Petersen's wife," the woman announced, holding out her hand.

"Pleased to meet you. I'm Meg Gallagher," she smiled.

Leona looked Meg up and down, making no secret of her curiosity. "Len said you were a looker, but he didn't tell the half of it. Aw, what do men know?" She laughed. ""You're here, aren't you, and a sight prettier than Sam's last wife."

Meg caught the inference and blushed. "As far as I know, Mr. Gallagher has only been married once before; she lies up yonder—" she gestured toward the hilltop, "with her little girl. To keep up the proprieties, we got married in Cheyenne, but for all practical purposes, I'm his housekeeper."

"I know. Isn't that Sam a corker!"

Meg frowned. "Excuse me? I-I'm not quite sure I understand—"

Leona threw a clean diaper over her shoulder and took a seat in the porch rocker. "I mean he's a pretty sly dog, advertising for a housekeeper when all the time he was wantin' a wife." She cuddled her sleepy baby, patting its rump. "I expect you'll be in the family way any day now."

A shock wave of indignation swept over Meg. "Is *that* what people around here think?" she gasped. "Well, I hate to disappoint everyone, but we are married in name only!!" Meg blushed, knowing no other way to preserve her reputation, but to tell the truth.

Leona shrugged. "Relax. Sam's an honorable man, ain't he?" A broad smile lit up the woman's face. "Didn't waste any time, did he? No sooner off the train—"

If it was possible, Meg's face heated up even more. "No, you don't understand. Mr. Gallagher only married me because the children needed a home."

"What!" The rocker stopped creaking, and Leona Petersen's face turned as red as Meg's. She gaped in open-mouthed disbelief at Meg.

"Not only that," Meg went on smiling politely, "I filed my own homestead on the property immediately adjoining Mr. Gallagher's."

As soon as the truth was out, her neighbor began to laugh. "Well, don't that beat all! I can't believe it! Sam got himself saddled with a wife and a passel of kids. That must have come as a surprise."

Meg found herself squirming under Leona's amused scrutiny. "I must take part of the blame for that. You see, the Christian Aid Society hired me to help place orphans all the way across country. I still had three who needed homes when I got to Cheyenne, so I—"

Leona kicked out her feet in front and set the rocker to careening. "This tale gets better and better," she chuckled. "Old Sam must be in knots, waitin' his turn after the lights go out at night."

"That is not our agreement," Meg said primly. "Mr. Gallagher knows my feelings on the subject. We married to give the children the security of growing up with a mother *and* a father."

"Maybe so, but I also know human nature. If you and he aren't spooning long before winter sets in, I'll be mighty surprised. And if he don't suit, go find yourself a man who will!"

At this point, both women realized that Len's three daughters by his first marriage were lapping up gossip like cats fighting over spilled cream. Leona began directing the girls to carry everything up on the porch. "You there, Tessie and Hildy and Katarina! Hustle your bustles, girls! Mrs. Gallagher will show you where to put the vittles. You'll have to excuse me, Mrs. G. I need to nurse this li'l pumpkin of mine before I burst!" And with that pronouncement, she unbuttoned her blouse and put the baby to her breast.

Averting her gaze, Meg wondered if her other neighbors shared Leona Petersen's shockingly pragmatic views on marriage. She could see where preserving one's privacy might be difficult out here on the frontier. Everybody just naturally assumed that every woman in the territory *wanted* to be married. Single, widowed, separated, or divorced, ladies of all ages seemed to be fair game.

In fact, if she was to believe her ears, even if a woman was technically married, nobody thought twice about encouraging her to look about, with an eye to reducing the number of unmarried, untamed, love-starved males roaming around by one!

Badly shaken by Leona's blunt way of speaking, Meg scanned the corral and the chicken coop, hoping to locate her orphans. She hoped, by pointing them out, she might make the woman understand her situation better and become an ally. She certainly did not need advice!

Might as well get everything out in the open, she thought. "Mr. Gallagher and I are raising three orphans together. There's little Susie, and Davey, who is...well, he's different from most children. He doesn't talk much, and he has seizures once in a while," she explained, outwardly calm. "And then there's Jimmy. He's twelve—oh, there he is, hanging by his heels from the hayloft." She cupped her hands around her mouth and yelled, "Jimmy! Come down from there, this instant!"

While she sought to explain the uniqueness of her marriage to Mr. G, Davey came around the corner with the two Petersen toddlers clinging to his suspenders and tugging him along. All three boys looked as if they'd been rolling in a field of tumbleweeds.

Leona rolled her eyes toward the heavens. "Covered with dirt already!"

"Leave them be. They're washable," Meg shrugged, and went to help the Petersen girls carry their baskets of food inside, away from the flies.

~ * ~ * ~ * ~

Within the hour, several more families arrived, all of them breaking a record, to hear them tell it, rushing through chores and getting to Sam's ranch ahead of schedule. None of them made any secret as to why they'd come either. They were there to inspect Sam's new wife—or 'bed-warmer-to-be,' they laughingly amended, when Meg tried to set them straight.

"You will be, soon enough!" said the oldest grandmother present, waving a gnarled finger under Meg's nose.

"No, I am a homesteader, like yourselves," Meg said, holding her head up high.

"Shucks, I got here long before they started givin' out them fancy pieces of paper," said the old woman. Shooing Leona aside, she commandeered the porch rocker.

"Granny is a true pioneer!" chimed in a young girl in pigtails.

"Oh, pshaw! Fetch me my knitting, child. Make yourself useful," the old woman said.

Surrounded by so many frankly curious stares, Meg tried to disguise her blushing confusion. Keeping track of names had never been easy for her. Now *she* was in the unenviable position of everyone knowing who *she* was—a fact she could only credit to one person: Mr. G. When she referred to him as her "employer," they all looked at her funny. "*Who?*"

"Oh, you mean, Sam," said another woman. "Your *husband*."

Well, it was just too complicated to explain their agreement, so Meg finally gave up trying. In all, there were twenty-eight adults, not counting a plethora of babies, small children, and teenagers. They were all here at Sam's invitation. And they all arrived way too early! She decided she could either get into a staring contest, or she could treat them as if she'd known them all her life and make them welcome.

That led to another problem: There were only a few places to sit, and while they all grinned and assured her that they'd come to work, not "set around jawing," Meg knew they'd all be worn out long before Sam's ranch hands returned with that last wagonload of timber.

Quickly she directed some of the teenage boys to raid the bunkhouse and carry all the tables and benches and chairs into the shade beneath the big cottonwood trees. Mr. Frockmeyer and his brood carried the benches and tables out of her cabin as well.

Things were going so well that Meg decided to have the Petersons' giggly girls fetch water from the well, so the women could make plenty of coffee and sun tea. Soon a fine array of picnic baskets, carefully covered to keep out dust and flies, occupied two tables, and the women got busy scrubbing down the rest of the table tops in preparation for the noonday meal later on.

Small children entertained themselves, playing with balls and hoops, while the older girls picked wildflowers to decorate the tables. Meanwhile several teenage boys joined their fathers, pacing off exterior walls on the new ranch house. Another group of men went through the stack of lumber, piece by piece, selecting and setting aside the straightest beams.

Led by a handful of men with carpentry skills, the neighbors just pitched in without waiting for Sam to show up. Having raised cabins and barns before, the men soon had the cornerstones set. Sticks were pounded into the ground at regular intervals, and strings pulled taut to designate elevations for the exterior walls. Every few feet, the men rolled stones into place to support the outer walls and braces beneath the hypothetical new wood floor. Before long, the nearly deafening clack-clack-clack of hammers began, as the framework began to take shape.

Mark and Tim Ryan, the only bachelors in the crowd, got busy repairing the stone barbecue pit on the lawn. They had it fired up, with a side of beef cooking over mesquite wood by the time Sam and his cowboys returned with another load of timbers.

Jumping down from the wagon, Sam slapped his gloves against his thigh and looked around with satisfaction. "I never expected you'd have the house all laid out before we got back with this final load of wood. Well done, men!" He began shaking hands all around.

Meg stepped away from a cluster of men who were studying Sam's sketch of the house plan, drawn on a rumpled paper sack. Rolling up the paper, she walked over to Sam, her apron ties fluttering in the breeze.

"Here's your house plan." She handed him the drawing and planted one hand on her hip. Her other hand shielded her eyes from the sun. "Your friends rolled in here right after you left," she said, her manner slightly defensive. "What did you expect? I had to give them *something* to do!"

A slow admiring grin spread over his handsome face, as he looked first at her and then studied the changes made to the layout of his house. "I'm impressed," he said. "Maybe I shouldn't have hurried back so quick. You seem to have matters well in hand."

"Yes, well, maybe you should have been here when they arrived. We've got the house pretty well laid out now, but if you want any changes, you'd better see to it yourself." And with that rejoinder Meg turned with a toss of her head and took refuge among the ranchers' wives. They had finished the initial setting up for lunch, which was still a long way off, and many were busily occupied stitching quilt blocks or doing mending.

"Just as long as it suits you, little spitfire," Sam said under his breath, watching her stomp off in high dudgeon. He shook his head, chuckling, and walked around to the back of the wagon. Grabbing hold of a large support timber, he called to his neighbors to lend a hand unloading the wagon.

In a comparatively short time, the men had the outside walls framed and standing, and the roof trusses nailed in place. Every so often, Sam would drag Meg away from her coffee klatch to ask where she wanted openings for the windows or if she wanted the front porch to wrap around two or three sides. A couple of the men hooted and called him, "hen-pecked," but it was all in good fun.

Meanwhile Meg began to warm to the other ranchers' wives and make friendly conversation. The women were mostly in their twenties and thirties, except for Granny Benson, who had gone through three husbands during her fifty years in the high country.

It had been so long since Meg had had other women to talk to that it was a real treat to sit down and chat, even if children, housekeeping, and "keeping the menfolk civilized" were the dominant topics. She hung on every word hungrily, and when someone mentioned a potluck and dance at the grange hall at the end of the harvest, her spirits *really* perked up.

Sophie Bartlett paused in her sewing. Her soft brown eyes twinkled at Meg over the tops of her wire rim glasses, and she patted her hand. "You and your husband must come," she said.

Delia Watkins nodded. "Be sure to bring lots of blankets and quilts. These get-togethers tend to keep us up half the night, so those of us who live at a distance usually bed down at the grange, right after the dance."

Leona Petersen giggled. "Sure beats driving off a cliff in the dark!"

Mitzi Gunderson bit off a thread on the quilt block she was sewing. "Now when's the last time that ever happened?" she asked, lifting her eyebrows in dismay.

A peal of laughter set the women to rollicking back and forth. Granny Benson got so carried away with merriment that her guffaws turned to snorts. "Not since the blizzard of '68, when my second husband, Charlie Elrod, wandered off without me and the boys. He was so liquored up, and a-whoopin' and a-hollerin' so loud, why, I could hear him all the way down the mountainside."

Meg's eyes widened with surprise. "He fell off a mountain?"

Granny Benson slapped her knee. "No, dearie, he started an avalanche. Didn't make no sense at all to fetch the undertaker. His blood must've been 90 proof, because he was still warm when I found him in the spring." And the old lady, catching Meg's look of utter consternation, laughed till she scarce could catch a breath, so pleased was she with her ability to stir up a little excitement among the ladies.

Leona and Sophie leaned in close from either side to comfort the newcomer to their quilting bee. "Don't pay Granny no never mind, Meg," Leona whispered.

"She's an absolute terror," Sophie confirmed. "I hear she got that way living among the Indians with her first husband."

Annie Benson, who was related to Granny and Two Bear by marriage, leaned forward to confide, "Zach was a trapper. Used to leave her alone for months at a time."

"Of course, she had a gun," Delia added.

"Of course," Meg said, looking with new interest at the old woman.

Sophie's eyes were round with awe. "Doesn't seem fair that she was left to fend for herself most every winter.

"Had her second son in a *tipi*," Leona divulged. "Rumor has it, the baby looked nothing like her husband. In fact, he had such dark hair that her husband accused her of having an affair with the chief's eldest son."

"No!" Mitzi and Delia and Sophie clapped their hands over their children's ears.

"Of course, that was pure nonsense," put in Sally Lassiter, who up until now had refused to join in the gossip.

"Of course, it was," said Annie Benson, who was married to Granny's second son. "As soon as Two Bear lost that baby thatch of black hair and red face, he looked just like his Daddy."

"But by then his father had skedaddled. Took their older son Zeb and made his way West over the Rockies."

"What!" Sophie's lips tightened with indignation. "You mean he left a defenseless woman and her new baby in an Indian village?"

"Went off in a drunken rage," Annie affirmed. "But not before he fought the chief's son and nearly got killed. After that Granny wasn't welcome either. But I wouldn't call Granny defenseless. Not if you value your scalp." She bent over her sewing with a sly smile. "Why, she raised Two Bear all by herself in a cave!"

"Lord a-mighty!"

Granny tilted her rocking chair back, breaking her rhythm. "You got that much right anyway," she said, squinting at the young women through opaque blue eyes. "The Lord a-mighty was with me every step of the way. I learned to rely on Him for *everything*."

Delia had the good sense to blush. "Why, Granny. I didn't know you were listening."

"I may be blind, but I ain't deef! And I ain't stupid, neither!"

Annie patted Granny's wizened old hand. "No, but you were mighty brave."

"I weren't no different than any of you," said the old woman. "I just asked the good Lord, and He gave me the strength to take care of myself and that baby boy o' mine." She chortled. "Some say I even strangled a wolf with my bare hands, but it just ain't so. Oh, I did shoot me a wild critter or two, so I could keep me and that man child o' mine warm that winter, but I had some help, too, includin' the chief's own daughter, bless her heart! She saw to it I didn't leave that camp without provisions."

Meg nodded, taking it all in. She could see why the other women made allowances for the old woman's eccentric ways, viewing her as a dying breed. Clearly Granny Benson had lived through some remarkable experiences. "Praise God," she said softly, as a new respect began to dawn for the elderly pioneer in their midst. "It's a real honor to meet you, Mrs. Benson."

"All the credit belongs to the Lord," the old woman cackled. "I'm just happy to be on this earth long enough to watch my grandchildren grow up to praise His name."

Annie smiled, glancing around the circle of women. "Granny is something special, let me tell you."

Chapter Fourteen

All through the morning, Meg basked in the kindness of Sam
Gallagher's neighbors. In so many ways she felt their acceptance—
through an understanding wink, a smile, a joke, all the shared
laughter, a friendly hand clasp—so many seemingly insignificant acts
of kindness. A word of encouragement or praise. Someone showing a
genuine interest in her orphans.

After struggling to make her way alone since her own parents'
deaths, it felt wonderful to feel accepted once again into a group of
women who enjoyed sharing friendship and life experiences from the
heart. Slowly as the day wore on, she began to relax and enjoy herself
more and more. Oh, how she longed for Susie and Davey and Jimmy
to find their place in this ranching community. How wonderful for
them to share the nurturing values and opportunities for fellowship,
like other children. Jimmy and Susie already seemed to be making
friends among the other children.

Davey, on the other hand, seemed to be having a difficult time of
it today.

During the noon meal, when the children lined up first to get their
food, Meg cringed inside when Davey suddenly appeared at her side,
eyes rigid and staring, arms jerking strangely. He seemed disoriented.
In all the excitement of playing with the younger children earlier, he
had become highly energized. Now it dawned on her that his behavior
might be a sign of a seizure coming on.

Taking him by the hand, she retreated inside the line shack,
hoping to avert an incident. Breathing a prayer, she took his bottle of
medicine from the shelf and knelt down to give it to Davey, who sat
on the floor, rocking back and forth agitatedly. He ignored her,
staring straight ahead, as she poured the liquid into a spoon and
gently pressed the silver tip to his lips.

"Come on, Davey. Time for your medicine," she coaxed.

Wham! Without any change in his expression, he raised his fist
and punched her in the face. Meg fell over backwards, the spoon

flying across the room. Cherry-red medicine splattered down the front of her dress. Taken by surprise—although she knew nothing should come as a surprise anymore—Meg grabbed his flailing arm and, picking up the spoon, jerked him to his feet.

"No, Davey," she said firmly. "Mustn't hit. It's not nice."

"No, no, no," Davey chanted, fighting to get away.

"Listen to me, young man. You *are* going to take your medicine!" Meg's intentions were clear, but how to keep the eight-year-old from thrashing wildly was beyond her strength. She kept a firm grip on his arm, even when he resorted to kicking and tried to bite her. She grabbed the bottle, determined not to spill any more of the precious liquid, but not daring to pour a dose either, when Davey was so out of control. "Hold still, Davey!"

"Got a problem here?" Sam's deep voice said behind her.

Meg didn't have time right now to deal with her employer. Davey had worked himself into a terrible state, and she was close to despair. For an eight-year-old he was extremely strong, and she could barely hold him in check.

"Don't just stand there!" she snapped. "Help me get his medicine into him." She braced herself against the wooden sink, fighting to free Davey's clenched fingers from her hair.

"Easy, partner." Taking the spoon and medicine bottle from her, Sam began talking to the boy in a quiet tone that had an almost hypnotic effect on Davey. In less than a minute, the boy stopped fighting and established eye contact with Sam.

"That's better," Sam said approvingly. "Open wide now." He shoveled the dose in, got him to swallow with a gentle chuck to the chin, then held out his arms to take the boy from her.

Meg surrendered the boy without argument. "Your timing could not have been better." Getting to her feet, she returned the medicine to the cabinet and set the spoon in the sink.

"He's a regular bearcat when he gets wound up," he observed, bouncing Davey lightly in his arms.

"I guess all the excitement set him off." Finger-combing through her dark auburn braids, she managed to get her hair into some semblance of order and it at the nape of her neck with a few hairpins.

"Well, he should be fine now. Right, Davey?"

Davey made no response, but at least the crisis had passed.

"I'm sorry," Sam apologized, knowing how upset she was by Davey's seizures. "I meant to give him his medicine earlier, but it completely slipped my mind when people started arriving early."

"I can take him now," she offered, and he handed the boy over. "I don't know how I would have managed without your help," she added shyly.

The corners of his mouth turned up in a beguiling smile. "Anytime." He touched two fingers to the brim of his hat in a friendly salute.

"Uh, wait!" It dawned on her that he must have been on an errand when he suddenly appeared on her doorstep. "Was there something else you needed?"

"Now *that* could be considered a leading question, Mrs. G, but for now, I need to warn you that we're working overhead, connecting the line shack to the main part of the house. As a spare bedroom. You and Davey would be safer outdoors, in case we have any falling timbers."

Meg blushed. "Yes, of course. Davey and I will rejoin the ladies at once."

He nodded. "Wouldn't want anyone to get hurt." He left her gaping at the empty space where he'd been standing.

My stars! she thought, still flustered by their encounter. *How can one man be so helpful and endearing, and at the same time be so provoking?*

~ * ~ * ~ * ~

With Davey already calmer, Meg's spirits lifted once again. *Time to get to work,* she decided. Besides three children to keep an eye on, she had a swarm of neighbors, come to lend a helping hand and needing to be feed. Never in all her born days had she seen such an outpouring of good-natured generosity. Such kindness was humbling, not to mention inspiring. Clearly these people thought highly of Sam Gallagher, to drop everything and spend the entire day framing walls and putting a new roof over their heads.

As she stepped out of the cabin, she saw a lot of hungry men clambering down off the roof, brushing off sawdust, and joking with each other, while they washed up before lunch. Everyone gathered around the tables in the shade, lured by the delicious aroma of barbecued beef and more side dishes than any of the young'uns could count.

Waiting for a break in the conversation, Sam Gallagher gestured with his hat, deferring to her as the lady of the house. "Mrs. G, will you ask the blessing?"

Caught by surprise, Meg reached out her hands to the women standing on either side of her. "Why don't we pray together?" she said quietly and bowed her head. "Our Father in Heaven, thank you for bringing all of us together today. We are so grateful for the fine fellowship and the food provided. Bless our labors, and bless our friends. Amen."

A hearty 'amen' was followed by the men taking their seats at the tables. Filling their plates, they passed steaming hot casseroles, baskets of hot biscuits and gravy, potato salad, and platters of barbecued beef. Meanwhile some of the wives and young daughters poured glasses of lemonade and sweet tea and passed them down the line to their menfolk. Meanwhile Archie kept a sharp eye on the extra side of beef on the spit, making sure it got turned at regular intervals.

After the men had eaten, many of them wandered off toward the creek for man talk and a smoke break. Meanwhile the women cleared the men's plates and put them in a deep pan of simmering hot water to soak. "Now it's our time to take a load off," Leona announced.

Filling plates for Susie and Davey—Jimmy had insisted on eating with the men—Meg took them under the trees to eat. Clearly on her best manners, Susie sat beside her on an old Army blanket, eager to impress all the young girls and their mothers. Feeling mellow since he'd had his medication, Davey sat in Meg's lap and let her feed him, opening his mouth like a baby bird for every bite.

A few of the ladies exchanged questioning glances, but nobody commented on his immature behavior. Many of the women sent their own rambunctious children off to the creek with their husbands and joined Meg in the shade, so she wouldn't feel left out. As she laughed and shared in their relaxed, good-natured banter, she was again struck by their genuine kindness. The way they reached out to her touched her deeply. She was already looking forward to being a part of this ranching community.

~ * ~ * ~ * ~

Before the women and children finished eating, the men were hard at work again on the roof, hammering, sawing, singing ditties slightly off-key, and trading jokes, as they nailed off plywood sheets.

Almost immediately Granny Benson was up on her feet—"taking my constitutional," she called it, as she hiked up the first two rungs on a ladder to inspect their progress—and subsequently got hit by a hammer that fell off the roof.

With a startled cry, she took a step back, teetered, then lost her balance. She sat on the ground, waving her fist and scolding John Lassiter for being careless. "Butter-fingers!" she hollered.

Of course, all work stopped while Sam made sure that Granny hadn't broken any bones. Then her son, Two Bear Benson, carried her to the sidelines beneath a shade tree. Named in tribute of the young Indian brave his father had nearly killed in a jealous rage—and knowing Granny had probably named him to spite his father for running off—Two Bear displayed an inordinate amount of patience with his cantankerous old mother. "Now, Mother," he gently chided, "can't you stay out of mischief for five minutes?"

"Don't you go lecturing me, Two Bear!" she snapped, yanking on his yellow beard with a wizened hand. "Don't be bossin' me neither, or I might start calling you 'Zach,' like your pa."

"Keep on callin' me Two Bear," he laughed, and winked at his fellow carpenters. "Annie thinks it's more romantic, bein' married to a wild frontiersman."

"Wild—huh! Them Injuns were more civilized than Zack Benson ever was." She cackled, enjoying the attentions being paid her, as several strapping men solicitously tucked a blanket around her and plumped pillows behind her back. "Aw, quit yer fussin'! I'm startin' to feel like some belle of the ball what's got me a flock of admirers. Gonna drive your wives pea-green with envy, if you keep it up!"

"You stole my heart long ago." Two Bear gave her a smacking kiss on the cheek. "Now hush up, and keep an eye on my kids, so Annie and the other ladies can get their chores done. I gotta get back to work."

Reluctantly the wives took the hint and began to clean up. Sending the children off to run and play hide-and-seek, they took turns washing dishes and whatever flatware they'd brought from home, and repacked picnic baskets. Once their chores were finished, though, the women went right back to sewing beneath the big shade trees. Excusing herself, Meg took Davey by the hand and took him inside the bunkhouse. With all the excitement he was more than ready for a nap.

All afternoon the men worked, almost without ceasing. Three men finished sheathing the rafters, while four others came along right behind, nailing on a cedar shake roof. Mr. Frockmeyer installed a new lightning rod, to prevent another fire. On the ground, four other men split logs into long thick planks.

Tim and Mark Ryan cut an opening in one wall of the line shack—the one that adjoined the ranch house—and while Mark framed in a doorway, Tim built a door to fit. In jig time, the line shack became an integral part of the main house, with two entrances; one into the main living area, the other exiting directly outdoors.

While all that was going on, Sam's foreman, Slim Rowlands, and neighbors Len Petersen and Two Bear Benson divided the ranch hands into teams on all four sides of the house. For every two men nailing on rough hewn siding, two teenage boys came along behind them, caulking the overlapping boards with oakum.

Determined not to accused of being a shirker, despite his stiff joints, Archie hobbled around, showing the teenage boys how to mix a daubing compound to fill in knotholes and chinks. "Pack it in tight, lads. We don't want no peepin' Toms around here," he said, glancing at his employer with a twinkle in his eyes.

Inspecting the men's progress from the sidelines, some of the women overheard the old man's ribald remark, Meg among them. She might have been able to ignore the remark, if Delia Watkins hadn't called out to her son, who was holding the door in place while the Ryans secured the hinges: "Stanley, stuff a plug of oakum in that keyhole!"

"Why?" the youngster asked, wide-eyed and innocent.

Ted Bartlett grinned, despite the mouthful of nails stuck between his teeth. "There's no key, that's why."

Young Stan bent to examine the latch, then straightened, scratching his head. "There's no keyhole neither."

Al Gunderson waved his hand drill. 'In that case, I reckon I'd better drill a keyhole!"

Delia rolled her eyes, enjoying the joke. "Well, that'll make it real convenient, won't it?"

"Easy," Sam started to remonstrate, but his mild protest only served as a goad for more good-natured ribbing.

"What's 'convenient,' Mama?" chimed in the Frockmeyer's daughter Mitzi, causing some of the men to guffaw and add a few of their own ribald suggestions.

Sensing Meg's discomfort, Sally Lassiter slipped an arm around her waist. "Don't pay these crazies no never-mind." She settled her gentle gaze on her husband. "John dear, be sure to install sturdy bars on both doors. I know it will ease Mrs. G's mind a good deal to know she's safe. Especially with rustlers roaming the countryside these days."

"All that extra work seems kind of unnecessary, since Sam and she just tied the knot." Grinning, Leona bent her head to nip off a loose thread on the sewing in her lap.

"Sorry to disappoint you ladies," Sam said, willing to make himself the scapegoat. "My wife and I haven't had much time for billing and cooing yet. I guess I'm getting old and set in my ways—"

"Hogwash," Granny Benson blurted out.

"Then why's she livin' here?" Mark Ryan wanted to know.

"Landsakes, she showed up here with three young'uns. Are you sayin' she has a husband back East?" old Granny asked the crowd.

"She don't look like no bigamist to me," said Delia, keeping the razza-ma-tazz going.

"Maybe she's a runaway wife or a widow," Emma Frockmeyer speculated.

A shocked silence settled over the crowd. One man, still driving nails, hit his thumb with his hammer and cursed. Sam's foreman Slim quietly set down his end of a board. Over two dozen pairs of eyes turned to study the blushing new bride in their midst.

"Mr. Gallagher hired me to be his housekeeper," Meg said, red-faced from all the attention. "I traveled West with the orphan train. When I got to Cheyenne, three of the children still hadn't been adopted, so Mr. G graciously volunteered to help me raise them."

Sam nodded. "It takes courage for a young woman to move out here and establish a new life out here among strangers." Looking around at his friends, he added, "To show her heart's in the right place, she even filed a homestead on the land next to mine."

"That so?" Len Petersen clapped a hand on Sam's shoulder. "How long have you had an eye on that bottom piece?"

"Eight years." Sam shrugged. "Amie never got around to filing. But I've promised Miss Wolfie —I apologize, Mrs. G—that I'll help her with spring planting."

Two Bear exchanged a look with his wife Annie, but said nothing. So did a number of ranchers and their wives.

Meg had no trouble reading their minds. Most of them probably felt uncomfortable about an independent-minded woman living in close proximity to an unattached male. The fact that their marriage hadn't been properly consummated seemed to call into question how durable it was. She suspected only their friendship for Sam kept his neighbors from expressing their disapproval out loud.

Only Granny dared to call a spade a spade. "But you *are* married, ain't you?"

"Yes, we are," Meg cleared her throat and glanced down at her ring finger, which was missing a wedding ring.

"Rev. Schroeder tied the knot in Cheyenne." Sam explained. "Not exactly a whirlwind romance, but we felt it was best for all concerned."

"So—just for the record: You're legal?" Delia Watkins persisted.

"Yes, you could say that." The words stuck in Meg's throat. "We did it for the children's sake, you see."

Leona Peterson had no trouble speaking her mind. "So you could always get a divorce, if things don't work out."

Her husband Len spoke harshly from across the clearing: "Hush up, Leona. You're gettin' a mite too fond of that word 'divorce' lately."

Leona's face turned beet red. One hand fluttered protectively to her swollen belly; the other covered her mouth. She turned away, eyes bright with unshed tears. "It's none of my business, of course," she choked. "Please forgive me for speaking out."

"It's none of *any* of our business," Sophie said softly, and turned to Meg. "But if you ever need a friend to talk to—"

"Thank you," Meg said. "I do thank all of you for showing up and helping."

"No problem. What are neighbors for?"

"Happy to do it."

"You'd come a-running if we had a problem."

Suddenly Meg and Sam were surrounded by neighbors congratulating them on their marriage and wishing them a long and prosperous life together.

Finally Stan Watkins called the men back to the main reason everyone were there. "Hey! Let's get back to work, shall we?"

"Yeah," Al Gunderson said. "Only a couple hours of daylight left."

The men went back to nailing off the shake roof, and framing inside walls for the main house, and the women resumed their needlework.

Meg smiled apologetically at the women clustered around her. "Thank you so much for all your help and encouragement. Next spring I plan to start homesteading across the creek, but no matter which side of the creek I'm on, I want you to know you're always welcome to stop by when you're in the neighborhood."

Most of them accepted her open invitation graciously, but Emma Frockmeyer was squirming like she had a crawdad stuck in her corset. Her nostrils flared with disapproval. Lips pursed, she cast aside her knitting and stood up. "Liza and Flora, it's time to load up the wagon!" She turned a cold gaze on Meg. "The children and I need to start back, if I'm to have supper on the table when Mr. Frockmeyer rides in. Goodbye, Mrs. Gallagher." She held out a limp hand, which Meg took hesitantly.

"Thank you so much for coming." Meg said, while the chilling censure in the woman's eyes seeped through her bones. *Whatever did I do or say to turn the woman into an icicle?* she asked herself.

Soon after, the other women began to make their excuses. Some took longer to gather up their children and belongings than others, but everyone seemed intent upon returning to the safety of their own homes before dark. Even doe-eyed Sophie seemed tongue-tied, though she reached out and gave Meg a hug. "Come see me soon?" she urged.

"I'd be more than delighted. Thanks for inviting me." Waving goodbye, Meg stepped back as the Barrett's wagon lurched on the hard, rutted dirt road, following the other ladies at a distance.

Meg had just located Davey and was walking him up the steps to take a peek inside the new ranch house, when Sally Lassiter, the last of the women to leave, loped around the side of the house astride her husband's horse. "Hope you don't mind. I've left John the wagon. I'll make better time on horseback." She leaned down, smiling into Meg's startled gaze. "I'd love to stay longer, but I've got livestock to feed."

"Oh! Yes, I quite understand," Meg stammered. "It has been such a wonderful day, and I already look forward to more good fellowship with my neighbors. I do hope it won't be long before we meet again?"

Sally's eyes twinkled good-naturedly. "That Davey's quite the handful, isn't he?"

"Yes, he certainly is." Meg put her arm around Davey and gave him a hug.

"He's a handsome little boy. So often they are." Sally's gaze fixed on the horizon, as if seeing some far distant event. She sighed and straightened her shoulders. "I had a little boy like Davey once. Well, not *exactly* like him. Still Jeremy *was* different, so I know what you must be going through."

Meg's eyes widened with surprise. "I didn't realize—"

"Not many people do. John feels it's best not to talk about it. Some people might not understand." Her hands tightened on the reins. "It broke my heart when our sweet little Jeremy died."

"He was sickly?"

Sally's blue eyes pooled, as memories returned in a flood. "He was born with an open spine. He put up such a valiant fight, but he only lived two months."

Meg clapped a hand over her mouth. "Oh, Sally, I'm so sorry!"

"Don't be," Sally said, a touch of iron creeping into her voice. "John's a fine man—stuck by me through thick and thin. But it took little Jeremy to bring him to his knees—and to the Lord."

"Still, it must have been painful, losing your baby—"

Sally nodded. "The pain was unimaginable." But then her face brightened, suffused by an inner peace. "We learned not to view it as a punishment for sin. God helped us come to terms with our loss. What a comfort, knowing our little Jeremy is safe in His care!"

Meg stared up at Sally, awed by her faith. In her early thirties, Sally exuded such an air of quiet confidence, as she gazed up into a distant bank of cotton candy clouds and bright blue sky. "All of it was worth it, Meg—*all* of it. God in His infinite mercy makes it bearable."

Sensing a kindred spirit, Meg reached out and touched her friend's hand on the horse's bridle. "Sally, could we— Would it be all right, if we talked about this again, sometime?"

"I'd like that." Sally adjusted the reins, and the horse tossed its head. "Bring the children. You're welcome at my hearth any time."

Sally's horse was champing at the bit, eager to go, so Meg stepped back, her hand raised in farewell. "Until we meet again."

"See you in church!" Sally slapped her reins lightly against the horse's withers, and it surged forward, carrying the graceful young woman on its back toward the sunset.

Chapter Fifteen

Sam removed his wide-brimmed hat and wiped beads of sweat from his forehead, as the last of their neighbors rode off in the twilight. Then he turned to Meg with a satisfied grin. "We made an excellent start today, wouldn't you agree, wife?"

"Yes, Mr. G, I'm amazed at the progress you and your friends have made." Blushing at being addressed so familiarly as his "wife," she began sweeping wood chips and sawdust off the new verandah.

"Our house is better than ever," he affirmed, gazing at the sturdy joists overhead. "Built strong enough to last a hundred years."

"Or until the next lightning strike," she said under her breath. "Or rustlers' raid."

He shook his head. "Now, now, Mrs. G," he chided gently. "Let's think positive."

"I suppose you're hoping I'm a dead shot with that rifle of yours."

He smacked his hat against his thigh with a hearty laugh. "No, but you sure do handle yourself well in difficult circumstances." He squinted good-naturedly at her through the honest sweat of a hard day's work. "My first wife Amie, God rest her soul, got rattled over the least little thing, but not you. I've been watching you, Miss Wolfie." He wagged his finger at her. "You stand your ground, even when those otherwise delightful neighbor ladies decided to give you a piece of their mind." Pausing to shake dust and wood splinters out of his hair, he put his hat back on. "Any woman who can stand up to the neighborhood gossips should be able to handle a few outlaws or renegade Indians from time to time."

He was just stepping off the porch when Meg playfully swung her broom and connected with his backside. Not enough to smart. Just hard enough to let him know her mind.

Sam gave a playful yelp and backed away, rubbing the seat of his sturdy levis. His tawny brown eyes were dancing, as he circled just out of reach with a wily grin. "I pity the man who comes around here looking for trouble."

Meg cocked her head to one side. "And what about yourself, Mr. G?"

He raised both hands in mock surrender. "Whoa! I'm a peace loving man, lady. You'll get no back talk from me, as long as you keep me and the men in this outfit well fed."

She planted one hand on her hip. "Hah! The amount of work to keep you and your men looking half-way civilized is more than one lone housekeeper can do!"

"What's that?" He gestured for her to continue. "Don't be shy. I value your opinion."

"Well," she hesitated. "I hope you won't take offense, but the men—well, they stink to high heaven! Either they need to spend a few hours every week bathing and washing their clothes, or you need to hire a couple of full time washer women!"

Sam rolled his eyes heavenward. "There you go! Isn't it a little mean-spirited to criticize, when they've been working so hard today? Look at all they accomplished!"

"I know. They got an amazing amount done today, laboring side by side with your neighbors. But that's not my point. Most of your men are of marriageable age—"

"So?" He stuck out his jaw—a little *too* defensively, she thought.

"My point is that if they had half a brain, they'd realize how many eligible young ladies came with their parents to this house-raising. With men outnumbering women here in the territory, your men should spruce up more often. Think of it as survival of the species. How can they expect to find a wife, if they don't even shave?"

"Men sweat when they're working hard." Sam scowled, suddenly touchy as a bull. "Care to smell my armpits?"

Meg extended both hands to ward him off. "No, I most certainly do not! How could you even suggest such a thing?" She began to pace. Somehow she had to educate Sam about the finer social amenities. "What I'm trying to say is that the odor of sweat was really noticeable when the men were standing upwind. Now, I know they're all decent, hard-working men, and maybe they think they can get away without bathing out here in the wilderness, but as their employer and friend, I can't believe you didn't at least mention—"

"Maybe I'm dense, but I thought everybody did just fine. The whole purpose of getting together today was to build you and the kids a decent place to live!" he said, a vein standing out on his forehead.

"Yes, but it was also a missed opportunity!"

"Sounds like you're picking a scab to see if it will bleed!"

"I have no idea what you mean," she said, realizing she had struck a raw nerve in her boss's makeup. "I am totally in awe at all the work that was accomplished here today. Mr. G, I'm not trying to diminish their abilities. Far from it! I'm just trying to say that maybe if they bathed more often, they might attract the eye of some pretty girl—"

"Oh, good Lord!" he thundered, slamming his hat on the ground and giving it a kick.

Meg backed up. He was definitely not in the proper mood to discuss personal hygiene!

Come to think of it, she wasn't either.

"Mr. G—uh, Sam, I was only suggesting—"

He shook his head, in bewilderment. "I know. I totally get it: Women's minds run in the complete opposite direction from men's. Counter-clockwise. While *you* aspire to being a matchmaker, all us sweaty, *stupid*, uncouth males are busting our balls to build you a HOUSE!"

Meg's jaw dropped. How could she have been so blind? And as she stood before this man, hot blooded, heavy breathing, red-faced—well, maybe it was red because he'd been out in the sun too long. He might be bull-headed, but he had a perfect right to express his opinion. And he *did* make a valid point. As a matter of fact, her employer— Correction: Husband. Legally he was her husband, she reminded herself. If he wanted to give her a swat for getting him all riled up, he'd be perfectly within his legal rights. But the frustration in his eyes told her how greatly she had erred. He was bigger than her, true, but he wasn't trying to be mean-spirited. He was just trying to get through to her that he and all the men slaving away the entire day had done it to provide for her warmth and safety and comfort!

Sam Gallagher had a more realistic grasp than she on what really mattered, she was ashamed to admit. And if she wanted to keep him as her friend, she must try to make it up to him. Right away. Without pausing to figure out all the ramifications, she lowered her head and walked straight into his arms.

"I'm sorry. I am so so *so* sorry!" she said. "I *never* meant to belittle the magnificent work you and your men did today. I was just trying to increase everyone's chances of finding the perfect mate. So they w-won't be lonely anymore!" Bawling, she buried her nose in his smelly shirt. "Help me, Sam. I'm not very good at apologies."

Caught by surprise, Sam folded his arms around her. "Why, Miss Wolfie. Whatever did I do to deserve you?" His shoulders shook with silent laughter.

"I'm a fine one to advise anyone how to behave," she sniffed. "I'm not really as ungrateful as I appear."

He planted a kiss on her unruly mop of hair. "You're a holy terror, my dear."

"I really want to do better." She lifted her head, her eyes full of penitence. "It's the family curse, having red hair and a temper to match," she told him solemnly.

"Open your mouth," he told her.

"Why?" She eyed him suspiciously.

"Because a wife should do what she's told, at least some of the time."

She smiled mischievously. "I guess you think I need my mouth washed out with soap."

"No." His eyes smiled into hers. "So I can kiss you."

Blushing, she puckered up her lips.

She looked so adorably serious that he burst out laughing.

"Oh!" She squirmed to get loose.

"Open up," he gently urged. "Wider, now—"

She stuck out her tongue.

"Haven't you ever kissed a man?"

"No, never!" she averred. "And don't poke fun at me!"

"I'm just trying to establish a family tradition," he said.

"What kind?" She frowned, not trusting him for a second.

"It's called Kiss and Make Up. Surely you've heard of the custom? Oh! Look!" Sam feigned surprise, pointed at the ceiling, and when her gaze followed his, he captured her luscious mouth in an ardent kiss.

At first Meg struggled, but soon changed her mind. Or rather, he changed it for her. Kissing was rather a delightful pastime, she soon discovered. Besides, it didn't require nearly as much energy as arguing did. Gradually she relaxed in his arms, appreciating the tenderness and passion of her first kiss *ever*. It was also her very first kiss as his bride, and though he certainly knew how to enflame her senses, she realized that it was *his* very first kiss as her husband, too.

In seconds she became as involved in the whole kissing process as he was. Her whole body began to tingle with excitement, and her heart took off racing. Standing on tiptoe, she strained to gain better access to him, when the earth began to shake beneath their feet.

Next thing she knew, her senses picked up on the sound of wild hoof beats and the clatter of wheels outside the cabin door. Assuming his men must be moving horses and heavy equipment, Meg threw herself against Sam, backing him up against the wall. "Oh, Mr. G, your kisses positively set my lips on fire," she panted, tugging on his hair to pull his head own to hers.

"Hey, let's not get carried away just yet," he breathed in her ear. "We haven't a stick of furniture in the place. No place to carry this to the next level."

"Does it matter?" she gasped, wondering about his sudden concern about furnishings. "All your friends have gone home, so we needn't–"

"Oh, Miss Wolfie, you are something else," he chuckled, shaking his head. "Still, it's a little awkward doing our sparking standing up, but here goes."

Lifting her up on her tiptoes, he covered her face and throat with passionate, open-mouthed kisses until her head was positively spinning. Encouraged by her moans, Sam nuzzled her breasts, and she went weak in the knees. As woozy as a child imbibing too much of Grandma's elderberry wine, Meg threw her arms around him. "Oh, Sam, I think I'm going to faint!"

"I've got you, sweetheart." His voice grew husky with excitement. "Take a deep breath. Plenty of oxygen now—"

Suddenly a loud rumbling interrupted her focus. "Oh, my stars! What's that terrible racket?" she gasped.

"Uncle?" A bewildered adolescent voice cracked. "What's going on?"

Glancing around, the guilty pair discovered young Daniel gawking at them from the doorway.

Meg pushed Sam away and nearly lost her balance. "Uncle?" she repeated. "Why would he call you 'uncle?'"

"Maybe because he's my nephew," Sam said calmly, holding her up, wobbly knees and all.

"Your *what!*" She stared at him in dismay.

"I-I-I didn't mean to intrude!" Daniel stammered, about to take flight.

"That's quite all right," said Sam. "What's going on out front?"

"Mr. Turner's here with some furnishings you ordered."

A blond, blue-eyed giant of a man stepped into view, carrying pieces of a walnut bed frame under each burly arm. "Howdy, Sam. I tried to get here this morning, so I could lend a hand, but the roads were a mess and it took me forever to get here."

"Come on in, Byron." Sam waved him inside. "Mrs. G, I'd like you to meet Byron Turner, one of the best freighters in the territory."

"Howdy, ma'am. Happy to make your acquaintance," Turner grinned. "Where should I put these?" He looked around with a shrug. "I see you're not quite ready to set up housekeeping, but I've got a few more pieces in the wagon."

"Oh! Prop them against the wall, I guess." Meg gestured vaguely. "Where would you suggest, Mr. G?" she asked, flustered.

"Until we finish installing the floor, how about the spare bedroom?" Sam suggested. "Come on, Meg, let's go see what else Byron has for us in his wagon."

"You're my last delivery of the day," Byron said, following them outside.

Never having seen a freight wagon before, Meg was wildly impressed by its enormous wheels and how large the wagon was. A canvas all-weather tarp protected the cargo, which was drawn by six oxen. As she walked around, taking it all in, her eyes got huge. "Why, the wheels are as tall as I am!" she exclaimed.

"*Much* larger than the Conestoga wagons that cross the plains," Byron said, proud to show off his rig. "Of course, it's built to haul heavier loads, including shipments of ore from the mines up north. I go all over the territory, delivering just about any commodity my customers have a hankerin' to buy."

"There's no better bullwhacker between Cheyenne and Hellgate Canyon," Sam acknowledged.

Just then a young boy, close to Jimmy's age, came up from the well, carrying buckets of water to the oxen. "Hey, Pa!" he called, wiping his brow. "Are we about done here? I'm starved!"

"Now, Troy, we're only a half-hour from home," his father chided. "Sorry, ma'am, you know how the young'uns are. Impossible to fill 'em up at this age."

"Well, Mr. Turner, you and your son have come at the right time." Meg smiled at the boy. "I have loads of leftovers from the house-raising—cookies and cakes and pies. I do hope you can help make some of them disappear?"

Young Troy looked at his father, seeking permission.

"Oh, all right," Byron conceded. "Can't thank you enough, ma'am. Though I'm warnin' you, he's a bottomless pit."

So while Meg and Troy raided the cookie jar, and Archie put another pot of coffee on the pot belly stove in the bunkhouse, Sam and the freighter made quick work of assembling the four-poster, complete with bed railings and springs. They had about run out of room in the line shack addition to the house, and were carrying a large dresser up the porch steps, when Meg waved them over to the picnic tables under the cottonwoods.

"We better leave the dresser outside," Byron said, glancing around the cluttered line shack.

"Good idea," Sam nodded. "I hope you found us a comfortable mattress."

"Nice and thick. Gave it a good shake before I loaded it onto the wagon this morning." Bryon Turner accepted a cup of steaming hot coffee from Meg with a wink. "Ah, thank you kindly, ma'am. Sure hits the spot."

"Please call me Meg," she said, reaching over Sam's shoulder to pour his coffee. "That's what my friends call me, isn't it, Mr. G?"

Sam casually looped his arm around her waist. "When they're not calling you 'Miss Wolfie' or 'Mrs. G.'"

Seeing Meg blush at her husband's teasing remark, Bryon chuckled. "I never thought I'd see the day, Sam—you bringing home a beautiful new bride. Ah, 'tis a happy day!" He stuck out his big calloused hand, first shaking Sam's hand, and then Meg's. "The luck of the Irish to you both. I couldn't be happier for you."

After several trips back and forth, cramming the porch and line shack full of useful household items, Byron and his son departed for home, burdened down with pies and cookies for his other four children. "Carolyn will be dropping by in a day or two," he promised, flourishing his bullwhip to impress Sam's new missus and the brood of orphans Sam had taken under his wing. "See you real soon!"

A little overwhelmed by the bombastic Mr. Turner, Meg suddenly felt like her feet were clean wore out. What a day it had been! Exciting and exhilarating, but also exhausting. But they had made a tremendous amount of progress, too. Not to mention the lightning rod Mr. Frockmeyer had installed.

Hobbling around on tired feet, Meg carried the gift of embroidered pillows made by Byron's wife and filled with downy feathers into their "catch-all bedroom." *Mercy sakes alive!* There was no place to sit and barely room for all Meg's and the children's belongings, plus two beds. Trunks were stacked on top of each other, and clothing scattered all over the place.

And where was she supposed to cook breakfast? The stove pipe had been removed, and still needed to be installed in the new kitchen. Turning around in the midst of all this confusion, Meg bumped into Sam.

"My goodness! Do you really think we'll need such a big bed?" she asked, suddenly nervous about sleeping arrangements. "And where do you think you're going with that grandfather's clock?"

"Relax. We can surely squeeze everyone in together for a night or two." Brushing off his trousers, Sam gave her a wink. "A few more days roughing it, and we should be ready to set up housekeeping."

She looked at him, thinking, *One inexperienced housekeeper. Three orphans. One large husband. Not to mention an adolescent nephew. Where will we all sleep?* In her mind's eye she could envision six pairs of bare feet sticking out from beneath one coverlet. A tight fit, indeed!

How would anyone get a proper night's sleep?

His twinkling eyes met hers. "Some folks call it bundling."

"It sounds a bit crowded to me," she countered, retreating outside to the porch.

While Daniel and Jimmy wrestled the new mattress and a couple of matching chests of drawers through the front door, Sam commandeered the rocker on the porch step and stretched his legs to get the kinks out. Even seated, his tall powerful stature made Meg feel tiny by comparison, and the devil was sure dancing a hoe-down in those twinkling brown eyes of his. She felt like he could see right through her clothes.

"The right word of encouragement, Meg," he said in a quiet drawl, "and life could start humming between you and me like a hive of honey bees."

Refusing to let him know how jumpy the bold message in his eyes made her, Meg clutched her broom handle to her breast and frowned. "I believe you'd be better served by pouring a bucket of cold water on your head, Mr. G. And while you're cooling off, I'll go warm up some leftovers for you and your ranch hands."

The corners of his eyes crinkled at the sight of his wife brandishing her broom. As if he could be so easily intimidated! After that brief session of sparking, he knew for a fact that the attraction crackling in the air went both ways. Still, he wasn't in a hurry to claim his marital rights just yet. First he needed to earn her affection and trust. Right now she was walking a tightrope between playing the proper lady–prickly on the surface, and wound up tight as a drum inside–and jumping his tired bones.

The War between the States had dealt the nation a catastrophic blow. Most everybody he knew had come West, hoping to start over. Nothing to return to. Miss Wolfie was no exception. Regardless of what she said, she hadn't come West in search of adventure–far from it! And neither had those orphan kids. They'd all come, looking for *home*, a settled place where they belonged.

Admittedly he'd lost his religious bent during the war; he didn't know *what* to believe anymore. But from the second he opened her letter, he knew in his gut: Margaret Wolverton–"Miss Wolfie"–was The One. And, God helping him, he wasn't going to mess things up this time. Meg was like being given a second chance for happiness.

But he wasn't about to rush her off her feet, or push his luck. She needed time to catch her breath. To know she was safe. And that she had a future here.

Watching Sam out of the corner of her eye, Meg tried to fathom the wicked thoughts that surely must be churning behind that handsome façade of his. But when he finally spoke, she was completely taken by surprise. "Anyone ever tell you how beautiful you are, with the sun setting behind you, and your hair all lit up like a ball of swamp gas?"

"Beg pardon?" She let out a nervous laugh, not sure she'd heard correctly, but not willing to be mocked either. "Did you say...'swamp gas'?"

"Caught your attention, didn't I? Better than me spouting off about angelic halos." He grinned, amused that his backhanded compliment had slipped past her defenses. "Besides, I've never seen a real angel—though I must say your hair sure does shine like a bright copper penny, Mrs. G."

Falling in with his foolish talk, she touched her hair self-consciously. "Are you trying to infer that my hair—?"

"—has devilish highlights?" They were standing toe to toe now, though he had the advantage of height. "No, but it's sure giving *me* plenty of ideas." He gave her a slow wink.

At this, Meg exploded with laughter. Didn't that beat all! Either Mr. G. had the strangest notion of how to romance a lady—or he was just playing with her. More like a cat tormenting a mouse, she decided, recollecting how easily she had succumbed to his kisses.

"Why, thank you, sir," she fluffed her hair flirtatiously. "That is without doubt the most entertaining compliment I've ever received from a gentleman."

"You're welcome, ma'am." Smirking, he made an elegant bow and started walking backwards toward the barn. "See you at supper."

She gave him a little finger wave and skedaddled inside, dropping the bar across the heavy oak door in case he was tempted to waste any more of her valuable time making improper advances. *What fun!* She'd outmaneuvered him again. She smothered a mischievous giggle behind her hands and did a merry little jig.

~ * ~ * ~ * ~

Sam touched his hat in mock salute and wisely kept out of her hair. He knew exactly what his spunky little wife was up to. Trying to tie him in knots and test his patience. But that didn't dampen his admiration for the lady. Miss Wolfie was sure an original. Any woman who could mingle and hold her own today among such an odd assortment of neighbors deserved his respect.

Over the years, all sorts of women had come to this valley, many of them still pining away for what they'd left back east. One woman had taken one look, promptly left her husband, and taken the train back east. Two had taken to their beds when the isolation got too hard to handle. One had since died. The other, heavily addicted to laudanum, moved silently through her days like a ghost, while her husband and four young children tiptoed around her.

He counted the women who'd accompanied their husbands to today's house-raising to be among the survivors—those who were good for the long haul. His spunky little wife stood head and shoulders above most. Yes, Sam conceded, not for the first time, Meg had what it took to become a first rate pioneer. She had courage and determination. And no matter how often she held him off with her snippy little nose in the air, he wasn't about to give up believing that one of these days, Miss Wolfie would be as crazy in love with him as he already was with her.

It hadn't taken him long to realize that Meg was the woman he'd always dreamed of, and no court in the land could stop him from loving her. No somber Judge of the universe either! He figured if there really was a God in heaven, He'd have to judge him *not* for his clumsiness or his wrong-headedness, but for the intentions of his heart. Because, hell or high water, he wasn't about to abandon his claim on the heart of Margaret Wolverton Gallagher!

~ * ~ * ~ * ~

Though legally man and wife, the Gallaghers were still a long way from sharing the intimacies of a conventional marriage. Indeed, all Sam's teasing and levity hinted at a closer relationship between them than was strictly true. So *why*, Meg kept asking herself, did he persist in calling her "Miss Wolfie" and "Mrs. G?" He knew her Christian name, Margaret, so why didn't he use it?

And that knowing smile of his was beyond infuriating! Even made the hairs rise on the back of her neck! Every time she turned around, she found his eyes on her—watching her with a whimsical smile—as if she were an unfathomable puzzle he was trying to figure out. Or maybe find fault with? Or make fun of. If Sam was trying to make her feel jumpy as a cat, he was certainly succeeding!

So why would he do such a thing? Could he be having serious doubts about hiring her? Or marrying her? Was he worried about the difference in their ages? Or did he wonder if she lacked sufficient experience to care for the children properly? Had he overlooked the fact that she hadn't been under his roof a month yet—*if* one could even call it a roof! A half-finished shell of a house was more like it! At least he should allow for the difficulties she'd had to deal with since her arrival. She still had no place to put her things or the children's. It was hard enough getting meals on the table for him and his men without benefit of an organized household!

And there he stood, still making light of her name. And calling her "Mrs. G," as if they really were man and wife! Why, they were barely friends! She still thought of herself as the hired help, for goodness sake!

Even so, she was willing to accept his stated reason for marrying her—that the children needed the stability of a loving home and oversight by two caring parents. *Their* needs must take precedence over Mr. G's or her own personal wishes. It only made good sense that he had given her his name to protect her from the unwanted attentions of men she might come in contact with. His ranch hands knew instinctively that they'd have to reckon with the boss, if they didn't show her proper respect.

Still, Meg kept coming back to her role on the ranch. For all practical purposes she was doing what he'd hired her to be: his housekeeper and cook. He even promised to pay her at the end of each month! Though lately she'd come to believe her responsibilities needed to be redefined a bit. Cooking, mending, washing and cleaning up after Mr. G and his men, not to mention all the outside chores, gathering eggs, milking, slopping hogs, gardening, plus watching over three lively children and the like, was a daunting job, to say the least! Not that she suspected her boss of piling on so much work intentionally. And never let it be said that she was a whiner or a shirker! But she *did* hope that once the house was finished and life settled into a more predictable pattern, he might see his way clear to dividing up the work more equitably.

For one thing, during the house-raising she'd seen with her own eyes how skillfully Archie prepared a barbecued side of beef. He also kept the coffee pot going nonstop for over forty people! She'd also heard how he took charge of the chuck wagon on cattle drives, so it didn't seem unreasonable at all, if Sam were to have Archie take over cooking breakfast for the ranch hands on a regular basis. That seemed only sensible to Meg. Even though Archie was getting on in years, he still had a fair amount of kick left in his gallop. Of course, she'd be happy to make pies and lend a hand as needed, but the men in the bunkhouse shouldn't expect her to wait on them hand and foot, as a matter of routine.

Also, was it too much to expect his men to start taking more pride in their appearances? With the exception of Zeke, who kind of overdid it with his waxed mustachios and long flowing hair, the rest of them were an unwashed disgrace! Surely it wouldn't hurt if they shaved and cut their hair once in awhile, or took a bath on Saturday nights. With Daniel beginning to sprout peach fuzz, hopefully someone would take him in hand and help spruce him up a bit for church and other social events.

But regardless. It shouldn't be up to *her* to nag a bunch of grown men. *Sooner or later, there's going to be a showdown,* she vowed, tossing a few sticks of kindling into the bunkhouse stove, and rattling her pots and pans. As soon as Mr. Gallagher's house was habitable, she planned to have a serious talk with the man.

~ * ~ * ~ * ~

Weeks passed, while Sam and his men divided their labors between moving cattle "here and there" to graze, and putting the finishing touches on the ranch house—getting it "right and tight" to withstand the coming winter storms, he kept telling Meg. Meanwhile friends from all over the valley dropped by to give advice or lend a helping hand. Some brought spare building materials, a length of stove pipe, a set of bunk beds, or a window or two left over from their own house-raising. Useful things mostly, just lying around in a barn or shed, or so they claimed.

Of course, some donated items were mostly decorative, like a big clump of crystal rock, or an Indian basket, or a butterfly collection. "It'd be a darn shame to leave such treasures lying around," Tim Ryan said, showing up one day with a set of rusty wagon wheels.

Invariably Meg made sure all such contributions were properly acknowledged. She never sent anyone away without a hearty meal of biscuits and beans and a cup of coffee, topped off with a helping of Apple Brown Betty or a slice of her raisin pie. Everyone in the valley was a jack-of-all-trades, willing to swap and trade, so everybody went away happy.

In between such visits, a few of the ladies stopped by, mostly arriving on horseback, to see how things were going and to invite her to the upcoming sewing bee. Still not unpacked, Meg didn't have much to contribute in the way of fabric, but the ladies insisted that she come anyway, so she dug around in her portmanteau, found her sewing kit, full of needles and thread and her mother's thimble. She still felt a little hesitant, not knowing how Sam might feel about her abandoning her post in the middle of the day, but when she asked, he very kindly sharpened her scissors for her. This she took as a very good omen.

On the appointed day, she baked a shoe-fly-pie and apple-pan-dowdy to share with the women during refreshment time. Leaving the boys in Mr. G's capable hands, she led Susie out to the buckboard.

Several of the ranch hands were standing around, but she managed to get Susie and the shoe-fly-pie safely on board, then braced herself to take up the reins.

Never having driven a buckboard before, she had asked Archie to hitch the S-G-S's gentlest horse to the buckboard. "You want me to drive you?" he asked, watching her step daintily onto the front wheel and climb aboard.

"Oh, no. I've watched you do it so often, Archie. I feel certain I won't have any difficulty at all," Holding onto her hat in the breeze with one hand, she took up the reins. "Besides, the grange hall is only a few miles down the road."

Here goes, she thought, and winged a prayer to the Almighty. Susie held onto the seat for dear life, while Meg slapped the reins against Molly the horse's backside. "Giddap!" she cried.

No response. That darn horse just stood there, flicking its tail at a buzzing horsefly.

Oh, goodness gracious, this will never do, Meg thought. Having Sam and his men watch made her extra nervous! She hauled back on the reins, hoping to get the horse's attention. And oh boy, did she! Old Molly reared back with a shrill neigh of protest. And then ambled over to the horse trough.

"Well, I certainly made a good impression, didn't I?" she groaned. "That's all right, Susie. Me and Molly are just getting acquainted." She waved and smiled to the cowboys sitting along the corral fence, hoping they would all take a hint and disappear.

Instead their heads suddenly swiveled toward the horse and rider racing up the road in a cloud of dust. "Hold on there!" shouted the rider, a woman as trim and petite as Meg, only she was a fireball of energy and had complete control of her mount.

"Oh, fine," Meg muttered to herself. Being a tenderfoot wasn't bad enough. Now she had to compete with a talented equestrian! Her ears burning with embarrassment, she yanked on Molly's reins again, fighting to get the darn horse's muzzle out of the water trough.

Meanwhile the cowboys started cheering, as this fine looking, dark-haired lady on a strawberry roan swooped past Meg, and circled around, glad-handing several of the men in passing.

"Hey, there, Carolyn!" Sam hopped off the corral fence and warmly clasped the lady's hand.

"Good to see you, Sam. I got here as soon as I could," she said, striding with him to where Meg sat dejectedly in the buckboard, while old Molly drained the trough. "Byron's riding herd on the kids today. The whole lot of 'em are just getting over the chicken pox. Can you beat that?" she laughed. "Anyway I figured I'd stop by and kidnap your wife for a few hours."

Without further ado, Carolyn tossed her horse's reins to Sam. "Take care of Snappy for me, will you, Sam?" With a big smile, she reached up and shook Meg's hand. "I'm Carolyn Turner—Byron's better half! Sorry it took so long to make it over to your place, but with five kids sick—well, you know how *that* goes! Anyway, after all the good things Byron told me about you, I decided to escort you personally to our sewing bee today." She sprang nimbly up to the seat and settled between Meg and Susie. "Hey, little Susie, I bet you're wondering how come I know your name."

The three-year-old narrowed her eyes accusingly. "You weren't here when all the people came to build us a house."

"No, darlin', I wasn't, and for good reason. My kids broke out in big spots, and I didn't want you to catch what they had." Laughter just bubbled out of her, as she turned and gave Meg a quick hug. "Well? Are you ready to get out of here and have some fun?"

Chapter Sixteen

"Hold onto that young'un of yours! Gee-hah!"

Without even asking, Carolyn gave the reins a couple of quick jerks to get Molly turned around, and away they went down the bumpy road. Just as soon as they were out of sight of the S-G-S cowboys, she handed over the reins to Meg.

"Oh, but I never–" Meg protested.

"Aw, you'll get the hang of it in no time," Carolyn said with a rascally grin and a quick wink. "First I had to get you away from all those smart alecks back there. Men just *think* they know everything about horses, but they don't. Not really. Now, let me show you how it's done."

For the next half-hour or so, they rattled along at an easy pace. To Meg's surprise and delight, driving a buckboard wasn't such a terrifying experience, after all. Carolyn showed her how to hold the reins, and how to keep old Molly from bolting, or just plain acting mulish.

Before long, both women were laughing and bumping shoulders companionably, as they drove along. Susie hung on tight on the curves and held her breath, but before long, even she began to relax. "Make the horsey go faster, Mama!" she giggled, swinging her legs.

"This is fast enough for a beginner like me," Meg smiled.

Up ahead, just off the road was a lone building–or was it a barn? At any rate, several other wagons and buggies were parked in the shade of a mesquite tree. "Is that the grange hall? Already?" she asked eagerly.

"Sure is," Carolyn confirmed. "Pull off and stop between that piebald pony and the green buckboard."

"Like this?" Meg yanked on the reins, heading for the closest horse and buggy.

"No, not *that* horse. The piebald!"

They were about to collide with a big black gelding, when Carolyn's hand covered Meg's, and together they managed to guide

Molly past impending disaster. A few heart-pumping seconds later, they pulled in beside the Benson's green buckboard.

"Whoa!" Meg gasped. "We made it! Just barely."

"You did just fine." Carolyn set the brake, which Meg had forgotten to do, and hopped down. "Let's go meet the rest of the ranchers' wives."

Handing Susie down to her amazing new friend, Meg rescued the shoo-fly-pie from the buckboard and, arm in arm, she and Carolyn stepped inside the hall.

~ * ~ * ~ * ~

Five hours later, Meg was on her way back home again.

Never had she met a friendlier, more practical group of women, or laughed so much. Working in groups, they had tied three quilts, and accomplished so much that Meg was truly in awe. Although she had attended sewing bees back East, the women she met that day inspired her *so much* with their wit, their wisdom, and their kindness. Moreover, the colors they used lifted her spirits, and the patterns were so original! Talk about creativity!

As for Carolyn, the woman didn't have a negative bone in her body. Everybody was her friend, the sky was always blue, and even if it wasn't, she found a way to make people smile.

During the circle's potluck, she kept everyone in stitches, as she shared how she battled cabin fever while nursing her children through chicken pox. While being stuck inside for weeks with five sick children didn't seem like much to laugh about, Meg had laughed as hard as everyone else. No doubt about it, the sewing circle ladies were a bunch of unpolished diamonds, and Carolyn...well, she was the rarest gem of them all.

"I cannot thank you enough for rescuing me," Meg told her new best friend, who was busy checking the cinch on Snappy's saddle.

Carolyn grinned up at her, her dark brown eyes twinkling with the sheer joy of living. "We had fun—didn't I tell you we would?"

Without further ado, she kneed the strawberry roan in the gut, forcing it to let out a belly full of air. Brushing off her hands, she came around to where Meg stood, and they hugged.

"Guess I better go feed Byron and the kids," Carolyn said, "but I'll be back!"

~ * ~ * ~ * ~

Over the next several days, Meg received visits from some of her other neighbors. Naturally the ladies wanted to see all the progress that had been made on the new ranch house. They also shared favorite recipes and the latest gossip. Since most of them also belonged to the sewing circle, the subject came up frequently about her favorite colors, and how she planned to decorate the house.

"Basically I'm drawn to colors from nature, blue and gold and tans and orange," Meg shared with her callers one afternoon. "Almost anything except bright pinks and reds."

"What a coincidence! I feel the exact same way," trilled Delia Watkins. "Though muted colors are considered more relaxing, I suppose."

"Magenta and purples are my favorites." Sophie Burnett peered over her wire rim spectacles as if to dispute Fannie Mae Gehrhart, a temperance thumper who invariably wore drab olive green.

"To each her own," said Fannie, knitting away on a dark grey sweater for her husband. She raised a few flock of sheep, which caused talk among the other ranchers' wives. Though a prosperous cattleman, her husband harvested the wool for her, and she dyed and spun her own yarn.

"I do so admire that stitch you're using," Sally Lassiter sighed, hoping to distract Sophie from taking another jab—no pun intended—at the knitter in their midst.

"It's a cable knit stitch. I'd be happy to show you how," Fannie offered, turning her work. "It's actually quite simple to do."

"You know, Meg, I just happen to have a yellow dress I've outgrown," Delia interrupted, patting her expanding belly. "Perhaps you'd like to use it to make a quilt?"

"Oh, but won't you be needing it? For the baby, I mean—?" said Sophie.

There was an awkward pause, for nobody liked to talk about the unborn. Once their babies were toddling about and misbehaving was an entirely different matter. Soon enough the competition would begin—"bragging rights," it was called, if Meg remembered correctly from the sewing circles she attended as a child with her great-aunt Gladys.

"Speaking of discards, my father-in-law dropped off a pile of worn out dungarees last week. They're still in my workroom," Delia giggled. "Though what I'm supposed to do with them, I have no idea!"

"Meg, maybe you could make Davey a pair of coveralls?" Sophie suggested.

"Pish!" said Delia. "My father-in-law is so portly, you could make coveralls for *both* those orphan boys!"

"Thank you," said Meg, not wishing to ruffle any feelings. "I just may take you up on your offer, Delia. Jimmy and Davey are growing by leaps and bounds, now that they're eating regular. And Susie, why, she's been wanting her very own denim riding skirt!"

"I have a better idea," Sally butted in, hoping to keep the ladies from forever unloading unwanted used clothing on each other. "Why don't we gather up all the beat-up denim jeans we have lying around and take them over to Carolyn? She can turn them into beautiful, warm quilts faster than you can whistle "Buffalo Gal, won't you come out tonight—"

"Come out tonight," Susie piped up from the corner, where she was playing with her dolly.

"And dance by the light of the moon!" Sophie and Delia harmonized, and everybody hooted with laughter.

Well, *almost* everybody, because Fannie Mae was, after all, a staunch prohibitionist and found songs about saloon girls offensive. Calmly folding up her knitting, she placed it in her work bag. "Well, ladies," she said calmly, "it's been delightful visiting, but I have a lot of mouths to feed at home, so I guess I'll be seeing you all next Sunday at church?"

~ * ~ * ~ * ~

Finally the ranch house was "right and tight, and ready for winter storms," or so Sam informed his chatty wife with a wink. Meg could only wonder what the wink meant to convey—especially since he hadn't tried to kiss her even once since the house-raising! Not that she had any objections or felt neglected. *Landsakes!* She was *much* too busy for such foolishness.

At any rate, all the windows and shutters had been installed, and the cedar siding on the exterior walls had been carefully caulked. Two Bear and his son-in-law, John Lassiter, had rebuilt the old fireplace, using leftover mortar mix and flat rocks from the creek.

By late August a rack of elk antlers hung over the mantelpiece, and Granny Benson had sent over hand-tied bunches of fragrant onions and herbs from her garden, which Meg gratefully hung from the rafters near her wood-burning cook stove.

On the table a tin can was crammed with daisies and Queen Anne's Lace—a gift from Susie. Curtains created out of a discarded patchwork quilt had been transformed by Meg's very own hand into cheerful yellow and blue curtains to grace the kitchen windows. There was still plenty of work to be done, but gazing around at all that had been accomplished thus far, Meg was frankly amazed.

At long last, the place was starting to feel downright homey!

~ * ~ * ~ * ~

"I know it's your very first night together," Carolyn said, reining in her strawberry roan, Snappy, in front of the S-G-B ranch house. All five Turner children accompanied their mother on horseback.

"Can't stay long. We're expecting Byron by mid-afternoon," she explained. "He's been on a long haul, and leaves again in the morning, so we can't *not* be there, y'know."

"Still, I hope you can all come in for a few minutes," Meg said, thrilled to see her friend.

"Just for a quick look around." Beaming, Carolyn dismounted and secured her horse's reins to a fence post. "All right, kids. Come say hello to Mrs. Gallagher. She's the lady I've told you so much about."

"Nice to meet you, ma'am," sang out a chorus of five, three girls and two boys.

The oldest, a blonde, took off her cowboy hat. "I'm Missy," she announced.

"Howdy, Mrs. Gallagher," said Troy.

A pretty brown-haired girl stepped up next to shake Meg's hand. "I'm Shelley. Is it true people call you 'Miss Wolfie?'" she giggled.

"Why, yes. Some people do," Meg smiled.

Carolyn rolled her eyes. "Now, Troy. Did you put your sister up to that?"

"Aw, Ma."

His face turned beet red, but before he could open his mouth again and get into more hot water, a bewitching little creature butted him aside. "I hear you bake yummy molasses cookies." She licked her lips and smiled up at Meg like a cat.

"Now, Velma, what have I said about your sweet tooth?" Carolyn smiled apologetically at Meg. "I swear, if I hadn't taught Missy and Shelley how to bake, I'd never get out of the kitchen!"

The youngest member of the Turner family tugged on Meg's hand. "I'm Duane, and I think you're pretty."

"Why, thank you, kind sir!" Meg laughed. "And you're a very handsome young man." She smiled at everyone. "Not to give you children a big head or anything, but *I* think you're all pretty amazing. And very good looking." She took in a deep breath, and looked around the circle of children. "Guess what?"

Carolyn threw her hands in the air "Don't encourage 'em, Meg. They're already too full of mischief, as it is."

"Aw, Ma!" all five protested.

"Good word," said Meg, and winked. "*Encourage* is exactly what I'm going to do."

The children looked at her. Eagerly waiting.

"I'm going to give each of you two cookies, on one condition." Again she held her breath. "Can you wait until you get home to eat them?"

"Noooo," a forlorn chorus of five groaned.

"Oh, good! Because these cookies need to be eaten *right now*!" Meg shared a helpless shrug with Carolyn. The children began jumping up and down in their cowboy boots, clapping.

"Come on in, everybody." She held the door open, and the Turners made a beeline for the table, where cookies and a pitcher of milk awaited them. "Sorry, Carolyn," she said out of the corner of her mouth, as she followed them in. "I hope this doesn't spoil their appetite for dinner."

Carolyn laughed heartily. "Be careful, or they'll be over here constantly pestering you for sweets. They're like a hoard of locusts, always munching."

"I've also got lumps of sugar for their ponies," Meg hinted. "Unless you're worried that the children might eat them first?"

"Hold that thought," said Carolyn. "Keep an eye on my kids, Meg. I'll be right back."

Though intrigued, Meg hurried to pour milk and to see that the children all got their fair share. But the minute she had things divided up equitably, Susie, Davey, Jimmy and Daniel showed up and began circling "the eats" protectively like sharks, sizing up their guests, and filling up on their own fair share of refreshments.

Daniel already knew Missy and Shelley and Troy from school the previous year, though the Turners were younger than he was. Susie and Velma instantly bonded and started chatting about their dollies. Fortunately everyone got along well, which made Meg breath a sign of relief. Leaving Daniel to supervise, Meg went outside to see what was delaying Carolyn.

Her friend was pulling on a huge package, wrapped in brown paper and tied behind Snappy's saddle. It was rather bulky, but evidently not very heavy, because once it was untied, Carolyn was able to drag it off her horse and carry it over to the porch without any help from Meg.

"I've been waiting until you got the house rearranged a bit." she said, and held it out to Meg. "Here, take it. It's a wedding gift for you and Sam."

Caught by surprise, Meg was so deeply moved she could scarcely talk. "Oh, Carolyn, thank you. I— Are you positive—? I mean, really, you didn't need to do this—" She shook it, and while it was a bulky package, nothing rattled. Whatever it was, it felt soft and kind of, well, flexible.

"It's just a little something from me and Byron." Her brown eyes twinkled, and Carolyn couldn't have grinned any wider, if she'd tried.

Meg peered around the giant package. "Do I need to wait and open it with Sam?"

"No. But he'll get as much enjoyment out of it as you will. Especially when the wind gets to blowin' and temperatures drop below zero," she said, throwing Meg a big hint.

"Is it a bunch of saddle blankets for the horses?" Meg asked, dragging out the suspense. She knew that couldn't possibly be true, but she felt a case of the sillies coming on and couldn't help herself. "Oh, I know: It's a giant oven mitt, to keep the kettle of water on the back of the stove from freezing in the middle of the night!"

Carolyn burst out laughing. "Now I *know* you're pulling my leg, Meg!"

Rollicking back and forth, helpless with laughter, they both took hold of the package. Every few seconds, they would look at each other and started laughing again. "C'mon, let's get this thing inside," Carolyn said, being the practical one. Between them and the package, they could barely squeeze through the front door.

"Where to?" Meg laughed, bumping into the wall.

"Wherever Sam set up that four-poster," Carolyn grinned.

"So, is it some kind of medieval curtain to keep out the wind?" By now Meg and Carolyn were giggling so hard they dropped the package and slid down the wall, landing on their rumps. Somehow they just brought out the sillies in each other.

Suddenly they were surrounded by nine worried young faces. "Are you all right, Mama?" "Can we help, Miss Wolfie?" they clamored.

Meg and Carolyn doubled over with laughter. "No. Just eat your cookies, children!" Holding their sides, they went off again.

Daniel frowned and shook his head. *Such behavior. Surely adults are supposed to act more dignified,* his expression said. "Should I put the package somewhere?" he asked, after both women *appeared* to be coming to their senses.

"In the bedroom with the four-poster," Meg said in a muffled voice.

Carolyn held out her hand, and Daniel pulled her to her feet. "Thank you, kind sir. Help Miss Wolfie up, as well." She glanced cautiously at her gleeful partner in light-hearted lunacy. "Whoever tagged you with such a name?"

"My orphans." Meg took a few steadying deep breaths. "The less said about that, the better." Finally in control of her dignity, she led the way into the bedroom she and Sam would be sharing, starting tonight.

Carolyn sized up the package on the bed, then grinned at Meg. "Do you think we dare open it?" she asked. "Or will we lose complete control again?"

"Just as long as we don't crack a smile," Meg said, eager to see the contents. "Ready? Get set, *rip!*" She tossed aside the paper, and with trembling fingers, spread wide the most beautiful blue denim quilt she had ever seen. Never had she seen anything so functional, yet so creative. The pockets, the zippers and buttons—even flaws in the rugged work pants—were all there to marvel at.

It was like being able to open a private journal and experience events, or a tiny piece of the original owner's personal history. A cattle brand or spark from a campfire left a scorch mark on the fabric. And here was a tiny brush stroke of barn paint. And a well mended tear on one knee.

Spotting a folded piece of aged paper sticking out of one pocket, Meg pulled it out and read a wife's love note, left for her husband to find during the heat of the day. It read, 'Every time I think of you, my heart begins to sing.'

"Oh, Carolyn, thank you so much!" she whispered, and reached for her friend's hand. "It's so beautiful! What an amazing gift you've given Sam and me."

"It's my way of saying that the little things in life may seem small and insignificant, but it's the little things that make or break a marriage. Like that love note from a woman to her man." She gestured to the scrap of yellowed paper and smiled. "I always go through the pockets of discarded levis people drop off, before I start to put together all the pieces. You'd be surprised what I find."

Meg nodded. "I shall always treasure your friendship, and your wisdom."

The grandfather clock sounded four o'clock in the front room, calling them back to their responsibilities.

"Reckon I'd better round up my little cowpokes and get on home to that man of mine," Carolyn sighed.

"I'll get those sugar cubes I promised for the children's horses," Meg responded. "Ride safe. We'll talk again soon."

~ * ~ * ~ * ~

Coming up from the barn, Sam waved goodbye to the Turner family as they rode away. Then he turned to Meg with a grin. "Our new house looks mighty fine," he declared, watching her busily sweep wood chips off the new verandah. "Built to last a hundred years."

"Or at least until the next gang of outlaws comes roaring through," Meg said facetiously.

"They wouldn't dare." He laughed. "Now that I've got you and Dusty watching over the place, I guess it's time to put up a 'No Trespassing' sign."

"Oh, really! I suppose you figure I'm a good enough shot with that shotgun of yours," she scoffed. So far, Sam had only taken her out behind the barn twice to try her hand at target shooting. The first time she squeezed the trigger, the gun kicked so hard she landed on her backside. It took a lot of sweet-talking before she agreed to try again, and even then she was shaking in her boots.

"Trust me," he had told her. "I have the perfect solution." So he had led her farther into the woods, stood her against a tree trunk, and told her to fire off a round from Daniel's Henry rifle. That time she nearly dislocated her shoulder and had to wear a sling for two days, so it seemed only reasonable that she was still a little skeptical of all his good advice.

"We'll find a gun you can handle," Sam promised. "But even more important than learning how to defend yourself is the fact that you instinctively know how to handle yourself under duress." He squinted good-naturedly at her through the honest sweat of a hard day's work. "My first wife Amie used to get rattled by the least little thing, but not you, Meg." He waggled his finger at her. "You stand your ground. Remember that first night you spent in the line shack, when the old hoot owl and the rattlesnake got into a fight? You calmly slept through the entire life-and-death struggle. Now *that*, my dear, is what I call true grit."

Meg blushed. "Oh, Sam, that's not how it was at all. I was just too exhausted that night to care. Plus it was pitch dark. Under different circumstances, I probably would have hollered loud enough to raise the dead."

"And what about when all your delightful lady friends give you advice on how to raise *the* perfect children?" Shaking dust and wood splinters out of his hair, he put his hat back on. "Anyone who can keep a straight face when they share their favorite nostrums should be able to help teach our kids to read."

Here he goes again, she thought, and decided it was the perfect opportunity to speak her mind. She planted one fist on her hip. "When do I have time for teaching? What spare time is left when I'm not busy keeping house, being a washerwoman, pickling beets—" she held up her stained fingers as proof, "—raising poultry, slopping hogs, and cooking 'round the clock? Tell me that!"

Sam planted one boot on the porch step and leaned forward, grinning at her. "Ah, but I also need you to be my wife, and a mother to our children. In other words, my helpmeet."

Meg cocked her head to one side, pondering how *not* to kick up more dust than she could handle. "Well, Mr. G," she said sweetly. "I hope you won't get upset by what I'm about to suggest."

"Sweetheart, I am waiting with baited breath," he grinned.

"I am well aware that you're a highly educated man—a doctor, in fact. So instead of passing the evenings playing poker in the bunkhouse and swapping jokes with your men—"

"Mmm. This is beginning to sound interesting, Miss Wolfie. Go on," he invited.

"Now I fully understand that you and your men may feel the need to blow off steam at the end of a hard day's work—" Truthfully she had a *lot* to get off her chest, but just then something totally unrelated, but equally important, popped into her head, so she decided a short detour around the barn was in order first.

"Oh! Before I forget... With four more people living here, and all the visitors we've had lately, we need a new outhouse—something that will accommodate a larger number of people. So there won't be a big line of people every morning." She paused to get his reaction to *that* idea.

"I plan on getting to that—soon, actually. Don't you worry." A quizzical frown appeared between Sam's eyebrows. "Anything else, dear heart?"

"I am, of course, concerned about hygiene," she added, ignoring all his smoochy-smooch endearments. "Being a doctor, you are, too, I expect."

"I'd be happy to show you the plans I've drawn up." He rubbed his hands together. "Now, let's get back to discussing a more profitable way of spending our evenings, shall we?"

What? Meg's jaw dropped. True, her train of thought had been temporarily diverted elsewhere, but surely he hadn't said what she *thought* he implied—*especially* with Susie only ten feet away! Temporarily rendered speechless, she stared at him in disbelief.

"Uh-uh-uh," she stammered, her mouth suddenly as dry as the Mojave Desert.

Sam leaned forward in a proper show of concern. "Are you all right? Miss Wolfie? Should I get you a glass of water?"

Meg sucked in a deep breath, forcing herself to address the murky depths of the male mind. "No! Though I confess I'm somewhat taken aback, that a man of your obvious education would— Frankly, sir, I find your suggestion rather bold!"

Giving her a strange look, Sam clapped his hand across her forehead. Finding no fever, he checked her pupils.

"Don't you dare!" She backed up, convinced he was up to no good.

"Have you gotten into locoweed, or eaten any bad food?" he demanded, puzzled by the sudden onset of symptoms.

"I have not!" Meg drew herself up to her full five feet one inch. "I am simply fed up with your cavalier attitude! 'More profitable use of our evenings,' indeed!"

"What?" he said, and then laughed. "Oh, that. I fear you've been out in the sun too long, my darling."

"I have not! And I'm *not* your darling!" she snapped.

"No, I guess not," he agreed, humoring her. "Come sit down, while I try to get to the bottom of this. One minute your face was beet red, the next you're pale as a codfish." Trying not to laugh, he supported her solicitously over to the porch rocker.

She struggled to rise, but Sam was too busy checking her pulse to heed her wishes. "I am not that kind of a girl," she muttered faintly.

"No, of course you aren't." He was hovering over her, his fingers searching in her hair. "Can you recall if you were bit by a wasp or a bee?" he asked, looking properly worried.

"No." She tried to bat his hand away from the buttons on her dress. "Mr. G, stop! You are carrying this 'doctor' business too far." Her voice was stronger now, and she was getting up her nerve to wallop him on the nose. Of course, after she did, she would probably be obliged to resign...

He straightened, still pondering her odd behavior. "Perhaps it's a passing episode of some sort," he said, stroking his chin. "You seemed perfectly all right before you went all strange."

"I would be strange, indeed, if I allowed you to make such improper suggestions," she huffed indignantly.

Being pragmatic, Sam had pretty much figured out the cause of his wife's witchiness, so he stopped the teasing. "All right, let's back up, shall we? What were we talking about when you had this hyper-reactive response?"

"Idiot!" She pushed him away. "You were talking about spending our evenings 'more profitably,' if I'm not mistaken. Oh, now you've got me all confused!" Flustered, she looked up at him hopefully. "Maybe you didn't actually mean what I thought you did?"

"That is entirely possible," he said, straight-faced. "Men and women have a tendency to talk over each other. In the process of translation, almost anything can happen." His shoulders began to heave with silent laughter. "What were you trying to say to me, Meg? Right before all that gobbledygook about latrines."

She saw the mischievous twinkle in his brown eyes and realized he'd been playing her the whole time. She decided now was not an appropriate time to talk about the children's education.

"Oh, dear, it seems to have slipped my mind." Smiling, she stood and brushed her skirt off. "But I'm sure it will come back to me soon enough," she said cheerfully and went to round up the children for supper.

~ * ~ * ~ * ~

Later that evening, after the boys were finally asleep in the bunkhouse, and Susie in her usual place in the add-on to the new house, Sam invited Meg outside to relax beside a crackling bonfire. She didn't ask '*why*,' which he felt was progress. They were still feeling each other out, trying to find common ground, but little by little they seemed to be making headway. So when she set aside the sock she was darning and went to find her shawl, a deep sense of relief swept over him. They had been sparring a lot lately, and he was hoping to get beyond all that and establish a more intimate bond.

And so they built the fire together. He wasn't looking for conversation so much as he sought human warmth. It had been a tough day, and he suspected they both needed to unwind. Across the creek, where Meg still planned to homestead, a grove of birch trees cast a silvery light, reflecting off the leaping flames of their fire. Sparks spiraled toward the night sky, surrounded by deepening shadows, and a symphony of insects and creatures rustling nearby in the fields lulled their senses...

"What triggered our misunderstanding earlier?" Sam asked her after a long silence. "I'd really like to know."

Meg nibbled her fingernail, pondering both the question and the strong planes in his handsome face against the flickering flames. "I think it started with feeling like I'm constantly being pulled in every direction, and wanting you to become more involved with the children's care. Does any of what I just said make sense to you?"

"Sounds like a legitimate concern," he agreed. "Well, my hard working wife, what kind of tasks do you have as a mother that you'd like me to help you with? As your husband?"

As his warm brown eyes searched her bright blue eyes for answers, a curious connection, far deeper than mere friendship, began to blossom. Not all flowery-bowery, like a mushy Valentine. No, this *thing*, this growing warmth and attraction, felt far more substantive.

For Meg, it entered her bones like an ancient fire, kindling a renewed confidence that her life was on the right path. Slowly it spread inside her, warm and comforting. Though the words weren't spoken aloud, she felt almost as if Sam was seeking permission to become a permanent part of her life, and asking her to allow him to do the same for her.

The intimacy of that shared moment went deep, to that secret place where Meg didn't even trust herself to explore. Sam made her feel wanted. Not just needed, like a paid drudge. It felt more like being included. Or invited to share a dream.

Not necessarily always being in total agreement, but each having the liberty to celebrate their differences, male *and* female, and together to become part of something bigger than just the two of them. Something that mattered greatly and was attainable.

A dream that would last a lifetime, perhaps even longer.

Watching the logs burn and slowly collapse into hot embers, Meg and Sam swallowed a yawn and smiled sheepishly at each other.

"Bedtime, Meg." Getting to his feet, Sam doused the fire with a bucket of water. They stood quietly, their arms around each other, while they watched the fire fizzle and die out.

Meg nuzzled her cheek against his arm. "G'night, Sam," she sighed, and lifted her face to smile at him sleepily.

He kissed the tip of her nose.

"We have some serious catching up to do, young lady," he reminded her.

She opened one eye. "We do?"

"Later. When you're not asleep on your feet." He kissed her lips softly.

He waited for her to kiss him back, and she did. Not once, not twice, but three times. Friendly little pecks.

"You're a very kind man," she mumbled drowsily.

"Why, thank you—I guess." Smiling, he swept her up in his arms and carried her up the porch steps and into the cabin. "I'm all for kindness, Meg, but it doesn't hold a candle to the joys that are yet to come."

Roused by the passionate timbre in his voice, Meg gazed up at him.

Not for one second did she mistake the bold message in his eyes. Blushing, she closed her eyes dreamily. *At last*, she smiled to herself. *The day has come when this polite little marriage of convenience turns into the real thing.*

~ * ~ * ~ * ~

If Sam was guilty of anything, it was of being *too* considerate of her feelings, Meg raged, pacing around their bedroom like a tigress.

Was he *ever* going to claim her as his bride? And why would he lead her on, and then just leave? *Either he's chicken-hearted, or he's too polite*, she decided. Too handsome and rugged, and—too *cautious—yes!* That was the word she was looking for! *Cautious.*

So what was she supposed to do? Drag him out of the bunkhouse, or wherever he had gone?

This was *not* the way things were supposed to happen. At least not according to what some of her married cousins used to giggle and whisper about! Of course, she herself had no idea what a wife should expect on her wedding night. But for Sam to carry her into their bedroom, drop her on the bed with a polite little kiss, and then *leave* was unforgivable!

It was...the ultimate insult.

See if she ever forgot such a snub. *Ooh!* Sam Gallagher had a lot of admirable characteristics, but he was way too bashful—*whatever!* Working up a full head of steam, Meg took another turn around the room. She grabbed his pillow off the bed and hurled it at the door.

But then another thought struck her: God forbid he was merely *indifferent* to her! *Aarrgh!* She let out a little scream of frustration and kicked the bedpost, then hopped around on one foot. Her big toe was throbbing. Her heart was broken. Nothing was working out the way she had hoped.

If it weren't for the children, she would— Well, she hadn't made up her mind what to do just yet, she realized, and burst into tears. Here she was, out in the wilderness with no one to love her...

Meg was too busy plotting revenge to notice when the bedroom door swung open behind her. Suddenly a pair of muscular arms closed around her and lifted her clear off the floor.

Of course, that about gave her heart failure. With a shriek she spun around, arms flailing to ward off her attacker.

"What in the world are you pitching a fit about now?" Sam exclaimed.

She collapsed against his hairy chest, trying to catch her breath. "Oh, Sam, I thought you left me," she blurted out. "I thought you didn't want me. I was so scared!"

"Sshhh, my fierce little mouse." He gathered her close, turning back the sheets and warm quilt with his other hand. "I just wanted to give you a few minutes to get ready for bed."

She looked up at him, hoping he could understand how afraid she was. Not just of being intimate with a man she barely knew, but of potentially finding herself all alone in the world again. Only now she had three children to care for, too. How was she going to do it all by herself? Even with her faith in God, sometimes life could be...truly exhausting.

"I don't ever want to sleep in this big bed alone," she confided.

"I'm not much for sleeping alone either." Grinning, he gently kissed her tears away. "Do you usually wear a nightgown?" he asked to break the awkward silence.

She nodded, then asked daringly, "You?"

"Not unless it's winter and the winds are howling like banshees outside. Then I wear my longjohns and pile on the covers."

"Oh." She stared at her hands, folded primly in her lap.

"May I help you unlace your shoes?" he offered.

"I stubbed my toe," she confessed, feeling like a fool.

"In that case, maybe I'd better take a look." He bit back a laugh. "As your private physician."

"I am not helpless," she told him. "I can take off my own shoes."

"By all means, be my guest," he said, with a twinkle in his eyes.

She stood up. "Perhaps I should use the privacy screen." Her unsteady gait as she rushed across the room nearly made her trip. "I-I won't be a minute," she assured him and ducked behind the screen.

Fascinated, Sam watched as her tiny hand tossed various articles of clothing helter-skelter. Soon the screen became so burdened with a gingham dress, followed by various items of intimate apparel, stockings, garters, corset, and chemise, that the framework began to wobble and sway, as if ready to capsize.

"Can I be of any assistance?" Sam asked, his imagination running wild—not to mention other anatomical parts!

Were all women burdened by such heavy feminine trappings? he wondered. *If so, such fashions were downright cruel and unjust!*

Barely able to restrain himself, Sam strode across the room, his teeth clenched. He had but one goal: to free his unhappy little wife from such tyrannical and restrictive garb.

He came within three feet of rescuing Meg, when the privacy screen teetered under the weight of eleven layers of clothing and fell to the floor with a loud crash.

Trying to shield her nakedness, Meg assumed the fig leaf position with her hands and screamed. Towering over her was Sam, glaring down with bared teeth.

Not about to test an obviously rocky relationship further, Meg took off running. Sprinting around to the other side of the four-poster, she dove under the covers and burrowed down, shaking like a leaf.

"Don't you come near me," she shrieked. "It's not my fault the screen fell over."

The crackling sound of Sam's boots trampling the screen signaled his approach. He smoothed his hand over the covers hiding her trembling body, and in particular her curvy little rump. It was pretty hard to miss something that delectable, when it was sticking straight up.

Giving her a friendly pat, he sat down on the side of the bed and gave himself a moment to reconnoiter. After seeing his wife streak across the room with nothing left to the imagination, it was hard not to double over and laugh until his ribs ached. But that wasn't all he had to be concerned about.

Daniel and Jimmy were pounding on the bedroom door. Davey was also awake and prowling around the house, whistling to bring the dog inside, and raiding the pantry.

"Uncle Sam!" Daniel called. "We heard a terrible crash. Are you all right?"

At least Daniel has the good sense God gave him not to open the bedroom door. Sam thought.

"Stay right where you are, Miss Wolfie," he whispered to his wife, who was squirming under the covers. Until he got the boys settled down for the night, there wasn't a chance in hell of enjoying a relaxing romantic interlude with his wife.

In fact, viewing the situation under the harsh light of reality, he figured things had gone about as haywire as they possibly could for one night.

~ * ~ * ~ * ~

Bribing the boys with a pan of sweet rolls Meg had baked and set aside for Sunday morning breakfast was easy. Persuading them to go back to sleep required almost an act of Congress. And certainly a great deal of firmness. Daniel and Jimmy were in an extremely talkative mood, which delayed getting back to his bride any time soon.

Nearly two hours passed, while in whispered tones, he answered their questions about why he decided to raise cattle, and what breed did he like best, and where the S-G-S Ranch got its name, and about the Indians... Sam felt his eyelids grow heavier and heavier. When the clock struck two, he jerked out of a stupor. Those two rascals looked as wide-awake as ever.

Exhausted, he confiscated Daniel's tobacco pouch, cigarette papers and matches, and escorted the two older boys out to the barn to camp out for the rest of the night.

"Behave yourselves," he counseled the pair, and provided them with blankets. "No smoking, y'hear? And keep Dusty with you."

"Sure thing, Mr. G," said Jimmy, who'd consumed a batch of sugar cookies, in addition to the sweet rolls.

"G'night, uncle," Daniel said with a wink. "Pleasant dreams."

Right then and there, Sam realized he'd been *had*. By his wily young nephew! And by that smart-aleck kid from Hells Kitchen. They probably had their ear glued to the wall all evening. Spying on him and Meg.

Shaking his head, he trudged back to the house. Removing his boots, he left them just inside the front door. Already feeling foolish, he checked on Davey—*sound asleep, thank God.* So far, so good. The house was totally silent. Not a cricket or a mouse was stirring.

At last, Sam thought, rubbing his hands together to warm them. *A man should never lay cold hands on a hot woman,* he reminded himself, and tiptoed inside the master bedroom.

Stripping down to his skivvies, he felt around in the dark, trying to locate his wife. He certainly didn't expect her to be still burrowed under the covers at the foot of the bed, and she wasn't.

Sometime during his exhausting man-talk with the boys, she had actually gotten up and put on a nightgown. It felt soft and fleecy to the touch. Inhaling her sweet scent, Sam cautiously cuddled up behind her, spoon-fashion, and nuzzled her hair. Not having been put through hours of senseless interrogation by the boys, his bride was deep in dreamland.

Needing a few hours sleep himself, he slipped his arm around her waist— and then froze. What in blue blazes? Raising up on one elbow, he peered into the angelic faces of two very precious members of his household: Susie, with her thumb in her mouth, and 'Miss Wolfie,' unofficial champion of every homeless or needy creature between New York and the S-G-S Ranch. *Both so innocent and beautiful.* Looking at them, all snuggled up together, Sam felt his heart melt with tenderness. What he wouldn't give to be welcomed into her arms like that?

But not tonight.

Pressing his lips to Meg's wildly scattered tresses across his pillow, he sighed deeply, then rolled over to face the other way. As aroused as he was, lying there beside his wife, the night hours had flown by. The clock chimed, reminding him that it was near dawn.

In a few short hours, a full day's work lay ahead for him and his men. *Plenty of time for loving tomorrow...* Yawning, he closed his eyes and drifted into an exhausted sleep.

Chapter Seventeen

The next morning Meg woke to find Sam and his ranch hands gone. Evidently Archie had fed the men breakfast, so at least that chore was done. Rushing around to get her outside chores done, she came upon Daniel wrestling with Jimmy in the barn. Both were covered with dirt and straw, but otherwise seemed to be enjoying themselves. No black eyes, nothing like that, though she was a little surprised to see them, since they usually rode out with the men.

However, today was Sunday, and she wasn't about to miss the opportunity to take them with her to church.

Hmm, Meg thought. Could Sam and his men be avoiding church, too? *Typical!*

"Where's your uncle?" she asked Daniel. He had Jimmy pinned down, and she figured by distracting him, she might make it a fairer match.

"Oh, Sam rode out hours ago," he said, trying to get a half-Nelson on his wiry opponent.

"Do you know where he went?" she persisted. "Now, *James,* you should be able to get out of that hold easily!"

"I know, Miss Wolfie," Jimmy grunted, getting one arm free. "All I gotta do is grab him where the sun don't shine—"

Blushing, Meg turned away, refusing to look. "Stop it, this instant!"

Both boys sat up, panting from their exertions.

"Did you boys eat breakfast with the men?" she demanded, arms akimbo.

"Sure, but we're always ready for an extra helping of good eats," said Jimmy, brushing himself off.

"Me, too." Daniel snapped his suspenders to show how empty his belly was.

"Good. Now go wash up. And don't forget to put on your Sunday-best clothes," she added. "I'll see you back at the house."

"Soon as I milk the goat," Daniel stalled, grabbing a milk pail.

"And I better collect the eggs," said Jimmy, another artful dodger.

Davey, still rumpled with sleep, appeared in the barn doorway, barefoot and in his pajamas. "Sue and I already got the eggs, Miss Wolfie."

"Come with me, young man." Meg took the eight-year-old's hand. If experience had taught her anything, she needed to give Davey his medication right away, before she got sidetracked.

Jimmy and Daniel exchanged a trapped look. Clearly they'd run out of reasons not to attend church.

"Everybody else clean up for church—no stalling, you hear?" She narrowed her eyes, warning the two older boys not to take off for the hills. She set her jaw, trying for a stern look, but somehow her heart wasn't in it. Those two were just too lovable and rascally.

"Hurry now!" she urged. "I'll have breakfast on the table faster than Dusty can chase her tail!"

~ * ~ * ~ * ~

"Daniel, you drive," Meg said, climbing into the buckboard and handing him the reins. By separating the two older boys, and letting Daniel drive, she hoped to keep the peace. With Davey and Susie perched on bales of hay directly behind her seat, she'd have instant access to them, in the event of an unexpected mishap.

Also in back, Jimmy had an incredibly fast reaction time—probably the result of years spent running with the child gangs in New York. Normally he and Daniel got along like most fun-loving youngsters, but once in a while Daniel plus Jimmy turned into instant combustion. All it took was a spark to set them off. She never could predict when the fireworks might start.

Yes, she had to admit, there was method to her madness. If *she* did the driving, who would keep a close eye on the mischief-makers in back? Or keep the little ones from falling out? This way Davey and Susie could enjoy a fine view of the hills as they rolled along, but without any mishaps that might land them all in a ditch.

Most Sundays the congregation held a potluck after church, but this particular Sunday, Pastor Tindle was supply-preaching at a small start-up church at a settlement thirty miles north along the river. Since two deacons had agreed to accompany the pastor, and several ranchers were in the midst of harvesting alfalfa and corn for their stock, Meg didn't expect a large attendance. Neither did she expect to spend half the afternoon chatting with neighbors and catching up on the latest news.

Erring on the side of caution, however, she had four jars of sun-sweetened tea and a batch of chocolate brownies stashed inside her picnic basket. Of course, none of the children knew about these treats, hidden away under the buckboard's front seat.

A reward for well-behaved children, she smiled to herself.

Of course, the Happy Valley Church met at the Grange Hall, where all social events of importance to the community were held. Early arrivals that morning, Sally Lassiter, Stan and Delia Watkins, and Mike Gehrhart were already busy sweeping and straightening benches. Mrs. Maybelle Ralston was setting the stops on the organ, while Fannie Mae distributed hymn books at the end of each row.

Daniel pulled into the yard and parked in the shade. Hopping down, he hurried around back to fill a bucket with water for their horse.

Meg shook her head at his forgetfulness in failing to help her down from the buckboard. Being able-bodied, she hopped down and retrieved her Bible and the picnic basket, while the three in back climbed over the side. Thank goodness Jimmy saw Susie hanging over the side and came to her rescue! Giving a nod of approval, Meg gathered her flock around her and ushered them up the steps, vowing to give the boys a few lessons on how to treat a lady.

The instant they entered the grange hall, all three boys began to drag their feet. Even though church was a good place to meet girls, worship hadn't become an established habit—*yet*. Despite all her best intentions, they arrived with only seconds to spare—"barely squeaked under the wire," was how her Aunt Gladys would have described the boys' lagging enthusiasm.

Scuffing their feet, they barely made it inside, before Mrs. Ralston cracked her knuckles, a clear signal that she was ready to start pounding out the opening hymn.

With so few people present, it made no sense trying to hide out at the back of the hall. Smiling and nodding to her neighbors, Meg led her reluctant brood down the aisle and scooted into the front row. Not that she was counting, but she saw more children in attendance this particular morning than adults! Everyone else within a ten mile radius who was absent was either playing hookey from God, or harvesting crops so their families and livestock could survive next winter.

But she was here for her weekly "spiritual vitamins," not to count noses. Even if nobody else came to worship, she planned to be here every Sunday, in rain, sleet, hail, or sunshine. (She hadn't decided about blizzards yet.)

Mrs. Ralston got to pumping away at the organ, which had made its way across the plains in a prairie schooner in 1854. And shock of shocks, who should be filling in for Pastor Tindle this Sunday but one of Sam's ranch hands, Walker Simmons!

Since her marriage to Sam back in early June, Meg had come to respect the ranch hands at the S-G-S for their many fine qualities. Walker, however, had such an unassuming way about him and was so soft spoken that he was the last person she ever expected to see standing up front, Bible in hand, leading in worship! *Oh, well,* she thought. *Judge the Good Book by its contents*, immediately came to mind, followed by *Judge a man by his character.*

Standing behind the pulpit, Walker had somehow lost his customary bashfulness. He invited people to call out their favorite hymns and led the singing in a clear, ringing baritone. Then he asked for testimonies, something Meg had never heard of before—until Mike Gehrhart stood up to share how he met Jesus, and got all choked up, relating how grateful he was for his wife Fannie and the children. A lot of hearty "amens" were offered up, and he sat down.

Walker led the congregation in singing all four verses of "No One Ever Had a Friend Like Jesus." Then he asked if anyone else wanted to share. Delia Watkins popped up and said a few words about being convicted of her sins, due to her wicked tongue. She alos vowed to be more grateful for her blessings from now on. Her husband Stan applauded her for her courage, and they both sat down.

Next Jimmy surprised Meg by getting to his feet. He thrust his thumbs in his hip pockets self-consciously. "Hello. Hi, everybody. I'm Jimmy. I want to thank God for my new family, Mr. and Mrs. G." He wiped his eyes on his sleeve. "And for a bed, and food to eat, and a dandy horse to ride." He took a faltering step toward Meg and fell into her arms. "You saved my life, Miss Wolfie."

Well! After that emotional confession, there wasn't a dry eye in the place.

While Maybelle Ralston played gospel hymns softly, adults and children alike clustered around the boy who had been rescued from Hell's Kitchen, New York. Words of encouragement were shared, along with hugs and quiet pats on Jimmy's head, until gradually voices grew hushed with reverence and everyone returned quietly to their seats.

Walker flipped open his Bible and cleared his throat. "I *was* going to preach this morning about the Prodigal Son. But I kind of think we've already witnessed the outpouring of Father's love on one of our own, so let's turn to Luke 15, verses 23 and 24, where Jesus tells us, 'Let us have a feast and celebrate, for this son of mine was dead.' Folks, by 'dead,' our Lord means, dead in trespasses and sin, if you get my drift. "

Stan Watkins shot to his feet and pumped a fist in the air. "Preach it, brother!"

Mrs. Ralston sang out, "Glory to God!" and played an arpeggio up and down the organ's keyboard.

Walker waited for things to settle a bit, then went on with his sermonizing. "The Father in Jesus' parable said, 'My son is *alive* again. He was lost and now is found. And so they began to celebrate.'" He closed his Bible and leaned across the pulpit. "That's it, folks. Celebrate God's love. Can't get any simpler than that."

After a quick prayer, everyone gathered around, the grown-ups shaking hands, while their children made short work of Miss Wolfie's double batch of brownies. Then everybody went home, relieved to know that even an orphan from New York's toughest neighborhood could be saved.

~ * ~ * ~ * ~

As soon as Meg returned with the children from church, she dished up a spicy chili with fresh baked bread and peach cobbler for dessert, then sent everyone out to play. She felt a little disappointed that Sam and the ranch hands still hadn't returned home, but instead of moping around the house all afternoon, she decided the sunshine was too nice to waste. Soon enough, cold northern winds would arrive from Canada, stripping the trees bare, and creating lots of extra work raking leaves.

Besides, there was still one task she had set for herself, before the house-raising, and it had begun to prey on her conscience of late. Leaving things half-done just didn't seem right, especially when she had plenty of free time this afternoon. Now was the perfect time to finish decorating Amie and Beth Gallagher's graves.

Gathering together a few garden tools, she put on her apron to protect her Sunday-go-to-meeting dress and went in search of the boys.

She found Daniel in the corral, showing Jimmy how to throw a lasso around various fence posts. "Boys, I need your help," she called.

Daniel pursed his lips. "What can we do for you, Miss Wolfie?"

"I've been looking everywhere for Sam's wheelbarrow."

"The last time I saw, it was behind the outhouse," he said.

"Yeah," Jimmy piped up. "It's behind that smelly old place."

"Well, perhaps one of you fine gentlemen could go fetch it?" Meg hinted. "Susie and Davey and I are heading out on a special mission this afternoon, and it would make things so much easier if I had that wheelbarrow."

"What kind of special mission?" Daniel asked, intrigued. "Maybe we could be persuaded to tag along."

"Now, why didn't I think of that? You boys are certainly welcome to join us. First we're going to climb that hill—" She indicated the direction they planned to take. "And when we reach the top, we're going to plant wildflowers on your Aunt Amie's grave, and your cousin Beth's."

Jimmy's face fell. "You're going to visit a graveyard?"

"They died an awful long time ago," Daniel pointed out. Still, he was always ready for a new adventure. "I suppose we could go with you, Miss Wolfie."

"Yeah, sort of as protection," Jimmy nodded. "You know: in case we run into any venomous snakes."

Meg smiled at them. "Oh, I doubt we'll run into any dangerous creatures."

"I'll take my rifle, just in case," Daniel decided.

"And I can push the wheelbarrow for you, Miss Wolfe," Jimmy insisted, not wanting to be left behind.

And so the entire clan set out on their grand adventure. The boys took the lead, carrying such essentials as a jug of lemonade, a canteen of water, and a sack of ginger snaps in the wheelbarrow. Davey carried a shovel over one shoulder, "like a real soldier."

And, of course, they *had* to take Daniel's gun, "just in case."

Halfway up the hill, Susie's short legs grew tired from trying to keep up, so she cadged a ride—where else?—in the wheelbarrow. Of course, this gave her instant access to the cookies, but since she was small, and not likely to consume more than two or three—oh, surely no more than four!—the boys saw no real harm in giving her a ride.

Even with the extra weight, Jimmy managed to push it nearly to the top. But then Daniel spotted a deer, and off all three boys went, with their floppy-eared pup Dusty loping along beside them.

Left to fend for herself, Susie scrambled to her feet. "Boys are so mean!" she screeched, shaking her tiny fists.

"No, they're just excited," Meg said, brushing dirt off the child's dress.

"Are they really gonna shoot the deer?"

"Oh, I doubt it," Meg laughed. "That deer can run much faster than they can."

Collecting the shovel and other items, she pushed the wheelbarrow the remaining distance, with Susie trudging along at her side. From the hill, they could see the boys—including Davey—leaping and tumbling in the field far below.

Arriving at the gravesite, Meg found everything pretty much the way it was, weeks before. She looked about, searching for plants that would survive the winter snows and bloom again in the spring. Of course, she immediately rejected berry bushes, as their sweetness would attract foraging animals, including bears, to the site. Since she needed to remove the weeds first, Meg began moving a few medium-sized rocks to form a nice headstone.

Suddenly Susie ran up to her, clutching several wild roses in her hand. "Look! Flowers," she panted, and dropped them in Meg's lap.

Of course, the plants were exactly what Meg needed to decorate the graves: beautiful perennials, and hardy enough to endure all seasons. "Show me where you found them, darling." And so together, with Susie chattering excitedly, they made their way down a rocky slope that was ablaze with wild, pink primroses.

Excited by their find, Meg retrieved the shovel and handed Susie a trowel. Over the next hour, they dug up dozens of plants. Emptying the wheelbarrow of edibles, they soon transferred the wild roses to the gravesite. Carefully Meg and Susie turned over the top layer of earth, removing pebbles and tenacious weeds in the process. Using the canteen, she helped Susie moisten the plants. "Use it sparingly," Meg cautioned, "just enough to give the roots a drink of water."

Time slipped away, as they very carefully transplanted the wild roses, spacing them a few inches apart. Sitting back on her heels, Meg regarded their hard work and smiled. "With luck, these roses will spread and form a beautiful blanket of bright pinks and greens."

Susie nodded. "This is a happy place."

"Shall we celebrate a job well done with cookies and lemonade?" Meg unscrewed the jar lid on the lemonade and was about to pour, when she heard the loud boom of gunfire echo off in the distance.

Concluding that the boys and Dusty had finally run the deer to ground, she didn't get up to investigate. Instead she handed Susie a cookie and took a long sip of lemonade. *Ah, yes, this is the life*, she thought, and lay back, totally relaxed, her eyes half-closed.

A few minutes later, the loud crack of a gun discharged again. This time it was closer. Evidently the boys needed a little target practice. *Oh, well*, she thought, *I suppose we can survive without venison steak tonight.* She closed her eyes for a catnap. Soon enough the boys would come charging up the hill with one of their tall tales...

~ * ~ * ~ * ~

"Margaret!" Sam roared. "Where the Sam Hill is everybody?"

He and his men had ridden in the back way, fully expecting to hitch up the buckboard and bring in the load of medium growth timber they'd cut for the new outhouse. The buckboard was in plain sight, and Molly the horse was chomping on hay in her stall, but there wasn't a human in sight. The place was deserted; almost like history was repeating itself. A eerie feeling settled in Sam's gut, bringing to mind that horrific day in 1868, when he rode in and found Amie hanging by her neck in the barn, and little Beth dead in her cradle, up at the house.

Get a grip, man, he told himself. Dismounting, he started hurling orders left and right, sending the men to check every building, every shed on the premises for signs of life. When they rode in, it had felt like just another lazy Sunday afternoon. Locusts droning in the trees overhead. Birds singing. Chickens clucking out back of the barn. The mother sow and her young napping...

Even with so much tranquility, something felt terribly wrong.

Miss Wolfie and the children were missing.

Yanking off his Stetson, he wiped the sweat streaming down his face. *Let's not jump to wild conclusions,* he thought, bracing himself, in case his absolute worst nightmare was about to repeat itself. *No, dammit! No sane woman just disappears in the middle of the day. So maybe the orphans and Dusty wandered off, and she went looking for them. If so, she probably took Daniel with her. He knows the area—better than she does, anyway.*

Hoping this was the case, Sam retrieved his shotgun from his saddle and fired off both barrels. As a signal, to let them know he was home.

Still, the place felt too damn quiet. He walked through the ranch house again, searching for clues. The stove was cold. No supper tonight, he figured.

"Archie, better rustle up some supper for the men," he muttered in passing.

"Sure thing, boss."

Not wanting to break down in front of his men, Sam took off running toward the cemetery on the hill. By now he was near panic. *Oh, God! I'm going to lose my mind if something bad has happened,* he grieved. *I love Meg so much—the children, too. Please, God, don't let any harm come to them!*

He fell to his knees, full of self-loathing. *Why* hadn't he told Meg how much he loved her? Would she have believed him, even if he had? He should have spent more time courting her properly. Yes, they'd shared a few kisses, but there was so much in his heart that he'd never revealed. And now it might be too late.

"Margaret!" he bellowed. "Come back!"

Suddenly he heard a rifle fired nearby. It sounded like a Henry rifle.

Daniel! Getting to his feet, Sam stumbled toward the thickly wooded area ahead.

Chapter Eighteen

He was met at the edge of the clearing by three dirty-faced, grinning boys. Never had he seen a more welcome sight. His heart tumbling in his chest, Sam reached out and grabbed all three in a huge bear hug. "I've never been so glad to see anyone in my life!" He looked into their eager faces, checking to make sure no harm had come to them.

"We shot a deer!" Daniel and Jimmy babbled excitedly.

"A big fat one," Davey confirmed.

"Just as long as it wasn't a doe. Did you see a foal?" Sam asked. As concerned as he was about the prospect of a motherless foal falling prey to wolves, he was even more ecstatic, knowing his boys were safe.

"It had antlers." Jimmy spread his fingers over his head. "Big ones."

Daniel nodded. "It's that old moss-eared stag that tore up our garden two years ago."

"Then no harm's done," Sam said, relieved. "Do you need some help getting it back home?"

"Well, yeah," Daniel said, looking at his uncle strangely. "Are you all right, sir? You look kind of weird."

"Oh, I'm all right, now that I know you're safe." Sam gave his nephew a kiss and ruffled his unruly hair.

"Never better, sir."

"Great. Good job, men." He wrapped them all in another tight embrace. "I'm so proud of you all."

"We could use some help dressing out the deer," Jimmy hinted, looking up at Sam with adoring eyes.

Sam hesitated, suddenly realizing that he still needed to find Meg and little Susie. "Ordinarily I'd say 'yes.' You know I'd love to help you pack in that old stag, but—" He raised his hand as they started to whine and beg. "Whoa. Hold on. When's the last time you saw Miss Wolfie, boys? And little Miss Susie-Q?"

"Musta been hours ago," said Davey, scuffing his shoes in the dirt.

Jimmy nodded. "Yeah. Hours ago."

"It was quite a spell back, Uncle," Daniel confirmed. "I'm sure they're all right—"

"Where did you last see them?" Sam said, ready to put the fear of God in his boys if they didn't get more specific.

"Right over there, halfway up the hill," Daniel pointed. "Paying their respects to Aunt Amie and little Beth, I reckon."

"The graveyard?" Sam shook his head. "Now, why the Sam Hill?"

"Are we in some kind of trouble?" asked Jimmy, starting to look worried.

"No, of course you're not. I just never expected—" He took off his hat and scratched his head, perplexed. "Will I *ever* figure out the way that woman's mind works?" he asked himself.

"Do you want us to go with you?" Daniel asked.

"No, that won't be necessary." Sam had a faint smile on his face. "Thanks, boys," he said, swallowing them up in another big hug. "You hurry back home and saddle up a couple of horses. Tell Slim I want him to go with you. He can help you dress out the meat. He's one of best hunters I know. Now you boys get moving!"

He strode away, moving fast. A man with a firm purpose.

Jimmy scratched at a chigger bite. "Is Mr. G gonna give Miss Wolfie a spankin'?"

"I dunno," said Daniel, "but he's acting mighty strange."

"Mr. G loves Miss Wolfie." Since Davey rarely spoke, his opinion carried great weight.

"You think maybe?" Daniel shouldered his rifle. "All I know is that's the first time Uncle's ever kissed me." He shook his head in disbelief. "And all those hugs—eeeiiuu!"

"Weird," Jimmy agreed.

Halfway across the field already, Sam turned, walking backwards. "Quit your jawing!' he yelled. "And make tracks. Before a cougar or wolf pack steals your prize!"

~ * ~ * ~ * ~

No stranger to the bleak cemetery, Sam was breathing easier by the time he reached the hilltop. He was well acquainted with the scattered pebbles and rocks, the barrenness of the place. He certainly hadn't chosen the spot for its beauty. Out of his mind with grief at the time, he had just wanted a safe place for Amie and Beth that wouldn't attract predators. Wolves, cougars, coyotes, wolverines and bears had an uncanny knack for sniffing out carrion and dead bodies, even buried deep underground. Fearing what these natural enemies of man might unearth, he had chosen the hardest, most storm-ravaged rocky soil he could find for their graves.

Being tender hearted, Meg had no doubt hoped to surprise him by rearranging a few rocks and doing a bit of weeding. Sort of like how she'd begun to decorate the front room of their new house. Women enjoyed doing that sort of thing—call it instinct. And it was nice, really nice, the little feminine touches that made things homey for him and the children. *However,* he hoped to God he never walked up this hill and found a bunch of blanched bones scattered around.

He quickly spotted his hard-working wife and her small accomplice snoozing in the tall grasses, not far from a small patch of half-wilted flowers—some kind of wild roses, if he wasn't mistaken. Nearby lay a jar of lemonade, judging by its smell, and an empty canteen. Deciding to look around, he stepped around the angelic pair and went to see what other mischief they'd been up to.

He walked to the edge of the hill, looked in every direction. He recognized the overgrown bramble bushes, the thickets of scrub oak. Following the wheelbarrow tracks down the slope, he saw red boulders and rocks where they'd always been. He hadn't prowled around much of late, but everything looked pretty familiar. Only thing missing was the resting place of his first family. Where the Sam Hill had they gone to? Were his eyes starting to play tricks on him? Sure, he was in his mid-thirties, but he could have sworn he knew this place like the back of his hand.

Come on, Miss Wolfie, where'd you hide them?

He imagined himself groveling at her feet, and her smiling down at him with a teasing little smirk. *'Why, Mr. G, I hid them in plain sight,'* she would reply, in her best New York accent.

While this dialogue was going on in Sam's head, Meg and Susie continued to catch up on their rest, following what must have been demanding work, considering the large patch of flowers they had planted. With nothing better to do, Sam gathered the shovel, hoe, and several hand tools, and stacked them next to the wheelbarrow. He kept glancing over at Meg. She was likely to get a sunburn on that cute little nose of hers. Even so, she looked so relaxed, he hated to disturb her.

Pulling off his Stetson, Sam cautiously stuck it on the hoe handle and positioned it *just so*, where it would shade her face and block out the sun. Of course, the sun kept moving, so he had to adjust the hat's position periodically. After adjusting his hat several times to no avail, he sat down beside his sleeping beauty, using his body to block the sun's rays.

Watching her up close, he realized this was the first chance he'd ever had to study Meg when she wasn't in constant motion—or talking a blue streak! Grinning, he shifted his body, just enjoying the view, while he protected her fair skin from the elements. Over the summer she had acquired a few freckles on her cute little nose and the backs of her hands. *Never noticed those before.* And her fingernails were rough from digging around in the dirt. Sam lowered his head to examine a tiny blister on her thumb.

What a kind and generous and loving spirit she had, to create a flower garden in Amie and Beth's honor. Deeply moved, he buried his face in her long, tangled hair and breathed in her scent. He smelled vanilla and lemons, not to mention a hint of the chili powder she used to spice up her bean dishes. Just one of many ways she catered to the men's taste buds.

Reclining beside her, Sam marveled at how delicate and beautifully made his wife actually was. But what drew him to her went deeper than physical attraction. She was bright, courageous, strong in faith— By comparison, he saw himself as large, muscular, and brainy, but also quite undeserving of this amazing creature.

Even taking their differences into account, he still believed that in some mystical way, they had been drawn to each other over thousands of miles—or to put it in spiritual terms, *destined* to live in joyful harmony and love. Sam had no idea what the future held, but gazing down at his drowsing bride, Sam silently pledged himself anew to make Miss Wolfie's happiness his first and foremost priority.

Whatever it takes, Lord, he conceded, sitting up and reaching for a long-stemmed blade of prairie grass. Cherishing benevolent feelings toward his wife was one thing, but he was almost certain she would chew him out if he let her sleep through supper. Especially when Archie was serving up venison steaks tonight!

He tickled her nose with the long stem of grass, flittering it lightly over her skin, like an annoying bee or a butterfly. When he touched her lips, she came out of her 'coma' in a hurry, waving her arms and sputtering.

"Wh-what was that?" she exclaimed, squinting up at Sam. Even with his head surrounded by the sun's halo, she knew he was no angelic being.

"Wake up, sleepyhead," he crooned, stealing a kiss.

"Mmphf!" Startled, Meg waved her arms some more—until she realized what he was up to. Then she wrapped them around his neck and gazed into his smiling face "My goodness. It's you, Sam."

"Indeed, it is."

"How long have you been spying on me?" She sat up, rescuing loose hairpins and neatening her appearance.

"Maybe an hour, maybe longer," he teased, making her feel guilty for loafing. He reached over her and started tickling her small accomplice. "Arise, fair princess," he commanded.

Instantly awake, Susie climbed into Meg's lap. "I helped Mama plant the flowers," she told Sam.

"I saw that," he acknowledged. "And a fine job you did, too."

"We had to do *all* the work by ourselves." Susie puffed out her scrawny chest. "The boys ran away and deserve a spanking." She peered up at Sam to get his reaction.

"I'll have a serious talk with them after supper," Sam promised, biting back a smile. "Most ungentlemanly of them, not to help their baby sister."

"They spotted a deer," Meg said, hoping to lighten their punishment.

"I ran into them on my way up the hill," he divulged. "We're having venison to celebrate all your hard work this afternoon."

"I've been wanting to decorate these graves for some time," she confessed.

"Well, I wish you'd told me your plans in advance. I nearly had a heart attack when I returned and found everyone gone. For a moment, I thought something terrible had happened to all of you."

"Oh, Sam, I'm so sorry," Meg said. "You and the men were gone when I awoke, and church was so interesting, actually *more* than interesting this morning— Did you know Walker is a preacher?"

"No," he shook his head. "Walker never struck me as being a Bible thumper."

"Well, he did a fine job in Pastor Tindle's absence," she said, her eyes all lit up. "Anyway—"

"Jimmy got religion," little Miss Know-it-all slipped in edgewise.

"Yes, dear, but don't interrupt. Mr. G and I were talking first," Meg went on as smooth as silk. "When we got home from church, as you said, there wasn't a soul around. I had no idea where you had gone—

"My men and I were busy cutting down trees to build you a new outhouse," Sam started to explain.

"On a Sunday?" Her jaw dropped. "Oh, surely *not* on Sunday!"

Uh-oh. Back on the hot seat, Sam tried to maneuver the conversation away from church attendance. "Ah, but I don't see *you* objecting to the *work* you and Susie have been doing up here on the Sabbath!" He folded his arms across his chest, as if to say, *I will not be made the villain here!*

Meg stared at him hard, letting his words sink in. And then, she felt something let go inside, something she had held onto for a very long time. Call it pride, or the need always to be right. Perhaps it was the spirit of God speaking to her heart, but suddenly she saw her stubbornness in a whole new light.

"Sam, I apologize," she said, and thrust out her hand. "I shouldn't have said what I did. Please forgive me. You are right! Work is work, and us getting into a power struggle makes no sense at all."

Seeing Sam's harsh expression soften made her want to weep. He took her hand and gathered her close in his arms. "Oh, my darling girl!" he whispered hoarsely, burying his face in her hair. "I never meant to offend you."

"We need always to be open with each other. Like lifelong friends." She smiled up at him, and tenderly stroked his ruddy cheek. "I guess I got my priorities mixed up. I thought— Well, I was wrong to berate you."

He chuckled deep in his throat. "My righteous wife. I know you've been after me forever to attend church. And what did I do? In the middle of the night I got this brilliant idea about how I was going to surprise you! By building an outhouse." He rolled his eyes. "No wonder you got upset."

"How can I be mad at you for doing a good deed?" A nervous hiccup escaped her. "Oops, sorry." She ducked her head sheepishly. "Besides, you're in good company: Jesus healed on the Sabbath. So who am I to criticize, when you and your men were willing to use what little spare time you have, doing something that benefits every single person on this ranch."

"God, I love you," he exclaimed. "I'm so lucky to have you in my life."

Suddenly an impatient little hand reached up and tugged at his sleeve.

"I need hugs, too," Susie insisted.

And so he reached down and drew the child into the circle of love. *What a great day this has turned out to be,* he marveled. It hadn't turned out even close to what he expected. Still, he had learned a valuable lesson that day. Meg, too, he suspected.

And if it took a little squabble to put them on the same page, so be it, because this wasn't a case of who had spent his or her day more profitably. They had both been motivated by a desire to bring benefit to the other. Each of them had done something to please the other, and at the end of the day, both were richer for it.

"Thank you for the new outhouse you're going to build," Meg told him, as they loaded everything up in the wheelbarrow and set out for home.

"And thank you both for planting such beautiful flowers," Sam said, giving Susie a piggy-back ride down the hill.

"It was supposed to be a surprise," Susie confided in his ear.

He reached over and plopped his Stetson on his wife's head. As always, trying to protect her from too much sun. "Your willingness to plant a garden in Amie's and Beth's honor," he nodded toward the blanket of pink roses, "is one of the finest gifts I've ever received."

"I know how hard it is to lose the most important people in your life," Meg said, put to the blush by his praise.

Ah, thought Sam, ignoring the tear sneaking down his cheek. *My wife may be young in years, but inside she has the makings of a wise old woman.*

~ * ~ * ~ * ~

That night every man, woman, and child on the S-G-S Ranch feasted on venison. After dinner, Manuel strummed softly on his guitar, and everyone sang songs under the cottonwood trees. The moon shone bright, lighting up the children's eager faces, as they tossed popcorn in the air for Dusty to catch. A couple of the men took out their utility knives and whittled wooden decoys to use in the fall when thousands of ducks and geese flew south from Canada. Every man had a tall tale to tell, it seemed, but the mightiest hunter among them that night was young Daniel. At least in his own mind.

"I'll get Jimmy moved over from the bunkhouse tomorrow," Sam told Meg. They were sitting together, propped against a tree trunk, sharing body warmth. Things were winding down for the night, and he was eager to try out the big four-poster, especially since he'd installed a latch to keep the children from "sleepwalking" after dark.

"What about Daniel?" she whispered, so as not to waken Susie, who lay sprawled across her legs, fast asleep. "He's part of the family, too, isn't he?"

"He's my sister's son."

"Where's his mother? Is he her responsibility, or ours?"

"A better question might be 'Where's his father?'" Sam said. "The last I heard, he was trying his luck at the gambling tables in some mining town in Idaho. May even be dead by now."

"So for all practical purposes, his father is out of the picture," Meg said, shivering.

"Are you getting cold?" he asked, happily distracted. "Here, put your hands in my pocket. Come on, snuggle a bit." He opened his coat and gathered her close to share his warmth.

"Mmm, better already," she acknowledged.

"What's mine is yours."

"So where's his mother?" Meg asked, burrowing her nose in his chest hair. "Has anyone told you you're warm as a bear rug?"

Sam laughed low in his throat. "I'm a whole lot friendlier than a bear. Easier to tame, too," he threw out, hoping to lure her into his lair.

Her eyes sparkled up at him, shining in the firelight. "I suspect you'll come in mighty handy when winter comes."

"Oh, yes," he drawled. "Enough to heat up our entire cabin."

"In the meantime, we need to move *both* boys out of the bunkhouse," she said. "We have plenty of room."

"No problem. Daniel and Jimmy can room together." *I'll just move their bedrolls in the morning,* he was thinking, driven by urges that his sweet, innocent wife seemed to know nothing about.

"They get along real well, almost like real brothers, don't you think?" She gazed up at him with such trusting eyes.

"When they're not fighting," Sam said, hoping to bed his wife without the constant chatter.

"We'll be a real family then," she sighed.

"It's a start anyway." He stooped to carry Susie inside, only to discover that his new 'daughter' had bladder issues. His right pant leg was soaked.

Ah, the joys of childhood, he chuckled softly. Once again, the laugh was on him. Only this time around, he had not one, but four children to raise. And a wife with a heart of gold, who hadn't a clue what sexual frustration can do to a man who hasn't had marital relations in six years!

Chapter Nineteen

Well, they got through the next few days better than Sam expected. He and Margaret had settled in together, sharing the same four-poster, his little wife talking a mile a minute about everything under the sun, sometimes never shutting up until far into the night.

They both worked hard all day, so he couldn't fault her for wanting to learn everything she could about how he spent his days. And likewise, a husband *should* want to know how the "little woman" spent her time. Who said what, and who did this or that. Who scraped her itsy-bitsy knee, and who got caught smoking behind the new outhouse—that kind of thing. The only problem Sam had with all this sharing was that morning came around way too fast, leaving him too dog-tired to focus.

Besides, if he so much as *looked* at her, he'd want to touch her, and that would lead to making love, or trying to, without offending her "delicate sensibilities." At least that's what Amie used to call it. She used to say he was "too big," and "too intense." Incomprehensible accusations that made no sense. What was he supposed to do? Chop the damn thing off? Prance around like some two-bit stage actor?

Most of the time his first wife Amie got her jollies playing cat and mouse games with him. Sam hated living like that. He never did figure out why Amie couldn't just be *real*. He had cared deeply for his first wife, but nothing he did ever seemed to be enough.

This time, however, his strategy would be different. He had already resigned himself to introducing his new wife to married life *gradually*. Offer her neck rubs, back rubs, foot rubs—anything to help her unwind. Unlace her shoes for her. Shave every morning—maybe even at night. Gaze tenderly into her eyes. Give her soulful looks. Whatever the hell it took. Just thinking about having to hold back and put on a show made his stomach churn!

Was there not one single woman left on the planet who appreciated a man for his maleness? Had women completely forgotten that "in the beginning God made them male and female," and that He wanted them to find pleasure in each other?

Of course, he didn't dare quote chapter and verse to Meg. A practicing Christian like her would simply throw everything he said back in his face. And wouldn't *that* be embarrassing! Anyway, he'd given up all that religious malarkey long ago—never worked with Amie.

So how could he win his bride's affection? No one could force another person to love him. And he wasn't looking for false love. Going through the motions was sheer hell. Love had to be freely given from a heart that was full to overflowing.

Another thought occurred to Sam: Family was important to Meg. And with a house full of orphans, perhaps she saw no real purpose in engaging in the marital act. Aside from procreation, Sam could think of plenty of other reasons why sex played a major role in civilizing the male animal. Hadn't he read a medical article recently about how frequent sexual congress helped liberate men?

While he wouldn't go so far as to say that sex helped rid men of warlike tendencies and make them more compliant to social mores, it *did* improve a man's disposition; it definitely did.

Maybe the author of that article *did* tend to stretch the truth a bit, but he made a very good point: Good sex could cure a lot of the world's ills. *So sayeth I, and every other male with an unresponsive wife,"* Sam muttered, and rolled over in bed, wondering what it would take to get some sleep...

"Sam? Sam, are you still awake?" his chatty little wife demanded. Perched on his shoulder for easier access to his left ear, Meg gave him an impatient shake. "I haven't finished telling you about—"

Sam reared up in bed, causing his bride to give a startled squeak. "Woman, you try my patience!"

She blinked. Looking surprised, she licked her lips. "I-I do? How?"

"Don't ask. You wear me out with so much chatter. What I really need from you is—"

Her blue eyes lit up. "A goodnight kiss! Yes, of course! Why didn't you just come right out and say so?" She pounced on him playfully, tickled him unmercifully. "Ready or not, here comes Kiss Number One. Pucker up, Sam." And she began to bombard him with kisses. By the time she got to Kiss Number Eleven, they were both laughing so hard that she let *him* assume the superior position.

"So you've lost count, have you?" He grinned down at her in the moonlight spilling across the bed. "The trick, my pretty little vixen, is never count out loud. Here, let me show you how it's done."

"I rely, of course, on your vast knowledge of anatomy," she said nervously wiggling around beneath him. "Being a doctor and all."

"I assure you, kissing techniques never came up for discussion during my service in the Fifth Army." Fighting to keep a straight face, he lowered his head and blew gently against her soft breast through her nightgown. "Mostly I was busy setting bones and treating gunshot wounds."

"Really?" Overwhelmed by the strange sensations his fingers were evoking, she lifted her head from the pillow and stared down at herself. "What on earth are you doing?"

"You could say I'm examining my wife," he chuckled, working his way down her torso.

"Ooh, that makes me feel so warm," she whispered. "Do you suppose I'm coming down with a fever?" Her eyes grew wide with concern. "I've heard about travelers dying of cholera on the Oregon trail—"

"Trust me, Mrs. G., you're in perfect health."

"It's not contagious?"

"Oh, yes, *very*." Secretly delighted by her responses, Sam playfully nipped her belly button through her nightgown. "You seem to be warming up quite nicely."

"Then why do I feel so strange?" She stared up at him, her left wrist draped fetchingly across her forehead.

"It is possible you may wish to disrobe." He cleared his throat to hide his amusement. "In order to further the, uh, examination."

"But that would require *you* to close your eyes," she said, hitching her little derrière to get comfortable. By this time, Sam had one hand caressing her secret place, for want of a better word, rather *intimately.*

"Better if *you* close your eyes," he suggested. "One of us has to see in order to proceed. Otherwise—"

"No!" she said, shoving him off the bed. "I am not the fool you take me for!"

The twinkle in his brown eyes, as he climbed back into bed, told her all she needed to know: Sam Gallagher was up to no good!

"Without mutual trust, my dear, we'll never cover all the kissing techniques," he sighed. "It's entirely up to you, Meg. Personally, I'd just as soon get a good night's sleep."

"So you're saying..." She nibbled her index finger, trying to figure it out for herself.

"Kissing is only limited by one's imagination." Folding his hands over his chest, he faked a yawn and watched her through his eyelashes.

"You mean—*everywhere*?"

"Mm." Sam smiled amiably, pretending to be asleep. In his head he was asking himself, *Will she or won't she stop jabbering, and jump my bones?*

Meanwhile Meg was trying to picture how it would be to kiss his big handsome body all over. *Just as an experiment, of course. And what would be the repercussions? What if I tweak his fur, or do something outrageous? Will he roar like a lion? Send me packing if I don't please him?* She muffled her giggles beneath the quilt. *What if he makes me sleep outside with the dog?*

At this point, her imagination was running wild. Her heart was racing, and her body fairly tingled—decidedly hot and extra sensitive to the touch. As a new bride, she still didn't know *what* to expect, but after several days of Sam putting out feelers, both of them were clearly at the place where they needed to take the next logical step. They needed to reach out in faith to each other, and form a bond that would stand the test of time.

But did she love Sam? More important, did he love her? For without love, she feared their marriage—*any* marriage, for that matter—would be like trying to make a painter's easel stand upright on only two of its three legs.

But enough fanciful thinking, she told herself. *Sam is too much of a gentleman to make my mind up for me. I must take the bull by the horns, to use the cowboy's vernacular. Otherwise nothing is going to hap—"Aawkkk!!"* she screeched.

Suddenly Sam was on top of her, and from the feel of things, every part of him was very much awake. "Let me put you out of your misery, Margaret," he proposed, already unbuttoning her nightgown. "Otherwise you'll be over-analyzing the physical side of our relationship from now until eternity!"

"Oh, I certainly don't want to do that!" she said, blushing. "Here, I can unbutton—"

"Not tonight, sweetheart." Capturing her busy little fingers, he guided them to the buttons on his skivvies. "You work on things down there, while I free you from this delightful but totally unnecessary nightgown."

"I suppose you're in a bit of a hurry—"

"Damn right!" Tugging her nightgown over her head, he cast it aside. "Much better."

"You popped my buttons!" she gasped, as his mouth came down on hers, and suddenly everything else she was going to say flew completely out of her head, including how she was going to recover all those buttons in the morning.

On a slightly different mission, Sam moved with great urgency, faster than she ever suspected such a tall muscular man was capable of moving. "Forgive me, Meg," he said, positioning himself between her legs.

"What are you doing?" She lifted her head from the pillow to discover what was causing so much friction and grew quite light-headed. "Are you quite certain this is neces—"

"You, my dear, are the most talkative female I've ever met!" He gritted his teeth and entered her sweet, hot haven with a single stroke. The fact that he could breach her hymen so fast was a real salve to his conscience. He was not an insensitive man; far from it. But to find her so moist and ready for mounting was a truly mind-blowing experience.

The difference between initiating his first virgin wife and his second made him realize that they were poles apart when it came to sexuality. Amie was stiff and dry as dust, scared out of her wits, viewing the whole experience as something to be endured Unfortunately that never changed.

Meg was just as inexperienced, but her eagerness to engage him in conversation was oddly endearing and presented a different challenge, to satisfy her wildest fantasies. "I'll lend you my anatomical charts, should you have any questions afterward."

Pushing deep and feeling her eager response, Sam began to ride her hard. "For now, just hang on tight and enjoy the ride!"

"Actually it feels rather...wonderful," she gasped, starting to get the hang of things. When he started to kiss and suckle her breasts, she became aware more and more of the powerful sensations that swept over her. The feeling was *glorious!* Her entire body was consumed by fiery impulses that heightened her excitement.

As her body started to soar, it was impossible *not* to respond. For in that sublime moment, Sam became totally one with her, just as she became a part of him!

Locked in this magical embrace, Meg knew what it meant to be a woman fulfilled. Every fiber of her being felt loved. It was as if Sam had opened Pandora's box of secret treasures and in this wildly tumultuous physical act, answered all the unspoken longings of her heart.

She *adored* what he did to her body. Intuitively Sam had awakened a hunger inside that she never knew existed before. All her life she had been searching for completion. Through all the long dark days of the past, her faith had sustained her, but she had always sensed that some essential ingredient was still missing. Somehow the answer had always eluded her. Until now. For the first time in her life, she *belonged*. She felt *connected*. She felt *well loved*.

At last she realized that *words* could never convey the love and joy she sought as powerfully as actions did. As intelligent as Sam was, he had gone with pure instinct. He had reached deep inside and fed her need to be loved as never before.

She stretched deliciously. "Oh, Sam," she cooed. "Do it to me again."

Without withdrawing, he rolled her on top of him. He couldn't remember his body ever feeling this good before. "Your turn, sweetheart," he whispered in her ear. "Do it to me, baby, do it to me. Don't be shy!"

She lifted her head, her tresses in wild disarray. "Do what?" she asked, with a silly smile on her face.

"Do unto me what you'd like me to do to you," he grinned, arms outstretched and totally at her mercy. "I'm yours, baby. Feel free to take full advantage."

"Oh!" she said, squirming around a little to make sure he stayed hard inside. Being on top had definite advantages. For one thing, she could ride *him*. She moved experimentally, enjoying the fullness as his phallus probed more deeply, provoking her to play the vixen. Bending over him, she rubbed her beasts against his chest fur. She played with his nipples, and felt his chest muscles contract. The excitement mounted. Fascinated by his responses, she flexed the muscles in her saddle and felt him begin to move inside her.

He threw back his head and groaned. "Do it to me, baby!"

And so she put her love into action, proving again and again that the miracle of love was meant to last forever. As often as they made love...the infallibility of love proved itself, over and over and over again. But alas, eventually they ran out of energy!

"Good night, Mr. G." Meg yawned and stretched like a cat. "That was so... liberating."

"Happy to oblige, Mrs. G."

She didn't say another word till morning.

~ * ~ * ~ * ~

Their practice sessions continued nightly with increasing enthusiasm. Every night after supper, while Meg washed the dishes and put Susie and Davey to bed, Daniel and Jimmy hurried to finish up their outside chores. Then the boys hightailed it back inside to dry the dishes and prepare for bed. Often the kerosene lights were doused and everyone was in bed before the clock struck eight.

After four days of observing the two older boys' unusual need for sleep, Meg's suspicions suddenly went on high alert. Usually Sam visited the bunkhouse each night to assign various duties to be done the following day, so he hadn't really noticed the boys' eagerness and, indeed, their *insistence* upon "hitting the sack" at such an early hour.

When she mentioned the boys' odd behavior, Sam dismissed her concerns, saying, "They pretty much do a man's work and never complain. Maybe they're having a growth spurt, Meg. It only makes sense at their age that they'd require more sleep."

"I don't know," she said doubtfully. "There's an awful lot of snorting and giggling going on in their room after dark."

"Oh, for the love of Mike!" Sam exclaimed. "Boys will be boys, Meg."

"So it's nothing I should be concerned about?" she asked.

"Perfectly normal." Eager to continue their ongoing experiment, he walked her inside their bedroom and barred the door. "Now where did we leave off last night, my love?" he asked, unbuttoning his shirt with a big smile.

Not about to be left behind, Meg ran behind the privacy screen and began discarding her clothes helter-skelter. "I think we're at Position Number Forty-six—or is it Forty-seven?"

"Close enough." Eyes partially closed, Sam solicitously waltzed his vixen wife toward the four-poster. They were right on the verge of taking their lovemaking to new heights, when...

They were brought back to reality by the ferocious pounding of fists on the front door.

"Sam! Sam! For the love of God, open up!"

Reluctantly Sam lifted his head from his wife's cleavage.

"What the Sam Hill—?" he grumbled.

"Open the door, Sam! It's an emergency!" The knocking grew more frantic, accompanied by kicking the door. "Open up, dammit!"

Giving Meg a conciliatory kiss, Sam rolled out of bed and sat up. "Hold your horses," he yelled. Making a grab for his trousers, he stumbled out the bedroom door.

In the living room, he spotted Daniel, sleepy and disoriented, standing on a chair in his nightshirt, reaching for the shotgun over the fireplace. Nearby Jimmy was busy loading shells into the Henry rifle.

"I'll handle this, you two." Sam snatched the weapons from their hands and set them on the mantelpiece. "It's all right, Daniel. No need to get so excited."

"Sam, I need you to come quick!" Several more kicks were delivered to the front door. The man on the other side of the door began to sob. "Please, Sam. It's Leona."

"Hold on, I'm coming," Sam said, calmly getting his medical bag.

Barbara Dan

Meg came out of their bedroom in her robe. "How can I help?"

"Just keep an eye on these two desperadoes," he said, indicating the boys. "I need to finish getting dressed."

Their late night visitor, now desperate, pounded his fist. "Have a heart, Sam. Open—" *Bang! Bang! Bang!* "—the—" *Bang! Bang! Bang!* "—door!"

"Coming!"

Meg held a finger to her lips to shush the boys, who were muttering threats through the door. "Stop behaving like a pack of wild dogs," she chided them.

Jimmy was shaking like a leaf. "It's some crazy man out there!"

"No, it's my neighbor, Len Peterson, if I'm not mistaken." Stuffing his shirt into his pants, Sam paused to ruffle the boy's hair. "Now calm down, partner. We're not in any danger."

With that, he picked up his medical bag and flung open the door.

Usually tough as nails, his long time friend stood on the porch with tears streaming down his face. "She's bleeding, Sam."

"I'll saddle up and be right there."

Slim Rowlands stepped out of the shadows, leading Sam's horse. "From all the noise, I figured you might be needin' your horse, boss."

Sam clapped his foreman on the shoulder. "Thanks, Slim." Securing his bag to the saddle, he stuck his left foot in the stirrup and swung into the saddle.

"I'll be back as soon as I can," he called, then turned to Peterson. "Let's make tracks, Len. You can tell me what happened on the way."

Meg waved to them from the porch. "Tell Leona I'm praying for her and the baby," she called.

The words barely left her mouth, when she heard the clatter of horses' hooves on the wooden bridge crossing the creek.

They were gone.

Turning, she bumped into Davey and Susie, wandering around like sleep-walkers. "All right, everybody, back to bed. March!" she said, herding everyone inside and barring the door. "Time for bed. I'll tell you everything in the morning."

~ * ~ * ~ * ~

Leona's screams could be heard even before her husband and Sam Gallagher reached the barn. Katarina, Len's youngest daughter from his first marriage, stood out in the cold, waiting by the gate with a kerosene lamp.

"Pa, you gotta come quick. I think Ma's dying!" She ran forward, clutching his hand.

"Where are your sisters, Jessie and Hildy?" Len frowned. "Didn't I tell you to take care of baby Joey?"

"Things are bad, Pa. Real bad," she said, running to keep up with his long hasty strides toward the house.

"And where are your brothers?" he demanded. "Didn't I tell you kids not to leave the house?"

"They're up in the hay loft. They got real scared, Pa. There's so much blood—"

"Calm down, Len," said Sam, interrupting Len's tirade. "Stop ragging on the kid, okay? We need to get Leona's bleeding stopped. I'll do what I can, but we need cool heads here."

"It's all my fault," Len blubbered. "I never expected this to happen."

"How is it your fault?" Sam asked. Pausing to scrape mud off his boots, he looked the man straight in the eyes. "What did you do to her?"

"I, uhm—I've been feeling edgy lately—not getting any lately, y'know—and I thought she wasn't very far along, so it shouldn't matter if I—" His gaze shifted to Katie, who was listening to every word like a bird dog on point. "Well, Sam, I thought if I could just knock off some rocks, I might get a decent night's sleep."

"Just how far along *is* Leona?" Sam's face turned grim in the lamplight.

Len scratched his head. "Hard to tell. She had little Joey ten months ago, and she's been nursing, so she never did get her monthlies after he was born. How should I know?" he burst out. "It's not as if I set out to do her harm!" He broke down, sobbing again. "I love Leona, Sam."

"Yeah, I know, man, but you've got to pull it together." Sam patted his friend on the shoulder.

As he entered the house, all three of Len's daughters from his previous marriage clustered around him with anxious eyes. To distract their fears, he began assigning practical chores. "Jessie, can you boil water? And, Hildy, I need you and Katie to bring me some clean sheets and towels. Meanwhile I'll take a quick peek at the patient, all right?"

As he entered the bedroom, Len started to draw back. "Hey, Len, toughen up. I need your help."

"I think I'm gonna throw up," Len said, his face ashen.

"Buck up, my friend. You made this baby, and I know how you love children, so roll up your sleeves and lend a hand." Putting words into action, Sam washed and scrubbed his hands, using water from the basin on the dresser. Then he opened his medical case and poured alcohol over his hands and forearms and dried them, before drawing back the bed sheet from Leona's inert body.

Between her thighs lay a premature baby, barely breathing. The cord was still attached. Sam grabbed a pair of sharp scissors from the nightstand and handed them to Len.

"Boil these for five minutes. Find some strong thread from your wife's sewing basket; boil that, too. And while you're at it, wash your hands with lye soap. Scrub hard. Clean fingernails, too. Now hurry!" He turned and picked up the baby, none too gently.

"Hey, watch how you handle my kid!" Len said.

"I'm trying to revive him." Clearing the phlegm from the baby's mouth, Sam began to blow gently into the infant's nose and mouth.

Hildy and Katie came running into the room, carrying a stack of towels and sheets.

"Is he going to live?" Hildy gasped.

Sam was too busy gently massaging the infant's chest with two fingers and breathing into its mouth to respond. "Come on, come on!" he said under his breath. "Come on, little one, *breathe.*"

A tiny hiccup, followed by the faint flutter of eyelids, raised Sam's hopes—but only slightly.

"How's he doing? Is he alive?" Tiptoeing in, Jessie held between two oven mitts the pot of boiled water containing the scissors and black carpet thread. She set the pot down on the bedside table and backed away, clearly terrified.

The infant chose that moment to take in a breath and let out a frail cry.

Everyone stood around adoringly. "Pa, it's a boy!" Katie said.

Len stood in the doorway, looking green around the gills. He raised a quavering hand, pointing toward the bed. "Wh-what's that sticking out of Leona's...b-bottom?"

Hildy was the only member of the Peterson family brave enough to look. "It looks like a baby's foot, Pa."

"Oh, my God!"

For the next few seconds, pandemonium reigned. Len fainted dead away. Sam cut Baby Number One's umbilical cord. And Leona regained consciousness just long enough to scream, "Get it out! Get...that thing...out of me!" and fainted again.

Fortunately, Sam didn't have a squeamish bone in his body. He'd only delivered a couple dozen babies during his military career, but one had been a difficult breech delivery. Plus he'd pulled a few dead calves over the past few years.

Hastily wrapping Baby Number One in a flannel blanket, he handed the young squirt to Jessie, and ordered her to sit down, while he attended to the next order of business.

"But he's peeing on me," she whined.

"Katie, go find a diaper and some safety pins," Sam said. "You and Jessie surely must know how to change a baby's diaper."

"Yes, Mr. Gallagher," said Katie, fascinated by the whole birth process.

Jessie wasn't as cooperative. After all, she was the one getting soaked in urine. "What about Hildy?" she whined.

"Hildy can help me. The rest of you, don't make a peep," Sam growled, trying to figure out whether Baby Number Two was coming through the birth canal facing forward or facing the spinal cord. The two feet already told him it was breech.

Hildy sidled over to the bed. "I promise not to faint, Mr. Gallagher," she whispered.

"Good girl." Sam probed Leona's belly, waiting for contractions to resume. There was a fair amount of blood on the sheets, and maybe it wasn't a terrible thing that Leona had lost consciousness. He would attempt to treat her for shock after he hauled the second infant out. Hopefully it was breathing.

He lifted his head and nailed Jessie with a stern look. "Now, Jessie, I need you to be my eyes and ears, so nothing untoward happens to your baby brother, while I'm busy over here helping your Mama. You got that straight?"

"Yes, Mr. Gallagher." She made a face behind his back, but at least she stopped jiggling her baby brother like she wanted to throw him in the air.

"He's doing fine, Mr. G," said Katie. "I'll make sure of that."

Meanwhile Sam had inserted the forceps and had a better idea how things were going. He moved his stethoscope across Leona's belly, checking for a heartbeat. Not finding one, he decided to make the delivery as fast and painless as he could, so as not to cause Leona to bleed out.

"Hildy, slide a thick folded towel under your Ma, while I lift her slightly."

"Like this, Mr. Gallagher?" she asked.

"Perfect." Saying a silent prayer, Sam removed the forceps. Assuming the worst, he was all set to haul the baby out, deliver the placenta, and stanch the bleeding—in that order. He reached inside and...

Len came to abruptly. He saw the baby in Jessie's arms. "Oh, good; the worst is over. How's Leona doing, Sam?" He stumbled over to the bed and crashed to his knees. "No more babies, sweetheart. I swear it," he crooned in her unresponsive ear.

Sam reached his free hand into his medical case and pulled out the smelling salts. "Here. Give her a whiff of this. Otherwise all those sweet nothings you're pouring into her ear don't mean a damn thing!"

"Uh, sure, Sam." Len took a whiff himself, then waved the salts under his wife's nose. "Seven is enough, sweetheart, just as long as you stick around." He covered her face with wet kisses.

"Shut up, Len, you're turning my stomach with all that mushy talk." Sam let go of Baby Number Two's tiny leg and sat back on his haunches. He was starting to get a cramp in his foot.

"Len?" A faint feminine voice drifted in the air.

"I'm here, baby. Haven't left your side for a moment," said her spouse.

Oh, brother. Sam rolled his eyes.

"Mr. Gallagher," Hildy tugged excitedly on his arm. "Ma's stomach is moving up and down kind of funny. I think you should look inside again."

So Sam looked. And then he laughed, because Leona was having a glorious contraction! Even with the baby coming feet first, there was still a good chance of making a safe delivery. The baby wasn't full term, which would surely help in a breech delivery.

"Hey, Len, I really hate to interrupt all the billing and cooing," he said sarcastically, "but your wife seems to be in labor again. Do you think you could send some of your children back to bed? No, not you, Jessie—sorry. You're not off the hook yet. And, Len, I need another lantern. It's kind of dark in here."

Forty minutes later, Sam was ready to repack his medical bag and head for home. He had finally delivered Baby Number Two, a red-faced little girl with a great pair of lungs that would keep her parents up for many nights to come. Both babies were busy getting acquainted with their mother, who was a little overwhelmed by her long and arduous ordeal.

"Thanks, Sam," Len said, wiping his sweaty brow with a handkerchief. "Man, you sure saved the day."

"Happy with the way things turned out?" Sam asked, tying his medical bag securely to the back of his saddle.

"Never happier. Imagine! Twins." He puffed out his chest and gazed up at the stars overhead. "Maybe we should try for triplets next time."

"Don't come banging on my door in the middle of the night, if you ever get a crazy urge like that," Sam warned.

"Huh! You're some neighbor," Len huffed indignantly. "Besides, Leona did all the work. You just were the baby catcher."

"I'm warning you, Len, give it a rest for a while. Leona lost a lot of blood tonight, and I sincerely hope you keep that promise you made to your wife tonight. Give her time to heal. If you don't, you may lose her permanently."

"What are you trying to say—that she'll divorce me?"

"Len, I love you like a brother, but you've got rocks in your head instead of brains." He leaned forward and tapped Petersen on the forehead. "No more babies, my friend. You have eight fine healthy children and a wife who loves you. What greater riches can a man ask for?"

"Yeah, you're probably right," Len grinned. "Even counting your sister's kid, I got twice as many as you."

"Ah, but I'm just getting started," Sam laughed, and mounting up, turned his horse toward home.

Chapter Twenty

The sun was just a sliver of light coming over the hill, as he rode into the barn. By the time Sam fed his horse and gave him a rubdown, the men in the bunkhouse were beginning to stir. Exhausted, he decided to catch a few hours of sleep before swinging into full gear. Whatever needed to be done would simply have to wait.

Making a quick stop at the outhouse, he ran across Jelly Belly and Moses, who started unloading a tale of woe about a dead cow poisoning the waterhole near the northeast property line.

"Sorry, fellas, I'm beat. Gotta hit the sack for a couple of hours," he yawned, barely able to keep his eyes open. "Have Slim check it out. I'll catch up with you later."

By the time he dragged his bones up the porch steps, his head was enveloped in a mental fog. "Damn it, somebody open the door," he muttered, finding the door barred. He gave the door a couple of half-hearted punches, then wandered around back, where Dusty pounced on him and licked his face. "Good dog," he mumbled, trying to push the pup off. "Down! Down, I say! Damn it, I said, down! Oww!"

Meg opened the window and peered out. "Who's there?"

"It's your adoring husband," he replied, about to drop in his tracks. "May I come to bed?"

"Why, certainly you may," she replied. "Come around front, and I'll let you in."

"I'm too dad-blasted tired to move. How 'bout I just climb in the window?"

"It's not that big a window—"

"Stand aside, woman. I'm coming in."

"You needn't be such a grouch," she said, grabbing hold of his jacket and helping him get a leg over the sill.

"Don't start lecturing me, wife. I've been up all night on a mercy call, and I'm tired." He landed on the floor and started crawling toward bed.

"Here, you dear man," she said, helping him to his feet. "How's Leona? Did she have her baby?"

"Twins. Never have twins, Meg," he admonished, and fell face first into the soft mattress.

"Well, of course, I'm not having twins," she said, struggling to pull off his boots. "At the rate our courtship keeps getting interrupted—" A soft snore came from the bed, convincing her that now was not a good time to fight the forces of nature.

"Sweet dreams," she whispered in his ear, and went outside to greet the dawn.

~ * ~ * ~ * ~

Sam was still sleeping when Meg returned from cleaning up after breakfast down at the bunkhouse. Slim had sent the ranch hands on an errand near the northeast property line—something to do with hauling a dead cow out of a waterhole and fencing off the area. Sensing the chance for adventure, all three boys had decided to tag along. But first, she'd given Davey his medication—couldn't forget that!

Susie, as usual, was playing part-time princess, part-time chicken thief. Hearing all the clucking and squawking in the hen house, Meg grinned to herself, as she made a beeline for the coffee pot in the kitchen. She took a deep breath—*aah!* The fresh brewed aroma still hung in the air.

Today was washday. She had piles and piles of clothing, separated by color, to prove it. She sat down at the kitchen table, preparing mentally for her weekly battle against dirt. "Stinky day," she called it.

First she had to build an outdoor fire. Then she had to haul out the big iron kettle, fill it with buckets of well water, and bring it to a simmering boil. Then she had to grind up soap chips, add lye and bleach, and stir until dissolved, *then* throw in a batch of clothes. In the process, the smoke and caustic fumes always got in her hair and spattered her clothes, sometimes doing irreparable damage. At the rate things were going, she'd have plenty of material to share with the other women at their next sewing circle.

Washday was her least favorite chore. That is why, today, she was hoping to come up with a valid excuse to delay washday. *Everybody needs a holiday once in awhile*, she rationalized.

For instance, Sam was taking the day off. Not voluntarily, of course, but because he needed to catch up on his sleep. Daniel and Jimmy and Davey had ridden out with the ranch hands, looking for adventure.

So why not her?

She supposed she could take Susie and go visiting. But judging by Sam's haggard appearance when he got home, she doubted that Leona would welcome a visit just yet. Twins meant twice as much work. And the Peterson's already had six to chase after, before this latest calamity. Twins! Judging by how worn out Sam was after being there to help with the delivery, having twins must be exhausting. *Poor Leona! No, no*, Meg decided, *if Leona is strong enough to get out of bed a month from now, it will be a blessed miracle.*

So, it looked like a day of drudgery was her fate, after all. Rising from the table, Meg tiptoed into the bedroom to fetch her most raggedy work dress. Sam was still sawing logs, so she tiptoed out, quiet as a mouse, without even giving him a friendly smooch.

~ * ~ * ~ * ~

It took her over a half-hour and several trips to and from the woodpile before she had enough chunks of wood, just the right size to build a fire that would last most of the day. Then she built a tripod and hung the kettle. Not an easy job, since everything had to be *just so* before she could fill the kettle with water. Then and only then could she set fire to the wood and get down to business.

Using the wheelbarrow, Meg began stacking baskets of laundry, and moved everything out of the storage shed out back. After lining them up on the porch, she checked on Susie again, making certain that she was safely playing indoors with her dolly. The scariest thing about washday was keeping the children away from the fire. In a way, doing the wash when the boys were gone made perfect sense.

Pausing to wipe the perspiration from her brow, she noticed a tiny dust storm on the horizon. It was getting bigger, and coming mighty fast. Just like—

Goodness gracious, Meg thought, stepping down from the porch. Hadn't she seen that cloud before? No! It couldn't be...

But it was. A few minutes later, Carolyn pulled up in front, her strawberry roan Snapper raising a whirlwind of dust. Her dark curly hair bounced around her shoulders, and the look on her face was grim, as she strode toward Meg. "Forget the wash. This is a real emergency. I need to talk to Sam."

"He's sleeping." Meg gestured toward the house. "He delivered twins at the Peterson's place and only got home a few hours ago."

"Well, wake him up!" Carolyn said. "I've come direct from Granny Benson's house. She's been throwing up all night, Meg, and she's so weak now—why, she may not make it through another day!"

"What's wrong with her?" Meg asked, leading her friend up the porch steps and into the house.

"Just wake up that man of yours," Carolyn huffed, out of breath and fanning herself. "Granny's real sick."

"I-I'll be right back," Meg promised, and made a beeline for the bedroom. "Sam...Sam?"

She paused, looking around. Where had he gone? She couldn't believe a man could be sleeping so soundly a short while ago, and then vanish without a trace. His boots were gone, too, so he must have gone somewhere. She looked out the open bedroom window, then retraced her steps to inform Carolyn. "He's gone! I thought he was asleep, but he's disappeared!"

Not sure she believed it, Carolyn checked for herself and had to agree. "Maybe he went to take a leak," she said.

This led to a frantic search outdoors, all of which turned up nothing. Even Archie and the chuck wagon were gone.

Trailing behind the two women, Susie tugged on Meg's apron. "I know where he went," she said.

"Where, sweetie?" Carolyn asked. By now she'd pretty much worked herself into a frazzle, dark curly hair flying every which way, her face red as a beet. "Where did you see him?"

"I saw him and Mr. Archie go...that way!" Susie pointed dramatically, and Meg's shoulders slumped in defeat.

"Northeast. Oh, Carolyn, I'm so sorry!" she exclaimed. "Sam mumbled something in his sleep earlier about a polluted waterhole, and a dead cow floating in the water. I knew his men were headed out that way to fence off the area, so none of the herd would get sick, but I *never* expected Sam would head out that way, too."

"Well, no point crying over soiled milk," Carolyn said. "Do you know where Sam keeps his medical supplies?"

"I know he keeps a lot of bandages and medicine bottles and vials in a cupboard, but—" Meg shrugged apologetically. "Neither of us has any medical training. I'd be afraid of giving Granny the wrong thing, don't you see?"

"Pshaw!" Carolyn snorted. "What have we got to lose? If we don't do something, she's a goner, for sure. Maybe we should take a peek. Might be something in there that will help pull her through. What d'you think?"

"Well, I feel like we're reaching into a grab bag for a cure." Meg nibbled her lower lip. She was scared, sure, but also emboldened by her friend's forthright manner. "I know: Let's at least see what's in the cupboard. I'll get the key."

"Good thinking." Carolyn looked down at Susie, doing figure-eights around her boots. "Let's go brush your hair, Miss Susie. You, me, and your Mama are making a social call this morning!"

Meanwhile Meg was rummaging around in the top dresser drawer and everywhere else she could think, searching for Sam's keys. Finally she threw up her hands in defeat. "He must have taken them with him."

"Well, hot Jehoshaphat!" said Carolyn, standing arms akimbo. "Find me a screw driver or a crowbar."

"Good idea." Truly amazed how her friend's brain worked, Meg ran out to the barn and began opening boxes in search of the correct size screw driver.

She was still hoping for a miracle, when a green buckboard rumbled up to the open barn.

"Hey, Sam!" Two Bear Benson bellowed. "If you can hear my voice, I need your help—*now!*"

Dropping a box of widgets and hoof picks on the barn floor, Meg hurried out to greet Granny's son. "Oh, thank God!" she exclaimed. "We need your help." Babbling on about finding the right miracle cure for his mother, she led him into the house and pointed to the lock on Sam's medical cabinet.

"You're strong, Two Bear. Can *you* unlock that cupboard?"

"Sure, no problem." Two Bear pulled his Navy Colt .45 from his holster. "Stand back, ladies, and hold your ears," he warned and, taking careful aim, pulled the trigger.

"That was incredible!" Meg said, picking up the mutilated lock, still hot to the touch from the explosive impact. Slivers of metal lay scattered all over the floor.

"A man after my own heart." With an approving nod, Carolyn removed her fingers from Susie's ears.

"That was loud," the little girl said, watching Two Bear reholster his weapon.

"Glad to be of service," Two Bear said. "Now—where's Sam? I need his help bad."

"Gone," all three females informed him.

"However," Meg gestured grandly at the splintered lock on the now open cupboard door, "we now have access to Sam's medical supplies."

"We're thinking there must be a cure for what ails Granny," Carolyn added.

"So what are we waiting for?" said Two Bear.

Shoving all the bandages aside, Meg called off the names of each medicine, one at a time, and handed them to Carolyn, who lined them all up on the dining room table. "Zinc sulfate." "Paregoric." "Laudanum—Is she in a lot of pain, Two Bear?"

"Lord, yes! But we need something to *cure* her, not finish her off! Keep looking," Two Bear urged.

The list went on and on. There were medicines for almost everything. Breathing. Heart disease. Indigestion. Finally, Meg called out, "Dr. Philips' Milk of Magnesia," and Carolyn grabbed the blue glass bottle and held it up.

"Eureka!" she yelled, doing a happy dance. "I think we've found the Granny cure."

"Are you sure?" Two Bear lowered his eyebrows.

"My Aunt Elizabeth back East wrote me about this product two months ago," she explained. "Her friend Mildred complained of feelin' all blocked up. Well, things got worse and worse. She drank prune juice and hot lemon juice and special teas—nothing worked. Then one day she started throwing up for hours and hours. Couldn't stop. Finally the druggist gave my auntie a bottle of this here milk of magnesia. Gave it to her *free*, mind you, 'cause it had just come on the market. And wouldn't you know—it worked! Now her friend Mildred is feeling brand spankin' new— singing all the time. 'Course there *is* one drawback." She winked at Two Bear and Meg.

"What?" Two Bear squinted suspiciously at the label on the bottle.

Carolyn laughed. "Why, Mildred has got a new lease on life! Mind, she's in her sixties, but she has been carrying on like a wild woman with the male boarder who lives upstairs—"

Meg planted one hand on her hip. "Now I *know* you're pulling my leg," she said, shaking her head.

Carolyn laughed heartily. "Maybe I *did* embellish the story a little, but—" she turned to Two Bear, " you take this home and give it to Granny. Four tablespoons with lots of water. What d'you want to bet Granny is a new woman by tomorrow morning?"

"I'm not much of a gambler," he said sheepishly, "but if you ladies think it might work, who am I to argue?"

Meg walked him to the front door. "If it doesn't work, hopefully Sam will be home soon. I'll tell him you stopped by."

"Thank you, Mrs. G. I've been wracking my brain, trying to think of a way to ease her pain and vomiting. Maybe this will restore her to her old self!"

"Tell Granny about my aunt's friend Mildred," Carolyn called after him. "A good laugh always helps, especially when things are coming *up* instead of going *down*." She made a funny face, and they all laughed.

"Thanks, ladies!" Two Bear waved, flourishing the bottle, as he hurried over to his buckboard.

As they watched him turn the buckboard around and drive off, Carolyn let out a sigh. "Reckon I'd better be getting' home, too. Never know when I'll find my kids hanging off the roof, or some darn thing."

"Thanks for helping mess up my kitchen," Meg said facetiously. "And for finding Two Bear a cure to take home."

"Aw, all that it took was a little practical common sense."

"Do you think it will work?"

"*Could.*" Grinning, Carolyn grabbed her horse's reins and swung into the saddle. "You never know till you try."

"Give your children big hugs for me," Meg said, stepping back.

"Right back at you." And she took off down the road, maintaining a steady trot.

"*Could,*" Meg mused, heading back inside to tidy up before Sam came home and discovered the mischief she and Carolyn had been up to in his absence.

Could. Would. Should. Huh! At least they were sincere in their desire to help Granny. But was sincerity enough?

She decided washday could be delayed another day. At least until she got news that Granny was on the road to recovery.

~ * ~ * ~ * ~

Around about nine o'clock the next morning, Daniel rode up to the house with Jimmy and Davey. "Hey, Miss Wolfie!" he yelled. "I brought you a couple of helpers!"

Even from the porch, Meg would see that all three were covered with dirt. "It's a good thing I never got around to doing the wash yesterday," she smiled. "Come inside, boys. You better change your clothes while I fix you a snack."

"I sure missed your cooking," said Jimmy, stomping past her into the house.

"Me, too," said Davey, standing a far piece back from the other two.

"Come up here, and give me a hug," she beckoned, but he only shook his head.

"I stink awful bad, Miss Wolfie," he said, looking at the ground.

"We ran into a skunk," Daniel said. "I told Davey not to pick it up, but would he listen? *No!*"

Jimmy came outside, munching on a crisp red apple. "He's a regular stinkeroo," he confirmed, just as Meg reached out to give Davey a hug and recoiled. "Told you so."

"How about *you*?" Meg asked, turning to the two older boys. "I just bet you and Daniel put him up to it."

"Uncle Sam already raised the roof hollering at us," Daniel confessed. "But it wasn't really our fault. Davey *insisted* on petting it."

"Like it was a pussycat," Jimmy grinned.

"So what am I supposed to do with three such filthy boys?" she demanded, exasperated.

Their dog Dusty came bounding around the house to greet the boys. She took one sniff and ran under the porch, howling with distress.

What's the matter with that dog? Meg wondered, then shrugged. She had enough trouble without trying to console a traumatized dog.

"And what did Mr. G say about all this tomfoolery?" How she wished she didn't have to deal with de-skunking one very sad little boy.

"We're supposed to be your slaves, and do whatever you say," said Davey. "I didn't do it on purpose, Miss Wolfie—honest." He wiped his nose on his shirt. Getting a strong whiff of skunk, he began to retch.

"No, I don't suppose you did." Meg looked sternly at the two older boys. "Daniel, you go pick me as many ripe tomatoes as you can find in the garden. And, Jimmy, you drag the bathtub out here on the porch."

They both began to whine and complain. "Aw, do we have to?"

"Yes, and no back talk."

"What's wrong with Davey?" Susie asked, skipping around the corner of the house.

"Skunk," everyone told her.

"Try to stand down wind!" Meg choked, her eyes watering, and held Susie's nose. "Inside, young lady—go! This instant!"

Susie took one look at the boys' guilty expressions and balked. "Why should I? *I* didn't do nothing wrong."

"Right now!" Meg snapped. "I'll explain after I get Davey cleaned up. Play with your dolly," she added, more gently.

While Jimmy struggled to drag the bathtub *sideways* out the front door, instead of front end first, Daniel went through the garden, picking all the late season heritage tomatoes.

Meanwhile Meg stuck a clothespin on her nose. Then she stripped Davey naked as the day he was born. Since his clothing reeked of musk, she threw his clothes on the firewood she'd laid out the day before. The kettle had a couple of inches of water from a late night shower, so without further adieu, she touched a match to his discards. *Whoosh*, everything caught fire.

Davey strained to get away, but she nabbed him before he could escape. "Oh, no, you don't!" she exclaimed. "I'll fetch you clean clothes, but first we need to get rid of the skunk odor." Taking him by the hand, she marched him over to the bathtub.

Oh, drat! The plug was missing.

"Jimmy!" she hollered, still holding onto Davey. "Find me the stopper to keep the water from running out."

So while Jimmy ran around looking for the plug, Meg marched inside and added kindling to the kitchen stove. Daniel carried in two bushels of ripe tomatoes and looked at her with a hang-dog expression. "Where do you want me to put these?" he asked.

While they waited for more water to heat up on the stove, *she* found the plug for the bathtub—in plain sight beside the kitchen sink! Then she presented Daniel and Jimmy each with a potato masher and watched them pulverize the tomatoes. Then, because they did such a good job—and so quickly, too!—Meg had them carry buckets of warm water outside to the bathtub.

All this Susie observed with a rather supercilious air. Then she quietly went into the parents' bedroom and spritzed herself all over with a bottle of lily-of-the-valley cologne Sam had bought Meg the day they tied the knot in Cheyenne. Of course, she managed to get it in her eyes, and because Meg was busy helping Davey lather himself all over with tomato paste, and Daniel and Jimmy had snuck off somewhere to play, Susie had a screaming fit that must have lasted at least ten minutes.

In fact, she might never have got the cologne out of her eyes that day, had not Two Bear's wife Annie dropped by to report on Granny Benson's miraculous recovery.

Meg was on her knees beside the bathtub, squishing tomatoes through Davey's hair, when Annie arrived. "Goodness gracious!" Annie exclaimed, swinging down from her horse. "What's all the racket about?"

Meg pointed to Susie on the porch, hollering to beat the band. "She got some of my cologne in her eyes."

"Oh, I'll take care of that," Annie said, going to Susie. "My, what a fine pair of lungs you have, darlin'! And you're such a pretty little thing, too."

"There's clean rinse water in that bucket," Meg said, sniffing to see if Davey needed another treatment, or not.

Annie dipped a small tin cup in the bucket and held it to each of Susie's eyes, letting the water dribble down the child's chubby little cheeks. "It's going to be all better," she crooned.

"How's Granny?" Meg asked, scrubbing behind Davey's ears.

"Much improved, thanks," Annie grinned, drying Susie's tears.

"I intended to stop by this morning—" Meg rolled her eyes. "But that was before the boys ran into Mr. Skunk."

Annie nodded. "I totally understand. Wasn't it Robbie Burns who wrote, 'The best laid plans of mice and men often go awry'?"

Wrapping a towel around Davey, Meg gave him a pat on the rump and sent him scurrying for cover in his room. "Annie, if you promise not to be offended by all the mess, I'd be pleased to offer you a cup of coffee," she said.

"Why, I'd be honored." Annie gave Meg a quick hug and followed her into the house. "Granny sends her love, by the way—" She looked around the kitchen, her eyes twinkling. "Oh, I see what you mean about the mess." She burst out laughing. "It looks just like *my* house!" She rolled up her sleeves. "Let me give you a hand here, Meg."

Chapter Twenty-One

The following day was Wednesday. Having subjected the Monday wash to a strong lye solution through Tuesday night, Meg decided she was likely to get more accomplished if she did the cleaning and washing without so many "helpers" to gum up the works.

After breakfast, she sent Daniel and Jimmy back to Sam. In her note to Sam, she added— a bit facetiously, considering the chaos the boys had left everywhere—"Your kindness in lending them to me will not soon be forgotten, dear husband. I return them to you with all my blessings. —Margaret."

Of course, it wasn't very flattering to hear the boys whoop and cheer, as they rode off to help fence off the polluted waterhole and build a trench to reroute water to where the cattle could drink fresh water. "Scallywags!" she declared, and began to give the men's dirty levis a bit of rather rough treatment on the washboard.

At least now she had only two children to keep an eye on. Not to mention a ton of wash to do.

~ * ~ * ~ * ~

It took Sam and his men until noon Friday to finish moving the herd to safer pasturage and clean drinking water. They rode in late that afternoon with only one thought in mind: getting cleaned up and going to the annual Harvest Dance.

Meg met Sam at the door with a fervent kiss—and a slightly guilty conscience. Not wishing to spoil his enjoyment at the harvest time get-together down at the grange hall, she avoided mentioning the raid on his medical supplies, or the cabinet door left hanging by one screw.

Of course, the padlock was also destroyed, but she and Annie had swept away most of the evidence. Now all she could do was keep her fingers crossed that Sam wouldn't notice the damage, or the missing bottle of Milk of Magnesia, until after he'd had a chance to relax and unwind. And where better to have fun and forget one's troubles than at the Harvest Dance?

"How do you like my dress?" she asked, twirling around to show off her bright yellow dress and her ankles.

"Take care, my love, lest you blind me with your beauty," he joked, escorting her through the front door. He sniffed the air. "Ah, what *is* that delicious aroma?"

"Rabbit stew—for the potluck tonight," Meg boasted. She tugged on his arm, steering him past the medical cabinet and into their bedroom, where she had fresh clothing laid out for him on the bed. "Oh, Sam. I missed you so much!" she sighed, cuddling up to him.

But perhaps she'd overdone her affectionate welcome, because Sam raised his eyebrows and pulled back a little. "I hear you had a busy week while I was gone," he said, beginning to shuck his dusty clothes.

"Oh, a little of this, a little of that." She shrugged.

"Uh-huh!" he said noncommittally. Sitting down, he tugged at his muddy boots.

"Oh, let me help!" she said, rushing forward.

"Stand back!" He waved her off. "Much as I enjoy you lovin' on me, you'd better let me get out of my dirt first."

Meg threw up her hands in despair. She didn't want anything to spoil their fun at the harvest dance, but what if he discovered the damage to his medical cabinet, and hit the roof?

"I-I'll just take a quick peek at the stew while you clean up," she said, and skedaddled. Her petticoats flared, as she spun around in the kitchen, searching high and low for some way to conceal the damage. If only she had carpentry skills! She needed something to cover...

"Something wrong, Miss Wolfie?" Daniel asked, appearing in the open doorway. His hair was slicked back, and he wore his best shirt and levis.

Meg jumped guiltily. "Oh! You startled me," she gasped. "My, don't you look handsome? I almost didn't recognize you for a second."

"It's just me," he grinned, preening a little. "Hey, when are we going to tell Uncle about you-know-what?" He gestured toward the broken hinge hanging by one screw.

"Sshhh!" She looked around furtively. "Don't say anything! I'd rather he didn't find out until after the Harvest Dance."

"You want me to *lie*—?"

"No, no. Not lie. Just keep him from noticing—"

"Daniel," her husband's voice rumbled like distant thunder from the bedroom. "Fetch my tool box, will you? I need you to do a small repair before we leave."

Meg and Daniel froze. They looked at each other like criminals caught in the act.

"Uh, sure, Sam, I'll get right on it." Daniel said, clearing his throat. With an apologetic shrug, he took off, leaving Meg to face the music.

"Better take that stew off the stove before it catches fire." Sam stood in the doorway, wiping shaving cream off his jaw.

"Oh, Sam, I was going to tell you—" She gulped.

"I ran into Two Bear earlier this afternoon," he grinned. "How about a big smooch?"

Meg ran to him and threw her arms around his neck. "You're not upset with me?"

"Only for trying to sneak one over on me," he smiled. "I guess we both had a rough week, didn't we?"

"I really did miss you," she whispered. Standing on the toes of his boot, she gave him a proper welcome home kiss.

In return, he gave her a gentle swat on the rump. "Time to round up the children. I'll get the buckboard."

~ * ~ * ~ * ~

The Harvest Dance marked the shift between seasons, moving from back-breaking work, sun-up to sun-down, to the coming together of neighbors in celebration. Ranchers and farmers alike—made no difference how they earned their bread. They were neighbors in the best sense, and the bond between their families would remain strong forever. The friendships and spirit of cooperation would get them through anything old Mother Nature or fate could throw their way.

With the harvest in, and their barns bursting with feed to see their animals through the fall and winter, a festive mood fell over people all over the valley. And that meant gathering together for a night of square dancing and jubilation before the weather closed in once again.

People had a certain nostalgic feeling about the weathered old grange hall, too, and jokingly expressed an eagerness to return to the "scene of the crime"—referring, of course, to the plethora of weddings that frequently took place soon after the Harvest Dance. Many a romance had begun on the dance floor, and many a young couple had tied the knot after sparking too long in the moonlight.

Riding herd on the Gallagher family, Sam arrived at seven o'clock sharp. "1873 was a tough year economically for most of the nation," he told his blushing bride and those in the back of the buckboard who had big ears. "But we made it through, despite the odds," he grinned. "Hard work always wins out."

Helping Meg and Susie down, he waited for the boys to leap to the ground, then gave them a last minute inspection. "Boys, I'm damned proud of every one of you," he grinned. "Now, remember what I told you, and don't get into too much mischief."

Right away, all three boys, and even Susie, puffed out their chests with confidence. "Thanks, Mr. G," and "Gee, thanks," tumbled out of their mouths like an angelic chorus—*almost!* Then they scattered to check out who else their age was rarin' for a night of hijinks and celebration.

Not wanting to miss out on the fun, Susie stomped her foot and yelled, "Wait for me!"

When Davey came back and took her inside, Meg's eyes filled up with emotion. "Oh, Sam, they're starting to look out for each other."

"I credit you, my darling girl, with transforming all our lives," Sam put his arm around her and escorted her through the door and into the teeming crowd inside the hall. "In less than four months, you've presented me with three sons and one daughter. I think that must be some kind of a record, don't you, Miss Wolfie?"

"My goodness, I did no such thing," she demurred, then spotted several people she knew and began to wave. "Hello! Oh, look, Sam, there's Granny Benson, and Annie, and—"

"Right behind you, sweetheart." Sam was having a hard time keeping up with his diminutive wife. The changes Meg had wrought seemed nothing less than a miracle—and *he* was not even a professing believer!

"Sam," she called, beckoning. "Come and see. Granny is going to lead out with Mr. Pctcrson for the first dance!"

"I'm fit as a fiddle again, thanks to your missus," the old woman chortled.

"Well, you certainly *do* look fit," Sam agreed, searching Meg blushing face for an explanation.

Granny leaned close to confide: "Take it from me: Thet Magnesium is a miracle drug!"

"Meg? What's she talking about?" he asked, but Meg was suddenly too busy raving about his friend Len's daughters and their new dancing shoes to discuss Granny's intestines.

"How's Leona doing?" he asked Len out of the corner of his mouth.

"Huh? Oh, she's fine," his neighbor replied, almost as if he barely recognized his wife's name. "Babies are up a lot at night, but otherwise everything's fine."

"You sure about that?" Sam said, remembering the advice he'd given his neighbor.

"Y' know anyone with a mama goat?" Len asked, glancing furtively around.

"Sure. I could lend you mine—"

Granny cut in on their conversation. "Later, boys. I need to make sure Len does the two-step correctly. Can't have him trippin' me up." She led her partner away, talking a mile a minute.

Looking around, Sam spotted Meg halfway across the room, greeting some friends she'd made at the ladies' sewing circle.

With a sigh, Sam headed off to greet some of the old-timers. By now, people were pouring into the grange hall by the droves. Families mostly, bringing with them potluck dishes and everyone from the youngest baby to the oldest, most cantankerous, free thinking resident in the valley.

Leading the pack in that category was Jedidiah Whittaker, who ran for Mayor of Silvertun, population 30, in 1863, and *lost*. Old J.W. had been a sorehead ever since, but he was still the richest son-of-a-gun in the valley. Count on him to have the ear of nearly every cattle breeder and farmer present.

Due to his recent acquisition of a full-fledged family, Sam pretty much expected he'd get razzed for being so "prolific." So many of his neighbors exceeded him in terms of family size that he could hardly wait for the verbal jabs and the ribald jokes to begin.

But mostly the annual get-together wasn't about fertility. It was about sharing information about increased productivity and cultivating the land. Everyone wanted to know whose bull had produced the most calves and the breeding lines. Jedidiah Whittaker had all such information always at his fingertips. He also kept track daily of the fluctuating values of wheat, oats, and corn on the Chicago stock market, via telegraph. Except when there was a blizzard, he never failed to make his way to the telegraphy office situated .037 miles from the railroad's last stop for water, before taking the grade up to the Plinkton Mine.

~ * ~ * ~ * ~

But even J.W.'s wisdom couldn't compete with the potluck, which began at 7:30 P.M. The eats were mouth-watering. No man in his right mind passed up the opportunity to sample the ladies' cooking, and in the process, a few bachelors tried their hand at wooing some of the cooks away from their spouses on the grounds that any dang fool jackass who didn't fight to keep his woman around to provide a little body warmth during a blizzard didn't deserve her the rest of the year either! Of course, it was all done in jest—no hard feelings— and nobody threw any punches, although somebody *did* manage to spike the apple cider!

Before long, the sheer bedlam of so many people visiting back and forth became well nigh deafening. The jingle of silverware and the *clunk* of bowls of succotash, beans, whipped potatoes with gravy, and corn on the cob being set out on the tables nearly drowned out the musicians tuning up their instruments nearby. Knowing children, the women had kept back the cakes, pies, and cookies, out of sight in the kitchen.

Reverend Tindle stepped forward and led in a prayer of thanks. "For health, harvest, and all Thy bounty, we give thanks. Amen."

Then it was pretty much every man, woman and child for him or herself. Wearing an apron, Archie from the S-G-S stood behind the table, serving up his famous barbecued pulled pork. The Widow McAlister, who "enjoyed" a rather interesting reputation, having been married and widowed four times, stood beside him, serving up fried chicken and onion rings. Of course, she flirted outrageously with Archie, just as he did with her! (All innocent fun, of course.)

For practical reasons, those with young children went through the line first. Maybe the adults thought it would reduce the volume of loud talking, though it was hard to tell. The parents were twice as noisy, but at least with the youngsters stuffing their faces, it was easier to carry on a decent conversation.

The end of the line was reserved for the bachelors—those who still held out some hope, and those who'd pretty much gone sour on life. This particular night, several single men were present to check out the ranchers' pretty daughters—and a few who weren't real stand-outs, too.

Those bachelors who were gun-shy kept to the back of the line. Mark and Tim Ryan fell in that category. Not that they didn't appreciate a well-turned ankle and a pair of flirty eyes. They just weren't ready to sign on yet for a life sentence.

After supper, Sam put Jimmy in charge of Susie and Davey while he and Meg circulated through the crowd, greeting friends and catching up on the latest news. (Mostly they'd eaten too much and hoped to walk it off before the dancing began.)

Two Bear and Annie were keeping an eye on their brood, as well as on old Granny Benson, who was a little worse for wear after testing the heavily spiked apple cider.

Granny still had her eye out for the perfect dance partner, in case Len couldn't keep up with her. All this, despite her recent "close call with death." Being a good sport, Len Peterson gave the spirited old woman a twirl around the empty dance floor, before Sophie's husband, Ted Burnett, cut in "for old time's sake."

Over in the corner, Daniel and a bunch of his friends were busy laying on the charm, hoping to sweep Jessie and Hildy Peterson and Flora Frockmeyer off their feet and reap a reward— perhaps a stolen kiss or two—once the dancing began and their parents were temporarily distracted.

By now, close to two hundred people were crammed together inside the grange hall. The windows had been thrown open to let in the breeze and cool everyone off.

At last the moment they'd all been waiting for arrived: At 8:35 P. M. Jake McCandry mounted the platform and called the dancers to the floor.

~ * ~ * ~ * ~

Coming up behind Meg, Sam nuzzled her ear. "Mrs. G, may I have this dance?" he asked, a smile in his voice.

Turning, she felt his belt buckle press against her stomach, as he slid his arm around her waist and snugged her close. She laughed up at him, and in that moment, she forgot the jostling crowd. She no longer heard the flutist's shrill high pitch, or the accordion's strident tempo. They both stood transfixed, gazing into each other's eyes. The lines around his eyes crinkled with good natured fun, and in that magical moment, Meg somehow knew she was destined to love this man forever. Maybe he *was* more loose and relaxed than usual. And maybe they'd imbibed too much spiked cider, but it didn't really matter. Seeing him so eager and carefree and full of laughter, she caught a special glimpse of her husband with his guard down.

Finally! Sam Gallagher stood unmasked before her, his soul laid bare. In her mind's eye, he was transformed into a handsome knight who'd ridden in on a wild steed. Gone were the burdens and responsibilities he constantly carried on his big shoulders, day after day.

For the first time she saw her husband for the man he truly was. It came to her like a flashback, or a mystical vision, revealing him as young, with a generous heart, vibrant, full of dreams for the future, eager to share so much...and with *her*.

"Oh, Sam," she sighed.

"Now, Miss Wolfie!" His lips tightened. Clearly feeling the same powerful attraction, but tamping it down. "Whatever mischief you've got in mind, let's make it our little secret, all right?"

"But I just realized how much I love you," she blurted out—and waited to hear a similar pledge of undying love from him.

"Are you sure you can even hear yourself think in here?" he shouted against the noise all around them.

"Oh, I'm quite certain," she said earnestly, though disappointed that he wasn't more impressed by her announcement.

"Does it feel hot to you in here?" he asked, spinning her around on the dance floor.

"Actually, quite a lot. But what I *am* feeling deep inside surpasses even the joy we share when we're private!" She fluttered her eyelashes at him for fun.

"Hm. Sounds like a hot flash," he said, reverting to playing doctor.

"Why must you always do that?" Peeved, she stomped on his big toe, on purpose.

"Do what?" Sam raised his eyebrows, apparently impervious to pain.

Meg could have come right out and accused him of hiding his feelings. *'You love me. Admit it,'* she wanted to holler in his ear, but she didn't. Instead, she took another tack.

"Admit it, Sam. You like me a lot."

"Of course, I do. Wouldn't have married you, if I didn't."

Maybe the spiked punch *was* stronger than she thought. Whatever the cause, this convoluted conversation was making her confused. She shook her head to clear her brain.

"But didn't you say you married me because of the children?" she asked.

"That may have been a factor," he grinned.

"Oh! You are so—*obtuse!*" she flung at him, and lurched unsteadily toward the grange hall's front door.

Understanding her better than she knew, Sam swooped her up in his arms and carried her outside. "Take a few deep breaths, love. Enjoy the cool mountain air." Laughing, he set her on her feet.

"Darn you, Sam." Weaving, Meg took a puny swing at him.

He ducked. "Wait till you sober up, little spitfire," he advised, steering her toward their buckboard. "Then we'll see how much you love me."

"Are you taking me home?" she demanded, getting belligerent. "You think I'm intox—intoxified, don't you?" She wagged her finger under his nose. "You d-drank just as m-much as I did, Sam."

"A butterfly like you can get drunk on a thimble-full of cider. I, on the other hand, could drink a quart of that stuff—if I didn't know what was in that punchbowl! Up you go!" He picked her up and tossed her light as a feather onto the hay bales in the wagon.

Meg wasn't taking such treatment sitting down. "I can drive my—myself home, thank you very much." Climbing into the driver's seat, she nearly fell over the side.

Sam barely rescued her from doing a cartwheel onto the ground. "Hold on, sweetheart. I'd better get you some buttermilk to coat your stomach."

"Blaaagh!" She started wailing. "Please don't take me home, Sam. The party's not over yet."

"Hush, my darling," he crooned, petting her gently. "You just need to sleep it off."

Raising her head, she looked around. "Hey! It's dark out here. I might drive off a cliff."

"No, no," he reassured her. "We're staying here overnight. Remember?"

"I know," she said, wise to him. "You don't want your horse to get hurt." A hiccup escaped her. "Oops! Sorry." She leaned her head on his shoulder and shut her eyes.

"Don't worry about a thing, Margaret," he whispered. "I'll drive you and the children home in the morning."

Getting her settled down for the night in the back wasn't easy. Sam stretched out beside her in the hay and covered her with a blanket. *Just until she's safely asleep,* he told himself. Then he'd go find the children

~ * ~ * ~ * ~

"Shhh!" Daniel whispered, reaching down to help Jessie Peterson climb into the front seat of his uncle's buckboard.

"My Pa will skin me alive, if he catches us!" she whispered back.

"Relax. This is the last place anybody would dream of looking for us," he said confidently. The sky was pitch black, and inside the music was as loud and spirited as ever. Chances of being discovered were about nil, in his estimation.

Not that he was an experienced Lothario. He was still working up his courage to steal his very first kiss, and so far Jessie was holding out. Every time he tried to lay a big smooch on her, she moved her lips. He couldn't see well enough to see what was gong on, but most girl's mouths were located smack in the middle, not moving all over her face. "Jessie, this is never going to work, unless it's both our idea," he complained.

"I'm just so nervous, Dan," she said, wiggling around on the seat. "I never kissed a boy before."

"All you gotta do is pucker up," he said, now desperate. "I can take care of the rest."

"Have *you* ever done this before?"

"Well, no." He sounded annoyed. "That's why I need you to stop moving long enough for me to land one on you."

"Maybe you two should skedaddle back inside and practice the two-step," said an ominous voice behind them. "Before you venture into more dangerous territory."

Rising up from the crackling hay in the back of the wagon, Sam grabbed Daniel and Jessie, open-mouthed and about to experiment on each other, and gave them a little shake. "Besides, this buckboard is already occupied."

"Uncle?" Scared out of his wits, Daniel's voice cracked.

Jessie let out a scream and began flailing her arms. "Help! Rape! I'm being attacked!"

"Oh, for God's sake!" Sam growled. "Nobody even laid a hand on you."

"No, but what if my Pa finds out—?"

"Oh, be quiet," said Meg, sitting up with hay stuck in her hair.

"Mrs. Gallagher? Is that you?" Jessie gasped.

"Climb back here, Jessie, and stop your squalling," Meg said, annoyed. "Daniel, you walk back inside with your father—I mean, uncle. Just act casual, like you both came outside to use the outhouse."

"Yes, ma'am," he said.

"Good idea." Backing his wife's play, Sam vaulted over the side rail and beckoned to Daniel. "Come with me. I'd like to introduce you to a couple of wallflowers. One's a little on the shy side, but..."

Their voices drifted away as they left. For a second, Jessie hesitated, torn between not wanting to share Daniel, and coming up with a plausible alibi that her father might accept.

"I'm not fast," she said defensively.

"And neither is Daniel; that's obvious. You're both at the age when you're bursting with curiosity and want to try things out." Meg wrapped her blanket about them both. "Comfy?"

Huddled together, Jessie slowly began to relax. "What should I tell my father?"

Meg tucked a curl behind Jessie's ear and smiled. "What's there to tell?"

"Oh." Aside from the cricket sharing their bale of hay, there was a long silence. "Thanks, Mrs. Gallagher. I guess I'll go back inside now. Before Pa starts looking for me."

"I'll go with you," Meg offered, moving cautiously in the dark. The hay squawked a little, but as long as she held onto the side rail...

"Thanks for being so understanding," Jessie said, as they groped their way toward the main entrance of the grange hall.

"Don't thank me. Five years ago, I might have been tempted to flirt a bit."

"But you didn't?"

"No, Jessie," she said, her voice warm and understanding. "But only for lack of opportunity."

As the pair went up the steps in the pitch dark, Sam paused a few feet away, stunned by what he'd just overheard. The words, *'Five years ago,'* rang in his ears. *What had Meg meant by that?* he wondered.

Was she just trying to strike up a rapport with a naïve young teenager? Or was she talking about when she herself was fifteen—*five years ago!*

Simple math led him to an even more provocative question: *Just how old is my wife, anyway?* He stopped dead in his tracks, as another disturbing thought occurred to him: *If she's only twenty, then I'm almost old enough to be her father!* Well, maybe not quite, but still, he couldn't sneeze away fourteen years difference in age.

Oh, hell! he thought, shifting Susie to his other shoulder and herding Davey toward the buckboard. "Sleep tight, little pardners," he said, settling them down in the hay. "C'mon, Jimmy, keep a close eye on these two, while I go find Miss Wolfie."

Turning back toward the lively strains of fiddles and flute, accordion and bass and tambourine, he wondered what this world was coming to. Some of his friends would be shocked, if they ever got wind of his wife's age. They'd probably have a high old time, accusing him of robbing the cradle.

Maybe it *did* look a mite strange for a childless widower to suddenly return with three orphans and a spirited young wife. And then there was that little matter of raising his sister's son. 'No previous signs of insanity,' and *'plumb loco,'* he could almost hear the neighbors say behind his back.

Not that he gave a hill of beans for such talk. Still, he needed to have a little heart-to-heart talk with Meg. He hired her, thinking she was twenty-two. But twenty? That seemed a little young. If she fibbed about that, he was done.

Still, she's a real go-getter. Conscientious, too, almost to a fault, he thought, reconsidering. The least he could do was hear her side of things.

But no more sex for a while. A man had to draw the line somewhere.

Chapter Twenty-Two

Meg woke up to discover Sam up front driving the buckboard home in the silvery dawn. Molly the horse was plodding slower than usual, probably because of the extra weight of sleeping bodies and several bales of hay in the wagon. Daniel drooped beside Sam, his head nodding up and down in tempo with the horse's.

She and Sam had exchanged sharp words last night, after he rounded up the children, and then went back inside the hall, looking for her. He definitely was not pleased to find Jessie Peterson and her school chums hanging all over her and asking questions they should have been asking their mothers.

Maybe they felt drawn to her because she was closer to their age than the other ranchers' wives. Whatever the reason, almost the minute Meg walked in the door with Jessie, she found herself hemmed in by a clique of teenaged girls, treating her like an ally and confidante. Obliged to help raise her siblings after the war, she had never been all that popular growing up. Suddenly Meg felt like the Queen Bee surrounded by her court.

Of course, this outpouring of interest came as a big surprise. Mostly she tried to be empathetic and friendly. Responding to their questions mostly required good common sense. Still, it did surprise her that they wanted to know so much about her marriage to a prosperous rancher like Sam. What had she done to catch his eye? Did she have any beauty secrets? It was almost laughable, the questions they posed.

Slightly amused by all the attention, Meg did her best to put the girls at ease. Certainly there was no reason to reject their overtures of friendship. Overlooking their hunger for acceptance, she tried to listen to their concerns and what was on their hearts. After all, they were in the process of becoming women, like herself. They didn't deserve to be talked down to. They needed *sensible* answers, and by their very actions, clearly they longed to be treated with respect.

They were in the midst of a very serious discussion about skin care when who should show up but Sam.

The object of several young ladies' secret admiration.

The first words out of his mouth were, "Meg, I need you—*right now!*"

He made his request with great forcefulness and urgency.

Of course, having a handsome male stride into their midst brought about instant paralysis of the larynx, or vocal chords. (Meg had been secretly reading Sam's book on medical terminology, so she now knew the correct word to use.)

What she didn't expect was for Sam to quite literally sweep her off her feet in front of all these impressionable young girls. "Ladies, goodnight!" He gave a cursory nod and left, effectively breaking up the conclave of eager young misses who had been clustered around her.

"Sam, how *could* you be so rude?" she said, frantically waving goodbye to her new friends. "Put...me...down...this...instant!" She kicked her feet to lend special emphasis to her command, but to no avail.

In two shakes of a donkey's tail, she was outside the grange hall and—oh, she was *furious.* "How *dare* you humiliate me like that!"

She balled her fist, wound up and let him have it, right in the solar plexus. (Another term she'd recently added to her vocabulary.)

Unfortunately it had no appreciable effect on Sam. He had a muscular bread-basket that felt like a cast iron skillet.

"Ouch!" she gasped, shaking her dainty digits. She jumped up, this time targeting his nose, which was considerably higher than her own. She missed and sprang at him again.

The instant she was airborne, Sam tackled her around the middle, hoisted her onto his shoulder, and walked off into the dark.

Closeby a match flared, and a second later, John Lassiter shone his kerosene lantern on the pair. "Hey, Sam, that's some hellcat you're got by the tail."

Several other men, out for a smoke, materialized out of the dark to cheer him on. Now, Sam could easily have blistered his wife's bottom, but he hadn't the heart. Especially with a bunch of grown men there to witness her getting her comeuppance.

"Sorry to disappoint you, fellas," he laughed, "but we're just indulging in a little honeymoon hijinks. Sort of warming up to do a little cuddling later tonight."

"Could be she drank too much of that special deluxe cider," one of the Ryan twins called from the shadows.

"What? Why, *you*—" Raging, Meg swung again. This time her blow glanced off her husband's right ear.

"Oops! Guess I'll be sporting a cauliflower ear tomorrow," he grinned, patting her gently on the rump.

"She's got a vicious right hook, all right," Olaf Gunderson sympathized.

"What you just saw was Mrs. G goin' on a rip-roarin' tear, on account of all the hootch *I* drank tonight," Sam said good-naturedly deflecting the crude humor onto himself. "She doesn't take kindly to insults, so if you'll excuse us, gentlemen, we'll go bed down in the buckboard now."

"Don't believe a word he says," said Len, coming out the door to see what all the excitement was about. "I hear Mrs. G's in training to take on Jackie Sullivan— Hey, give us a drum roll, Ollie!"

Gunderson and a few other hecklers imitated a drummer by rhythmically slapping their thighs. "Gentlemen," he announced, "I give you Mrs. Sam Gallagher, the next lightweight champion of the—" He doubled over with laughter. "—the ladies' sewing club!"

Raucous laughter was followed by the raising of flasks.

"To Mrs. G!" they proclaimed.

"Hip-hip-hooray!"

"Down the hatch," Jedidiah Whitaker hollered, smashing his whiskey bottle against Tim Ryan's. The bottom cracked, and he watched a dark puddle form at his feet. "Aw, hell!" he said and passed out.

"To a better year ahead," Sam said quietly.

Meg said nothing, but he could feel her anger in every cell of her body, as they made their way to the buckboard with S-G-S branded into the tailgate.

~ * ~ * ~ * ~

The minute they rolled up in front of the ranch house, Sam knew he was in for it—was he ever! A man had a sense about things like that. Waiting for an outpouring of vitriol, he set the brake and hopped down.

Now, usually Meg waited for him to do the honors, but this morning she ignored the hand he offered and swung down to the ground on her own. She silently gestured for Jimmy to hand over Susie and, turning her back, marched straight to the new outhouse behind the big house. There wasn't a tear in her eye, but that didn't mean she wasn't suffering from a broken heart.

Sitting there, waiting for Susie to finish her business, Meg had a lot of time to think. There was no doubting the fact that she and Sam had reached a crisis point in their brief marriage. But how to repair the damage was beyond her ability to figure out. One could almost say that her marriage, and all the joy and pride she'd felt, had vanished like shite, down at the bottom of the hole.

She was as close to complete and utter despair as she had ever been, and that was saying a lot.

Life had never been easy growing up. But she'd always rallied before. She'd seen both parents underground and she had survived. But things were different now. For the one thing she needed so desperately was Sam's love.

The pain in her heart felt like a wound so great that it would never heal. She felt empty inside. Alone. Not bitter, for she was partly to blame. She had brought this on herself by being too full of herself—prideful. *How can I go on?* she agonized. For without love and acceptance, without forgiveness and human kindness, there was no hope. All she had ever wanted, and worked, and strived so hard for, had been truly lost.

She waited for Susie to finish her business, then pulled up the tiny panties. Deep inside, she felt burdened by a deep sense of failure. God forgive her, she had even failed the children.

Just as she had failed Sam. What a disappointment she was to them all.

Sooner or later, she would have to face...*him.* But how? After all that had happened last night, her spirit felt crushed. She had gone to the dance, looking for acceptance and Sam's approval. She had wanted him be so proud of her.

She threw a scoop of lime down the dark hole, and took Susie's tiny hand. She wondered if she could ever make it up to them all.

~ * ~ * ~ * ~

As she walked with Susie under the cottonwood trees, a soft breeze lifted her hair from the back of her neck. It felt like a light caress against her skin. Like a whisper of hope, reminding her that with God all things were possible. And that His love never fails.

Her gaze located Molly in a nearby pasture. Sam, or one of his men, had unharnessed the gentle, ever plodding horse. She wasn't the fastest horse on the place, by a long shot. But she was a kind and faithful creature. One of God's creatures. Just doing her job.

With a sigh, Meg followed Susie toward the barn. Somebody had removed all the bales of hay from the buckboard. While she was busy moping, life went on as usual, and the work got done. She was certainly not indispensable.

Out of the blue, Dusty came up to her, wagging her tail, and licked her hand. Meg smiled and stooping, put her arms about the lop-eared mongrel. Wriggling with delight, Dusty gave her a big slurp of affection.

At least somebody still loves me. She pulled the gangly pup onto her lap, big clumsy paws and all. Her dress was soon covered with dog hair and dirt, but at least somebody still loved her, despite all her faults. She sat on the dirt barn floor and thought about that a while...

Among other things she noticed was that one of the boys had milked their one remaining female goat. Len Peterson had borrowed the mama goat to help feed Leona's twins. Poor woman had eight children and a husband who didn't have a lick of self-control.

Meg got up and brushed herself off. She really should remind Sam to have a man-to-man talk with Len Peterson. And perhaps she should take a jar of her strawberry preserves over to Leona as a peace offering; maybe lend her a hand around the house for a few hours. If she did nothing else, she could crack the whip over Len's daughters by his first wife. Might keep them from day-dreaming the time away.

Yes! she told herself. Instead of moping around, she might as well go see someone who had *real* problems! Her own could wait.

~ * ~ * ~ * ~

When she and Susie got back from visiting with Leona, she put a pot of beef and chili on the back burner. She also made six loaves of bread, leavened with sour dough yeast, covered it with a dish towel, and left it to rise in the window, where it could catch the warm sun.

Oh, that Sam! He must have gone down to the mail drop-off at the telegrapher's shack on the way up to the mine. A great big pile of letters, catalogs and old newspapers were spread all over the dining room table.

Word from the outside world didn't arrive very often, but when it did, there was enough news to catch up on to keep from feeling lonely. Meg had received only two pieces of mail since June, but she still enjoyed re-reading a letter from back home. Just holding it in her hand was such a comfort.

This time she had two letters addressed to her. Steaming open the envelopes over the tea kettle, she stretched out on the divan and quickly perused the letter from the Children's Aid Society.

"Dear Mrs. Gallagher,

Thank you for informing us of your new address.

I want to congratulate you on your marriage to Mr. Sam Gallagher. It is also most gratifying to learn of the successful adoption of Susie Wilson, David Hale, and Jim Baxter.

Your role and your husband's in bringing about out the permanent placement of these children in your home is greatly appreciated.

Yours truly,

Rev. Todd Appleton, Chairman of the Board.

The other letter came from Aunt Gladys, with black borders around the envelope and the letter inside. Her heart sank, even before she began to read, knowing that the news was not good.

"My dear Margaret,

"With a heavy heart I write to tell you that your Uncle Henry is now sleeping among the angels. He passed very peacefully in his sleep during the night on August 4th. For him I rejoice, but oh, how my heart longs to fill the void left with his passing.

"Your sister and brother came for the funeral. Both are well and send their love. Lilabet's husband owns a prosperous business in Patterson, and they are expecting their second child in December. Jason is working for a lawyer in Philadelphia and hopes to pass the bar late next spring.

"As for *you*, my precious girl, I have nothing but praise. Your letter of July 9th causes me to rejoice exceedingly over your great good fortune. I can't believe you got married and became the mother of three the very next day after you stepped off the train in Cheyenne!

"I confess at first I was flabbergasted to receive the news, as you must have been, but immediately recognized the hand of God at work. And what a kind, chivalrous man Mr. Gallagher must be, to open his heart and home to your orphans without a moment's hesitation!

"I embrace you all. How I wish I could meet your delightful little family, but alas, with so many miles between us, I can only send my love. I am so happy for you all..."

A smudge on her aunt's stationery looked like shed tears, or perhaps from a cup of her favorite green tea? Meg held the letter to her lips. *Dear Aunt Gladys! If only she had her aunt's unquenchable faith in humanity!*

Getting up from the table, she made *herself* a cup of tea. Never in a thousand years would she ever disillusion her poor, grieving aunt. She already had enough heartache. Remembering her aunt's lessons in comportment, Meg set down her teacup. She straightened her spine and resolutely lifted her chin. She walked "majestically," to use her aunt 's favorite phrase, across the room and into the bedroom where she and Sam had spent several nights in passionate sexual congress.

How could she ever live up to her aunt's exalted opinion of her? Should she even try? Could this marriage rise from the ashes and recapture the spontaneity and joy she and Sam had enjoyed?

There was only one way to find out. She went to her knees in prayer.

~ * ~ * ~ * ~

That night at the supper table Sam kept a promise he'd made her months before. He caught up paying her overdue monthly salary. "Put it away some place safe," he advised, closing her fingers over the greenbacks he'd counted into her palm. "Keep it for a rainy day."

Meg's jaw dropped. She stared at the money, and then at those strong, work-roughened hands holding hers. Before, she would not have hesitated to follow his advice. After all, what she contributed to the ranch's success deserved respect and reward. But suddenly, out of the blue, she questioned taking money from Sam. Were not a husband and wife meant to be life partners? Risk takers together in this wilderness? Would it not cheapen their relationship, if she accepted the money?

For a second she was tempted to refuse. But then she tried to see it from Sam's perspective. Months ago, he had committed himself to paying her a monthly salary.

So did that make her an employee in his eyes, or his wife?

In an instant, the hackles on the back of her neck rose. Oh, the urge was undeniably there, just to throw it in his face and stalk off. Pick a fight. High drama and tears. Make him feel like an insensitive brute for what had transpired last night at the grange hall.

Her fist closed around the money. It was so tempting!

But then Meg looked into his eyes. Really looked. Those deep, rich brown eyes, usually so full of laughter and understanding.

She looked past all the hurt and humiliation she'd felt last night. She remembered his kindness to the children. And saw his love for her. His patience. The long hours *he* sacrificed to provide a solid roof over their heads. This was not just an employer paying off the hired help. This was the man she had fallen in love with. Maybe he loved her, too; maybe he didn't. But she would never know if she didn't listen to what her heart was saying: 'Try love. Love never fails.'

Someone once said the eyes were the mirror of the soul. And right now Sam's eyes were full to overflowing with apology. She also saw regret. And pain. He knew she was hurting.

He was also waiting for her to make the first move.

"Maybe we can use it for something we need around the house," she said, just to see what he'd say next.

"No, this is for you to squirrel away. Squander it, do whatever you want with it. We've got enough to get by on. Anything you need for you, or the kids, or the house, you just leave that to me." He tilted back in his chair, arms stretched wide to show how big his wallet was. "That's how important you are to me, Meg," he said.

It sounded a little like Sam was begging forgiveness, but was afraid to bare his soul, for fear of rejection. Unfortunately for him, Meg had already taken a peek in those brown eyes of his. She knew he was soft as a marshmallow inside.

Getting to her feet, she crammed his greenbacks down the front of her dress. "I could use a little help finding a good safe place to hide this cash," she hinted. "Maybe you could help me?"

Caught by surprise by her amiable suggestion, Sam teetered and fell with a crash to the floor, breaking a spoke in his chair.

Meg turned to the children. Their eyes were big as pitchers, as they absorbed every word. "Daniel, kindly help your uncle up. And the rest of you, it's time for bed. Scoot, now!" she said, shooing them off to their rooms.

Coming around the table, she helped Daniel free Sam from the broken chair. "Oh, are you badly hurt?" She solicitously put her arm around Sam's waist, like he was an invalid.

"Thanks for the assist," Sam growled at his nephew, and then raised a wicked looking eyebrow at his petite wife. "I may need your help, love. My head is spinning," he went on in a faint voice that hinted at laughter. "Maybe I should lie down for awhile."

Ah! So now it's his turn to play-act, she thought, frowning at her husband. "I'll take it from here, Daniel. You go check on the little ones," she smiled, then turned to the big handsome galoot in her arms. "Oh, Sam, I *do* hope you weren't seriously..."

"Please be gentle with me," he pleaded. Urging her to pick up the pace, he practically dragged her inside their bedroom "Ah! At last I have you alone, my dear," he began in melodramatic tones, and hastily locked the door.

"Here, Mr. G, let me help you get more comfortable—awwk!" Those were the last intelligible words out of Meg's mouth that night. Though there was considerable giggling and a few wild outbursts of laughter.

As Daniel explained to Jimmy and Davey the next morning, "Somebody must have a ticklish funnybone."

Chapter Twenty-Three

The ranchers' routines changed substantially with the changing colors and the falling of the leaves. Some of the older children in the valley were sent to school in Cheyenne. The Frockmeyers shipped off their two daughters, Flora and Lisa, to a finishing school for young ladies in Denver. Not having a local schoolmaster in the valley, most of the younger children either ran wild, or acquired the basics through home study courses that came in the mail every quarter.

Fannie Mae Gehrhart, being an educated woman, chose to tutor her children at home. She also took a few of the neighbors' children under her wing two days a week on one condition: They must bring their own slates and pack a lunch.

As for the wild bunch at the S-G-S Ranch, Sam chose to run the legs off his boys during the day, helping his cowboys herd cattle from sun-up till four in the afternoon. "It keeps them fit," he told his wife when she expressed concern about possibly overdoing the boys' level of physical activity.

"By evening, they'll be ready to concentrate on their lessons," he explained, dumping an armload of wood next to the fire crackling on the hearth. "Trust me, my love. I know what I'm doing."

"Well, I hope you're right," Meg said, busily darning socks. To tell one boy's socks from the others, she had devised a system whereby she used a different color of yarn for each member of the family: Forest green for Sam, navy blue for Daniel, purple for Jimmy, brown for Davey, pink for Susie, and white for herself. Sam had big feet, but with Daniel's recent growth spurt, she was determined not to be caught napping.

Soon they settled into a nightly routine: Susie and Davey drew pictures and went over the alphabet with Meg, while Sam tutored Daniel and Jimmy in reading, English and math in the evenings.

There was always a bowl of buttered popcorn in the center of the dining room table, in case anyone got the munchies. Dusty managed to get more than her fair share by being Meg's foot warmer on cool nights.

Meg and Sam were settling into married life quite nicely, now that the ranch house was finished. They had their children gathered about them. Evenings were a special time for family closeness, and a prelude to their own more private moments in the bedroom.

~ * ~ * ~ * ~

By mid-October gale force winds had begun to sweep across the prairie lands from Canada, replacing the balmy breezes of summer and fall. Leaves had been raked and composted into the garden. Anything that might get blown away in a storm was stored in the barn or storage shed.

Then the day came when all the younger children and their mothers gathered at the Grange Hall for Halloween treats and bobbing for apples. Spooky stories about ghosts and goblins held the children in thrall. Afterward the party was declared a great success. Nobody had nightmares, or wet the bed, or had to sleep with Ma and Pa because there was a bear under his bed.

The wolves continued to howl at night, but thus far, none of the ranchers had lost any of their cattle. Merging their herds together took care of that threat, for the time being.

But then the freezing time came. Several of Sam's men took off for a little excitement in Cheyenne. Others rode down to Texas, where the winters weren't so dad-blasted bone-chilling. Archie was among those who left for the winter; as always, they all promised to return in the spring.

Soon Meg got the bright idea of moving her chickens into the barn for the winter. With the boys' help, she fashioned a makeshift chicken coop insulated by thick bales of hay on three sides and on top of the wire cage. Susie and Davey still made their daily raids on the nests, looking for eggs. Culling less productive hens from the flock, Meg served chicken soup for lunch more frequently.

Occasionally Daniel and Jimmy accompanied Sam on hunting expeditions. Elk and deer tracks were often seen in the fields at dawn, so when the family larder ran low of red meat, they jumped at the chance to help. They learned to take care of their rifles and not waste ammunition. They also learned to pick up spent cartridges and make their own bullets in the evenings, after their other lessons were done.

When temperatures dipped even lower, the children stayed inside more often than not, playing checkers and Old Maid. They cracked nuts for Meg and helped mix the batter for cookies. Susie skipped rope—almost nonstop, it seemed.

The boys played ball with Dusty, who acquired a truly vexing habit of getting under the cook's feet, no matter where she trod. The barn cat had been promoted to permanent house cat. She dined on the occasional mouse and kept out of everyone's way by taking up residence under the kitchen stove.

Meanwhile Sam and Slim and Walker made their daily rounds, inspecting the herd and dropping off extra feed where needed. Soon a few casualties were reported. *Wolves!* They were like a voracious thermostat; their attacks on the herd usually coincided with another drop in the temperature.

Through all the snow flurries and ice storms, Meg made sure everyone was well supplied with mittens, scarves and knitted caps to keep them warm. *Thank goodness for Fannie Mae and her flock of sheep!* As the winter settled over the valley, ranchers' families forgot to grumble about Gehrhart's wife and her strange fondness for sheep. Unperturbed, Fannie kept her spinning wheel going to keep up with the demand for wool.

~ * ~ * ~ * ~

Suddenly the temperature dropped to forty below. Everyone basically went into hibernation mode. Nobody traveled past their barn and outhouse, if they could help it. All communication with the outside world ceased.

And then it began to snow. For five days a silent blizzard of white was the only thing Meg could see from her kitchen window. A blinding white. Even the trees were solid white.

Walker, now the lone resident in the bunkhouse, waited out the storm. He had food and heat, as evidenced by the barely visible plume of pale smoke rising from the smoke stack. But for those five days of isolation, nobody moved.

For the first time Sam was holed up inside with her and the children. He took naps—something Meg had never seen him do before. He also studied all the government pamphlets lying around the place, ignored for months, then crumpled them up and tossed them in the fire. He re-read all the personal mail, including hers, then quietly returned it to her. If he found anything interesting in Aunt Gladys's letter, he never mentioned it to her.

One day he whittled several pieces of kindling to make a jiggity-jig wooden puppet, got a splinter, and raised *such* a fuss that she had to dab it with iodine and wrap a bandage around his finger. When she asked, "Do you want me to kiss it all better," he wrestled with her playfully, gave her a swat on the rump, and sent her into the kitchen to make him a bacon sandwich.

He constantly challenged Daniel and Jimmy to play chess with him. He also made them rattle off their multiplication and division tables twice a day. He let Susie and Davey climb all over him, while he read them stories about a smart-aleck rabbit who outwitted all the mean animals who wanted to throw him in a briar patch. "Blip!" He slammed the book shut. "Time for bed, everyone."

As fascinating as it was to watch Sam interact with the children, Meg missed the friendly crunch of galoshes tramping through the snow. She missed her neighbors' frequent visits.

Now, even after the snow stopped falling, there was the daunting job of having to dig their way through eight-foot drifts. The ropes Sam and Walker carefully strung between the house and bunkhouse, barn, and outhouse, weren't of much use, once they were buried in the snow.

So life went on pretty much the same for the next few days, while Sam and Daniel shoveled a path from the house to the barn, to make sure the animals had survived. Meanwhile Walker tunneled his way from the bunkhouse up to the house to liberate Dusty and the cat, who were by now going berserk. (The less said about *that* the better!)

But then, *finally*, a Chinook wind blew down from Canada, and the snows began to melt. Rivers and creeks flowed over their banks and went raging through the low spots in the valley.

A few brave souls began to move about, though it took another two weeks before the roads were even halfway passable. Sam and Walker rode up into the hills, hauling feed to a bunch of stranded cows.

Meanwhile Meg was pretty much stuck at home. She'd been riding herd on four restless children for weeks, and she had finally figured out what 'cabin fever' was all about.

She was also the first person in the valley to learn about Sally Lassiter's husband. On January 14, 1874, the gigantic wheels on Byron Turner's freight wagon, defying all odds, including a four-foot flood of water, rumbled over the bridge and pulled up in front of the ranch house.

Not having seen a single living soul in quite some time—not counting Walker and her family—Meg made it to the front porch in record time. "Why, Mr. Turner, what brings you out on a drizzly day like this?" she said, with a big smile. "Come in out of the wet."

"I fear I'm the bearer of bad news, ma'am," he said, his boots sloshing through the yard. "Forgive me for tracking all over your porch," he said, scrapping off the worst of his mud. "Is Sam here?"

"No, but he's due back anytime." She gestured for him to step inside. "Let me get you a cup of coffee and a slice of my apple pie."

"Thank you kindly, ma'am." He ducked to get through the door, saw the children, and broke into a smile. "I see your young'uns are sproutin' up fast, same as mine. By the way, Carolyn says 'hi.'"

"Thank you. Please, do sit down," she said. "I know it must be something important, for you to come out this far in the rain."

"Yes, ma'am—"

"Now, Mr. Turner, how long have we known each other?" She tapped her foot and looked him direct in the eye.

He scratched his head, looking puzzled. "It was June, as I recall—"

"So don't you think maybe it's time we drop the 'Mr.' and 'Mrs.' and call each other by our first names? After all," she reminded him, "Carolyn *is* my best friend."

He grinned. "Yes, ma'am, I reckon so."

She laughed. "So, *Byron*, do you take cream and sugar in your coffee?"

"Cream, if you got any."

"Excellent! I like it that way, too." Spinning around, Meg poured his coffee and handed him the cream pitcher. "Help yourself, Byron."

Cutting him a piece of warm apple pie, she handed him a fork and sat down across the table. "How's the family?" she asked leadingly.

"Family's fine. Rambunctious as ever," he said, taking a bite. "Mm-mm!" His mouth full, he was incapable of saying another word until he'd consumed the whole slice.

"Good?" Meg asked.

"Yes, ma'am."

"All right, *Byron*, don't make me drag it out of you. What is the reason you came over here in a downpour?" She glanced out the window to make sure the weather hadn't changed in the last five minutes.

"I got very sad news," he said, stirring more cream into his coffee. "Really shocking news."

"*And*—?"

"I really hate to say."

"It can't be *that* bad, Byron."

"Worse than you can imagine." He ran his tongue over his teeth and shook his head. After a long pause, he looked her in the eye. "Avalanche."

"Where?" Meg demanded, her first thought being for the safety of her own husband. "What happened?"

"I was driving back from the Creswell mine up along the North Platte." His blue eyes clouded over as he visualized the scene. "John Lassiter and I passed, coming 'round the curve. We waved, each goin' our own way, you see. And then I heard a terrible rumble, so I turned around. The whole side of the mountain was coming down. Tons and tons of pure white snow! Mrs. G, I saw an avalanche of snow swallow him up—poor John! Buried on the mountain. Giant trees torn up by the roots like they were toothpicks. 'Twas a terrifyin' sight, I tell you."

Meg sat on the edge of her seat, too horrified to speak.

"If we're lucky, we'll find his body, come spring," he said, wiping his eyes.

A long silence fell, while they tried to assimilate the news.

"Has...has his wife been told?" Meg asked.

"I figure Sam should be the one to tell her—poor woman. In case she takes it real hard and needs—well, you know. Maybe he has something to calm her?" His chair legs scraped, as he rose to his feet. "Well, I'd best be getting on home, ma'am." He stood, hat in hand, a stricken look on his face.

Meg nodded. "I'll let Sam know right away." She reached out and touched his hand. "I know how difficult it is to lose a good friend, Mr. Turner," she said quietly. Inside she was thinking of all her family members who were lost in the war. *Somehow the pain of being separated from loved ones never goes away entirely.*

~ * ~ * ~ * ~

An hour later, Sam walked through the door, sopping wet and exhausted from a hard day's work. His mind focused on protecting his cattle from a pack of wolves he'd spotted on a distant ridge.

The absolute last thing he expected was to find Meg pacing the floor in her best dark wool dress. "I need to go with you, Sam, right away," she said, running to embrace him. "Byron Turner stopped by this afternoon, and I know Sally will take the news much better, coming from another woman."

"What news?" he growled, picking her up and moving her aside as easily as if she was one of his chess pieces. Brushing past Jimmy and Davey, he disappeared into the bedroom to change into dry clothes.

Meg hurried after him and helped him find dry longjohns and clean socks. "Oh, you poor darling!" she cried. "Soaked to the bone."

"Just give me a moment. Gotta get organized," he said, stripping naked and using a towel to dry off. Meg was flitting around, creating the kind of mental chaos guaranteed to make a man crazy. Finally he pointed at the bed. "Sit! I can't talk to a moving object right now," he said. "I need to get my thoughts collected. I've got cows to rescue from a pack of hungry wolves—"

"Oh, so now I'm an object, am I?" Meg handed him a thick flannel shirt.

"Please, Meg, not right now!" he said, grinding his teeth.

"I totally agree. Your pack of wolves can devour the entire herd, for all I care!" She helped him button his shirt. That way he couldn't ignore her. "The fact is, John Lassiter got buried in an avalanche earlier today, and it's up to you and me to let Sally know!"

"Holy—" he was all set to cuss when Meg clapped both hands over his mouth. He shook her off. "Who told you such a thing?"

"Byron Turner. He's quite worried about how Sally might take the news." Her eyes pleaded with him. "I suppose that means you should take your medical bag?" she suggested, wringing her hands.

"You mean you haven't ransacked my supplies yet?"

"Of course not! What a perfectly *stoopid* thing to say!"

Sam rummaged around in the closet, found his oil slicks, and handed her a second one. "Here, this is waterproof. Since you're determined to go, you'd better dress appropriately." He pulled hip waders over his boots, and clomped resolutely into the kitchen.

"Wait for me!" she shrilled, running to keep up with him.

When she got there, Sam had his nose in the stew pot "Daniel, I'm putting you and Jimmy in charge. *Mm.* This seems edible. Load everybody up with seconds, and make sure Davey and Susie get to bed by seven."

"Aw, no fair!" Davey whined.

Susie stuck out her lip, speechless with indignation.

"No bedtime story if you pout," Sam warned, yanking open the front door. "C'mon, Margaret. This is one helluva night to be making a house call."

"Wait!" She held up his medical bag. "You nearly forgot this!"

He rolled his eyes. "What would I ever do without you?" He gave her a quick buss on the lips. "Time to go, kids! For God's sake, try not to burn down the house while we're gone!"

"Why, they would *never*—" Meg gasped indignantly, as he dragged her down the steps.

"Hey, Walker!" he yelled, striding toward the barn. "Throw a saddle on my horse, will you? The missus and I are heading over to the Lassiters' place."

"Can't it wait? I thought we were going after those wolves—"

"Change of plans. John Lassiter died in an avalanche. Gotta break it to the widow." Sam checked the cinch, then mounted. He gave Meg a hand up behind him and winked at Walker. "Keep an eye on my kids. No telling what kind of mischief they'll get into!"

Chapter Twenty-Four

The rain was coming down with a vengeance, as Sam rode up the dirt road to Lassiter's cabin. Holding on for dear life, Meg tightened her arms around his waist. Repeated lightning strikes lit up the distant sky. His horse spooked and balked every time thunder rumbled.

Dismounting in front of the cabin, he tied the reins to the porch railing, knowing that his skittish horse would be gone in a flash otherwise. Meg handed down his medical bag, then slid off into his arms.

"I hate to be the bearer of such bad news on a night like this," she shouted over the fury of the storm. Carrying her up the steps, Sam sloshed through puddles and set her down at the front door.

"There's never a good time for such heartbreaking news," Sam said, hoarse with grief. "Let's just get it over with." Pounding on the door, they waited with water trickling down their necks.

Through the window they saw the light of a kerosene lamp moving toward them from the back of the cabin. A moment later, the latch was thrown, and Sally Lassiter stood in the open doorway, a tall, willowy figure in a rust-colored woolen dress. Her face looked drawn and pinched, almost as if she knew the reason for their visit.

She stood aside. "Please. Come in."

Sam cleared his throat. "Sally, I brought Meg with me."

Meg stepped forward and held out her hands to her friend. "Sally, please forgive the intrusion on such a wet night—"

"We came as soon as we could," Sam added.

Sally nodded. "Let me hang up your things. Did you ever see such terrible weather?"

After they hung their rain slicks on pegs by the door, everybody just looked at each other with tears in their eyes. Nobody quite knew how to bring up the reason for the visit.

Finally Sally, her chin quivering, broke the silence. "It's about John, isn't it?"

"He's gone, Sally. Killed by an avalanche up north of here," Sam said, and put his arms around her. "John loved you so much. I know you must have been in his thoughts and prayers when he took his last breath."

Deeply moved by Sam's gracious words, Meg stood on tiptoe and gave his grizzled cheek a kiss, then turned to embrace her grieving friend. "I know it comes as a terrible shock, but you and John have many friends here in the valley. All of us feel your loss deeply. If you need anything, all you need to do is ask, and we'll be glad to help."

"Wh-where's his body?" Sally pressed her hand against her trembling lips, looking from one to the other. "I want to see him, touch him."

"He's buried under a mountain of snow," Sam said. "I'm so sorry, Sally. We won't be able to get to him till late spring, at the earliest."

"I need John now, damn you!" Bursting into hysterical weeping, she pounded Sam's chest. "Don't you *dare* say I can't see my husband!"

"We'll all see John again in heaven," Meg said, trying to reason with her. "You're a woman of faith, Sally. You know that."

Sally flung herself out of their arms. "If you can't help me right now, leave! Get out of my house!" she screamed, then doubled over like an old woman and moaned. "Oh, my *God*, what am I going to *do*?"

Quickly stepping between the two women, Sam supported John's grieving wife to a nearby chair. "Easy now," he said quietly. "I know losing him is hard, but you're going to get through this. Trust me."

"You're a fine one, Sam Gallagher, to suggest I'm going to land on my feet!" she yelled, looking around her like a mad woman, her hair flying around her face.

"I took it hard, just like you, when my wife and daughter died," he said, holding her tight, while she continued to struggle. "I won't lie to you, Sally. It's hard to deal with. I felt like I had nothing to live for."

"I don't! I *don't!*" she shrieked. "Just give me a gun, so I can shoot myself. Where's your gun, Sam?" Suddenly her hands were all over him, searching his pockets.

"No, Sally, no." Weeping, Meg fell to her knees beside the chair and gripped her friend's balled fists. "Nothing is ever as hopeless as it seems. You've had a terrible shock—"

"I'd rather *die* than live without him." Sally bared her teeth, almost like a wild animal. "You don't understand what life was like before John—" She broke off, realizing what she'd nearly confessed. "Oh, my God, *please*. Please let me die!"

Sam motioned with his head toward his medical bag. "Meg."

Heartbroken to see her friend in such a state, Meg got slowly to her feet. "God loves you, Sally, no matter how dark things look right now."

"He took our baby!" Sally screamed, thrashing in Sam's arms. "Now He's taken John!"

Holding her close, Sam's gaze locked with his wife's, telling her what she must do. Biting her lips, Meg walked over to the medical bag.

"Open it," he barked. "I need the chloroform and a clean cloth. Hand them to me."

Meg gave him a puzzled look. "Don't you mean 'hypodermic syringe'?"

"Just do as I say, Meg!"

"Laudanum, give me a bottle of laudanum!" Sally sobbed, clawing to get free. "Let me kill myself!"

"Sorry. I never give narcotics to *anyone* who has as much fight in her as you have," he said, as Meg handed him the bottle of chloroform. "Hold still now." Shaking out several drops, he smiled into Sally's defiant gaze. "You, my dear Mrs. Lassiter, have too much to live for!"

She spat in his face. "I hate you! Let go of me!"

"Nighty-night," Sam said softly, and put Sally out of her misery with chloroform. "A temporary cure. When she wakes up, I hope she'll tell us what she's so afraid of."

~ * ~ * ~ * ~

Carrying her limp body into the bedroom, he laid Lassiter's widow on the counterpane and returned to the parlor for the kerosene lamp. "I need to take care of the horse, put him in the barn for the night. Meanwhile, don't let her out of your sight."

He stared for a moment at the figure lying on the bed like a broken doll, then shook his head. "Sure breaks your heart when something like this happens."

"She'll rally, I know she will." While Meg waited for Sam to return, she removed Sally's shoes and loosened her clothing. A leak in the roof near the bed needed tending to, so she tucked a quilt around her friend and hurried to the kitchen for a large cast-iron pot to catch the water dripping down off the rafters.

Then she pulled up a chair and held her friend's limp hand, all the while listening to the steady patter of rain into the pot. Prayer came hard. There were no glib answers to explain this terrible accident, or why John Lassiter happened to be in that exact place at that precise moment. *Why* seemed like such a pointless question. It didn't matter *why*. Sometimes things just happened, for no rhyme or reason.

So, how should a person pray in a situation like this? she asked, searching her heart. In the end, all she could do was ask God to watch over Sally and grant her *His* peace and *His* love. Also trust Him to supply all her needs.

A while later Sam came stomping back inside the cabin, his arms laden with firewood. Hearing him come in, Meg left her friend's side, hoping to render some assistance to her husband. Soaked to the bone, he dropped to one knee and put a split log in the potbelly stove. The flames flickered against the wall, revealing his face stricken with deep sorrow and fatigue.

"How's she doing?" he whispered, adjusting the stove's draft and adding another log.

"Still sleeping. Haven't heard a peep out of her."

Coming alongside, Meg removed his hat and tenderly smoothed a wet lock of his hair back from his forehead. "Let me fix you something to eat," she offered. "Then you should get some rest."

"You, too." Getting up, he wiped sawdust from his hands. "Let's find out what's in the kitchen cupboards, shall we?"

Together they explored the Lassiters' kitchen. "Why, there's hardly anything in here!" Meg exclaimed, after they'd made a thorough search for foodstuffs.

Gathering two cans of beans, a few condiments, and a bag of wormy flour from the shelves, Sam turned. "Why, they must have been on the verge of starvation!" he said in a low, urgent whisper. "I knew John was worried about making ends meet till spring, but I never imagined things were this bad! Can you make us some supper with a can of beans?"

"Yes, I can easily throw something together," Meg said. "But, you know, Sam, the neighboring ranchers need to be alerted about the situation here. No wonder she seemed so desperate!"

"I bet John was looking for work at the mines up North when that avalanche killed him."

"Oh, Sam." Meg's eyes brimmed with sympathy. "Let's start a neighbor-helps-neighbor food drive to replenish her pantry!"

"Yes. Starting with a raid on our root cellar," he agreed. Using his knife, he opened a can. "Here, heat this up, while I check on our patient."

~ * ~ * ~ * ~

News of John Lassiter's death had spread like wildfire the day before. Having heard her husband's first-hand account, Carolyn then passed the news on down the chain of command. Members of the sewing circle told their husbands, who spread the word throughout the valley.

As a result, people started showing up at the Lassiters' place with the usual array of casseroles and baked goods, starting at nine o'clock the next morning. Of course, the first to arrive were the in-laws. Showing up *en masse*, Two Bear Benson, his wife Annie, their children, and Granny Benson pulled up to the front door in their green buckboard.

Two Bear and his brood jumped down, just as Meg came around the corner of the cabin, following a brief visit to the outdoor "facility." (In her spare time, Meg had started trying out more gentile names.)

"Good morning!" she said, with a welcoming smile. "Here, let me help you up the steps, Granny."

"I'm not an invalid," the old woman snapped, moving Meg aside with her walking stick. "I'm here to do what I can for Sally."

"I—I'm not sure she's awake yet," said Meg, rushing ahead of the family. "Sam was just with her. Let's check with him first, shall we?" Her blue eyes flitted over the circle of impatiently waiting relatives. "I'll be right back!" Not sure what Sam might recommend, she slipped past the Bensons and, in her haste, closed the door in their faces.

Two Bear looked at Annie, who looked at Granny, who had never let anything or anybody stand in her way in her entire life. "Hm!" she said, "There's somethin' mighty strange goin' on around here," and threw open the door like she was storming a medieval castle's gates.

She raised her stick and shook it under Sam's nose. "Well?" she demanded. "What d' you have to say fer yourself, young whipper-snapper?"

Sam gave up chewing on a crusty old biscuit. "Good morning to you, too, Granny," he greeted her. "I haven't been called a 'whipper-snapper' in at least twenty years," he grinned.

Meg barely had time to warn him of the sudden onslaught of in-laws, before the whole bunch came surging into the parlor. "They're here to see Sally," she said, giving him a warning look. "Is—is she awake and presentable yet?"

"'Presentable?'" he weighed the question. "That's for her family to decide." He signaled with his eyes that all was not well in yonder bedroom.

Forcing a smile, Meg turned to Annie and Two Bear. "Sally had a restless night—quite understandable, considering. Perhaps it might be best if you go in to see her, one at a time?" she hinted.

"Of course," Annie nodded. "John's death must have come as a terrible shock."

"She and John were inseparable," Two Bear affirmed.

A small shriek of pent-up fury indicated that Sally was awake and very much alive—though none too happy about *that*, either.

"She's awake," Meg sighed. What more could she say?

"She's always been prone to panic attacks," Granny said, holding up her stick like Moses in the wilderness. "Temper, temper," she wagged her bony finger at the Benson children. "Never accomplishes a dang thing," she said, and marching into the bedroom, slammed the door behind her.

Everybody looked at each other worriedly.

"Leave it to Granny," Two Bear said, folding his arms over his chest. "If anyone can talk sense into my sister-in-law, she can."

Annie and Meg tiptoed across the room, each pressing her ear to the bedroom door. Annie gave her husband a thumbs-up.

"Don't come near me!" Sally hollered, loud enough to raise the roof. "My life is *over*! No disrespect to you, Granny, but I don't want anyone telling me what to *do*, what to *think*, or how I should feel!"

"Aye, you young rebel. Now listen to me, an' listen straight," said Granny. "I've had three husbands, and I survived 'em *all!* Whether they were good, bad, or indifferent."

The bed ropes squeaked audibly, as the family matriarch sat down. "My bones always creak when it rains, so if you don't mind, I'm gonna stretch out here beside you, girl, and we'll just have us a nice heart-to-heart talk," she chuckled softly.

Things got quieter after that. Sounds of weeping, followed by someone blowing her nose. Granny must have been whispering, because her voice was very soft and soothing.

"Most of the time her voice carries like a Union Army sergeant," Two Bear whispered to the other eavesdroppers. "But right now Granny's speaking to the spirit of an injured soul."

Sam and Meg raised their eyebrows at each other. "Goodness gracious," she whispered. "Could Two Bear really be part Indian?"

"Doubtful," Sam breathed in her ear. "He just *talks* like an Indian shaman."

Meg's lips formed an O, as if to say, "Impressive."

Annie took out her hankie and dabbed her eyes. "My brother John and she were so close." She hid her face against her husband's chest, and they waited. And then waited some more.

At last everything grew silent in the adjoining room. The Benson family communicated with signs to each other and left the cabin.

"I think Granny Benson has better medicine than I do," Sam whispered. "Can you hear anything at all?"

Meg listened intently at the door. "I hear something. It's not talking—" She checked again, then stifled a giggle. "They're snoring, Sam. Isn't it wonderful?"

~ * ~ * ~ * ~

Around noon, people from all over the valley began to show up. Most of them brought comforting words, along with casseroles, baked goods, and canned goods, to show their concern for the widow.

When Reverend Tindle and his wife arrived, offering comfort food and prayers, Sam figured it was time to head on home.

He gave Sally a mild sedative, feeling that he'd done all he could, for the moment. Still worried that Sally might harm herself, he stressed to Annie that her sister-in-law must not be left alone.

"She's still in shock," he whispered to avoid waking his patient. "I just hate to see her in such pain."

"I know. It must be hard, reliving how you felt when your wife and baby died." Annie patted his arm. "Go home, Sam, and leave her to us," she urged. "Granny and I will be staying with her for a few days. You mustn't worry so."

His hair rumpled, Sam looked like he'd been through the clothes wringer himself. He nodded, and raised Annie's hand to his lips. "I 'll rest easier, knowing you and Granny are in charge," he said gallantly, and went to saddle his horse for the ride home.

"If you're still that worried, maybe we should take her home with us," Meg said a few minutes later, as she buttoned up her outer garments. "It just seems wrong to leave her in this condition."

"Let's see how she does in the next day or so. Once she realizes how supportive everyone is, her outlook may improve greatly."

"I love you, Sam." Meg launched herself at him, giving him a smooch. "I'm so glad you have experience dealing with a crisis."

He threw her a skeptical look. "I'm not so sure about that," he said, securing his medical bag to the pommel. "I came close to punching out Sally's lights, a couple of times last night."

"Yes, but you didn't." She slipped her arm cozily through his. "You reminded her about your own loss, and how upset you were when Amie and Beth died."

"But hindsight doesn't come close to what she's going through right now," he reminded her. "That's why it's important for family to keep a close eye on her right now."

"I'll stop by and share your concerns with the ladies in our sewing circle," Meg said, and gave him a juicier kiss.

"Uh, thanks! Now, was that Kiss Number Five Hundred and Ninety, or—" His eyes twinkled, and he lightly tweaked her nose.

"All my kisses are only for you," she reminded him, fluttering her eyelashes at him.

"Good. You remember that," Sam grinned. "Now, up you go!" He tossed her up on his horse, then mounted in front, taking the reins. "You know, I'm downright homesick for our children."

"Me, too. I can hardly wait." Meg tightened her arms around him, as they ambled off toward home. It made her heart glad to know he derived so much comfort from spending time with the children.

Chapter Twenty-Five

Two days later, Sam's horse went lame about a mile down the road from Tim and Mark Ryan's old place. Being in a hurry to get home for supper, Sam dismounted, hoping to avoid further injury to his horse by taking the excess weight off and walking him the rest of the way.

As luck would have it, Mark drove past with his buckboard, testing out a matched pair of horses. Seeing Sam on foot, he pulled up, as any good neighbor would. Backing his new team at the next wide place in the road, he trotted back to shoot the breeze.

"Well, look whose horse pulled up lame," he observed. "Need a ride, Sam?"

"Sure do," said Sam, relieved. Tying his horse to the back of Mark's rig, he climbed aboard. "Thanks for stopping. You've got a fine pair of steppers there."

"I purchased these beauties from Mike Gehrhart," Mark bragged. "He still likes to race the back roads around here once in a while—just as long as his wife doesn't hear of it," he grinned, urging his horses to a trot. "Let me show you what they're really capable of," he offered.

And so the two men sped along, conversing about horses mostly, until they reached the turn-off to the S-G-S Ranch. Not knowing Mark's destination, Sam offered to get down at this point, since he only had another mile left between him and home.

"No, I might as well take you right to the door," Mark insisted. "Only minutes away."

"I sure appreciate this," Sam said, as they pulled up in front of the S-G-S.

"My pleasure," Mark said, shaking hands. "Say, what's this I hear about John Lassiter? I expect his widow is pretty tore up about his death."

"Yes, theirs was a real love match, from what I hear," Sam said, untying his limping horse. "Pretty much inseparable. You can imagine how hard this has been on her."

"Yeah. A real tragedy." Mark nodded, suddenly lost in thought. "Their property line runs parallel with the place I just filed a homestead on. Tim and I are getting a little tired of each other's company after all these years," he laughed. "I wonder—me being her closest neighbor and all— Do you think she might need a little help with the stock?"

"Now, Mark—"

"Or maybe you think it's too soon for an old bachelor like me to drop by and pay a call?" He glanced over at Sam with a wily gleam in his eye. "Maybe she and I could console each other from time to time. What d' you think?"

""No shenanigans," Sam warned, petting his horse. "I'd give the widow a bit more time to recover, if I were you."

"Ah, but you're not me!" Laughing, he whipped up his horses to make the turn in Sam's front yard. "See you around, neighbor!"

~ * ~ * ~ * ~

Until the body of John Lassiter could be recovered, Reverend Tindle found himself waffling back and forth, between a rock and a hard place. The burial was still a long way off—hopefully next May, certainly no sooner. So the most humane thing, he finally decided, was to hold a memorial service at the church.

Considering how distraught the Widow Lassiter was, that seemed the best thing for all concerned. John Lassiter was a man well liked in the community, and it couldn't be put off much longer. People needed to pay their respects, then move on with their lives. *Healthier that way*, he thought.

Only one hitch: The widow had come down with the sniffles and wouldn't be in attendance.

So the church leaders got their heads together and decided to hold the service anyway, followed by a potluck. For what would a funeral be without a potluck? they reasoned. Eternal life was something to *celebrate*, not take to one's sickbed and mope about. All that weeping and gnashing of teeth belonged to the crowd who were headed straight to hell.

Whether the widow appreciated their opinion or not, she continued to mope. She paced around her cabin, wearing her late husband's favorite flannel shirt and oversized pair of dungarees, plus two pairs of his old socks on her feet to save on fuel and prevent frostbite.

Her once beautiful black hair hung in lifeless strings about her thin shoulders. Her grey eyes, once so full of good humor, stared blankly out the windows, as if she expected her beloved John to come striding across the fields any second, and sweep her up in his arms.

Knowing how despondent Sally was, Meg elected to keep her company while the funeral was going on. Aside from cooking breakfast and keeping the potbelly stove stoked with firewood, she kept her mouth shut. She was here to support Sally, not intrude on her pain and make matters worse.

Off in the distance, the church bell rang out—a sound so mournful that Meg's young heart nearly broke. Would her friend's pain never end?

~ * ~ * ~ * ~

A half-hour later, a man on a flashy palomino loped across the fields to the Lassiters' place. With everybody else in church, he was gambling on finding the grieving widow home and alone.

Every other time he'd come to call, he saw buggies and wagons and horses tied up out front, and so he'd just ride on by. *No point in stirring a lot of old hens' feathers.* But this morning, led by the clarion call of church bells, he was bound and determined to make his peace with the widow. This, he thought, his chest swelling with confidence, was truly his date with destiny!

Circling around the cabin, he first reconnoitered the barn and outbuildings, including the outhouse, to make certain the lady was, indeed, alone.

There were four horses feeding in the barn, all wearing the JL brand. There was also a swayback old horse grazing under the trees beyond the corral. Certainly no serious competitor for the lady's favors would ride such a poor specimen of horseflesh!

Ah, perfect timing. The coast is clear, he congratulated himself. Turning his horse into the corral, he ran around the cabin, leapt over the porch railing, and began pounding his fist on the door.

"Sally, my love, open the door. Let me in!"

~ * ~ * ~ * ~

Taken completely by surprise, Meg reeled with shock. Who in his right mind would have the audacity to attack Sally's door with sledge-hammer blows? she asked herself. *Certainly nobody with an ounce of sensitivity,* she concluded, rushing to provide solace to the grieving widow.

"Do you have a gun?" she demanded nervously.

"Here, use mine," Sally said, handing over a heavy revolver.

Meg held it up by thumb and forefinger. "What is it?"

"Smith & Wesson, Model 3. Hey, watch how you handle a loaded gun!" Ignoring the pounding on the front door, Sally started loading her husband's shotgun.

"Let me in, Sally, or I'm going to break the door down!" the man roared. The door was shaking on its hinges.

"Oh, my God!" Meg cried. "Why would a perfect stranger try to batter down the door?"

Sally turned, a fiery look in her eye. "Oh, I know exactly whose voice that is. And he is neither perfect nor a stranger! He is a wicked Casanova, a—"

"Come on, sweetie, open the door."

"*Now* watch him grovel," the widow whispered, and cocked both barrels of her shotgun.

The look in her eye was truly diabolical, Meg thought.

"Honey, open the door," he pleaded. "I just want to talk to you."

"Get away from that door, Mark Ryan, or prepare to meet your Maker," Sally said, taking aim.

Terrified, Meg grabbed the barrel, wrestling for control of the gun. "You can't do that!" she gasped. "Murder is illegal."

"What about a little buckshot in his tokus?" Sally grinned fiendishly. Clearly all the excitement had brought her out of the doldrums!

"Have you lost your mind?" Meg held onto the gun for dear life. Whatever grudge Sally had against Mr. Ryan, it didn't justify a shootout.

"I have my reasons," her distraught friend said. She took a few deep breaths, trying to control the way her hands were shaking. "Look at me," she said. "Just thinking about that man makes me a nervous wreck."

"Well, you still can't shoot him." Scrambling to her feet, Meg gingerly carried both guns—the Smith & Wesson *and* the shotgun—to the kitchen and hid them in the woodpile.

Next, she put her arms around Sally and led her into the bedroom. "My life is a complete shambles." Sally broke down and sobbed. "I-I hope you don't think I'm a truly despicable person?"

"No, of course I don't. We'll talk when you're feeling more yourself," Meg promised. "Rest now. I'll see that nobody disturbs you."

As she drew the covers up, she glanced off to the East and spotted a caravan of people leaving the church. Knowing that many of the women would be stopping by to express their condolences, Meg hurried toward the front door, hoping to head them off.

Suddenly she spotted Mark Ryan chinning himself on the parlor window sill—a perfect target, if only Sally knew what he was up to!

Opening the window, Meg grabbed a fly swatter and smacked his fingers. "Shoo! Shoo! You must leave—right now," she hissed. "There's a whole bevy of church ladies headed this way."

"But I must see Sally!" he insisted, truly possessed of a one-track mind.

"Go home, Mr. Ryan. Your conduct is most unbecoming," she said primly.

He grinned. "Aw, Sally wouldn't have shot me."

"Maybe not, but *I* might have. Now good day, sir!" She slammed the window, barely missing his fingers.

Whew! She wiped her perspiring brow. *That was a narrow escape!*

~ * ~ * ~ * ~

Fortunately Mark Ryan had a fast horse and managed to evade the church ladies, which was more than Meg could say for herself.

However, the afternoon turned out much better than she ever expected. Annie Benson immediately took charge, assigning various ladies to make the coffee and heat up leftovers from the church potluck. Then, as soon as everybody was suitably occupied, Annie went in to greet her sister-in-law—and even persuaded her to put on a fresh gown, wash her face and comb her hair for company!

A born organizer, Fannie Mae had taken the liberty of drawing up a preliminary outline of duties and goals of a Widows' Relief Fund. While the ladies had discussed the possibility of forming just such a fund earlier at the church potluck, it was a totally new idea to Meg.

"Life is unpredictable—and not just for orphans and such," Fannie Mae reminded the ladies present. "I trust we can all speak freely, since none of our spouses is present?" Getting an "amen" to that, she continued. "We all know how devastating the weather can be, and the effect it has on our families' livelihood. Floods, drought, illness, or even an avalanche—such as the one that took John's life—can leave any of us homeless and financially bankrupt in an instant!" She snapped her fingers. "Any woman among us could easily find ourselves in Sally's predicament."

Carolyn raised her hand. "How can we contribute to a fund for widows? All of us are basically living from week to week."

All the ladies nodded solemnly.

Like a flash Annie came up with an idea. "All of us have things we do really well," she said. "What if— What if we pooled our talents?"

"I already tithe," Sophie Burnett butted in. "You'd better not expect me to take food out of my children's mouths!"

A wave of objections circulated around the room, all related to money being tight.

"Whoa! I'm not suggesting you rob the loose change in your cookie jars, ladies," Fannie smiled. "Or take your husband's hard-earned greenbacks. That would be wrong. But don't forget what

Annie said: We all make things. Wonderful things. *Valuable* things, like quilts and baby clothes and doll clothes."

Emma Frockmeyer's eyes lit up. "I already make recipe books for my friends. What if I made up a few more and sold them?"

"Oh, and I always put up more jams and jellies than my family actually uses," Delia Watkins revealed. "Maybe I could sell my surplus and donate the proceeds to the Widow's Relief Fund?"

"I already have a thriving business," Maybelle Ralston disclosed. "I sell, oh, thirty, maybe forty jars of my walnut-prune conserves every fall at the Cheyenne Emporium. Vernon takes a box in every time he goes to town, and we get paid cash on the spot!"

"There's a big market for your products, ladies!" Meg exclaimed. "Why, many of you are multi-talented! Have you seen the beautiful baskets Annie weaves, or her water color paintings?"

Fannie smiled. "I'm confident that each of us has hidden talents. Why don't we jot down a list of things we enjoy making? Before you know it, we'll have enough money set aside to help families in crisis all over our wonderful valley!"

Sally raised her hand. "I wish somebody had thought of doing something like this a long time ago. Maybe then I wouldn't find myself in such dire straits today!"

"Oh, but you don't need money to get involved," Annie said, patting Sally's hand.

"I have an Underwood typewriter," Sally said hesitantly. "Can I donate that?"

Sophie spoke right up. "No, but if you can type, you can write articles to the *Cheyenne Gazette* and other newspapers about our widow's fund and the articles we're selling for a good cause!"

By three o'clock the ladies had formed a sisterhood committed to supporting each other through good times and "not-so-good" times, to quote Granny. "I refuse to use the word 'bad,'" she declared. "You never know when something 'not-so-good' may turn out to be a real blessing."

Their business concluded for the day, the ladies stood and raised their coffee cups to toast the Widow's Relief Fund. "Through thick and thin," they pledged.

"And the 'not-so-good' times," Sally added bravely.

"Thank you all for coming, ladies," said Annie, embracing each of the ladies as they prepared to depart. "You've already done our hearts a world of good."

"Well, ladies, I see my driver's waiting," said Carolyn, bundling up against the gusty winds. "Guess I'd better not keep him waiting."

Halfway out the door, she came back to give Sally another hug, and looked her right in the eye. "I definitely want to see *you* at our next sewing circle." Then laughing and waving, she walked down the steps on her husband's arm. "Byron, honey, I have the most exciting news to tell you..."

Chapter Twenty-Six

A few days later, Meg went to check on Sally again. It was one of those rare moments when she found the young widow alone.

Still grieving and not sure how she was going to survive, Sally was packing her trunk. "I'm leaving," she announced.

"But why?" Meg asked. "Why are you doing this?"

"If I stay," she said, "I shall slowly go mad. Meg, I have no money! All John's ranch hands lit out for Texas the minute he told them money was tight." Frustrated, she threw her hands in the air. "How can I rescue John's dream, when I haven't the means to hire help!"

"But the Widow's Fund—" Meg said.

"Too late for me. Don't get me wrong, Meg. It's a great idea, but I need help now." She started sorting dejectedly through books and special mementos given her by her husband.

"Where will you go? What will you do?" Meg asked, suddenly frightened. She could hear the defeat in her friend's voice and saw it in her sad eyes.

"Wherever the wind blows," Sally said gloomily. "Maybe I'll get lucky and land on my feet. If not—" She fell silent. She had 'who cares' written all over her slouching, emaciated body.

"Here, let me help you—that's what friends are for, isn't it?" Meg said, hoping to keep Sally doing—*anything*, just to keep her from giving up and doing something she'd regret forever. "How about these sheets? Is there room in your trunk? And what about your favorite photos?" She went to the dresser and clasped Sally and John's marriage photographs to her breast. "I don't see how you can bring yourself to part with any of these!"

"Meg, stop! *Things* don't matter. Why, a hundred years from now, none of this will matter." Sally stared through watery eyes, almost as if Meg were invisible. "We only matter as long as we have someone to *love*." The cords in her throat constricted. "Yes, I have friends, but I'm still alone! My life is *over*, don't you *see*?"

"I-I still don't understand," Meg said, deeply troubled. "Could we just sit down a minute and talk?"

"Sure, why not?" Sally cleared a place on the bed to sit. "Let me tell you where I'm coming from, and why I will never fit in around here."

Meg got a sinking feeling. Like she was in over her head, trying to make sense of what she was hearing. Yes, she had faced a lot of challenges in her own life, but nothing like this!

What Sally desperately needed was to love and be loved, but for some reason, she didn't believe she was lovable!

Oh, how Meg's heart went out to this broken-hearted woman. Yet she felt so inadequate. How was she going to reach someone so lost and full of self-loathing? Was it even possible? Instinctively she realized that deep inside Sally had a wound so deep only God could heal it.

Knowing that she was not up for the challenge, due to her own weakness and inexperience, Meg decided to listen prayerfully and respectfully to what Sally had to say. That way, hopefully, Sally might find her way to the foot of the Cross and find healing.

"Let me tell you about a happy-go-lucky little girl," Sally began her story in a strained voice. "As a child, she always tried to do what was right. She obeyed her parents and never complained, even when she had to do chores she didn't like. She walked two miles to school every day and studied very hard to make her teacher and her parents proud of her. She went to church and answered the altar call when she was ten years old. Growing up, she tried to be her mother's 'perfect princess,' and never do anything wrong." She leaned toward Meg; her eyes intense. "Are you getting it so far?"

"Yes, of course," Meg nodded. "You were a beautiful little girl. You wanted everybody to love you."

"Some might say she led a charmed life. But all that changed when she was fifteen. And you know why?"

"Something happened?"

"Oh, I knew you'd catch on! Now listen up! My mother used to say, 'Into every life a little rain must fall.' I thought she was talking about the weather, but she wasn't. When I was fifteen, a new pastor came to our town. He had a family—a very nice family, including twin boys. They were eighteen and so handsome, I nearly swooned if they so much as *looked* at me. Especially the taller one. He had the loveliest red hair—"

"Did *you* look at them, too?" Meg asked, hoping to keep the story on track.

"Of course, I did! And pretty soon I did a lot *more* than look." Sally grimaced. Evidently the devil was *not* in the details, because she decided to go with the abbreviated version: "He got me pregnant when I was sixteen. When he refused to marry me, my parents drove me to Chicago and dropped me off on a busy thoroughfare—I haven't seen them since, by the way. I supported myself on the streets and gave birth to a stillborn baby. Eventually I made my way West, where I worked as a saloon girl, which is a polite way of saying I paid for my room and board by working on my back."

A deadly silence settled over the room, while Meg tried to figure out how to respond to what she'd just heard. When it dawned on her that Sally was being intentionally hard on herself, she decided to ask a more relevant question: "Where did you meet John?"

"Dodge City. He took one look and bought my freedom from the madam I was working for." Sally gave a deep sigh. "I had a good life here with John."

"But now you're afraid again." Meg's question hung in the air, demanding a truthful answer.

And she got it.

Sally's voice turned brittle. "I'd rather die than go back to being a saloon girl again."

"Stay, Sally. Don't run away! You can still make a good life for yourself on the ranch, even though John's gone."

Sally shook her head. "I can't, Meg. I fear my past is about to catch up with me," she said sorrowfully. "That preacher's son I told you about? He just filed to homestead the property next to John's."

"*What!*" A chill went down Meg's spine. "You mean—Mark Ryan?"

"The one and the only man I ever truly loved." Sally swallowed hard, her eyes reflecting all the anguish and suffering she carried with her through life. "*Now* do you see why I have to leave?" she demanded. "I can't let go of the pain and humiliation of what he put me through."

"Oh, my dear friend! How you have suffered!" Meg burst into tears, and suddenly they were in each other's arms, one seeking to comfort, the other broken and sobbing.

"B-besides John, you're the first person I've ever had the courage to share my story with," Sally said, wiping her eyes. "I've been hiding the truth so long, I hardly know what to do next: Run and hide, or—or shoot myself."

Meg smiled softly. "Maybe you could start by forgiving yourself," she suggested. "Do you think you can do that?"

Sally shook her head forlornly. "If I did that, I'd have to forgive Mark, and I'm not prepared to do that—*ever*. And then I'd have to stop hating all the other men who used me like I was a piece of trash."

"You're right, Sally. That's too much to ask, after all you've gone through," Meg said, holding Sally's face gently between her hands. "I cannot imagine the pain you must be feeling."

For a long moment they sat together on the tattered old quilt. Both grieving. Both casualties of life, but in different ways.

"You can't *ever* give up, Sally," Meg whispered.

"Give up what?" A tiny hiccup escaped, making Sally laugh cynically.

"Well—" Meg lightly bumped foreheads with her despairing friend. "For one thing, you can't ever give up on yourself." Smiling, she tapped Sally on the left side of her chest. "There's a 'precious princess' living inside you. She's still *screaming* to get out, don't you see?"

"Well, I doubt *that,* but go on," Sally said, raising her eyebrows. "Go on, Miss Wolfie, don't let me stop you."

"Ah! I see you know my nickname," Meg smirked.

"Other than that, you're squeaky clean. At least nobody around here knows anything bad about you," Sally teased, nudging Meg with her elbow.

"Everybody's gone through hard times—" Meg broke off, as a terrible bleak expression came over her friend's face again.

"Oh, honey, compared to me, you're an angel. Believe me." Sally's mouth twitched, giving her a bitter aspect.

"No, Sally, that's not true," Meg said, trying to raise her friend's spirits. "I've never had to walk in your shoes, but if it weren't for God's love, who knows what my life might be like?"

"Don't ever slip, is all I can say! Those good religious folk might decide to burn you at the stake!" She wagged her finger in Meg's face. "That's why I've got to get out of town while the getting's good!"

Meg looked in Sally's eyes and saw naked fear. She could see the battle going on inside her friend, and win or lose, Meg was not about to back off. *'Get thee behind me, Satan,'* she prayed, and went with gut instinct. It was now or ever. She had to fight for her friend, claim the victory!

"Frankly, I haven't run into any haters around here," Meg said, "but what I *have* seen are some mighty big-hearted folk. People who would give you the shirt off their back, Sally."

"I never said there weren't plenty of nice people," Sally said, trying to hold onto her defeatist position.

"*Including* those church ladies who came here the other day to pledge their friendship and support. They *love* you and John!" Meg had never felt so pumped up in her life; somehow she *had* to get through Sally's thick skull. "Don't you *see* what's at stake here?" she pleaded. "These are your *friends*, Sally, and they're mine. Sure, they hate sin, but so do you, Sally, from all you've told me. Didn't you tell me you never want to go back to the old life?" Meg leapt off the bed and shook her finger in Sally's face. "Come on. The truth now!"

"Sure, and I meant it when I—"

Meg cocked her head, waiting. "You know what *I* think, Sally? I think you're afraid of rejection. But you also want a new life. Don't lie to me! You want it so bad you can taste it! You want freedom, too, and real love. No more lies and pretend love!"

No sooner did she run out of things to say, when Sally stood up, her body shaking all over with violent tremors. For a second, Meg feared her friend was going to come all to pieces and have a seizure. Maybe something worse.

"I-I just don't want you to go to hell. I love you, Sally," she said and burst into tears. "C-can you ever f-forgive me?"

In the next instant, they fell into each other's arms. They kissed and hugged and cried some more. Finally things calmed down a bit. Being thirsty, after shedding so many copious tears, they walked outdoors, arm in arm—exposed to blustery weather, but not thinking much about it. Sally lowered the bucket into the well and brought up water so cold it made their teeth chatter.

"Well, we know a remedy for that, don't we?" Meg grinned.

"Let's brew us a strong cup of tea," said Sally, quite restored to her sensible self.

So they sat across from each other at the kitchen table, thawing out while the water heated. "Well! Where do I start? This has been the most extraordinary day of my life." Sally looked at Meg with a rueful smile. "I don't know if I can adequately describe what just happened, but if it hadn't been for you, Miss Wolfie—if I may call you that?

"You may." Meg reached out and squeezed her friend's hand. "After seeing you chase off Mr. Ryan the other day, I believe you also qualify as a member of the Wolf pack!"

Sally's eyes glowed with humor. "Thank you from the bottom of my heart, Meg, for what you said. I know it wasn't easy. But if it weren't for you, I might have given up and been on my way to one of the gambling halls in Cheyenne this afternoon."

"I hope what I said didn't hurt your feelings," Meg apologized.

"Truth hurts. But it also made me see things differently. For the first time I realized that I've been stuck in the past for a long, long time, letting all the anger and hate boil up inside me. I couldn't forgive myself, yet I couldn't stop being me, either." She shrugged her shoulders. "Suddenly I feel like I've just had a spiritual bath."

"'Old things are gone. All things are made new,'" Meg shared.

"Thanks for giving me a good swift kick!" Sally laughed. "I've had such a dark cloud hovering over me of late. But now, thanks to you and God, life looks brighter!"

"All you needed was the courage to take that giant leap of faith," Meg said, grinning with happiness.

The steam kettle started whistling. They both jumped up to respond, but Sally got there first. "*I'll* get it! *I'm* the hostess, don't forget!"

"Well, la-de-dah!" Smothering a giggle, her guest presented her teacup with a raised pinky. "I take my tea with sugar, ma'am, *if* you please!"

~ * ~ * ~ * ~

"Now you mustn't worry about a thing, Sally," Meg said. "Just sit tight till the rain stops. You have a good roof over your head—"

"It leaks like the dickens," Sally interrupted, pulling a long face.

"I'll ask around. I know Sam knows all the best carpenters—" She clapped her hand over her mouth, remembering that the Ryan brothers fell into that category. "Anyway, you have plenty of canned vegetables and a cellar full of potatoes and onions..."

"Maybe I'll try my luck hunting if the weather improves," Sally said, being facetious. "I'm sure I spotted a pheasant last week around here somewhere—or was it a duck?"

"Sally, really! You're far too near-sighted to be a good shot." Meg narrowed her eyes, realizing what was missing. "Why aren't you wearing your spectacles?"

"Maybe because what I can't see isn't likely to bother me?" Sally posed comically with her finger to her chin. Since confronting her fears, her spirits had greatly improved. She was more hopeful.

Her sense of humor was back, too.

"If you need anything, just throw a saddle over your favorite horse and come see me. Oh, dear! I can't *wait* to see the pile of dirty dishes in my sink!" Meg laughed, visualizing the chaos awaiting her at home. "But I'm sure Sam has everything under control. Oh, and don't forget, I'll be picking you up for the ladies' sewing circle on Tuesday."

"Yes, I'm looking forward to that," said Sally with a mischievous twinkle in her eye. "I have lots of dishes to return from the potluck. *If* I can sort out what belongs to whom, and all that."

"Well, I'm off!" Meg declared happily.

They embraced again, for the third time. "Oh, Sally–?"

"It's all right, you may go," Sally said, gesturing toward the door. "I am perfectly sane, dear Meg, and I'm certainly not alone, now that I have 'You-Know-Who' watching over me." Smiling, she pointed toward the ceiling.

Meg nodded earnestly. "God our Father."

"Quite so. My constant friend and protector."

"Oh, Sally! I feel like I have a new sister," Meg gushed.

"Well, little sister, I think your husband is probably ready to wring my neck for keeping you so long. As I recall, men sometimes have a short fuse when they're neglected too long."

They embraced again, after which Sally gave her 'new sister' a gentle push out the door and closed it.

"Whew! My new little sister is quite the chatterbox," she laughed. "Not that I'm complaining, Lord! I'm just so thankful you saw fit to send her my way!"

Chapter Twenty-Seven

The instant Meg walked in the front door, she knew Sam and the children would always mean Home to her: the place that kept her anchored and refreshed her spirit.

"Hello, everybody!" she smiled and held out her arms.

Sam got to her first in all the bedlam. "Thanks for stopping by," he said facetiously.

"Oh, you great big grizzly bear!" she laughed. The house was in total disarray, but having Sam's strong arms around her felt like a healing touch from God.

"I've missed you," he said in her ear. "The children have been driving me mad."

"Oh, Sam, how can you talk that way about our precious angels?"

"They're only angels when you're home," he teased.

"Oh, you *know* you love them as much as I do." Meg laughed, opening her arms even wider to include Susie, Davey and Jimmy, all vying with each other for her undivided attention. Somehow, her tail happily waving, Dusty managed to push her nose into the free-for-all for a lick, too.

Keen-eyed as always, Sam sensed immediately that his petite wife had had a taxing day. "How did your visit with Sally go?" he asked, when the excitement died down a bit.

"Oh, Sam! The most wonderful thing has happened. Only I can't tell you, except to say that she's staying."

"That sounds promising," he said. "Maybe we can talk about it later."

"I promised not to."

"Oh. Well, that's all right," he said agreeably. "I suppose you ladies like having your little secrets?"

"Something like that." She turned to see what Susie was holding up. "Oh, sweetie, did you make that for me?"

~ * ~ * ~ * ~

That night, while preparing for bed, Meg filled Sam in all the ways the ladies' sewing circles planned to raise money for the Widow's Fund. She also shared about Sally's miraculous change of heart, and how blessed she was to have such a wonderful friend. Of course, her lips were sealed about Sally's former life. Indeed, she would take her secret to the grave!

"We're just like real sisters now," she confided, fluffing her hair and snuggling against Sam's warm shoulder. "My goodness, you're warm," she exclaimed, running her hands over his body. "Why is that, do you suppose? Do men just have warmer blood?"

"The better to keep you hot, my dear," he said, capturing her squirming body beneath him.

"Oh, Sam, I missed you so much today!"

"I was right here, taking care of our children," he reminded her.

"Sweet man, you even did the dishes," she crooned, rewarding him with warm kisses. "What did you have for lunch—" But that was as far as she got with *that* line of interrogation. The combination of a warm bed and a very hot, eager man proved to be too irresistible! Especially after getting caught in the rain on the way home. But she had all day tomorrow to ask him about... *Oh, what did it matter?*

Happily distracted, she ducked under the covers to do a little exploring of her own. *How wonderful to have such a loving husband, always at my beck and call,* she purred.

"Love me?" he demanded, poised impatiently above her.

"Always," she assured him breathlessly, and as they came together, they were caught up in the most exquisite, rapturous joy.

~ ✦ ~ ✦ ~ ✦ ~

Word soon got around that Mrs. Lassiter's roof had a leak in her roof, right over the bedroom. Since Mark Ryan had had time to reflect on their last encounter, he decided perhaps it was time to let bygones be bygones. He would just ride over and "comfort the widow."

Well, maybe his motives aren't all they should be, but perhaps she still had a soft spot in her heart for him, even after all these years. He knew he'd treated her badly way back when, but that was then, and now they were two consenting adults—or at least he hoped that was how thing would go. Perhaps she'd take pity on a lonely bachelor, and in exchange for home cooking (*wink wink*), he would fix her roof and save her herd from starving or falling prey to the wolves.

Though eyeing his proposition with suspicion, Sally decided to take him up on his offer. After all, he *seemed* sincere in wanting to help. So she struck a bargain: She agreed to cook for him, but he must live in the barn, she insisted.

Indignant at the idea, Mark informed her that there was no heat in the barn. "It's freezing out there, Sally," he told her.

Almost she relented. "I'll feed you, but no funny business," she warned him. "Now scrape the mud off your feet before you come in," she said, not at all pleased to see him, but the Good Book *did* say to turn the other cheek, so she was testing the idea out.

But Mr. Ryan no sooner sat down to supper, when he started trying to play patty-cake with her fingers. So out he went again.

"And good riddance to you, sir," she shouted after him. *He should be glad I didn't shoot him,* she muttered to herself, slamming the door.

But at least she'd gotten her roof fixed. Score one point for her, and zero for the man who broke her heart.

~ * ~ * ~ * ~

But Mark Ryan was not easily discouraged. There lingered a strong fondness in his heart for the sweet lass of yesteryear, so he began to look about for other ways to win his way back into her good graces. She was still a fine, strong lass, shapely and, aye, he liked her spirit. Though not so much her temper, when he was the target.

Eventually he moved into a line shack on the western border between his new homestead and Lassiter's property. He might have continued to live with his brother Tim, but Tim was as fed up with batching it as he was, and was currently in serious negotiations with the comely sister of the rancher who lived on the *other* side of the Ryans' original homestead. A complicated business, to be sure.

In the end, he chose to part ways with his brother. At least for a time. They'd always be close, but right now they both needed a little room to breathe. Especially when Tim was shamelessly carrying on like that.

So Mark moved his things into the dilapidated line shack and saw to the widow's cattle. Didn't ask permission; just worked on the Q.T. Her husband's cattle tended to run with his, so it was an ideal set-up. But the *real* prize to be won was the widow herself.

At night, he would sit shivering in front of his little cook stove, feeding the fire with green wood, and muttering to himself. How long he would have gone on this way was anybody's guess.

Very soon Sam got wind of what was going on through his wife—who seemed well informed on such matters—and so he paid Mark a visit. "I brought you a bottle of fine whiskey to keep you warm this winter," he said.

Never one to look a gift horse in the mouth, Mark accepted the gift and invited his friend in. They had a lot in common, having come to the Territory about the same time.

They chatted awhile about cattle and water rights and pasturage, before Sam got down to business. "I hear you and the Widow Lassiter grew up together back East," said he.

"Oh, we knew each other briefly," Mark said casually, slanting his eyes in Sam's direction. "Her family belonged to my father's church for a time." He poured himself a drink and tossed it down with an appreciative sigh. "Ah! Goes down smooth, it does."

"Takes off the chill on a cold night."

Sam glanced around the drafty shack. "I think you could do better than this for yourself, Mark. Or are you doing penance for something in your past that's troubling you?"

"That's a cheeky thing to say!" Mark poured himself another drink. "It's out of the kindness of my heart that I'm helpin' that unappreciative woman."

Sam laughed. "Not many men would leave the comforts of a decent house to live in a dump like this. What really happened? Did Tim throw you out?"

"No, I went of my own accord," he said grumpily. "Couldn't stand all the billing and cooing that's going on between Tim and Donegal's sister Margie."

"From what I hear, they're seriously considering matrimony."

"Well, they had better!" Mark said indignantly. "Before her brother Walt hauls them up in front of the Reverend and makes an honest woman of her!"

Sam raised his eyebrows. "Sounds like you have strong feelings when it comes to shotgun marriages."

"Oh, don't get me started on the subject," Mark said testily. "Nearly happened to me once—" He switched subjects abruptly. "I just don't like seeing my brother get taken advantage of."

"What if a man gets the girl pregnant?" Sam looked directly into Mark's shifty eyes. "What if he abandons her, and she winds up on the streets with no one to love her and no safe place to go?"

Mark narrowed his eyes. "I don't know what the hell you're talking about, Sam. I never—"

"I think you know *exactly* what I'm talking about, Mark. My guess is that you were young and callous and scared. I think you ditched an innocent young girl who had stars in her eyes for you. I think you told her a lot of bunk, just so you could feed your vanity."

"Damn you, Sam!" Red-faced, Mark hurled the bottle against the wall. "What gives you the right to come in here and accuse me—!"

Sam smiled amiably. "I'm not accusing anybody. But let's just suppose a young girl in her mid-teens found herself in a similar predicament. Suppose her parents went to the boy's parents, hoping their son would do the right thing. He denies the whole affair, and his parents send him off to college to avoid any scandal..."

"I enlisted in the Union Army," Mark said defensively. "Let's get the record straight, Sam. *I* am not that man!"

"Sure you are, Mark. We're *all* vulnerable and do stupid things growing up." He stood up to go. "Either we take responsibility for our actions like a man, or we let someone else suffer the consequences."

"Sarah wasn't pregnant!" Mark blurted out. "Do you think I'd have left her in the lurch, if she was?"

"Then somebody in your family made damn sure you didn't find out, my friend!" Sam heaved a sigh. "Did you know that her parents disowned her? Or that they drove her to Chicago, dropped her off on a street corner and left her to fend for herself? They left her, Mark. All alone in the world and pregnant. Think about that for a moment."

"My God!" The blood drained from Mark's face. Speechless, he lurched slightly, and Sam grabbed his arms to steady him.

"Easy, my friend. It happened a long time ago, and while you can't undo the past, you need to realize how vulnerable she is now."

Mark wet his lips. "No wonder she hates me."

"I don't know the whole story, but I beg of you: Don't make things worse. She just lost her husband. She doesn't need you hanging around, trying out your old seduction tricks on her." Sam hoped he'd gotten across his point. "You broke her heart once, Mark. Now leave her alone."

"But she needs help with the herd," Mark said anxiously. "I can at least—"

"That shows your heart's in the right place," Sam agreed, "but Sally needs time to heal. She's been through a lot, believe me." He grasped the doorknob, ready to head out again into the drizzling rain.

"Wait!" Mark reached out, blocking the door. "How did you find all this out? Who told you? Did Sally—?"

"No. And neither did my wife—at least not intentionally." Sam grimaced, remembering Meg's nightmare the night before. "My wife is sworn to secrecy, and you and I should also respect Sally's right to absolute privacy."

"Then how the h—?"

"My wife sometimes talks in her sleep." Sam jammed his woolen cap down over his ears and put on his gloves. "Think about what I've said. And what Sally's life must have been like all these years."

"I feel like such a cad—" Mark started to say.

"Maybe it's time we saw you in church more often," Sam said with a wink.

"But didn't *you* give up church when your first wife died?"

"I did. But I've changed my mind," said Sam. "I hope you will, too." He tapped his forehead. "Think on what I said, my friend."

Pulling his horse's nose out of its feedbag, he mounted up and headed back home for a late night snack and a little pampering by his wife.

~ * ~ * ~ * ~

Sam's visit to the rickety line shack that rainy night was never spoken of to another living soul. Yet Mark continued stubbornly to watch over the widow's stock. During those lonely sorties through the canyons and wild passes in search of strays, his mind often drifted back to the things Sam had said.

He pictured the thin, black-haired young girl with glasses— actually very pretty when she took them off— and how her face lit up with smiles every time their paths crossed. And as he made his morning rounds moving the herd, he often asked himself, "What if—?"

To himself, in private, he could admit the truth: *He* had done her serious wrong. He had no one else to blame. He wept for the baby he never saw come into the world. And the more he thought about his own callous disregard for Sarah and their baby, and the way he'd abandoned her, the smaller he became in his own eyes. Some Casanova he was!

In his gut, he knew what her fate must have been—sixteen years old, homeless, left to survive alone on the streets. He thought about the days, months, and years that followed. Just thinking about the dangers and abuse she must have endured made him sick to his stomach.

Somehow he knew he had to make it up to her. Yes, he thought, hearkening back to his conversation with Sam Gallagher, maybe it was time for genuine, heartfelt repentance. *What if I could live my life over again and do things differently?* Here he was, crowding thirty-eight. This was sure one thing he'd do over, if he could.

But was it too late? Or had he strayed too far off the beaten path to make a new start?

Chapter Twenty-Eight

As always, the Gallaghers were running late. The church bells were ringing in the distance, and Meg and Sam and the children were still more than two miles from the grange hall.

"Church is going to start without us," she fretted. "Davey, sit up straight. Susie, stop fussing with your hair bow! Jimmy, brush the dog hair off your trousers. I want all of you neat as a pin when we get there."

"Let them be, Margaret," Sam grinned. "Who cares if we get there a few minutes late? The main thing is saying 'Howdy' to the Lord, and being thankful for a bright sunny day." He looked over his shoulder at the children. "Isn't that right, Daniel?"

"Uh, yeah. As long as Jesse Peterson is still speaking to me when the service ends." Daniel had his nose in I Kings. As an admirer of military campaigns, that had recently become one of his favorite books.

"Reverend Tindle must have more patience than Job," Meg said, clutching Sam's arm. "Watch out! There's a driver coming up behind you. He's going to run us off the road, if you're not careful!"

"I expect he's red-headed," Sam said, calmly easing his horse over to the side of the road.

"What sort of remark is that?" she demanded. "It's his reckless driving that concerns me—"

"Hey, Sam!" the other driver yelled. "I bet you a Jackson twenty I make it to church before you!" To prove it, he whizzed past them, leaving them all choking on his dust.

"Why, it's Mark Ryan!" Meg gasped, holding her handkerchief to her nose. "Now where do you suppose he's going?"

"He said 'church,' my love."

"Go faster," she urged. "See if you can overtake him. We musn't let him get there ahead of us."

"Yeah, Uncle. Our horse can beat his. Just give 'im a touch of the whip!" yelled Daniel.

Of course, Jimmy and Davey leaned over Sam's shoulder, shouting like drunken cowboys. "Gee-haw! Go faster, Pa!"

Hearing the orphans call him "Pa" filled him with so much pride, Sam almost ran the buckboard off the road. Fortunately he was more interested in what was about to happen at church, so he blinked away the moisture in his eyes and lightly flicked his horse's rump.

"Gee-haw!" he hollered, and drove under the mesquite tree, beating Mark out of the best parking place in the shade. Jumping down, he swung Meg and Susie down, and then it was every man for himself.

With Daniel leading, Jimmy and Davey made a beeline for the grange hall doors. Brushing off their skirts, Meg and Susie walked sedately behind the boys, who at the last second recalled their manners and held the door open for the ladies in the family.

'Thank you, gentlemen," Meg smiled and hurried inside.

Sam, on the other hand, was busy shaking hands with Sally Lassiter's archenemy. "Good to see you, neighbor!"

"It was a close race," Mark agreed, breathing hard.

"Let's call it a draw," said Sam, throwing his arm around Mark's shoulders. "Why don't we give the Reverend a conniption fit by splitting our bet fifty-fifty, and dropping it in the offering?"

"Sounds good!" Mark laughed. "Hey, I may grow to like goin' to church around here."

"Steady, man," Sam chuckled. "We'd best be on our best behavior, at least till we get back in the swing of things."

"Amen, brother!" And so the two black sheep cheerfully entered the grange hall. Being late, they even sat together.

~ * ~ * ~ * ~

The minute Meg spotted her husband seated with Mark Ryan across the aisle, she knew those two were in cahoots. Signaling with her eyes, she quickly jotted a note on the back of her prayer list and passed it to Carolyn. "Urgent! Let's sit with Sally," it read.

Carolyn showed the note to Byron, who gave their five kids a warning look to stay put. Carolyn then passed the note to Leona Peterson, who welcomed any excuse to take a break from her eight children. Leona gave husband Len the gimlet eye. He got the message and took over supervising the twins and his other six children.

Swiftly the note passed from one member of the sewing circle to the next, until Sophie Burnet, Delia Watkins, Annie Benson, and Mitzi Gunderson were ready to answer the summons to action.

As the congregation rose to sing the opening hymn, "A Mighty Fortress," all seven ladies unobtrusively stepped across the aisle and seated themselves like a bulwark of righteousness around Sally. They all faced forward with innocent expressions on their faces.

Startled, Sally nudged Annie. "What is going on?" she mouthed.

"We're being 'your shield and defender, a bulwark never failing,'" Annie sang out of the corner of her mouth. "'But still our ancient foe...'" She indicated the redheaded charmer seated directly behind them.

"Oh, I really don't think this is necessary," Sally whispered. "He hasn't tried to bother me in several days. I think he finally figured out that I'm just not interested."

"Well, just in case, we're here to protect you," said Sophie.

"'One for all, and all for one,'" pledged Mitzi.

At this point, Meg got a poke in the ribs from behind.

"What do you think you're doing?" Sam frowned.

"Why, I'm visiting with some of my friends," she said, fluttering her eyelashes at him.

"And who's watching our kids?"

"I thought you were."

"Guess again," he whispered. "Mark is my guest this morning. In fact, he and I plan to start attending church *regularly*."

Her blue eyes widened with surprise. "You are? When did you decide that?"

"Oh, awhile back," he shrugged casually. "Mark and I got to talking one day about how we needed to get back into church. You ladies can't have all the fun, you know."

Flabbergasted, Meg faced the pulpit and tuned him out. Every time she thought she had Sam figured out, he said or did something that completely threw her off kilter.

He tapped her on the shoulder. "We'll talk about it at home."

Oh, he's up to mischief, all right! she decided.

Just then Jimmy blew a spit wad and hit one of Leona's step-daughters on the neck. Katie twisted around in her seat to point out the culprit. Len, busy taking the offering, looked around, expecting his wife to deal with it, and found she'd moved.

"Excuse me, Carolyn. I've got a small discipline problem to deal with," Meg whispered. "The rest of you ladies, hold the line. We mustn't desert Sally in her time of need."

Practically crawling over the laps of her sisters in the faith, Meg reached across the aisle and dragged Jimmy outside. Naturally Daniel and the other two insisted on going along to see if he got a licking.

He didn't. Mostly all Meg did was pace up and down beside the buckboard, waiting for the service to end so they all could go home.

After what seemed like an eternity, Sam came out alone. He shook the pastor's hand at the door and ambled over to where she stood, looking more than a little cross.

"Ready to go home?" he asked blandly. "Pile in, everybody!"

~ * ~ * ~ * ~

"Despite all the disruptions," Sam said over the Sunday roast, "the pastor preached a mighty fine sermon. Meg, please help Susie cut her meat in tiny pieces. Anyway, Mark went down the aisle at the invitation to rededicate his life to the Lord..." He paused to redirect traffic. "Davey, just pass everything to the left. That way, the mashed potatoes and gravy and the carrots will get to everyone. Like a choo-choo train. That's right: Everything going in the same direction."

He beamed at his wife from the head of the table, and his handsome smile got her so flustered that she could not have cared less what Mark Ryan did in church. He could have stood on his fool head, for all she cared! Of course, she was grateful that the other ladies stuck around to protect Sally from harassment, but— *Oh, what does it matter?* she sighed. All she wanted right now was to enjoy the day with her beautiful family and count her many blessings.

~ * ~ * ~ * ~

Now that the weather was clearing, the women's sewing circle met regularly each week. In addition to tacking two or three quilts each week, each of the ladies brought craft items and homemade articles they'd made at home.

To get the Widows' Relief Fund off and running, Sally Lassiter put her typing skills to work, putting out the word that there would be a rummage sale at the grange hall every third Tuesday of the month, starting in April.

To prepare for the sale, each of the ladies carried in armloads of items each week: stuffed Raggedy Ann and Andy dolls, doll clothes, corn husk dolls, paintings, pine cone wreaths, embroidered tea towels, pot holders, canned preserves, jams and jellies, skeins of yarn, croqueted doilies, antimacassars, and tablecloths, plus knitted bootees, baby clothes, diapers, crib quilts and baby blankets.

"Well done, ladies!" Fannie Mae exclaimed, gazing in rapture at the amazing array of articles stacked on tables around the room. "Your versatility and creative skills do you proud!"

"The older girls came up with their own projects." Leona smiled benevolently at her three step-daughters. "With the twins and all, I have to give them most of the credit."

Katie Peterson made an awkward curtsy. "The whole family helped. Even Pa. He made the holiday wreathes in his spare time."

"I'm still putting together a Pioneer Cookbook," said Maybelle Ralston. "I'll be needing your typing skills, Sally."

And so it went. Everybody had caught the vision of neighbors helping neighbors; even the children found ways to be helpful.

Hoping to attract more customers, the ladies unanimously nominated Carolyn to lead the charge, because of her outgoing personality. And who did *she* nominate to help her? Her husband Byron, among others.

A shrewd trader, Byron Turner made frequent trips to the Emporium in Cheyenne, so it made perfect sense that he should act as the ladies' go-between, dropping off items for sale and collecting cash for the Widow's Relief Fund—and if a family was in dire need, trading with the Emporium for much needed staples. He even helped the ladies open a small bank account at Wells Fargo, so they could begin to make modest investments in the market.

~ * ~ * ~ * ~

Well, he had finally penetrated the widow's most intimate circle of friends. He was now a member of the church choir—one of the few who could actually carry a tune in a bucket. He also possessed that rare gift that Maybelle Ralston simply couldn't resist: a rich tenor voice.

Rather pleased with his progress, Mark Ryan dusted off his old King James Bible—a few damaged pages were proof of the mice who shared his line shack—and thus he began to refresh his memory. Before he knew it, he gave up his scheming ways, and he found himself pondering the Scriptures as never before.

Of course, he still had his eye on the main prize: Sally Lassiter. But now he wanted to win her, fair and square. Not try to con or exploit her, but to make amends for all the heartache he had caused her. Looking back, he now saw things very differently. As a callow youth, he had basically pursued selfish advantage.

Now he could see all the carnage and seeds of destruction he had sown. Not intentionally, but because he'd been spiritually blind. It astounded him now that a preacher's kid, living under the same roof with godly parents, could have behaved so badly.

He had even weaned his brother Tim away from an active faith and the church. Yes, the more Mark examined the past, the more truth emerged; he wasn't proud of what he'd done.

So anyway, he had Wednesday evenings covered, and Sunday mornings. The rest of the week, he took care of Sally's cattle, and a few chores around the cabin and corrals when she was busy at the grange hall. At night he focused on becoming a new man inside. *More sensitive toward the feelings of others, more aware. Less selfish.* He grew accustomed to reading far into the long cold nights, only dousing the light when the kerosene fumes began to sting his eyes.

Then he learned about the need for donated items to be sold at the ladies' rummage sale. Being skilled with his hands, Mark Ryan wracked his brain. *Hm, there must be lots of things I could make in my spare time,* he thought. He made a list.

Toys headed the list: string puppets, trains, a whirligig, baseball bats, fishing rods (if he could find wood that was supple enough), duck decoys, bread boxes, cabinets, children's furniture. Anything that had to do with wood was right up his alley!

Fortunately there was plenty of scrap wood in Sally's barn... *Whoa. Wait just a second! Hold everything,* he told himself. None of that wood belonged to him. He couldn't rob Peter to pay Paul. That was just wrong.

So what did he do? He packed up his gear and moved back to the cabin on his newly filed homestead. Why should he freeze in that dilapidated old line shack, when he had a perfectly good house to live in? It was waterproof, had a sound roof, and no wind whistling through the place. *Why, I must have taken leave of my senses, living out in the boonies,* he thought. Besides, he had a perfectly good lathe and all sorts of custom tools in the barn. He also had enough wood from the original cabin that had blown down in a windstorm. Why, he could set up shop and make enough toys to fill every kid's stocking in the valley, come next Christmas!

~ * ~ * ~ * ~

Ah! This is more like it! Stretching luxuriously, Mark rolled out of bed the next morning, ready to take on the world. He pulled on his levis and scratched his chest thoughtfully. First on his list was to get his caboose moving up to high ground and check on a couple of newborn calves. They weren't branded yet, but their mothers belonged to Sally— *Damn!* He still thought of her as Sarah, but he'd just have to get used to using her nickname, he supposed.

Anyway, he wanted to bring them down with their mothers and alert Sally to keep an eye on them. Otherwise some cattle thief might slap his brand on them and— He shuddered. He might have been tempted at one time, but at least he'd never stooped *that* low!

Coffee first, he reminded himself, then he'd ride out and take care of her calves. He scrounged around in the kitchen, fired up the stove, put on the kettle, and was about to go out the back door when something—some *human*—flashed past the window, all hunched over, pushing a wheelbarrow!

If he wasn't mistaken, that was his damn wheelbarrow! *Oops, excuse the bad language, Lord,* he thought, going out the door to retrieve his property.

As he rounded the corner of the wood shed, who should he run into but Sarah—correction: Sally. He wasn't worthy to kiss the hem of her tattered dress, much less call her by that dear name.

Why, that minx! She was pilfering his firewood! The cold wind buffeted her gaunt figure, whipping right through her thin shawl. This early in the morning, she must be chilled to the bone. Where was her coat? As his gaze fell to the thin-soled slippers on her feet in the snow, his heart turned over. No wonder she was shaking so violently and her face was so gaunt and pale!

"Sarah!" he cried, rushing to help her. "You shouldn't be out here. You'll catch your death of cold!"

"What are you doing here?" she yelled over the wind, her teeth chattering. "I thought you moved back in with your b-brother."

"Ah, so that explains you sneaking over here at the break of dawn." He wrapped his arms around her and half-carried, half-dragged her out of the wind. "Let's get you out of the cold," he insisted. "If you need firewood, I'll gladly get it for you."

He sat her down in front of his stove. "Now stay put!"

Stubborn minx, she stood up anyway. "You can't hold me here against my will!"

"Ah, 'tis the Irish pride in you, isn't it?" he said, chafing her hands and blowing on them to get them warm. "Why didn't you just ask, Sarah? I'd have delivered it right to your door, so you wouldn't have to dirty your pretty hands."

He lowered his head to kiss her calloused palm, and got his ears boxed for taking liberties.

"I thought you'd gone back to carousing with your brother." Her lip curled; clearly spoiling for a fight. Well, she'd come to the right place for that, all right.

"Sarah, Sarah. What a low opinion you must have of me." Hoping to give her a better understanding, Mark spread his arms wide. "Here stands before you a changed man. Ready to help in any way I can."

"Hah! I bet you can hardly wait to have me arrested for stealing." She raised her chin defiantly.

"Not likely, when I'm guilty of stealing so much more from you, dear heart," Mark said, meaning every word. "I know it's a lot to ask you to forgive me—"

"Oh, stop! If ever I saw a liar, it's you, Mark Ryan!" She poked her finger at his chest for emphasis, only to get her jagged fingernail caught in the red curls peeking at her over the top of his longjohns.

"Ooh!" she let out a squeal of frustration and turned away. "It's useless, trying to reason with you!" Pulling out her lace hankie, She blew her nose angrily.

The whistling tea kettle interrupted their spirited tête-à-tête.

"Excuse me, while I pour you some coffee." Mark found two chipped cups and set a cup of hot coffee before her. She looked at it dully, fumbled to pick it up, then her hand dropped limply to her side. He knelt by her side, concerned that she seemed to have lost interest in their dispute. "Here, let me hold the cup to your lips," he offered, puzzled by her pallor and dull glassy stare.

Suddenly she doubled over in a coughing fit. Overcome by a terrible breathlessness, she was clearly on the verge of collapse. One moment she'd been trying to carry the fight to him, the next the strength just seemed to ebb from her body. Shivering violently, she groped for the chair and sank down woozily, unable even to hold up her head.

A second later, she fainted into his arms.

"Sarah! Oh, my God!" Mark got to his feet, clasping her near lifeless body in his arms, his heart pounding with fear and despair. Was she dying? Had his selfishness brought her to such a terrible state of helplessness? "Please God, just let her live," he begged, the tears streaming down his face. "Send me to hell if you want, but don't let her die!"

She felt almost weightless as he carried her to his bed. He laid her down, noticed how chilly the room was; then he felt her forehead. *Oh, my God, she's burning up! What should I do?"* Frantic, Mark looked around. Obviously the kitchen was the warmest place in the house...

He heard a knock at the back door and nearly panicked. But then he realized that maybe it was God's way of answering his prayer.

"Anyone home?" a feminine voice called.

"Coming!" he yelled, and ran to let his caller in.

He found Meg Gallagher already standing inside his kitchen, bundled up in one of Sam's warm jackets and wearing a pair of ladies' size riding boots. She was looking at the two coffee cups on the table.

"Oh, Mrs. G!" he exclaimed. "Out so early?"

"Well, something woke me up around four, and I couldn't fall back to sleep. It's the strangest thing," she said, rather pensively, still looking around.

"But what brings you *here*?" Mark asked, wondering if he should let her know about the woman lying unconscious in his bed. If he did, what were the chances she'd blab to all her friends? The last thing he wanted was to ruin Sarah's reputation, but if she died, he'd have to answer to a Higher Power for that, in addition to all his other sins. Clearly he was between a tripping stone and a bloody boulder.

He took a deep breath. Obviously he was "in for a penny, in for a pound," as his grandfather used to say.

"Mrs. G, can I trust you to keep a secret?" he asked.

"I've come at a really bad time, haven't I?" She nodded, as if she understood his predicament perfectly. "You're keeping company with a lady friend, am I right?"

"Well, not exactly," he said, blushing guiltily—and silently cursed his forebears, who were also profuse blushers.

Meg put her mittened hand over her mouth. "Where is she? No, no, that's the wrong question! I hate to ask, Mr. Ryan, but is she–?"

"No, she isn't dead, and she and I aren't lovers," he said gruffly. "In fact, she quite despises me." He broke off and pointed toward his bedroom. "She's in there, Mrs. G. She appeared on my doorstep at five o'clock, asking to—um, *borrow* some firewood," he explained, following Meg to the foot of the bed.

"Yes, she mentioned being almost out of firewood yesterday afternoon," Meg said, walking around to the head of the bed like a detective searching for clues. She even sniffed the air for incriminating signs of lovemaking!

"Listen, nothing is going on here," Mark said earnestly. "I invited her in for a cup of coffee—it's freezing cold outside, as you must realize, having ridden all the way over from the S-G-S—"

"Then *how* did she get here?" Meg looked around his room, observing his messy clothes hanging out of a dresser drawer.

"I can explain my poor housekeeping, really I can," Mark said, totally sidetracked by his uninvited guest. He stuffed a few shirts in his bottom drawer to prove his good intentions, and folded his arms with a scowl. "I just moved back in last night, if you must know!"

"So you say." Dismissing his nervousness as a sure sign of guilt, Meg placed her hand on Sally's forehead, then shook her head. "She's got a high fever." Then she leaned down and listened to her friend's galloping heartbeat and congested lungs. "Mr. Ryan, she needs a doctor right away."

Mark threw his arms in the air, vindicated. "That's what I was trying to tell you! She fainted in my arms, and I had no choice but to carry her in here."

"I'll accept your version of the events—for now," said Meg, undoing her scarf and removing her outside clothing with deliberation. "I shall remain here, while you ride hell-for-leather to the S-G-S. My husband should still be home, no doubt preparing breakfast for the children. You bring him back here, Mr. Ryan, post haste!" She looked him in the eye. "Well? Is something wrong with your hearing, Mr. Ryan? I said, *'post haste'*!"

Mark stared at Sam's wife. This was the first time he'd ever seen her being anything but sweet and smiling and agreeable. The word 'harridan' came to mind, but he dismissed it quickly. Right now, Meg Gallagher might be all that stood between life and death.

Thrusting his arms into his heaviest coat, he looked down at the woman lying in his bed. "I love you, Sarah. No matter how much you despise me, I always will." He put on his hat and paused in the doorway. "And you, Mrs. G— You may be a real pain to live with, but you've got grit. I'll be back as fast as I can."

Striding out to the barn, he saddled his fastest horse, Thunder, and rode for glory, praying he'd catch Sam in time.

Chapter Twenty-Nine

"It's pneumonia," Sam announced, removing his stethoscope tips from his ears. "I'm afraid you have a long fight ahead of you, Mrs. Lassiter. I'll do what I can, and I'll show the ladies what needs to be done, but unless you—" He shook his head, for his patient had drifted off again, not seeming to notice her surroundings.

"What can *I* do?" Mark asked, drawing Sam aside. "I'll do whatever it takes, Doc. We've got to save her!"

"I don't know," he sighed. "Her lungs are badly congested, but I've heard worse lungs in an eighty-year-old patient and seen him recover. It's almost like the heart has gone out of her, Mark. She lost her husband recently, and a few years before that, her only child. It all depends on whether she gives up, or whether she rallies."

"I'll *make* her fight," Mark said, determination in his eye. "Just show me how to set up the steam kettle, and how to loosen up the mucous in her chest."

"She might prefer a woman attendant," Meg said from across the room, knowing Sally's fierce aversion to Mark.

"But lifting her, cupping her lungs, those are more easily performed by a person with upper body strength," Sam argued. "I know how much you love Sally, and your motives are sincerely meant, Meg, but for once I have to side with Mark. We are going to have to work around the clock to get the mucous out of her lungs. Every few hours, day and night."

"Oh, but—" Meg started to say.

Gently Sam drew his well-meaning wife out of the sickroom. "She's highly contagious, my dear, and frankly, I don't want our children exposed. That may sound selfish, but this is a very deadly infection. The kind of care she requires can be exhausting."

"What if we all take turns?" She looked up at him as if she was about to lose her best friend.

"That would just spread the contagion around," Sam said gently. "You can't ask our friends to endanger their lives, and their children's, now can you?"

"Can I at least come and hold her hand?" Meg asked forlornly.

"Not until she's well on the road to recovery. I know how tenderhearted you are, but this is a matter of community health," Sam stressed. The look of disappointment on her face almost made him relent, but what a nightmare he'd have on his hands, treating half the valley, if the illness spread. He smiled playfully, as if inviting her on a new adventure: "Now's the time for you and your ladies to test the power of prayer, don't you think?"

"Well, I don't know..." She nibbled on her lower lip, still determined to keep Sally out of the rather muscular hands of her archenemy.

"'If God be God,'" he reminded her. "We can't all be everywhere at the same time, but *He* can! Now, is it a deal?" Wrapping his arms around his rather balky little wife, Sam coaxed her to walk over to the buckboard, where his long-suffering nephew stoically watched over the children. Who were outside on a cold day, avoiding germs.

"Listen to me for once," he said, bribing her with kisses. "Your job right now is to get the prayer chain going. Reverend Tingle and his wife will help you. Now go do it!"

"Oh, all right," she said, kicking the buckboard wheel. "I know in my heart that you're right. It's just—well, why must it be Mark who gets to take care of her?"

"Because he's the key to getting Sally well." He winked at her. "Trust me. If he can't get her back on her feet, nobody will."

~ * ~ * ~ * ~

Breathing a sigh of relief, Sam sent off his family and got down to serious business. Dosing Sally liberally with cough syrup, he next set up a schedule for Mark to follow round the clock. "You see I've marked three columns here," he said, labeling each column on a piece of brown wrapping paper. You write the time, date, and dose in this column. Make sure you do it round the clock. No letting her sleep through the night. We're got to knock out the infection fast." He tapped his pencil on column one: "Write down her fluid intake: how much water, broth, or tea."

Mark nodded. "I'll mark everything down. What next?"

"Now this second column is for diet," Sam said. "Mrs. Lassiter's appetite will likely be poor for awhile, but offer her soft foods. Poached eggs, mashed carrots, soups, things she can swallow easily. You got that?"

"How about milk?" asked Mark, wondering if the new calves' mothers with their swollen udders might help.

"I'd go light on dairy for now." Sam labeled the third column 'Exercise' and underlined it twice. "This is extremely important, Mark," he looked directly in the carpenter's eyes. "I want you to find a sturdy board, at least two feet wide and about six feet long."

"I should be able to come up with that," Mark agreed, his mind racing. "I have a stack of twelve inch boards. Could I nail two together? Might that work just as well?"

"I'll let you figure out how to come up with the right size board," Sam smiled. "When you finish putting it together— By the way, it might be easier to complete the final stages of construction in the room where you plan to use it."

"Yes, yes, leave that to me," Mark said impatiently. "Just tell me what it's for."

"You elevate the board at one end and position the patient with her head down and her feet elevated."

Mark cleared his throat. "Why can't we call her Sally or Sarah? It sounds so cold and unfeeling to refer to her as 'the patient,' like she's an inanimate object."

"Right you are," Sam clapped his friend on the shoulder. "Let's call her 'Sarah,' since that's her given name."

"I'd feel more comfortable doing that," Mark nodded.

"Back to the board now," Sam said with a gleam in his eye. "It's a method where you let gravity help clear the lungs. You tip the board only slightly at first, and as the pa— as Sarah starts to improve, you can tilt it a little more each day."

"That's it?"

"Not quite. First you sand the board smooth and scrub it so clean you could eat off it, if you had to."

"Makes sense." Mark folded his arms across his chest. Sam was taking entirely too long describing what was essentially a teeter-totter. "What's next, Sam?"

"It's really quite simple: You position the patient correctly on the board," Sam explained. "And then you cup your fingers, like so, and rhythmically and *lightly* pound her back with both hands, starting at the bottom of the lungs and working you way toward the shoulders—"

"I got it. Top to bottom. Always moving in a downward direction." Mark frowned. "How will I know if it's working?"

"Oh, you'll know, all right," Sam grinned, drawing out the suspense. "She's getting better...when she starts to complain!"

~ * ~ * ~ * ~

After showing Mark how to mix a mustard plaster, Sam ran Mark through a couple of practice runs until he was reasonably sure he knew the basics of cupping his patient correctly. Relieved to see how dedicated Mark was to doing everything just right, Sam packed up his medical kit and rode back to the S-G-S.

After greeting his ranch hands, who'd returned as predictably as migrating birds to pitch in and prepare for the spring round-up, he moseyed up to the house to have lunch with Meg and the children.

When he got there, his wife was, as usual, in the midst of handling several tasks at once and relegating other jobs to her foot-dragging "helpers." Picking up dirty laundry lying helter-skelter in the bedrooms, she wasn't aware of Sam's stealthy approach until he scooped her up in his arms and tossed her onto their four-poster bed.

"Whaa—! Oh, it's you!" she gasped, bouncing upright.

Leaning over her, Sam gave her a lingering kiss. "*Mm*, you taste good. Is it too early for fooling around?"

Meg pulled the dust rag off her curls. "My, you have the most insatiable appetite!" she said pertly.

"Maybe when I get back?" he grinned suggestively.

"Oh, Sam," she pouted. "Right now I'm in the middle of doing laundry—"

He planted a warm kiss on the side of her neck. "*Mm-mm!* Carry on, Miss Wolfie. I'm heading off to the north pasture with Slim, but I sure look forward to getting some sugar later tonight."

With a parting wink, he left, taking all three boys with him. So there went her best helpers! Left in the lurch, Susie let out a howl and stomped her favorite blanket in the dirt.

Oh, that man. Meg shook her head, as flustered as she was amused. As busy as they both were, he always had time for flirting.

A few minutes later, Sam rounded back and stuck his head inside the front door.

"Expect just our family for supper," he informed Meg. "Mark was real keen on us bringing in those two newborn calves and their mothers. They belong to Sally, and he figures it might lift her spirits to know her husband's herd is increasing."

While his men caught fresh mounts for themselves and Slim Rowland, who'd just returned after nearly freezing off his backside in northern Texas, Sam and the boys hit the trail again. Loyal as always to the S-G-S, old Archie followed at a slower pace, carrying feed and other essentials in the buckboard for the ranch hands.

~ * ~ * ~ * ~

"What, Have you lost your mind?" Tim Ryan raged, pacing back and forth, and stirring up dust motes in the barn. "My own brother—playing nursemaid to a *widow*?"

"Not just any widow," Mark said, annoyed that his own brother was so preoccupied with Donogal's daughter that he had no time for his flesh and blood. "It's Sarah O'Connell—Lassiter's widow. You remember her—from way back, when we went to school?"

"Well, don't expect me to play errand boy, or help out. I can't believe that little witch has got her claws into you again," Tim snarled.

"Well, cock-a-doodle-doo to you, too," Mark replied, making another pass over Sarah's gravity board with his planer. "I just figured blood brothers might help each other in times of need."

"So what's this big favor you'd be askin' me?" Tim asked, pulling out his pocket watch. "I'm on my way to see my fiancée."

"I was hoping you'd get hold of Byron Turner for me. I'm starting to run low on a few things: Oranges, green tea, onions, carrots, a few marrow bones, things like that. Maybe you could ask him to pick up 'em up for me when he's in Cheyenne. I have the list right here—"

"Why don't you ask him yourself?" Tim was surly as ever.

"Because I can't leave Sarah for a minute," Mark snarled back. "This is a life or death situation, and I don't have time to ride all over the county, tracking down Byron!"

"Oh, all right. Gimme your damn list!" Tim grabbed the scrap of paper, stuffed it in his pocket, and stomped over to his horse.

As his brother galloped down the road, Mark rolled up his sleeves and got back to work, putting the final touches on Sarah's gravity board.

~ * ~ * ~ * ~

Slipping one arm around her, he raised her up a bit and gingerly touched the spoon to her lips. "Open wide," he crooned.

Sarah opened one eye. "Don't you ever sleep?" she groused.

Delighted that she had enough energy to speak to him, Mark quickly shoved the cough syrup between her lips. Next he helped her swallow an aspirin down with a few sips of water. Fluffing her pillow, he eased her gently down on the bed and pressed his ear to her chest. *Still way too noisy in there,* he decided. *Not quite as loud as a purring mountain lion, but somewhere between a lynx and a house cat.*

Her forehead was still hot to the touch, but also damp, which encouraged him to believe her fever might break during the night

To hurry things along, he unbuttoned her bodice and carefully placed another mustard plaster on her chest. Wrapped in flannel. He took a moment to admire her breasts, then gently did up all her buttons again.

Able to breathe again, Mark watched her drift in and out of sleep for a while. She seemed so subdued. Not at all like the raging creature who threatened to shoot him several days ago. Perhaps she might come to forgive him, he thought, longing to see her fully recovered.

Her hand lay so still and frail upon the coverlet. Slowly he lowered his head and touched his lips to her hand.

The next instant she walloped him with the bedpan, with a force that made his ears ring. Scrambling out of range, he gently pried it from her hand. "Dammit, Sarah, why'd you do that?" he complained, rubbing his head.

"Because." Her voice sounded weak and raspy, like a disembodied spirit communicating from across the universe.

"Oh. Just because you felt like it, right?" He pondered her behavior and decided that she was undoubtedly on the mend, just as long as he didn't overstep the bounds of propriety and provoke her further.

"Sleep now," he whispered, and tiptoed into the kitchen to keep vigil during the night—from a safer distance.

~ * ~ * ~ * ~

Sometime in the middle of the night, Sarah awoke to the shrill whistle of a tea kettle. The faint clatter of dishes being arranged on a tray was followed by a mild curse. Had Mark burned his hand, perhaps, holding the long toasting fork too close to the fire?

Ah! she mused, stretching. *He's still here, my ghost from the distant past. Still taking care of me, regardless of how often I reject his help.*

A few minutes passed. He was moving around in the kitchen, opening a drawer, moving a chair. *Must be looking for something,* she thought. Then the back door squeaked on its hinges, and slammed on his way out. *He has left me at last,* she concluded. *Hasn't changed one bit.* A tear involuntarily slid down her cheek. Not because she was sorry he was gone—*oh, no!* She'd cried herself to sleep too many times over the years to care about being abandoned again.

No, she told herself, it was being physically weak that was so vexing! Here she was, stuck in *his* house, and in his bed—yes, it was warm, but for how long? She felt the panic mounting inside.

Plus she didn't have a single change of clothing. No water, no food, and worst of all, she was so weak she couldn't even take care of her personal needs.

Worn to the nub, Sarah began sobbing uncontrollably. The least Mark could have done was dump her on her own back porch, where, eventually, one of her friends might find her body and give her a decent funeral!

She was hyperventilating so much that she got dizzy and very nearly fell out of bed.

"Whoa! What's going on in here?" Mark hollered. The gravity board fell to the floor with a loud crash, as he grabbed hold of her. "I've got you, Sarah! Are you—are you having a relapse?"

"I thought you'd l-left me." She clung to his neck, shaking like a leaf in a windstorm.

"As if I would!" he said, wrapping his arms around her. "Here now, love. Don't go falling apart on me." He reached around her and shook up the bottle of cough syrup. "Let's give you a swig of this."

She opened her mouth and took a swallow. "I was so scared of being alone, Mark," she whispered hoarsely

"Aw, your life's been upside down these past few days." He gave her a gentle squeeze. "But you're getting better, Sarah, trust me. I wouldn't lie about a thing like that."

Getting her temporarily settled on her pillows, Mark dragged the gravity board around to the far side of the bed and propped it up against the bed springs.

"Time for exercise!" he declared, flexing his fingers.

"What, more torture?"

"We've done this a few times already," he informed her. "You were pretty much *non compos mentis* at the time, so maybe you don't remember."

Sarah looked skeptically at the board. "Is that your version of making me walk the plank?" she asked, her chest gurgling ominously.

"Sam showed me how to break up the gunk in your chest," Mark assured her, and positioned her with head down on the board and feet elevated. Of course, her skirts responded right away to nature's gravitational pull—and wound up bunched around her hips. Deferring to her need for modesty, he quickly tucked everything in below the waist. "Sorry about that," he grinned.

"Oh, I just bet," she muttered sarcastically.

"Try not to talk, Sarah," he urged. "Now, what I'm about to do is called 'cupping.' It loosens the mucous and helps move it up in the chest so you can cough it up."

He moved her hair off her neck, and skimmed his hand lightly over her torso. She was a little twitchy, especially when he laid his ear to her lungs and listened: *Damn!* Still sounded like an angry cat in there.

Starting at the bottom of her lungs, he began a light but relentless percussive rhythm with his hands. Working his way along her ribs toward the top of her lungs, he paused every so often to wipe the sweat from his forehead. Then he'd continue the cupping, sometimes alternating with a shaking vibration to break things up.

Before long, Sarah began to cough and moan. Tilting the board's angle for better drainage, he handed her a handkerchief. "The more you cough up, the faster you'll recover."

Afterward Mark helped her back to bed. They were both pretty much exhausted from the workout, but if his smile was any indication, the congestion was much improved.

He made her a cup of tea and hovered over her like an old granny while she drank it. "Breathing better?" he grinned, leaning over her to check her color.

"Yes." Smiling for the first time in days, she patted his hand. "I don't know why you're going to all this trouble, but there's magic in your hands, Mark Ryan. Thank you."

"You're not out of the woods yet, m' girl," he said. "But I'm here for the duration, Sarah. As long as it takes." He winked. "I'll be your devoted slave, for as long as you can put up with me."

"Oh, dear!" She choked, a sudden catch in her throat. "Such a nonsensical idea!" She started coughing violently, and Mark pressed a fresh handkerchief in her hand.

"Try not to talk," he urged, stroking her back to calm her. "Listen to me, Sarah. We're going to breathe together—easy now."

Still struggling for air, Sarah clung to his hand. He rested his forehead against hers and gazed into her soft grey eyes. "I'm here, and I always will be. Everything's going to be all right," he promised. And in his heart of hearts, he meant every word.

~ * ~ * ~ * ~

Throughout the next two days and nights, Mark held Sarah in his arms increasingly often. Never more than a few steps away, he breathed with her, cared for her, prayed with her, until gradually Sarah was able to release the age-old fears. He laid hands on her—cupping, bathing, feeding—while slowly the congestion in her lungs began to clear.

Healing came on so many levels that sometimes Mark was reduced to tears of gratitude. He could never remember feeling this way before. They both sensed a deepening in their relationship, the release of old grudges, and the work of the Holy Spirit began ministering in ways they'd never thought possible.

On the fifth day, the ladies from the sewing circle descended upon Mark's house, laden down with lamb stew, fresh bread, eggs, butter, and two jars of applesauce.

"Ah! Just what the doctor ordered," Mark grinned, opening the door wide. "Come in, ladies. Welcome!"

"Just in the neighborhood," Fannie Mae said, leading the way inside. "We figured you might be running low on basics by now."

"How's our Sally?" the pastor's wife asked cheerfully.

"Stronger every day," Mark assured them. "Thank you all for coming. I'm not much of a cook, so this will come in handy! Especially since the patient's appetite is starting to pick up."

Maybelle Ralston shook her finger at him. "We missed you at choir practice, Mr. Ryan!"

The last to enter his warm kitchen, Meg went straight past the table covered with casserole dishes, cakes and cookies and into the bedroom with a bundle of fresh smelling clothes.

"I must say you're looking well, Sally!" They hugged, and Meg proceeded to confess how she'd snuck over to Sarah's house when Sam wasn't looking and gathered up all the dirty laundry. "Sam laid down the law about not coming over here till you were feeling better, but I took the liberty of doing your laundry."

"As always, I am overwhelmed by everyone's generosity and love," Sally said, blushing. "Mark has been busy enough taking care of me, without having to cook or clean up after me."

This last remark made Meg sit up and take note. Certainly Sally's friendly reference to Mark Ryan was a far cry from when she threatened to bring death and mayhem down on his head. "So, are you and Mark getting along better now?" she asked cautiously.

Sally laughed. "He insists on calling himself my slave. Can you imagine anything so silly? I reminded him that slavery has been outlawed, but he says that doesn't apply to a man whose heart is 'voluntarily enslaved'!" She pulled a long face, confiding, "Personally I think it's going to be difficult to persuade him otherwise!"

"Well, if he gets out of hand, let Sam know. He can talk good sense into anyone!" Meg nodded. "I wouldn't trust Mark Ryan as far as I can throw him!"

Sally smiled, unperturbed. "I shall certainly keep that in mind."

"Do you need help moving back to your place?" Meg asked, struck with another way to separate the pair.

"Perhaps soon," Sally said. "I'm still mending, and Mark is a big help with cupping. But don't you worry, Meg. I'll let you know when I'm ready to move home."

Having done all she could to rescue her friend, Meg gave her an affectionate hug. "Come see all the wonderful food the sewing circle brought you!" she urged.

Of course, the second Sally walked into the kitchen, all the ladies embraced her and exclaimed over the "fresh bloom of spring" in her cheeks. Mark received his share of compliments, too, for rescuing the widow Lassiter from freezing on his doorstep and a near brush with death.

Sally said, "I can't thank you ladies enough for coming," so many times that Meg began to wonder if it was a secret code for "Get me out of here. I'm being held hostage by this dreadful man!"

Meg was still scheming on behalf of her friend, when Carolyn, her husband Byron, and their lively five stopped by to deliver several items Mark had ordered from the Emporium.

While Mark settled the bill with Byron, Carolyn and young Troy carried all the booty into the kitchen. Forget the lemons and oranges and green tea, or the plucked chicken, carrots and potatoes. For there the damning evidence sat, in plain view:

A pink toothbrush and a tin of toothpowder.

A ladies' silver hairbrush, comb, and hand mirror.

A white lace negligée and peignoir. White bedroom slippers.

And a pair of size 6AA ladies' riding boots.

'*Scandalous!*' Meg could almost hear what the other ladies must be thinking.

It was now their sworn duty, she decided, to rescue their friend from the clutches of Mark Ryan. But how?

"I believe this is a matter best dealt with by my husband," said the righteous Mrs. Tindle, her false teeth chattering with indignation.

It was too late to find Sam and get him to intercede on Sally's behalf. And, she had to admit reluctantly, Mark's. Meg stepped bravely into the fray. "For me?" she cried, clasping her hands under her chin and fluttering her eyelashes. "Oh, that husband of mine! Always surprising me with gifts."

Mark picked Meg up bodily and beckoned to Sarah—aka Sally—to step forward.

"Nice try, Miss Wolfie," Sally said.

"Why, what did I do?" Meg said, looking around. "I was just—"

Mark held out his hand to Sarah. "Ladies, may I introduce Sarah O'Connell Lassiter, known in these parts as 'Sally.' I have a confession to make." The word 'confession' caused several 'oohs' and 'aahs,' but he pressed on. "I have fallen in love with this beautiful lady twice. She was sixteen the first time, and I was—well, I was young and too foolish to appreciate my good fortune. We lost track of each other for many years, and when we met again, she was married to John Lassiter—a fine man, as all of you know, and sorely missed by us all."

He cleared his throat self-consciously. "Recently Mrs. Lassiter fell gravely ill, and as a favor to Sam Gallagher, who was concerned about the illness spreading, I volunteered to care for Sarah here in my home. During the last several days, I realized that a love like ours never dies. Though we'd had our differences over the past twenty years, our love still shines bright."

He turned to Sarah and went down on one knee. "Sarah, you are the love of my life. Will you marry me?"

Sarah looked shocked. "First you tell everyone my age, and *then* you expect me to marry you? Oh, how *could* you?" She tried to yank her hand free.

Mark had a good hold on her hand and refused to let go.

"Ladies, I appeal to your good judgment: Does not love grow sweeter with age? Should we not benefit from the wisdom acquired with age?"

"You make us sound like we have one foot in the grave!" Sarah gasped.

"Behold!" Mark pointed to his fiery bride-to-be. "She's as healthy and spirited as ever she was at age sixteen!" He winked at her. "Marry me, Sarah?"

"Oh, all right," she conceded. "You're impossible, but—"

"Impossible, *yes!*" he laughed, drawing her into his arms. "But where there is love, *all* things are possible!"

Chapter Thirty

"I tell you, Sam, somebody needs to talk to that man," said Meg, pacing around their bedroom like a tigress.

Busy polishing his boots, Sam politely set aside his polish and brushes. *The better to hear her out*, he sighed. His wife had come home in a high state of agitation. Ranting and raving about how Mark Ryan had tricked her friend Sally into agreeing to marry him. The only thing worse, in her estimation, was if a hundred thousand buffaloes came stampeding through the valley and wound up drowning in the North Platte! Personally, Sam didn't see the correlation between Sally marrying Mark and having to deal with a river full of drowned bison, but who was he to judge?

"It's foolish to fight fate," he said, getting to his feet. Now where did he put that article on testosterone in the latest issue of his medical journal? It would be interesting to see if there were any new discoveries on the subject.

"Are you listening to me, Sam?"

Uh-oh, his wife was tapping her toe again.

"Just wondering... Do you think Sally's health has been adversely affected by the regimen I prescribed?" He rubbed his scraggly beard, wondering if he should shave. *Would that put her in a better mood?* "I gave Mark careful instructions, schedules—everything. Do you think he helped or harmed her?"

"Oh, she seemed pretty much her old self," Meg said. "Only she and Mark hardly butted heads at all." She sounded disappointed.

"And that's bad, I suppose?" Sam found the article on the endocrine system and flopped down on the bed to read.

"Clearly he's cast a spell over her— You know what I mean. Hypno—something?"

"Ah, so he's trying to hypnotize Sally. To what end, do you suppose?" he asked, hiding a wicked grin.

"Well, he recently bought the land next to hers," she said indignantly. "Maybe he has plans for taking over hers, too!"

"Smart man," Sam said, and nodded off.

~ * ~ * ~ * ~

The next morning Sam moseyed over to Mark Ryan's place.

"I hear you two are thinking of getting married," he said, finally getting around to the reason for his visit. He was on his third cup of strong coffee, and since three was his limit, he couldn't avoid the subject any longer.

"Ah, so you're hintin' around that you'd like to be my best man," Mark grinned.

"I would be honored," Sam said. "My wife, on the other hand—"

"Oh, I definitely want her to be my matron of honor," Sally said, seating herself across the table from Sam.

"She's convinced that you and Mark are mortal enemies."

"Are you serious?" Mark's jaw dropped. "Well, we *do* enjoy a little scrapping on occasion, just to make things lively," he explained.

Sam looked him in the eye. "You never laid a hand on Sally?"

"Depends on what you mean by 'hand.' I've never roughed up a woman in my life. Even cupping Sarah is hard for me." He reached over and gave her hand a gentle squeeze.

"I admit I've made threats in the past," Sally said. "I had a lot of anger bottled up inside me. But getting pneumonia made me see things in a whole new light. I think we both realized how important it was to let go of the past."

"For both of us, the past was a real hurdle to get over," Mark said. "I'm grateful she was able to forgive me for running out on her."

"I believe you, Mark. Love and forgiveness and acceptance are the three keys to happiness." Rising, Sam grabbed Mark in a bear hug, and bestowed a gentler hug to Sarah, since she was still on the mend. "Have you spoken to Pastor Tindle?"

"Oh, yes," Mark doubled over with laughter. "His wife must have lit a fire under him. He came pounding on my door an hour after the ladies' sewing circle left." His eyes crinkled with mischief. "We have two weeks to tie the knot, or risk getting run out of town on a rail!"

Sarah rolled her eyes. "To hear *him* tell it—" she nudged Mark, "— we're in mortal danger!" She shook her head. "The date is set for two o'clock two Saturdays from now."

"I'll alert my wife. I know she and the other ladies will be thrilled to get the good news." Sam paused at the door. "Mark my words: This is one romance that will go down in history!"

Watching Sam stride toward his horse, Mark whispered to his bride, "I hope they're not planning a shivaree!"

"We *could* elope," Sarah whispered back.

For a long second, they stood braced against the door, staring into each other's eyes. "No, I think we'd better get married the same as everyone else."

"I'm terrified," she confessed.

"My first time," Mark reminded her. "I know just how you feel."

"Oh, stop with the pity party!" she said, and gave him push toward the bedroom. "I want your hands all over me—*now!*"

"Sure. Cupping is good," he said, struggling to keep a straight face.

~ * ~ * ~ * ~

News of the wedding spread like wildfire through the community. By the next day, courtesy of the ladies' sewing circle, Sally had her choice of several slightly used wedding gowns.

"I am overwhelmed by everyone's kindness and generosity," she said, having finally decided that Fannie Mae's dress fit the best, since they were both tall and on the skinny side.

"Just don't have a relapse," Carolyn said, her mouth full of pins. She was in charge of making a few minor alterations. "We'll take care of all the wedding arrangements. You just catch up on your rest."

"You decide what kind of cake you want, and I'll see that it's done in plenty of time," Annie nodded.

"I can't decide between creamy vanilla and red velvet," Sally said.

"Well, you'd *better* decide," said Granny Benson. "Personally my favorite is chocolate."

"Pshaw! You're not the one getting married," Sophie reminded the wily old woman.

"Annie, you make the vanilla cream, and I'll bake a red velvet cake with chocolate icing," said Granny, ending the discussion.

"Everyone's coming from miles around," said Delia excitedly. "We'll need that much cake to feed everyone, and we'll have musicians—"

"Do you have a favorite song?" Maybelle asked, making notes. "How about 'Love Lifted Me'?"

"Do you need anything from the Emporium?" Meg asked, amazed at how quickly the color had come back into Sally's face. "Sam is taking the children and me to town next Tuesday. I could easily pick up any last minute items you might need."

"No, can't think of a thing," Sally said, stepping out of her wedding gown, and letting Carolyn do up the buttons on the back of her old housedress. "Mark and I can't thank you enough for all your help and encouragement."

Mitzi giggled. "That's what friends are for."

~ * ~ * ~ * ~

"Sally has made a miraculous recovery," Meg informed Sam that night after the children had gone to bed.

"I hear the wedding's going to be a major social event," Sam said, sorting through a seed catalog at the dining room table. "Maybe we should drop by Putnam's Nursery and pick up a few young cherry and apple trees for your homestead, what do you think?" He looked over his reading glasses at his wife.

"Think of all the pies I could bake!" she exclaimed, hanging over his shoulder. She licked her thumb and helped him turn the page. "Oh, look! Walnut trees, and grape vines! Think of all the fruit we could raise!" She pushed up his glasses and planted a kiss on his sunburned nose.

"Hold on! This catalog is from Ohio. Some of these trees might not survive our harsh winters," he said, suddenly engaged in a tug-a-war with his wife for control of the latest U.S. mail. A letter fell from the pages of his catalog, and he quickly shoved it in his pocket.

"But we could *try* growing our own fruit—maybe buy just a few trees," she wheedled.

"Certainly, my love. Anything to humor you," he chuckled. "Have you decided on a gift for Mark and Sally yet?"

"Silk stockings and garters," she said dreamily. "Maybe a pretty flower vase for the kitchen." She crinkled her nose. "Nothing practical."

"Sounds like *you* might like a pair of silk stockings," Sam glanced at her. "For special occasions?"

"Not for me." She looked at him, surprised. "Just to cheer Sally up on a rainy day, don't you see? She's gone through so much lately, and so I thought something pretty, not too expensive, so she won't feel embarrassed."

"How about a rose bush?" He showed her a rose in his catalog.

"Oh, I knew you'd think of something romantic, Sam!" She threw her arms around his neck and deluged him with kisses.

He circled 'rose' on his order sheet. "One rose bush for Sally."

She nibbled on her lower lip. "I suppose we should get something for Mark, too."

"Not if you don't want to," he said, knowing her ambivalent feelings regarding the man.

"No, I think we should get him gift. Or a gift both of them can use."

"I'll buy him a shovel," Sam said, turning to 'shovels' in his catalog.

"No, that would be a little tacky, don't you think?" She frowned, trying to think of something.

"Two shovels," he pretended to write, pulling her leg.

"Absolutely not!" She jumped to her feet and began to pace. 'That's as bad as giving a couple of newlyweds a gallon of kerosene!"

Sam laughed till the tears rolled down his face. "All right, minx, you decide."

"Well—" She plunked herself down in his lap, almost destroying his catalog in the process. "Maybe we could buy them a tea set. Have you noticed the ugly, chipped mugs he drinks his coffee out of?"

"No, but I imagine you've noticed." He smiled indulgently.

"Exactly. Now that they're getting married, they need a proper set of tea cups, and saucers that match."

"Uh, huh!" he said. "I shall rely on you, my pretty, to select the perfect tea cups and saucers when we're at the Emporium."

"You know, Sam, Mark really has changed."

"Glad you think so. No more objections to the marriage?" he asked.

"No. He seems utterly devoted to her. He saved her life, you know."

He yawned. "I seem to recall him telling her, 'I'll be her slave for life,' or some such nonsense."

Meg narrowed her eyes at Sam. "Why is it 'nonsense'?"

"Oh, because..." Evidently ordering turnip seed was more important than answering her question.

"I have decided to forgive him for his cavalier treatment of Sally," she announced.

The silence pulsed between them like an unfulfilled expectation.

Sam ordered enough seed to plant most of Meg's homestead in wheat that spring. When the clock chimed nine-thirty, she got up and set things out for breakfast. Unobtrusively Sam marked "two tea sets" on his list of purchases to make while they were in town.

She'd about given up waiting for Sam to give her his undivided attention when *finally* he set down his catalog. Getting out of his chair, he stretched, muscles quivering all over, and ambled over to where she stood at the counter, head down, gripping the frying pan.

Carefully, lovingly, he removed it from her fingers before she did something she might regret.

"I'll be your love slave, Meg," he murmured in her ear. "Any time, any place."

"Oh, Sam!" she cried, and threw herself into his arms.

"I take it you may require my services, *madame?*"

"Oh, yes, Sam, *please!*"

~ * ~ * ~ * ~

The days leading up to their departure for Cheyenne were unbelievably busy. There was so much to do around the ranch, even though there was still more than a month before the round-up started. Then the men would brand new calves, geld steers, and divide the herd, before making the trip to the railroad pens.

Eager to begin a new season, Sam and Slim and the men took Daniel and Jimmy and Davey under their wing and headed out on an overnighter. Archie carried all the grub in the chuck wagon, along with eighteen bedrolls, give or take a few. All the men had returned, except for Zeke the lady killer, who was trying his luck at the tables in Deadwood, and Jelly Belly, who'd hired on with the Wells Fargo stagecoach, riding shotgun throughout the territory. "My legs ain't all they used to be," he told Sam, "but I still have what it takes to protect the gold shipments up north."

So while Sam and the S-G-S cowboys worked the kinks out of the herd, and did a quick count of new calves, and assessed how many steers to deliver the following month to the rail cars in Cheyenne, Meg and Susie rode herd on the brand new baby chicks in the barn and made sure the mama sow didn't eat any of her latest brood of piglets. Not having to cook for a crowd made it almost feel like being on vacation.

Only she *did* so miss Sam and the boys. Even Dusty was gone; she missed that pesky pup, especially at night, when the winds came whooshing through the trees. She guessed she was still a tenderfoot at heart. Either that, or she was pure chicken, through and through.

If she couldn't survive one night without Sam, she was sure a sorry excuse for a rancher's wife. She was ashamed to admit how much she depended on him emotionally. What a patient man! And though he teased her unmercifully at times, she knew better than to take it to heart. Oh, how she missed that man!

~ * ~ * ~ * ~

At daybreak that fateful Tuesday, Meg gathered the eggs, slopped the hogs, and fed the baby chicks. While the Gallaghers were in Cheyenne, the ranch hands would be watching over things at the ranch. It would be a quick trip, Sam had told her, just long enough to get the children outfitted with new clothes and replace the shoes they'd outgrown. *Mind-boggling, how fast the children were growing!*

"We'll soon be on our way," she told Susie, while they ate their oatmeal. "I want to buy you some new hair bows while we're in town."

After tidying up after breakfast, Meg hurriedly put together a few essentials for their trip, including two quart-sized jars of sweet tea and a batch of snicker-doodles. Then she and Susie sat in the shade on the porch, all spruced up and ready to go.

By eight o'clock she had begun to worry. Had Sam forgotten? What if something had happened on the trail? It was not like Sam to be late.

~ * ~ * ~ * ~

While the boys washed their hands and faces in the creek, Sam finished harnessing two of his steadiest goers to the buckboard. He was running a little behind schedule, but there was still plenty of time to pick up Meg and Susie and make it to the train depot in time.

Trains were often late, but on the outside chance the westward bound train arrived on time today, he was bound and determined to get there on time. He had a special surprise for his bride up his sleeve, and he didn't want to be late.

"All right, boys!" he yelled. "Time to go! *Move* it!"

They all came running and piled into the wagon. Davey gingerly set his latest prize, a tortoise, in the wagon bed, and climbed up front beside Sam. "Don't forget my medicine, Pa," he reminded him.

"Got it right here," Sam responded, patting his breast pocket. "Gee-haw!" He flicked the reins against the horses and started off at a brisk pace. The sun was shining and the sky was a brilliant blue as far as the eye could see, as they set out for home.

"'Bye, Walker. 'Bye, Slim. 'Bye, Moses! Bye—!" the boys yelled, waving to all the ranch hands, who would spend the day rounding up strays and unbranded new calves.

And away they went, following the rutted road over the hill. Forty minutes later they rumbled up in front of the ranch house. Daniel and Jimmy jumped down and threw Meg's bag of essentials in back, then gently swung Susie up and over the railing.

While the horses got a quick drink, Sam leapt down to greet Meg. "I missed you last night," he said with a twinkle.

Meg smiled and, preferring action to words, gave him a kiss that made the adolescent members of the family groan.

"No need to be so dramatic," Sam said, rolling his eyes, then turned his attention back to his petite wife. "Got any cookies?" he whispered in her ear.

"Right here in this paper bag," she said, putting it under the front seat. "I've got sweet tea, too."

As soon as the horses' thirst was slacked, Sam carefully counted heads. "All present and accounted for," he declared. "Now hold on tight, kids. We're gonna make tracks!"

Everyone cheered, as Sam and his noisy brood headed off to enjoy a touch of "civilization."

~ * ~ * ~ * ~

The last mile into Cheyenne, suddenly Sam decided to race neck-and-neck with the West-bound train as it approached the station.

"Hooray! We beat that train by a mile!" Jimmy yelled, shaking his fist at the engineer.

"Ee-iiuu!" said Susie, holding her nose.

"Look, Pa. That smoke stack sure can belch," Davey said, and gave a loud burp.

Having won the race, Sam pulled up next to the horse trough outside the railroad depot and hopped down from the buckboard. "Come on, everybody," he said. "While the horses cool down, what d' ya say we go inside?"

Perturbed, Meg squinted up at him from beneath her sunbonnet. "Why are we stopping here, Sam? Wouldn't it make more sense to go directly to the Emporium?"

If ever Sam's behavior seemed outlandish, it was today. *Racing a train—what was that all about?* she wondered.

"But, sweetheart, have you no sentimental attachment to this railroad station?" he exclaimed, escorting her and the children into the waiting room. "After all, *this* is where we first met face-to-face ten months ago!"

She narrowed her eyes, now convinced he was up to mischief. The trip into town had been hard on her backside. She would rather not waste time with further delays. "We have a lot of shopping to do," she reminded him.

"Well, I just thought you and Susie might want to visit the ladies' comfort station. I know I need a short break," he added, looking shifty.

"Oh, all right, yes, that's a good idea," she conceded.

Just then a stream of arriving passengers entered the depot behind them. There was the usual hubbub, people queuing up to get their luggage, one or two children pushing through the crowd...

Meg took Susie by the hand and made her way through the crowd toward the comfort station. "I'll be right back," she told Sam.

Meanwhile Sam kept a sharp eye out. There was one passenger in particular he was searching for. He was certain he would recognize the lady when he saw her. Surely there'd be a family resemblance? And without doubt she'd be short, like his wife.

Signaling the boys to stay close, he made his way through the new arrivals from back East. *What would a widow look like?* he kept asking himself, looking for anyone wearing black crepe.

A voluptuous woman in black—rather well preserved and possibly in her mid-fifties—bumped into him. *No, couldn't be her.* The woman seemed far too cheerful to be a bona fide widow, he concluded, and kept looking.

His search went on for several minutes. He stuck his head out the door and looked up the track. The only passengers out there were boarding the train for Utah and California.

"Who're you lookin' for, Pa?" Jimmy asked, abandoning his post inside. "That lady with the big bosoms went that way." He jerked his thumb toward the ladies' comfort station.

"Ssh," Sam said. "I'm looking for a tiny little old lady, about Miss Wolfie's height." He indicated where his wife's five-foot-one came on his shoulder.

"Uncle, what's the delay?" Daniel said, joining the discussion.

"Yeah, I thought we came to get new boots," said Davey, scuffing his feet.

"We'll go over to the Emporium, just as soon as I fi—"

A wild scream came from the ladies' comfort station. "Aunt Gladys! What are you doing here?" Meg's voice was unmistakable.

"Looks like we've located 'Aunt Gladys,'" Sam laughed, ruffling his kids' hair. "Let's work our way over to that side of the waiting room."

"Who is Aunt Gladys?" Jimmy and Daniel looked at each other.

"She's your great-great-aunt by marriage and adoption," Sam said, grinning ear to ear.

"Is she gonna be visiting *us*?" Davey asked.

"For as long as she wants," Sam affirmed.

"Oh, boy," Davey moaned, and crumpled to the wooden sidewalk.

Chapter Thirty-One

Instantly Sam jumped into action to avert a seizure.

Fortunately Davey was only being dramatic. Giggling, he sat up. "Fooled ya!"

Down on one knee, Sam was helping the eight-year-old up when Meg and Susie—and the most voluptuous widow he had *ever* laid eyes on—walked outside to confront him.

"Sam, what on earth? Is Davey all right?" Meg asked.

"Yes, we're all fine," Sam said, dusting off his pants. "And who might this lovely lady be?"

"As if you don't know," the lady cooed. "I am Meg's Aunt Gladys, of course. And who are these charming young rascals?" Her bright blue eyes glittered mischievously behind her wire spectacles.

Trying to maintain discipline, Sam scowled at Daniel and Jimmy, who had a hard time keeping their eyes off the lady's rather splendid "accessories." Being shorter, Davey found it even harder not to look.

Racing through the introductions, Sam sent the boys to the baggage room to collect Aunt Agatha's many trunks and suitcases. When he originally wrote her two months prior, she apparently took him at his word, when he invited her to make her home with them. The result was that she had, indeed, brought with her any and all "items that were of special sentimental value."

Well, he had certainly stuck his foot in his mouth this time, he realized. But the lady seemed in good health and of a cheerful disposition, so perhaps all was not lost?

While he "repented at leisure," Sam arranged with one of the baggage handlers to have Aunt Gladys's bedroom furniture and velvet settees with fancy antimacassars and china closet hauled out to the ranch in a separate wagon.

"Oh, Sam," Meg said, throwing herself into his arms. "What a lovely, thoughtful man you are, to invite Aunt Gladys! Oh, thank you, thank you, thank you!" And she covered his face with happy kisses.

"Anything to make you happy, my precious," he smiled, moping his brow. "A bit warm, isn't it? Why don't we take Aunt Gladys and the children over to the café for a dish of ice cream?"

"Oh, Mr. Gallagher, however will I keep my girlish figure?" Aunty gushed. "But perhaps just this once, since it's such a special occasion—?"

"Oh, but I insist," Sam said, putting on his Stetson. With his eyes he directed the boys to hop in back and stand guard over all the luggage, while he handed up first Aunt Gladys and then his ecstatic wife to the front seat of the buckboard. Of course, Susie insisted on sitting in her new aunt's lap.

~ * ~ * ~ * ~

The rest of Sam's plans went fairly much the way he'd planned, including the purchase of new outfits and shoes for the children. Realizing that Sam had paid her aunt's train fare, Meg insisted on making new dresses for Susie and herself to wear to Sally's and Mark's wedding the following Saturday. They purchased a tea set as a gift. So far, so good.

Next they stopped off at the local nursery to buy Sally a rose bush. There were several bare root roses to choose from: yellow, white, red, pink, and even orange. But for some reason, Meg and Aunt Gladys simply couldn't agree on which color to pick.

"What's Sally's favorite color? Sam said, hoping to speed up the decision-making process.

Meg was nibbling her lower lip—never a good sign. "Well, Mark's house is painted brown, so almost any color would look nice."

"Definitely not orange, my dear," said Aunt Gladys.

"How about red?" said Daniel, unfamiliar with how women's minds worked.

"Too bold!" Aunty declared. "After all, she's a new bride."

"No, Aunty, this is her second marriage," Meg said.

"What about yellow? That's always a cheerful color," said Sam. "What difference does it really make? It's a flower!"

"It makes a *big* difference," Meg said, lining up her favorites: white, yellow, pink and red.

"I know what." Sam threw his hands in the air. "Let's buy all four, and you and Aunt Gladys can figure it out when we get home."

"Oh, Mr. Gallagher, you are the height of generosity!" Gladys gushed. "Meg, you are so blessed to have such a kind and thoughtful husband!"

"No, I just want to get home before the round-up is over," Sam said through gritted teeth.

"Silly! You know that's not until June," Meg giggled.

Sam beckoned to the nurseryman and got out his wallet. "We want these four."

So while the boys twiddled their thumbs, Susie got to ride piggyback on Sam's shoulders and put the four rose bushes in the buckboard. Meanwhile Meg and Aunty noticed some interesting six-foot 'sticks' with roots wrapped in burlap and put their heads together to plan an orchard.

Being from Pennsylvania, Aunt Gladys had very definite ideas about which fruits to plant, whereas Meg, remembering how harsh Wyoming winters were, felt Sam would be a better judge about what to plant on her homesteaded property.

By the time Sam returned with Susie from the buckboard, Meg was near tears. She dearly loved her aunt, but their ideas on how to do things were so different, she was getting a headache.

"What am I going to do, Sam?" she sniffed, drawing him aside. "She is the dearest soul, but, oh, I *wish* you hadn't invited her to live with us!"

Suddenly realizing that he could be living in the doghouse if he didn't straighten things out fast, Sam put his arms around his wife and murmured sweet nothings in her ear. "Sweetheart, maybe you haven't noticed, but there is a great shortage of women in the territory."

"So? What difference does *that* make?"

"There are lots of men out here who would love to pay court to your aunt."

"Well!" she sniffed. "I hope you find her a husband before I go stark raving mad!"

"Yoo-hoo, Mr. Gallagher!" her aunt called from across the nursery lot.

Reluctantly he trudged over to see what he could do to placate the widow. "Yes, ma'am."

"I was just talking to the nurseryman about these peach trees—"

"Whatever you say, Aunty." He winked at the nurseryman, who was trying to signal *not* to buy them. "Daniel, will you take Aunt Gladys over to the buckboard, while I pay the man?"

"Whatever you say, Uncle."

As soon as Aunt Gladys was out of hearing range, Sam took the nurseryman over to a stack of bare root apple trees. "I'll take ten of these, and five cherry trees."

"Yes, sir!" The man grinned. "I *told* the lady peaches don't grow in this climate, but she just wouldn't listen."

"We'll just play along with her," Sam grinned. "Tell her these are all peach trees, if she asks. What she doesn't know won't hurt her!"

~ * ~ * ~ * ~

They stayed the night at the Bradford's Boarding House. Aunt Gladys shared a room with Susie and volunteered to oversee the boys in the room next door.

Sam and Meg occupied the bridal suite down the hall. They made sweet, sweet love most of the night, and woke up refreshed the next morning, in spite of getting very little sleep.

In the morning Aunt Gladys and Meg escorted the children downstairs to breakfast, while Sam hurried down the street to the Emporium to make a last minute purchase: a surprise gift for his wife that he should have given her months ago.

They were on their way back to the ranch before ten o'clock. By the time they pulled up in front of the ranch house, who should they see but Byron Turner, offloading all of Aunt Gladys's "priceless" furniture in the great room.

~ * ~ * ~ * ~

Almost immediately the household was afflicted by an explosion of activity. Aunt Gladys took over the main room as her "command center." To give her credit, her bedroom suite "only" occupied one large corner. In no time at all, Daniel and Jimmy were busy hanging privacy drapes to afford her a modicum of privacy.

But her main focus from the very outset was making sure that Meg and Susie were properly attired for the upcoming wedding. Fortunately Aunt Gladys had brought her Singer sewing machine with her, so in three days, by the ladies' eager calculations, Meg and Susie would both have new dresses for the wedding.

During this time, the dining table was taken over, temporarily banning its use for meals. Sam and the boys very wisely retreated to the bunkhouse, where Archie took over the cooking chores—"on a temporary basis, ma'am," he assured Meg, who apologized profusely for all the chaos.

On the second night, Sam knocked over an adjustable manikin in the middle of the night, when he dared to pay a visit to his wife—*his own wife!* Realizing that his peaceful household had been taken over by forces beyond his control, he gritted his teeth and bided his time.

Meanwhile the dining table remained cluttered with dress patterns, fabrics, velvet trim and lace collars, to say nothing of tape measures, needles, pins, and spools of thread that kept rolling about the floor. Fascinated by all this feminine industry, Susie was constantly skipping about, or climbing onto a chair to see what Aunty and Miss Wolfie were up to.

The boys were strangely absent—up in the hills with the ranch hands most of the time. Sam knew better than to retreat completely from the scene of action. After all, this was his home, and he was fighting to retake control. A man did not surrender, just because his very charming and savvy "enemy" had gained a foothold.

No, no. Strategy was the key to regaining territory.

~ * ~ * ~ * ~

The ladies were still frantically hemming their dresses on Thursday. They had less than two days to go, but with both of them working into the wee hours of the night, they felt confident all would be ready in time for the wedding.

Susie's dress was finished in a day, but the full skirts and petticoats on Meg's dress were a real challenge. *Never again*, Meg vowed. Her fingers were getting blisters from all the hand sewing. Aunt Gladys had taken over hemming the petticoat, made of a light cotton, but this was absolutely the last time Meg got talked into making a dress with a skirt shaped like a bell! On top of that, all the velvet trim, buttonholes, and covered buttons had her patience worn thin!

By the time the clock struck ten, she could barely keep her eyes open. "Aunt Gladys, let's finish this up tomorrow."

Still working nonstop, her aunt looked up. "You do look a little peaked, dear. Why don't you toddle off to bed now?"

"You need your rest, too." Meg yawned so wide her jaw felt like it was cracking.

"Now don't you worry about me," said Aunt Gladys. "I'll just finish these last few stitches and scoot off to bed in a few minutes."

"'Night." Meg kissed her aunt on the cheek and wandered off to bed.

In the morning, the rooster crowed loud enough to wake the dead. Still tired, Meg wandered into the kitchen. Behind the drapes hanging catty-corner in the main room, her aunt was softly snoring.

And draped over the back of Sam's easy chair were Meg's beautiful new dress and petticoat trimmed with lace. Everything finished in tiny, perfectly even stitches the way only her aunt could sew.

Overcome with love, Meg lowered her face into her hands. Aunt Gladys might be a well meaning tyrant, but she always came through in a pinch. *Teach me patience, Lord,* she prayed. *Teach me to see only the good in others.*

~ * ~ * ~ * ~

The wedding of John Lassiter's widow and Mark Ryan came as a major surprise to those who knew them best. Sally's friends, in particular, were completely caught off guard. They knew how close she and her late husband John had been during their marriage—none closer. And while she was known for reaching out to those in trouble, and for her close ties to the Benson family, nobody had reason to believe that she and Mark Ryan had ever met prior to her illness. Indeed, it seemed preposterous that they could have ever shared a personal history or had anything in common.

Mark and his twin brother Tim had proven up a homestead in recent years and were known to be confirmed bachelors. They came of good New England stock, and were both handsome enough to attract the ladies, but up until Tim's recent obsession with Donegal's sister, they had both escaped getting roped into matrimony.

As fate would have it, Mark had decided to sell out to his brother and buy the parcel of land located next to the Lassiters. No ulterior motive, except that his herd was growing, and he needed land to expand his operation. A perfectly innocent transaction, in other words.

However, rumor now had it that when Sally fell ill, Sam Gallagher, often called upon to act as the local doctor, had played cupid in order to avert a full-fledged epidemic. Whether that was true or not, one thing had led to another, and Mark Ryan was about to get leg-shackled for the rest of his life.

Speculation was rampant on that fateful Saturday afternoon. Attendance was standing-room-only by one o'clock. The local ladies had gone all out, providing refreshments, including *four* wedding cakes, fancy watercress sandwiches (or a reasonable facsimile), with coffee and fruit punch to wash everything down.

Daniel and Jimmy helped escort family and friends of the bride and groom to their seats in plenty of time. Sam did the honors for Aunt Gladys, who created quite a stir wearing her best black lace gown and leghorn hat with its artfully draped veil. Indeed, several gentlemen of a "certain age" insisted on being introduced and stayed to keep her company, while Sam went to steady the bridegroom's nerves through the coming ordeal.

Arriving early, the bride and her three bridesmaids hid out in the janitor's broom closet, applying the final touches to their gowns. The bride was highly emotional, and definitely in need of moral support.

"You don't have to go through with this, if you don't want to, Sally," Meg said, blotting her friend's tears with her lace hankie. Though a romantic at heart, she still stood ready to defend her friend's right to change her mind.

"Oh, Meg, I-I'm so happy!" her friend broke down and blubbered against Meg's shoulder.

"Then why are you crying?" Delia asked, fluffing her hair in front of a small cracked mirror.

"Why? Because she's madly in love," Carolyn said, incurably cheerful as usual.

"Being in love must be scary," Susie the flower girl observed. Since nothing was in bloom yet, she would be throwing homemade confetti.

Over the noise of neighbors greeting neighbors, Maybelle Ralston played the first robust notes of the wedding march.

"It's time, Sally," said the pastor's wife, peeking around the closet door.

"Almost ready!" Meg reported, and hurriedly picked up the bride's veil. Together, the three bridesmaids carefully arranged it over Sally's dark curls and stood back to admire their handiwork.

"Beautiful," Delia sighed.

Two Bear appeared at the door, handsomely attired. "May I escort the bride down the aisle?" he asked with a bow.

"Indeed, you may!" Sally took his arm and smiled bravely at her bridesmaids. "I can't believe this is really happening!"

"You deserve all the happiness in the world," Meg said, picking up the bridal train. "Now remember, ladies: Susie goes down the aisle first, followed by Delia and Carolyn, then Two Bear and Sally."

"Wait a minute," Carolyn interrupted. "Meg, *you* arrange the bride's train, and then follow Delia and me down the aisle. *Then* Sally walks down the aisle on Two Bear's arm."

"Oops!" Meg smiled apologetically. "I'm so excited, I nearly forgot."

Two Bear gave his sister-in-law a hug. "No more jitters, Sally. Your future awaits you at the altar."

~ * ~ * ~ * ~

A ripple of excitement swept through the hall as Maybelle pulled out all the stops on the old church organ and played a fanfare. As she seguéd into the wedding processional, Susie came skipping down the center aisle, tossing confetti hither and yon. To her it was all a lark. To the bride and groom, it was a date with destiny, long overdue.

As the three bridesmaids came forward with measured steps, necks began to crane for a glimpse of the bride. Trembling slightly, Sarah O'Connell Lassiter clung tightly to her brother-in-law's stout arm. In lieu of flowers, she carried Fannie Mae's white Bible—one of several items she'd borrowed for good luck—and every step of the way, her eyes never left the face of her first love.

A love lost to her for so many years.

Her beloved Mark.

Halfway down the aisle, Sarah's steps faltered, as she silently thanked the Lord for John Lassiter, the dear, faithful man who had rescued her from the pit of ruin and despair. He would always live in her heart. *Thank you, Lord, for the mysterious ways in which you work.*

As she blinked back a tear, a ray of sunshine fell across her tall, slender figure. And then suddenly Mark came striding toward her. Claiming his bride. He clasped her hands and led her up the steps, to where the pastor stood ready to lead them in their vows.

"Mark?" she whispered, but he impatiently shook his head.

"Just follow my lead, Sarah," he whispered. "My heart is bursting with joy, and I need to share it with all these folks."

As if on cue, Maybelle began softly to play the old hymn, "Love Lifted Me."

"Friends and neighbors, if you will indulge me, I'd like to sing a song about the power of love to change lives. Feel free to join in on the chorus." Mark gave a nod to the organist, and gazing intently into Sarah's soft grey eyes, began to sing to her in his soaring tenor:

"I was sinking deep in sin,
Far from the peaceful shore,
Very deeply stained within,
Sinking to rise no more.
But the Master of the sea
Heard my despairing cry,
From the waters lifted me,
Now safe am I."

"Men's voices only on the first chorus," he told the congregation. "Sing it to your lady." And to Sarah's surprise, they did—*twice!*

"Love lifted me. Love lifted me.
When nothing else could help,
Love lifted me!"

Then he turned back to his bride. "This is my vow to you, Sarah, so listen carefully." She was already so emotional that she barely managed a nod, before he burst forth with a highly personalized version of the second stanza:

"All my heart to you I give,
Ever to you I'll cling,
In your blessed presence live,
Ever your praises sing.
Love so mighty and so true
Merits my soul's best song,
Faithful loving service to you belongs!"

Wrapping his arms around Sarah's waist, Mark whispered in her ear, "Sing with me, lover." And so with tears rolling down her cheeks, Sarah and the entire congregation—wives and husbands, sweethearts and beaus—joined him in singing the entire second stanza and chorus.

"Well," said Pastor Tindle, dabbing his moist eyes with his handkerchief. "If we all sang that verse to our spouses every day, Mark and Sarah, the world will be a lot happier place to live."

"Amen," said Meg, passing a fresh hankie to Sarah. "Keep it," she mouthed.

"Now, who gives this woman in marriage?" Already knowing the answer, the pastor saw that Two Bear was momentarily distracted by his wife Annie. "Two Bear?"

"Oh!" Granny Benson piped up, punching her son's arm. "Two Bear, stop mooning around and say 'I do.'"

"I do," Two Bear said, still busy hugging his wife.

Pastor Tindle decided to tackle the basics before things got any more out of hand. "Now repeat after me: I, Sarah O'Connell Lassiter, promise to love you, Mark Ryan..."

Chapter Thirty-Two

For the newlyweds, the rest of the afternoon and early evening passed in a happy daze. Mark and Sarah looked radiantly happy, as they cut the cakes and greeted their neighbors. Even brother Tim showed up with his fiancée and helped move chairs against the walls, so there'd be plenty of room for dancing—compliments of Jake McCandry and his merry band of musicians.

By six o'clock Susie was pretty much played out and was snoozing on Sam's shoulder while he made the rounds, chatting with friends. Having alerted the boys that it was time to leave, Sam made a beeline for Aunt Gladys, who was enjoying a tête-à-tête with Jedidiah Whitaker, who seemed quite overwhelmed by her charms.

"Ah, Sam! I see you've been keeping this lovely lady's existence a secret," Jedidiah chuckled. "Be careful, or I may steal her away permanently," he said daringly.

"Oh, Mr. Whitaker!" Gladys blushed. "How you do go on!" She playfully tapped the old gentleman on the arm with her fan.

"Aunt Gladys, I regret to spoil your fun, but it's time to say good night. The boys are already waiting in the buckboard."

With Susie sound asleep, Sam figured Gladys would be glad to be rescued from her ancient beau. Instead, she fluttered her eyes at the old coot and pouted.

"Oh, dear, must I leave so soon?" she protested. "Perhaps Mr. Whitaker could drive me home later—?"

"I'd be dee-lighted, dear lady!" said Jedidiah, patting her plump little hand. "As a matter of fact, I was just going to ask you for the next dance."

"Well, aren't you sweet! How can I refuse such a kind offer, sir!" Old Jed and Gladys had their heads together, like two lovebirds. Gladys waved her hand, shooing Sam away. "Now, don't you and Meg wait up late. Why, I expect Mr. Whitaker and I may just dance the entire night away!"

Jedidiah looked like the proverbial fox in the hen house. The grin stretched across his sunburned face fairly shouted, "Eureka!"

~ * ~ * ~ * ~

"Anyone seen my wife?" Sam said, looking high and low, as he made his way through the crowd. "Come on, Miss Wolfie, darling.' Show yourself."

Hearing her infectious laugh, he wrapped Susie in a blanket and made his way over to his petite wife, who was chatting it up with the Turners. Sometime during the evening, Carolyn had changed from her bridemaid's dress to a denim skirt, matching jacket, and boots. She and Byron had had a grand time square dancing together earlier. Carolyn and their five children were all mounted up, ready to hit the trail for home.

However, Byron, it seemed, just couldn't tear himself away from all the festivities. He stood beside his quarter horse, Scooter, well over sixteen hands high, feeding it sugar cubes and telling jokes.

"C'mon, Pa," young Troy called. "Duane's gonna fall asleep if we don't get home soon."

Byron threw his hands in the air. "Who's the Boss of this outfit, I ask you?" he laughed, still clowning around. "Well, Sam, I reckon I'd better get these rascals home, so me and the missus can do a little spooning."

"Thanks again, for helping," Meg said, shaking hands with two of her favorite people in the whole wide world. "That was sure a beautiful wedding."

"Sure was," said Byron, sticking his left foot in the stirrup. His weight shifted, as he threw his right leg over Scooter's back. Suddenly the saddle flipped under the horse's belly, and Byron found himself upside down in the dirt.

"Dag-nab-it!" he said, shaking his head. "Now you know why my friends call me 'Lucky.'"

"Oh, no, not again, Pa," his kids groaned.

"Byron, when are you going to remember to check the cinch before you ride that horse?" Carolyn said, barely able to keep a straight face. "Scooter just loves to play tricks on Byron," she explained to the Gallagher kids, who stood with their mouths open.

"Aw, sweetheart." Byron picked himself up and dusted off his trousers. "The reason I love that horse is 'cuz he has a great sense of humor." He shook his fist at Scooter, who responded by showing his big teeth. "Y'see? That's his horse laugh."

Meg looked at Sam, and they both doubled over with laughter.

Meanwhile Byron tightened the cinch and remounted without incident. "Don't take any wooden nickels," he shouted and spurred his horse to a fast trot, passing his kids and taking the lead with his wife right beside him as they headed home.

~ * ~ * ~ * ~

"Nice moon tonight," Sam said, gently nudging his wife awake. Setting the brake, he jumped down from the buckboard and carried her up the porch steps and into their bedroom. Somewhere between the grange hall and home, his amazing young wife had finally run out of steam. After helping with all the preparations for Mark and Sarah's wedding and reception, plus trying to keep up with Aunt Gladys, who was, to put it mildly, a human dynamo, the love of his life clearly deserved some serious pampering.

It might not be how he originally envisioned spending the rest of the evening, but only a selfish cad would turn a blind eye to all that she and the other ladies had accomplished. Yes, his amazing wife deserved a few days of being waited on, hand and foot.

So even if Aunt Gladys didn't crawl in the door until dawn, he was still putting her in charge of the children, while he took his wife somewhere quiet for a few days. Some place where they could talk without constant interruptions. A place where there was no cooking, no laundry, and no chores. Where there was nothing but peace and tranquility—and each other. Nothing but bliss, in other words.

Having decided on the ideal way to reward Meg for all her hard work and ingenuity and the love she lavished on others, Sam carried Susie and Davey inside and put them to bed.

Daniel and Jimmy must have sensed his need to be alone with Meg, because they decided to camp out overnight in the barn.

Ah, peace at last, Sam thought, stripping down to his skivvies and slipping into bed beside his warm, curvaceous wife. He inhaled, savoring her luscious scent. *Ahh!* He controlled his first unworthy impulse, which was to make love to her all night long. *No, not a good idea. She needs her sleep,* he thought, yawning. To do otherwise would be selfish. *At dawn he would spirit her away to some rustic getaway in the hills, where they could renew their vows of love...*

~ * ~ * ~ * ~

Around 2:00 A.M. Dusty began to bay at the moon. She scratched frantically at the front door, demanding admittance into the family circle.

Awakened from a delicious dream, Meg sat up in bed. Outside her window, she heard soft laughter and whispering. Whoever they were, Dusty seemed determined to get her humans to protect her. *Probably mischief-makers*, she thought. All she knew for sure was that Dusty did *not* want to confront them.

Some watchdog! she thought, searching in the dark for her slippers. Finally she pulled one of the flannel nightshirts Sam refused to wear over her head and crept toward the front door to let Dusty in. She was hoping that whoever was prowling around out there couldn't run fast enough to get through the front door before she dragged her cowardly dog inside and dropped the bar in place again. It was a risk she'd just have to take, she supposed.

But first she tiptoed back to their bedroom to enlist Sam's help.

"Sam? Sam, are you awake?" she whispered. No response.

She even tried to pry open his eyelids. No such luck. He was in a deep, *deep* sleep.

She peered through the back window and saw a shadow move. Someone was using the new two-seater outhouse Sam had built.

Meanwhile Dusty was still on the front porch, carrying on something fierce. Working up her courage, Meg opened the front door and hauled the dog inside, then slammed the door shut. *Whew! That was a close call*, she thought.

But then she peeked out the front window again. Someone had parked an expensive looking carriage over by the corral. And harnessed to the carriage was a black horse drinking from the water trough. For a second Meg almost thought she'd faint. What if it belonged to J.W.? Hadn't he promised to bring Aunt Gladys home?

How embarrassing! Still, she reminded herself, they'd been out there quite some time now, despite the dog creating all that racket. Why hadn't they called out for help? *Their behavior seemed very odd to her.*

Whatever was going on, it could surely wait till morning. She yawned, climbing back into bed. Sam's arm came around her, pulling her close. "What woke you?" he mumbled.

"Nothing important," she said, running her fingers through his curly chest fur. "I think my aunt has a new beau."

~ * ~ * ~ * ~

"What a lovely way to get waked up—thank you, Mr. G!" Meg gazed up at him with glowing eyes.

"No, thank *you*." Growling like a tame bear, he pinned her to the mattress. "You stay put while I put the coffee pot on."

"I will not!" Giving him a push, she slipped past him and though he pursued, she had the kettle on before he had his pants buttoned. "We're running low on kindling," she hinted, rummaging in the cupboard for their favorite coffee mugs. Not finding them in their customary place, or even in the drain, she turned to find herself pinned between the counter and one very hairy chest. "Sam? Where are all the coffee mugs? I saw them here yesterday—"

"Surprise!" He produced a cardboard box he'd been hiding from her. "Your own special tea set, *madame,* for when you're entertaining company, or your husband."

"What?" She eyed him suspiciously.

"Open it," he said, so she did.

"But isn't this the exact same set we purchased for Sally and Mark?"

"No, theirs is lavender blue. This one is yellow and green. See? Same manufacturer, only this one is more colorful."

She gave him a quick buss on the lips. "Thanks. I hope you didn't spend—" Again she was silenced by a kiss. "Sam, there was no need to squander money."

"Hush. It's for special occasions. Enjoy."

It was hopeless, trying to reason with him, when he was in such an amorous mood. She tossed a few sticks of kindling in the stove and struck a match. While the water heated, she ground the coffee beans.

Meanwhile Sam unpacked the Oriental basket with its cups and saucers and teapot. "I need to wash them before we use them," she told him, still wondering where he'd put the coffee mugs.

"Whatever you say, grumpy," he said, giving her another kiss. When Dusty started whining, he decided to let her out.

Standing in the doorway were Jedidiah Whitaker and Aunt Gladys.

"It didn't seem right to leave without telling you—" They looked at each other, then announced, "We're eloping!"

"Love at first sight," J.W. confirmed, puffing out his chest.

Meg hurriedly embraced her aunt. "This is so sudden!"

Aunt Gladys smiled and primped her hair. "We slept in the barn last night," she divulged in a low voice. "I must look like a scarecrow!"

"No, no, you look...quite lovely!" said Meg, brushing a few flecks of straw off her aunt's black lace gown. "At least you didn't catch a chill last night."

"No, we found a quilt hanging on the line, so we kept plenty warm."

Ah, yes, Carolyn's magic quilt, Meg smiled to herself.

"I'll just go pack a few things for the trip to Chicago," Aunt Gladys said, already throwing things into a suitcase. "We'll send for the rest when we get settled."

"Surely you have time for a cup of coffee? Eggs and toast?" Meg offered. "Won't take but a minute."

"Aunty," said a small sleepy voice. "Where are you going?"

"Oh, dear child!" Gladys gave a violent start. "What are you doing up so early?"

"I smelled warm maple syrup," Susie said, rubbing her tummy.

"Pancakes," Meg said, hoping to tempt her aunt into abandoning her impetuous trip. *Perhaps with something in her stomach, she might reconsider?*

"When you get to my age," her aunt said cheerfully, "you tend to eat less. Got to keep my girlish figure, y'know."

For all Meg's attempts to delay the inevitable, the lovebirds could not be dissuaded from their folly. "There's no place like Chicago for a honeymoon," J.W. said, rubbing his hands in anticipation.

And so with mixed feelings, Sam and Meg bade the elderly bride and groom a fond farewell.

"It'll take me two days at least to pack all her things," Meg sighed, and came back inside to find the coffee pot jumping. "Sam! Quick! Throw me a potholder. It's about to boil over!"

Working together, they rescued the coffee before the air filled with the aroma of burned beans. While she cleaned the stove top, Sam pulled two mugs from under the sink.

Happy to see them again, Meg set the cream and sugar on the table, and grabbed the coffeepot. But before she could pour, Sam casually tossed something shiny in her cup.

Clink!

Frowning, Meg picked up a gold ring. "What is going on, Sam? I saw this same ring in your breast pocket yesterday. I left it there, thinking you were holding it for Mark."

"Mark gave Sally his own ring. *This* ring—" he took her hand and slid it slowly onto her ring finger, "—is my pledge to love and cherish you always." He kissed her lips and then the ring on her finger. He cleared his throat a couple of times. "I have a confession to make, my dear Miss Wolfie—*Margaret*," he added for emphasis, because he wanted her full attention.

"*Ooh*, you sound so serious," she teased, nipping at his earlobe playfully.

He clasped her hands in his. "Without you, I might still be sleeping in the bunkhouse."

"Oh, Sam, that's pure nonsense. Why, the thought of you out there, and me all alone in this big house is just ridiculous—" For a moment she thought he was going to say he'd fallen madly in love with her and— She blinked, bringing herself back to the moment. *My goodness, where did that come from?* she thought. *It must be all the excitement of the wedding yesterday...*

Sam captured her hands in his and slowly kissed each of her fingers and then her calloused palms. By the time he finished, Meg was hanging onto his big strong hands with bated breath.

"The truth is, Meg, I fell in love with the *idea* of you the minute I read your letter, giving me your expected time and date of arrival. It took a little longer for reality to set in." He smiled sheepishly. "Remember the day you refused to go back to Cheyenne, because this was your home and the kids'? And you looked me in the eye and told me we were going to rebuild our dream home together, from the ground up.

"*That*, my sweet termagant, was when I fell deeply in love with the *real* Margaret Wolverton. Not with the pretty façade, but with who you really are inside. I fell in love with your courage, your strength, your unquenchable spirit. My fearless Miss Wolfie! You know, our orphan kids had you pegged right from the start. The truth is, I've been afraid ever since that I might scare you off, if I told you how much I love and adore you—"

Meg gazed into the most soulful brown eyes she'd ever gazed upon. "Oh, my dearest one!" she exclaimed. "How could you even think such a thing? Why, without *you*, I might still be sleeping in an unheated, one-room basement apartment in New York!"

His dark eyes registered surprise. "A well educated lady like you?"

"Life is never easy." She gripped his hands hard for emphasis. "I lost both parents during the Civil War, and if Aunt Gladys and Uncle Henry hadn't taken me in, I probably would have starved! But in recent times they fell on hard times, and, well, I didn't want to be a financial burden, so I moved to New York City, hoping to find work. Times were tough all over, Sam."

His brow furrowed slightly as he saw the distress in those sky-blue eyes of hers. "Well, hell," he growled, and pulled her into his arms. "You and those renegade kids are the best thing that ever came my way. Daniel, too. I'd be lost without the whole lot of you."

From the warmth and safety of his arms, Meg gave a tiny sniff. Not because she was weepy or ashamed of anything she had said or done, or because she wanted to be anywhere else. She belonged right where she was, she realized. In the arms of *this* man, whom she'd come to rely on to love, protect, and cherish her all the days of their life together.

She dug her little nose into his shoulder and sniffed again. He even smelled right. Just the way a man of strength and hard work should smell. Earthy. Down home delicious, and downright sexy.

Yes, Sam Gallagher would always represent Home to her. Like no one else, he understood the risks she and her orphans had taken to embark on this perilous adventure—and what it had taken to find that safe haven called Home, where through good times and bad, they would always find an abundance of acceptance and love and forgiveness. Where, together, he and Meg and their children—maybe even their grandchildren—would prevail, and the love they shared would grow even stronger.

For *all* of them, but especially for her, the S-G-S Ranch would always be that forever place called Home. *Still Going Strong.*

~ The End ~

Romance Novels by Barbara Dan

Petticoat Warrior
McGregor's Bride
O'Rourke's Bride
Silent Angel
The Outcast: The Long Road Home
Lady in Pink Tights
Family Friends and Lovers
Fair Winds to Jamaica
Fair Winds to Muscovy
A Bold Wager (Regency)
Trouble in Paradise

Other Books by Barbara Dan

Chasing the Brass Ring to Success:
My Journey to Broadway, Hollywood and Beyond

Survival Strategies for the Holidays
At the Foot of the Cross: Easter Dramatic Readings
Vicky: God's Angel in Our Midst
Power to Choose (coauthored with John Dan)
Screenplay: Appointment

For more information about Barbara Dan's books:
Visit: http://barbaradan.com

For book signings, interviews, or large orders:
Contact S-G-S Promotions, 268 NW Hayden Court,
Hillsboro, OR 97124 or the author at
barbgdan@yahoo.com

About the Author:
Barbara Dan

First published in her teens, **Barbara Dan** has enjoyed a variety of life experiences, including working as an professional actress, model, night club comedienne, singer/dancer, comedy writer, puppeteer, theatrical producer in Hollywood, screenwriter, publicist, fund-raiser, real estate saleswoman, hands-on builder of houses, escrow officer, co-teacher of couples' communications workshops with her family therapist husband, as well as publisher, editor, and adjunct college professor. But by far her biggest joy has been the grand adventure of being the mother of four now grown children, grandma to five grandchildren and great-grandmother of three toddlers.

With family roots planted deep in New England history, Barbara is a voracious reader of history, loves quilting, gardening, oil painting, tracking genealogies, and prowling around in old graveyards and musty museums while doing research for her latest novel.

She is currently a member of Women Writing the West and Western Writers of America, Inc. Her novel *Silent Angel* won Best Historical Novel Award in the Colorado RWA's Heart of the Rockies competition in 1992.

Besides degrees in Theatre Arts and Advanced Accounting, she earned her M.A. in Humanities (emphasis: history and literature) from California State University in 1988, but feels that life experience is the most valuable tool any writer brings to his or her work. (A good sense of humor helps, too!)

Visit http://barbaradan.com to learn more about this prolific author's books.

COMING SOON!

News Flash! Her next writing assignment is an exciting 3-book series about French emigrées who fled the Reign of Terror during the French Revolution and settled in Pennsylvania. This writing project is especially close to Barbara's heart, because of strong family connections through marriage to some of the survivors. Stay tuned at http://barbaradan.com for updates!

Proof

Made in the USA
Charleston, SC
24 August 2015